Jigsaw

Also by Campbell Armstrong

CAMPBELL ARMSTRONG

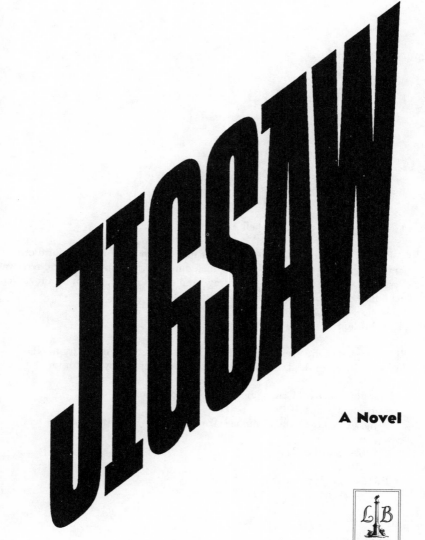

JIGSAW

A Novel

LITTLE, BROWN AND COMPANY
Boston   New York   Toronto   London

First Edition

Library of Congress Cataloging-in-Publication Data
Armstrong, Campbell.
    Jigsaw : a novel / by Campbell Armstrong.
        p.   cm.
    ISBN 0-316-04821-6
    I. Title.
  PR6052.L25J55   1995
  823'.914—dc20   94-44130

10 9 8 7 6 5 4 3 2 1

MV-NY

Printed in the United States of America

For Patrick Janson-Smith, Prince of Blackness

Jigsaw

LONDON

I

Bryce Harcourt said good night to the duty officer, a briskly courteous young marine from Alabama, and stepped out of the American embassy. In Grosvenor Square he was assaulted at once by the numbing chill of the early evening. It had been a winter of uncommon savagery across Europe. Ships locked and forlorn in ice-choked Baltic seaports, relentless blizzards in Germany and the Low Countries, scathing frost in the southern regions of Italy; nothing had escaped the ferocity of the arctic months. London, encased in ice, vandalized by rough winds, was a city embalmed.

Harcourt, hurrying to catch an Underground train, considered it a miserable place altogether, the gray parks immense and dismal, drones scuttling into buses and tubes to escape abrasive winds that snapped down the streets of Mayfair with the tenacity of hounds. It had been grim enough when the city had been adorned by Christmas lights — then at least you had an illusion of warmth and cheer — but the decorations were long gone and the first month of the new year had passed with no relief in sight.

Muffled in a heavy black overcoat, Harcourt had an intense longing for his native Florida, some burning Miami heat, palm trees and high blue skies and pastel buildings. He imagined himself in cotton shirt and Bermudas on a balcony overlooking the sunlit ocean. He could taste a lime daiquiri in his throat. He saw flamingos against a red sun and bronzed babes strutting across sands. A fantasy — but hell, it was one way of getting through these god-awful times when the mornings were dark and the afternoons icy and short.

He shivered as he entered the tube station. The rush-hour crowds thronged around him with the concentrated brutality of people anxious to get to their homes in the suburbs. He was jostled by the mob pushing toward the turnstiles. A city of moles, he thought. They had pinched, pale faces. They'd surrendered to the glum season, hostages of winter, yet they went about their business with that peculiarly English stoicism Harcourt could never understand. They waited in disgruntled silence for buses that were late or stood in underground trains too crammed and overheated for human dignity. The Spirit of England, ho hum; an empire had disintegrated into incompetence and indifference.

Harcourt clutched his briefcase against his side and stepped onto the escalator, where he collided with a woman trying to rush past him. Her mouth was covered by a red wool scarf, but even so Harcourt was immediately struck by familiarity.

The woman stared at him, then was swept down the escalator by the crowds pushing at her back. Puzzled, Harcourt watched her disappear. He'd seen her before, he was sure of that. He couldn't remember where or when. He ran into a great many people through his work with the embassy; he couldn't be expected to recall every one of them. He went to dinner parties and receptions and first nights. He was sought out by anxious matrons in Knightsbridge and Swiss Cottage when an amiable bachelor was required for dinner or as an escort. He was deliberately visible, a charmer known to enjoy the company of women.

When he stepped off the escalator, he saw the woman again. Her black hair was cut very short and side parted. She had a strange white-tinted shock of hair on the right of her skull, a touch of punk. She wore small round glasses. Attractive, Harcourt thought, in spite of the curious hairstyle. An idiosyncratic loveliness, high-cheekboned, bold, intelligent.

There was more than appreciation to Harcourt's reaction. Something buried and forgotten, an old bone. His memory was normally a sharp instrument and this unexpected failure concerned him.

For a second she looked around, caught his eye through the crush. He thought he saw recognition in her expression, perhaps even an element of anticipation, as if she expected him to approach and engage her in conversation. *Don't I know you from somewhere?* But the very idea of stopping to talk was crazy. He had no choice except to keep moving, squeezed toward the platform by the single-minded momentum of the moles. Maybe she'd get on the same train and stand very close beside him, which would be a good opportunity to clarify this feeling of familiarity in circumstances of forced intimacy. A captive audience, so to speak. She might even be obliged to press against him, especially when the train lurched.

Where have we met before? he'd ask. It was a bad line, but you did what you could to divert yourself from the horror of the Underground rush hour. And maybe she'd remind him, and they'd straphang together, and her breasts would touch his arm, and who could predict where that might lead . . .

The air in the tunnel was hot and unbreathable. The train would be even worse, a clammy ordeal, a sauna on wheels. He wondered about the woman. He wondered why, out of nowhere, he was filled with uneasiness. Was it a result of his own nervous state?

Lately he hadn't been sleeping well. The apparent calm he demonstrated daily at the embassy was all surface. He'd been smoking too many cigarettes, sitting up late at night scanning magazines in the fretful manner of a man whose aids to sleep — brandy and downers — couldn't quite push him over the edge. Insomniac moments, pockets of drowsiness, and then before dawn the blessed vacuum of sleep, albeit shallow and chaotic with dreams. Sometimes Jacob Streik was in these dreams, fat and scared.

Whenever he dreamed of Streik, Harcourt always woke tired. The weary mind, that prankster in the head, played games after a time. You began to imagine things. The woman, for instance. In which compartment of his life did she belong? Or was this mere imagination, the result of his fatigue? She was memorably good-

6 / CAMPBELL ARMSTRONG

looking and she appeared to recognize him. How *could* he have misplaced her?

The train was heard rolling in the darkness of the tunnel. The crowd moved expectantly toward the edge of the platform. Harcourt was urged forward. He felt powerless. A stick on a tide.

He saw the train appear and slide to a halt. The carriages were already overcrowded, every seat taken, every strap seized, aisles packed. He wondered why he hadn't tried to catch a taxi home, instead of suffering this. He'd begun to vary his routine during the past few weeks — bus, tube, taxicabs, his Mercedes, although the Merc was presently off the road, courtesy of some recent vandalism.

He didn't travel the same way two days running. It was a simple precaution. Sometimes he thought Streik's decision had been correct and that he should have followed Jacob into obscurity. But he had a position to maintain at the embassy, Streik didn't. He had career notions, whereas Streik was strictly freelance. He was also less prone to panic than the fat man. Streik jumped at the least thing, yielded to intimations of doom, and saw devils after his fourth martini. The last time they'd talked, Streik, calling from a public pay phone, had said: *They are going to kill us, Bryce. They are going to put us on ice. Because we know too much.* Jake had been drunk that day, possessed by dark menace.

Bullshit. What do we really know, Jake? We shuffled some money around, that's all. That's all we did.

Streik had said: *Get your head outta the clouds Chrissakes, Bryce. This ain't your basic laundering operation. You know and I know that money's going into some very strange places. And these guys play for keeps. If they think we know too much, hey, end of song. You think I'm being paranoid, huh? So why is somebody always following me? And why's my home phone tapped? Lemme tell you what I think, Bryce. I think I've kinda outlived my usefulness and now, shit, they see me as a threat.*

In his drunkenness, Streik had rambled on about strangers watching him, cars parked outside his flat at all hours, inexplicable clickings on his phone. To him, all this amounted to a death sentence. *See, Bryce, they only trust you so far. Soon's you know a little too much, down comes the fucking black curtain. I shoulda known better from the git-go. But no, I had to get myself involved. Stoopid, huh?*

Streik's concerns were contagious. Harcourt had begun to wonder if he were being watched too. If his life were being quietly ransacked. Some days after the conversation with the fat man, he'd thought long and hard about the money. It had been irregular, sure, but he'd done as he was asked, nothing more. You took orders. You didn't probe, didn't raise needless questions. But it had begun to trouble him ever since Streik had vanished from his small two-room basement flat in Islington, and a week ago he'd ignored protocol and asked for an appointment with the ambassador, William J. Caan, who wasn't available to certain staffers. So Harcourt had been shuffled into Al Quarterman's office and Al, the ambassador's lackey, had seemed impervious to his misgivings about the money. *It comes with the territory, Bryce. You knew that going in. It's a bit late in the day to be having qualms, don't you think?*

Qualms, Harcourt thought.

Now, briefcase jammed against his chest, he was forced into the carriage, thrust against a tall West Indian girl and a man attempting to hold a fragile bunch of flowers aloft. Harcourt had always been acutely conscious of smells, and they came to him now in a clamor — roses, sweat, bad breath, damp clothing. A bit late in the day, he thought. Quarterman's words had contained a warning, as if locked inside a very simple statement was something deeply sinister. It had been a mistake to approach Al Quarterman. He saw that now. He should have said nothing. He should have left it alone. It was none of his business in the end. His function had been to gather the funds delivered by Streik, who carried credentials that established him as a diplomatic courier, and then disperse the monies in accordance with coded instructions he received weekly from Quarterman's office. *Qualms*, he thought again. The word troubled him. Qualms were luxuries you came across unexpectedly in the bargain basement of morality, where you had absolutely no right to be rummaging.

The fluorescent tubes in the carriage flickered a moment. Harcourt thought: Terrific. A power failure. All we need is for the train to stall and the lights go out. All we need is anarchy.

He twisted his head in the direction of the doors. He saw the woman with the red wool scarf on the edge of the platform, watched her thrust out her hand as the sliding doors began to close, saw a dark leather purse fall from her fingers and drop inside the carriage. She made no effort to recover the purse, showed no sign of panic or loss. Instead, she hastily withdrew her hand before the doors finally shut. And then the train lurched forward and Harcourt saw her staring at him from the platform. She drew her scarf from her mouth and smiled at him as the carriage pulled away and she was drawn slowly out of sight.

Something is wrong, Harcourt thought. Something doesn't make sense here. He wasn't sure what.

A skinhead close to the doors had picked up the purse and held it uncertainly. It was too late to return the thing to its owner — what was he supposed to do with a lady's purse, for God's sake? A woman's purse didn't go with the tattooed hands and the gold ring through his nose.

The train cranked into the blackness of the tunnel, then came to an unexpected stop. Passengers lost their balance, collided with one another, shook their heads with restrained impatience.

Harcourt considered the woman. *That smile.* He had the feeling it had been intended only for him. He ransacked his memory. For God's sake, where had he seen her before? And if there was meaning in the smile, what was it? The train jumped forward abruptly. The man with the bouquet of flowers said, "Bloody hell. Where's this train going? Dachau?"

Harcourt turned his face away from the man, who had the irrational look of the frustrated traveler. Bodies pressed against unfamiliar bodies; the people in the carriage might have been guests invited to an overcrowded party none had any desire to attend.

The train halted yet again. Harcourt's face was jerked toward the bouquet of flowers: stop and smell the roses, Bryce. Who was the woman?

"It's just like the Nazi transports," the man with the flowers said. "A journey to hell."

The overhead lights blacked out for about five seconds. The dark was hot and total. When the lights came on again, the train was still motionless. To distract himself, Harcourt stared at a map of the Underground system, all those colored lines leading to obscure destinations. Cockfosters. Harrow-on-the-Hill. Rayner's Lane.

The mysteries of the grid.

The mystery of the woman with the red scarf and the strange white streak of hair and the way she'd smiled. You're making too much of this, he thought. You haven't been yourself lately.

Sweat had begun to collect on his forehead. He tried to raise a hand to loosen his necktie but his arm was jammed between the West Indian girl and a sturdy long-haired young man in a fawn duffel-coat. Harcourt experienced a passing light-headedness. He concentrated on the map. The Victoria Line. The Circle Line. The Jubilee Line. Colors shimmered in his vision.

The woman.

It came forcefully back to him then, a name, a photograph stapled to a document, a file in the Security section. The certainty of recognition jolted him. His throat was dry. He had a desperate urge to get off the train. She'd changed her appearance, the hair was different, the glasses were a new attachment, but he knew. Panicked, he stared into the roses, absently noticing droplets of water trapped in the petals. Sweat slid into his eyes and blinded him. He thought of the purse, the way it had fallen from her hand into the carriage just before the doors closed.

No. He opened his mouth as if he were about to address the man who held the flowers.

There was a sudden searing flash of light and for a second Harcourt wondered if he were undergoing a form of seizure, a visual hallucination, but the flash became a fireball that flared the length of the carriage and the West Indian girl screamed, the man with the bouquet looked astonished, the youth in the duffel coat cried aloud in anguish.

The roses burst into flame.

And Harcourt himself, even as he remembered the woman's name and its disagreeable connotations, felt an excruciating friction burn through his body. All around him was chaos, screaming, heat, flying glass, and the scent — obscene, redolent of an ancient smell long forgotten — of human flesh on fire.

LONDON

2

The woman, who carried an American passport in the name of Karen Lamb, had reached the street when she heard the explosion. It was far-off, muffled, but she felt it more than she heard it; it might have been the aftershock of a small earthquake. She walked quickly, turning away from Piccadilly in the direction of Shepherd's Market.

She entered a crowded pub, all brass and open fires and businessmen trying to get a little extracurricular activity going with their secretaries. She immediately headed for the toilet. She locked the door and took off the wig, which she tossed up into the cistern. She removed the glasses, snapped the frames in several places, then dropped the fragments inside the toilet, which she flushed. One lens was sucked away, the other floated back and lay on the surface of the water like a strange transparent eye.

She left the pub and continued to walk the narrow streets of the neighborhood in the general direction of her hotel. Although it wasn't quite dark, a few girls were already trawling the alleyways and passages, black girls mostly, with moussed hairdos and too much lipstick and street expressions — something of boredom, something of nonchalance. They were hard girls. They'd seen everything and were beyond shell shock. Nothing about human behavior astonished them.

Karen Lamb thought of the Underground train. She thought of fire and destruction and the massacre of passengers trapped in a metal tube hundreds of feet below street level. An extravaganza, a light show of death. She was suddenly buzzing, heart hammering, adrenaline humming through her.

She stepped into an alley. Lost in the glow of her own imagination, she was unaware of the chill on the early evening air. Lights illuminated shop windows, people drifted in and out of pubs, a few bars of synthesized rock music floated a moment through an open doorway. Life went on in little moments, cameos, apparitions. She felt distant from the general flux of things, outside of the human race, a spectator. She looked in a store window, gazed without interest at framed prints of Victorian hunt scenes.

She pressed her forehead against the glass. All at once she was aware of a familiar sense of crashing. Anticlimax. You were tense and electrified before the event, but afterward there was something unfinished, a craving. It was always this way. The edge had gone and there was a downward rush. Destruction, a craft in which she'd served a long apprenticeship, wasn't enough. It kindled other urges.

She wandered down the narrow street, moving slowly now. The sense of urgency she'd had before was gone. The planning was over, the work accomplished. She entered a callbox, stuck a phonecard in the slot, and dialed. On the second ring a man picked up.

Karen Lamb said, "I scored." She pictured him in his hotel suite. He always had suites, never rooms. The idea of him in a simple room was inconceivable.

"Excellent," he said. He paused before adding, "See you soon. Take care of yourself." He hung up before she could respond. She replaced the phone and continued to walk. She reached a corner, stopped, observed one of the hookers strolling along the sidewalk.

The girl wore a short black leather skirt and a jacket of imitation leopardskin. Her hair was piled up on her scalp and her lipstick was glossy pink, almost luminous; she had a mouth that might shine in the dark. She was maybe sixteen, seventeen, you couldn't tell. A child. Karen watched her for a time before she said, "You must be very cold."

The girl looked at her. "Freezing," she said. "You American?"

"God. Does it show?"

"The accent," said the girl, drawing the collar of her jacket up to her chin.

"You can't hide anything." Karen Lamb touched the girl's sleeve and let her hand linger. She was thinking of the man's parting statement. Take care of yourself. What did that really mean? Stay out of trouble? Keep cool? How typical of him not to ask questions, not to ask after details. Somewhere along the graph of his life he'd developed the capacity for shunting distasteful images into a remote siding of his head where they became unreal. He had places where he was able to park unpalatable matters, as if they were worn-out cars. What he didn't know couldn't hurt him.

"You got something to hide, have you?" the girl asked.

"Don't we all," Karen Lamb said, and laughed.

The girl smiled and looked for a moment oddly innocent. In the expression you might imagine her background, school dropout, pregnant, family squabbles, a quick abortion followed by flight from somewhere like Luton or Northampton to the streets of London, where the only thing she had going for her was her body.

"What's your name?"

"Candice."

Candice. Sure. She would be a Rita or an Angela. Candice would be her working name. They always had working names, fanciful or exotic, dream names. "Do you have a place, Candice?"

"Yeh. I got a room."

"Where?"

The girl appeared hesitant, licked her lips, looked sideways at Karen Lamb, who wondered: Does she smell blood? Is there danger about me, something of desperation? Maybe the girl saw into a core of loneliness and didn't like it.

"This way," the girl said. She moved off. Karen Lamb, watching how the leather skirt attracted creases of light from windows, followed.

The girl turned. "I don't get many like you."

"Like me?" Karen Lamb asked.

"You know."

Karen said nothing. She walked with the girl down an alley and through the doorway of a narrow building. A corridor led to a wooden staircase. A wall light in the shape of a clam shell threw out a thin glow. Cans of paint were stacked against a wall. The air smelled of fried bacon, turpentine, bleach. Signs of cluttered lives, scuff marks, footprints on the steps. Karen climbed after the girl. On the landing she put her hand against Candice's thigh.

"Now now, patience is a virtue," the girl said and stuck a key in the lock of a door.

"What would you know about virtue?" Karen asked.

"You'd be surprised."

The room was furnished plainly. A double bed, a nightstand on which lay combs, hairbrushes clamped together, mouthwash, a jar of moisturizing cream, an ashtray filled with cigarette ends. A simple brown velvet curtain hung at the window. The girl dumped the ashtray into a trash can.

"Sandra," she said.

"Sandra?"

"I share with her. She smokes and I get the dirty work."

Karen Lamb put her gloved hands on Candice's hips and drew the girl toward her. She heard the buzz of blood in her head.

"Let me get out of this first," and Candice took off the jacket, placing it carefully over a chair as if it were genuine fur.

Karen sat on the edge of the bed. "Take everything off," she said. "Everything."

"You're in a right old rush," said the girl. She stripped briskly, stepping out of the leather skirt, then removing her blouse. She wore dark green satin underwear, which she discarded quickly. She balanced nimbly on one leg as she slipped out of her panties. With no sign of self-consciousness she stood in front of Karen, who looked at the white breasts, the nipples that were barely visible, the bony angle of hip. She ran her palms across the girl's stomach, passing over a small appendectomy scar. She moved her hands between the girl's thighs.

"You shave," she said.

"It's healthier," the girl remarked.

"I like it." Karen pressed her face against the girl's stomach and shut her eyes. For a long time she didn't move. She enjoyed the faintly soapy scent of flesh, the softness. In this place it was possible to imagine you never knew solitude, that your world wasn't one of disguises and fake passports, that you had no connection with violence and death. A fragile illusion. The trouble was, you kept coming back to yourself in the end. All you know is destruction, nothing of love. The blood in her head roared now.

Candice sat on the bed. "We need to talk money."

"Later," Karen said.

"Not later. Before you go any further."

Karen pushed the girl back across the mattress, straddled her. Just a whore. A streetwalker. Disposable human material. Garbage. She caught the girl's wrists and forced them to her side. She kissed the chilly unresponsive mouth. The taste of lipstick was strong, candy-like.

"Wait," the girl complained.

"Wait for what?"

"You don't think I do this for free, do you? I'm not running a bleeding charity. Dosh first. Goods later."

Karen pressed her hands to the sides of the girl's thin face. *Goods later.* She was thinking of the Underground again. The man's eyes, his puzzlement. She saw him being drawn into the darkness of the tunnel on a train going nowhere. She envisaged broken glass, molten plastic, a furnace.

"You're hurting me," the girl said.

"I don't mean to. I don't want to hurt you." The blood hammered, pounded, her brain might have been filled with hot mercury.

"Then fucking let go of me."

Karen squeezed her palms harder upon the girl's cheeks. Candice twisted her face away. "Hey, I don't like this. I'm not into this. Why don't you just leave."

Making a claw of her hand, Karen pressed her fingertips tightly around the girl's lips and silenced her. From nearby came the noise of sirens. Ambulances, fire engines, police rushing through the streets of Mayfair and along Piccadilly. Too late.

She stared into the girl's face. Candice's eyes registered fear, uncertainty. A volatile customer, the hooker's nightmare: in bed with
the deranged. She struggled to free herself. She raised her legs as if
she might kick Karen.

"Don't," Karen said.

The girl looked at her imploringly. Karen lowered her face,
brushed the girl's forehead with her lips. She had the urge to tell
this child about the Underground train, the explosive in the purse.
This idiot desire to talk — what did it mean? Guilt? But that was
absurd. She never felt guilty about anything. She had nothing to
confess. Maybe it came down to something else, the need to shock
and impress.

Suddenly she released the girl, who sat upright and moved to the
other side of the bed, where she covered her breasts with her hands.

"I don't do this. I don't do this sick shit. I'm not into pain. Get
somebody else. Plenty of people do pain. I could give you names."

"I don't want names." Karen rose, strolled to the window, drew
the curtain back. The alley below was dark save for the yellowy stab
of a single lamp. Was it sick to look for a human connection, something to fill the void? She heard the hum of her blood change suddenly; a tumultuous melody echoed inside her skull.

The girl said, "I want you to go. Now."

Karen let the curtain fall and approached the bed. "I didn't mean
to hurt you."

"Right. You didn't mean to hurt me. But you did." The girl
touched her mouth as if she expected to find blood. "I told you. I
don't do pain."

"Everybody does pain," Karen said.

"You maybe. Not me." The girl gestured in the direction of the
door. Her fear had yielded to sullen defiance. "Just go. You scare
me. Just get the hell out. Go on."

Karen didn't move. The room seemed altogether confining to her
now, and the child on the bed plain and unappealing. What was she
doing here? It was weak to give in to these yearnings, to seek out
these situations. She always came to the same conclusion: she didn't
belong. She was a captive in that other world of featureless air ter-

minals and drab railway stations and night journeys, hard concrete and steel, a world of strangers, passengers shuttling through the dark to unknown destinations. It was a place of casual monosyllabic conversations with men who, drawn to her looks, wanted to force themselves on her, men she never encouraged.

She sat on the bed and reached for the girl's hand, but Candice drew her arm away. "Piss off, for Christ's sake." The girl pressed her back against the wall.

Karen caught the girl's chin and twisted the small face to one side. "I leave when I want to. Only when I want to. Do you understand that?"

"Fuck sake. You're hurting me again."

Karen squeezed the girl's lips between her fingers. A loose crowned tooth popped unexpectedly out of the girl's mouth and bounced across the back of Karen's hand. Candice yanked her face this way and that, unable to free herself. She brought up her hands, flailed. She kicked her legs, moaned, twisted her body around, tried to bite into Karen's palm. Again the whine of sirens filled the small room.

Karen gazed into Candice's face and thought: the pain of other people is as near as you ever get to them. She was aware of the girl's warm saliva in the palm of her hand. The human condition: spit and fear and a sad little broken false tooth. It didn't amount to very much in the long run.

She released Candice, who gasped for air and tried to scramble from the bed. She looked undignified, undesirable, her white buttocks upraised. Karen caught her, dragged her down, pinned her to the mattress. Tears flooded the girl's eyes.

"Stop crying," Karen said. "I don't like to see anyone cry. Stop." The melody had changed. There was a drone in her skull. She imagined a graph of her brain, an unbroken green line on the screen of a scanner. She heard sounds: *beep beep beep beeeeeep.*

The girl opened her mouth to speak, but then — seized by an inappropriate sense of vanity about the missing tooth — closed her lips and turned her face to one side.

"I won't hurt you again," Karen Lamb said. "I promise." She drew the bedsheet around the girl's shoulders, then picked up a pillow, which she smoothed between her fingers. She listened to the freezing wind roaring through the streets of Mayfair, rattling shop signs, window frames, fluttering ribbons and scraps of trash.

■

Later, she sat in a chair by the window and took off her black silk gloves and laid them in her lap. With her eyes shut, she rocked very slightly back and forth. After a time she got up and walked toward the bed. The lamp shade was askew. She adjusted it carefully. She noticed how a few spots of blood adhered to the surface of the cheap shade. For a moment she saw them, not through her own eyes, but as if from a policeman's perspective of clues and signs. She put her gloves on and, tapping her hands against her thighs a moment, she smiled and gave in to an impulse that hadn't been any part of her original plan.

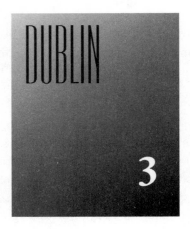

DUBLIN

3

Six weeks into a leave of absence he hadn't asked for, Frank Pagan sat at one A.M. in the lounge of the Shelbourne Hotel on St. Stephen's Green. Here and there groups of wearied tourists, many of them Americans seduced by off-season prices into visiting glacial Europe, sat over pots of tea or glasses of stout which they drank with exaggerated lip smacking — as if they'd discovered the elixir of life. The lounge had a dislocating sense of unreality; in this place clocks meant nothing. Only the darkness pressing upon the windows reminded you that it was night outside, and wintry.

Pagan sipped his Guinness. His fifth. Pack it in, he thought. Go upstairs to your room and sleep. But he didn't get up from the table. He took a picture postcard of Bantry Bay from the inside pocket of his beige woollen jacket and scribbled a message to his associate, Robbie Foxworth, in London. He wrote: *What the Yard calls a leave of absence is probably more like a midlife crisis. My future is about as bright as that of a man selling gynecological instruments door to door.* He put aside his pen and realized the tone of his language came off as more self-pitying than flippant. Flippant was what he wanted. In truth, he was a little dejected. And the Guinness, although it had befuddled his senses somewhat, hadn't elevated his mood.

He was still an unemployed cop, and you could dress that fact up in any euphemistic phrase you liked, it didn't alter the reality, the savagery of office politics, power struggles, departmental warfare. When Martin Burr, Pagan's guardian angel, had retired as commissioner, he'd been replaced by a brutal upstart called George Nimmo, whose "radical reconstruction" of departments had amounted to a Stalinist purge. Heads had rolled and more than a few people had bloody hands and Nimmo, contriving to rise above the mayhem, had conducted press conferences at which he spoke officiously of necessary reforms. And these so-called reforms had resulted in Pagan's banishment. *You're due some vacation time, Frank. Why don't you have an extended leave of absence and we'll figure out your future when you're gone, old boy.*

I never kissed the right ass, Pagan thought. And I never liked Nimmo.

So, rejected, he'd driven for six weeks around the frozen wastes of Europe in a purposeless way, a man chasing unreachable destinations. In a rented Nissan, so unlike the red Camaro convertible he kept in London — a car to which he was irrationally attached — he'd played his vintage rock and roll cassettes at maximum volume as he'd driven through Germany from Hamburg to Frankfurt and down to Munich, where he'd spent too many nights in one beer hall or another, vast tabernacles of lager consumption in which people became more and more sentimental as the hours wore on. There was laughter that would sometimes disappear inside moody silences, as if a sudden cloud of collective sorrow had descended. When he found himself imagining the beer halls were filled with boisterous Brownshirts, he knew it was time to move on again.

From Germany he'd gone into Austria, where, in Vienna, he'd passed his time uneventfully in dark coffeehouses flicking the pages of foreign newspapers in the manner of a man stripped of language. It was eerily comforting, he thought, to scan newspapers he didn't understand; it was as if the events of the world were filtered through an awareness from which he was excluded. Greek newspapers, Hungarian, Italian; he avoided the French and German press because he had a working knowledge of those languages. He might have been marooned in a space station orbiting earth, quite forgotten by those who'd sent him zooming into the heavens in the first place. He was hounded by a feeling of dislocation.

He drove into Italy without a particular destination in mind. It was another country on the map, that was all. He went to Milan, and to Florence, and found himself one night in an inexpensive hotel room in Rome, pacing up and down, walking back and forth from door to window, a man trapped in a silent box. What the hell was he doing here? he wondered. What was he looking for? Even the small Christ on the wall gazed at him with neither understanding nor pity, more a kind of puzzlement.

He spoke to no one. He lived deep within himself. Four nights ago in the town of Alba — why in God's name had he traveled to Alba anyway? — he'd come belatedly to the conclusion that his disaffection lay in the fact he was running from his own history, from anniversaries, from memories of loss.

He'd watched a full moon sail in the direction of the Mediterranean and he'd thought how obvious it was: he was a fugitive from himself. The moon, charged with all the desolation of the season, was as indifferent to him as the Christ in the hotel in Rome. He'd driven back to France and taken a ferry to Ireland, imagining he might try his hand at fishing, but a few days on a numbing West Cork riverbank had persuaded him the fish had succumbed to winterkill and he didn't have the patience in any event. The solitary angler, demented in the cold, stubbornly watching his float vibrate to the drumming rain — that wasn't for him.

He didn't finish writing the postcard. He stuck it back in his pocket, rubbed his eyes, stretched his arms. He realized he was more inebriated than he liked. The condition tended to arouse a maudlin streak in him. *I want the impossible*, he thought. I want things the way they were. Roxanne resurrected from the dead, my job back, everything reassembled and welded together, history rewritten. He stared into his glass and contemplated the somber fact that old sorrows were never quite buried, and more recent grudges hadn't lost their bitter sting.

Irritated by the tide of his thoughts, he lit a cigarette, then immediately crushed it out. Get a grip, Pagan. Face it. The world isn't the way you want it to be. You're not the architect of the universe. And five pints of Guinness aren't going to make you so. Five pints of Guinness: he was half-drunk. He had no great capacity for the black stuff.

He rose a little unsteadily — the old Guinness shuffle — left the lounge, walked to the elevators, pressed a button. The doors slid open immediately. He rode up to the sixth floor. He unlocked the door of his room, stepped inside, flicked a light switch. Kicking off his shoes, he lay down on the bed. He didn't feel sleepy. He picked up the TV remote control and pressed a button and gazed at the picture. He hadn't looked at TV in days, nor had he felt inclined to buy newspapers.

There was an item on the screen that depicted a street corner in Belfast surrounded by scene-of-the-crime tape and cops whose faces were red from the cold. A Catholic taxidriver had been shot dead by Ulster Loyalists.

The momentum toward peace in Ulster was always fragmented by the same old sorry sectarian violence, the same lust for bloodletting. Pagan remembered his last experience with Irish terrorism, when he'd been in pursuit of the curiously discriminating Irish-American assassin known as Jig. He hadn't thought about Jig for a long time. It was an odd consideration now. Jig represented — if indeed such a thing existed — the acceptable face of terrorism. Casual violence, the random killing of taxidrivers because of their religious affiliations, the butchery of innocent people caught in bombings and crossfire: these things were beneath Jig. He regarded them with contempt. There was, Pagan thought, a certain nobility of purpose about the young man; in a sense he was a throwback to the days of the old IRA. His targets were always political. He always made sure that innocent bystanders were never caught up in his activities.

Pagan had gone to the young man's funeral outside Albany, an affair attended by thousands of mourners, Irish-Americans from New York and the New England states, from Chicago and California. An Irish Republican flag had been laid across the coffin. A solitary piper had played laments. Pagan had watched the coffin being lowered into muddy black ground on an incongruously gorgeous spring day and he'd thought how Jig's enthusiasms and passions, his belief in the rightness of the Irish Republican cause, had been responsible for his own destruction. Pagan had been struck that day by a sense of waste so potent he could almost taste it in the sunny air. The waste of money donated by misguided Irish-Americans to the Cause, the wasted fervor — and above all, the waste of the young man's life.

He'd listened to the bagpiper, watched a lark hover in the high clear air, and he'd realized that in another reality he and the dead young man might have been friends. Jig, finally, had died for nothing. The real tragedy. Lives gutted — and for what? He remembered Artie Zuboric, the acerbic FBI agent who'd grudgingly worked alongside him in pursuit of Jig, standing in the funeral crowd and whispering, "I don't get you, Pagan. The guy was a fucking assassin. A terrorist. So why are we here? Why did I let you drag me to this goddamn gathering of the clans? What was he supposed to have been — some kinda saint, Chrissakes?"

"If you don't know, I can't tell you," Pagan replied quietly.

"Sometimes you come out with this mystifying bullshit," Artie Zuboric had said, and sighed with irritation. "I must be missing something."

Pagan switched off the TV. He got up and went to the window and looked down at Stephen's Green. A man and woman walked arm-in-arm below, lovers under cold lamplights. Theirs was not a world in which terrorism intruded. They were secure in each other's company. Pagan experienced a pang, a rush of blood to his heart. Terrorism could touch anybody at any time, it came out of nowhere and twisted your world beyond recognition; he knew that only too well.

Inevitably, he thought of Roxanne. He'd long ago given up the sad regular trips to the cemetery, the bouquets of flowers laid against his wife's simple stone. Now he went only once a year on the anniversary of their marriage. The graveside visits were morbid; he'd always felt locked inside a love that no longer existed. He'd stare at the name on the headstone, shocked by the fact of death, of endings. There had been a time shortly after her death when he'd sensed her presence in the apartment, when he'd heard her voice, the movement of her body, and he'd gone from room to room looking for her, calling out her name in the dislocation of grief.

Let it go, Frank. You can't change it now. He closed his eyes; he had a sense of gears grinding without purpose in his brain.

His telephone rang. The sound, so unexpected, shocked him. He picked up the receiver.

"Frank?" It was Robbie Foxworth calling from London.

"Foxie," Pagan said, astonished. "How did you hunt me down, for Christ's sake?"

"It wasn't easy," Foxie said. His next words were partly lost amid whistling sounds, interference. "You leave a pretty tangled trail. I've probably talked to every hotel between Cork and Connemara tonight."

"Now that you've found me, what do you want?"

"There's a problem."

"What problem?"

"Something in your line of work."

"I thought I was supposed to be on—quote unquote—an extended leave of absence."

"Hearts have obviously been changed, Frank. Your expertise is needed. They want you back here on the next plane."

"Do they, now?"

"That comes straight from the top. From Mr. Nimmo."

"The bastard could have called me himself," Pagan said.

"Mr. Nimmo doesn't make conciliatory calls, Frank. Don't shoot me. I'm only the messenger."

"So they want me back."

"Call me when you know your ETA. I'll meet you."

"What if I told you to tell Nimmo to fuck off?"

"Somehow I think not. I know you better than that."

Pagan smiled. It was strange how exuberance could come out of nowhere, how quickly your blood could be made to surge. It only took a disembodied voice at the end of a telephone.

"Have you been listening to the news?" Foxie asked.

"I've made a point of avoiding it."

"I'll bring you up to date when I see you. But you'll read about it in the papers before then. It's a biggie, Frank."

"How big?"

"Disastrously so."

"I'll be in touch." Pagan put the phone down.

They want me back, he thought. They find my presence necessary. Well well. Hearts had indeed been changed. He was going home after all.

DURBAN, SOUTH AFRICA

4

Tobias Barron was driven north out of Durban in an air-conditioned limousine with tinted windows. The heavy sunlit humidity, which bore the gaseous stink of the streets, seemed to penetrate the car in an unpleasant way. Barron sat in the back alongside a small man called Mpande, who represented the Department of Education and who kept wiping streaks of perspiration from the lenses of his glasses. At one point on the outskirts of Durban, Barron pressed a button to roll down the electric window of the car and found himself gazing across a vacant lot where a crowd of black kids in American-style jeans watched the limo with an almost hostile curiosity. Mpande reached out, touched the button, the window rolled shut.

"A car of this kind makes certain people both envious and suspicious," Mpande said, and smiled.

He smiled, Barron thought, a great deal. Perhaps he was proud of his two gold front teeth. Barron settled back and after some miles felt the rhythm of the car change as it moved from a paved surface to dirt. Mpande was fond of talking, usually in statistics, which bored Barron more than a little, but he listened anyway and sometimes nodded his head. The percentage of blacks enrolled in universities — this was one of Mpande's favorite themes, and he rattled off a sequence of stats concerning the number studying the humanities, or engineering, or medicine. Mpande talked in the sepulchral tones of a born-again actuary.

Two hours out of Durban the car finally came to a stop. Mpande said, "Be warned. There will be a welcoming committee. You will find its members perhaps a little overenthusiastic, but that is understandable. After all, you are a celebrity. A philanthropist. You bring, shall we say, hope into their lives?"

Barron said nothing. He wondered if there might be a slight sarcastic edge in Mpande's tone. He stepped from the car when the driver opened the door. The heat was horrendous, a force, a great white foundry of light. Unaccustomed to this blinding ferocity, Barron took a little time to absorb his surroundings and the people who were waiting under the shade of a blue canvas awning to greet him. Mpande made polite introductions, the mayor of the township, various elders, a minister, a schoolteacher — more faces and names than Barron could possibly remember. Later, he'd reflect on how indistinct everything was, the smiles, the harsh sunlight, the scrubland, the aroma of putrefaction that came from an open sewer nearby, the shanties cobbled out of any available material, cardboard, corrugated tin, flimsy wood, metal pipes.

The mayor made a speech in English expressing the huge gratitude of the people of the township for Barron's extraordinary generosity in establishing an educational trust fund for the youth of the place. Now the brightest children could go on to colleges and universities. Now they had — and here the mayor paused and closed his eyes, swaying a little as if to give his choice of word extra significance — a *benefactor*. The crowd sighed with satisfaction and pleasure. Barron, sweating and uneasy in his white suit, listened with disguised impatience to all this. He wanted to get back to his air-conditioned hotel in Durban. He didn't enjoy the feeling he had of himself as the great white savior. He was only doing the kind of thing he'd done before in many underprivileged parts of the world — Guatemala, Somalia, Ethiopia: if it wasn't money for education, then it was medicine; if it wasn't medicine, then it was nutrition. Philanthropy — it was just one of the things he did.

Somebody took his photograph and he smiled, a reflex gesture. Then he was escorted across a dusty plaza to the local school, which was clearly an establishment of some pride in the township, even if the gray concrete was cracking in places and weeds grew from fissures in the play-yard and windows were broken. He was shown inside boxy rooms where rudimentary desks and chairs had been neatly aligned for the occasion of his visit. The rooms smelled of chalk dust and rust and were filled with flies. He noticed a blackboard on which had been written the phrases *Welcome, Mr. Barron* and *Thank You, Mr. Barron.*

Kids clustered around him, pressing themselves against him, as if any brief contact with his flesh might bring them good fortune. A nun, Irish and freckled and withered from years in a climate vastly different from that of her native County Clare, said *God bless you.* She had tears in her pale green eyes. Barron modestly dismissed his contribution as a drop in the ocean, and the nun agreed there was much to be done in the world, but if there were only more men like himself so *willing* to give, wouldn't life be better . . .

"Education," she said with all the solemnity of belief, "is one means of curbing violence."

Barron agreed with that.

He was escorted back to the shade of the blue awning, where he was expected to give a speech to the people of the township. He looked out across the five hundred or so black faces and spoke, as he always did on such occasions, in platitudes concerning the fulfillment of ambition and how, if you had the right attitude, anything was possible. He wondered if anybody ever *truly* understood what he was saying, or if the message was somehow too *American* in its optimism, too foreign — but they always applauded and cheered him anyway. A small pigtailed girl in a gingham dress was ushered forward to present him with a keepsake, a tiny handcrafted copper medallion in which his initials had been inscribed.

When the visit was over, he waved and stepped back inside the limousine, accompanied by the smiling Mpande.

"You have made them happy," he said to Barron.

"Perhaps."

"No perhaps. When you provide hope, you are also providing a lifeline to joy."

Barron settled back in his seat for the trip to Durban. He stretched out his legs and noticed that a streak of pale red dust adhered to the cuffs of his white pants.

■

His hotel suite had a view of Durban Harbor in which ships of varied registration lay at anchor. The sun was slipping out of the sky but the enormity of the day's heat hadn't dwindled. The sky over the harbor was hazy. The windows of the suite were warm to the touch. He poured himself a glass of ice water and sat at the table by the window, where the air-conditioning unit was located.

He spread before him several folders that contained information about some future projects. He had plans to raise money for a glaucoma clinic in Haiti and an agricultural research center in the Guantanamo Province of Cuba — if he could ever find a way of bypassing Fidel's leaden bureaucracy. He skimmed through the files, evaluating the reports of experts and bankers, which were written in the kind of droning English guaranteed to induce sleep. Tired of reading, he pushed the folders to one side, then looked at his watch. It was a few minutes after seven; he was due to leave South Africa in an hour.

He rose, wandered the room, listened. At seven-fifteen precisely he heard the sound of Nofometo knocking on his door — a distinctive two raps, a pause, then three further raps. Barron unlocked the door and Nofometo, a lean black man whose face was scarred from the lobe of his right ear to the corner of his mouth, a puckered zigzag disfigurement, entered the room. Nofometo wore a red T-shirt and baggy beige shorts; he had simple open sandals on his bare feet.

They shook hands. Nofometo walked to the table, opened the folders, scanned the pages, laughed. Barron had always thought Nofometo's laugh suggestive of an exotic bird.

"You are still busy doing good, I see," Nofometo said. He had the accent of a man educated in an English public school. He lay down on the sofa and put up his feet. He closed his eyes and added, "You are too perfect, Tobias. A perfect man in an imperfect world. How do you manage it?"

"Practice," Barron said.

Nofometo opened his eyes, the whites of which were faintly pink. He twisted his face, looked at Barron. "A perplexing saint. Saint Tobias. Saint Toby has a better ring to it, I think."

Barron sat in an armchair facing his visitor. He said nothing.

"Don't I merit a welcoming drink? Have you mislaid your manners?" Nofometo made a clucking sound of disapproval.

Barron smiled. "I have a plane to catch."

Nofometo swung himself into a sitting position. He tapped his bare knees with his fingertips. He took from the back pocket of his shorts a folded brown envelope. He gave it to Barron, who opened it and scanned the two handwritten sheets of paper inside.

"Fine," he said.

"Now you are going to ask about money," Nofometo said.

Barron said nothing. He had times when he enjoyed silences and the small discomfitures of other people. He stared quietly at the black man. Nofometo got up from the sofa and walked to the table, where he filled a glass from the jug of ice water. He took a sip and ran the back of one hand across his lips. "The usual wire transfer," he said. "Into the usual bank, I assume?"

"You have the account number."

"Scorched into my heart," said Nofometo. He gazed at the envelope in Barron's hand. "When can I expect delivery?"

"Three or four days."

Nofometo nodded in a pensive way. "The world looks at South Africa and sees this laudable movement toward democracy." He gave the word "democracy" a derisory inflection, as if it were a term of contempt. "But what nobody really sees is that the change is somewhat superficial. You don't revise history overnight. You don't just mark a ballot — and lo and behold, old animosities and racial conflicts disappear at the stroke of a pen. Democracy isn't the great panacea Americans always want it to be, Tobias. Of course, it may create a new class of black entrepreneurs. It may smooth the paths of a few. But what about the rest? What about the hopelessness in the townships? What about the masses that have suffered for generations in poverty? There is still anger, there is impatience, and people are restless because the political process is a slow one. Even as men drone on endlessly in one committee after another, there is an enormous raw undertow of discontent. As I see it, violence is inevitable in South Africa. And some of us want to be ready."

Barron had the thought that violence was inevitable everywhere. He said, "I'll do everything in my power, Nofometo."

"Don't you always?"

"I try," said Barron. *Saint Tobias*, he thought.

Venice

Barron slept on the private Learjet that took him to Marco Polo Airport. He boarded a motor launch named *Desdemona*, which ferried him toward the Grand Canal. In Venice he felt more at home than anywhere else in the world — of which he owned a considerable amount, including property in Telluride, Hong Kong, Costa Rica, and Coral Gables. He collected apartments and houses the way some men are driven to accumulate butterflies, rare coins, or women. He stood alongside the driver of the launch, a squat Venetian called Alberto, and he sniffed the night air, which was cold — especially after Durban — and smelled faintly of old herring. A pale moon was visible in the sky, illuminating the palaces in their splendid clutter along the banks.

Alberto said, "Welcome home, Signor Barron. You will find nothing changed. Venice. Does she ever change?"

Tobias Barron said only that he was glad to be back. He wore a black cashmere coat over his white suit, and a black silk scarf knotted at his neck. Gulls, disturbed by the engine of the launch, flew out of the *vaporetto* stations and winged toward the moon like large moths mesmerized by light. Barron gazed at the lit structures that leaned against the water, admiring as he always did the sheer persistence of beauty, the way grandeur prevailed against floods and pollution.

The imagination of men, he thought. It encompassed creation and destruction; but he found no paradox in this. The same inscrutable organ that could build was also able to destroy with equal facility. The human heart was a chamber in which dark and light might coexist. Only when these elements warred was there uncertainty.

He drew his scarf a little tighter at his neck. Venice was icy, cold to its soul. The *Desdemona* left the Grand Canal, steering into quieter waters, passing under low bridges. There were lights from cafés and trattorias. Lovers stood on a bridge and watched the launch pass under them. Laundry flapped against the sides of crumbling houses. Discarded plastic bottles that had once contained mineral water were agitated in the quiet wake of the boat and shuddered in pale white eddies. The smell here was stronger than it had been on the Grand Canal, danker, greener, as if just beneath the surface of water, fish mysteriously decomposed.

"We have arrived," Alberto said. He moored the launch and made sure in his fussy fashion that Signor Barron disembarked without hindrance. Then he gathered together Barron's suitcases and stacked them on the dock, where another man waited, Schialli, a taciturn fellow who had been Barron's servant for years.

Schialli and Alberto gathered the luggage and walked alongside Barron down a narrow thoroughfare called Calle dei Avocati, where at number 3720 Barron owned a house. He used only the upper two floors, converted into a large apartment; the rest of the place, although sumptuously decorated, was usually unoccupied.

Schialli, who always made a great business of the heavy keys, rattling them with a show of importance, unlocked the big door, which was sixteenth century and adorned by the carved heads of angry lions. The three men entered a flagstoned foyer, then stepped into an elevator. Schialli pressed a button and the lift rose with a quiet cranking sound.

"Is the woman here?" Barron asked when the elevator stopped.

"She is," said Schialli, with a slight inclination of his head.

Barron got out of the elevator, followed by the two men hauling his bags. The upper two floors of the house were joined by a spiral staircase; Barron's bedroom was directly above the drawing room. He directed the suitcases to be unpacked as soon as he entered the drawing room. The central heating system was blowing forced air throughout the apartment. He removed his coat and scarf and walked to the unlit marble fireplace, where he stood with his back to the hearth, as if this were the source of heat. Alberto had silently withdrawn, and Schialli, having unpacked the luggage in the bedroom and hung the clothing away, brought Barron a negroni and soda.

"Wait fifteen minutes, then send the woman to me," Barron said.

"Of course." Schialli went out.

Barron sipped the drink and moved around the room, which was furnished in an eclectic way with pieces purchased here in Venice. There might have been an uneasy juxtaposition of periods in the eye of an antique dealer, but Barron bought whatever appealed to him, regardless of the century to which the furniture belonged. A room was your own because you made it so. It was the same with the world, he thought. It was whatever you wanted it to be — if you had the power and the urge to shape it.

He wandered for a time, rippling the keys of a seventeenth century spinet that occupied the window space, where amber and claret brocade draperies hung. Possessions and belongings: one might enjoy them, but never to the point where they owned you. Everything was dispensable in the end. Everything could be returned to the auction room. He went back to the fireplace, the mantelpiece of which was littered with framed photographs.

There was a picture of Barron arm wrestling with the late Ferdinand Marcos in the Raffles Hotel in Singapore. In the shot Marcos was smiling, but behind the smile was the stress of a man whose sleazy machismo was on trial. Other pictures showed Barron in the company of Yasser Arafat, George Bush, Albert Reynolds, former *taoiseach* of the Republic of Ireland, the late Indira Gandhi, Al Gore, and William J. Caan, the United States ambassador to Britain. Good old Bill had his arm linked with Barron's in the shot, the big breezy ambassadorial smile in place.

Somebody had once half-jestingly said of Barron that he knew everybody in the world. He was on first-name terms with a variety of pols and show-business types. He'd known Visconte and Truffaut. He'd spent time in the company of Ronald Reagan and Jerry Brown. Barron seemed to exist in that shadowland of fame where politics and show business become one and the same, that place of dreams and power. He'd fallen under the spell of this hinterland; its landscape enchanted him. Men of power had about them a special presence. They moved through the world with a disregard for the banal demands of life. They rose above the commonplace; they ascended into their own heavens.

Barron saw his reflection in a mirror over the mantelpiece. No matter the season, he always had a suntan. He habitually wore white or beige suits to underline his bronzed features. He seemed never to age. Rumors of surgical adjustment were always smilingly denied. Despite his public image, he remained a private man. He was congenial, wealthy, handsome, he had a marvelously photogenic face — but what did anybody really know about him? Where did his bucks come from? How did he get to be such a high roller?

On the dinner circuit that rolled from Gstaad to Aspen and then to Monte Carlo, there were those who said he'd inherited wealth, while others spoke of a portfolio — suspect, nefarious — put together over a period of twenty years; there was also a wildly implausible story in which he'd gained access to Marcos's legendary cache of Japanese gold. None of these rumors had any basis in truth.

As for his origins, he always said he came from the obscure Californian town of San Luis Obispo, but he'd never been near the place, never seen pictures of it. In the end he was a mystery.

And that was precisely the way he wanted it.

He turned away from the photographs and unlocked the door of a small antechamber, a chilly space. An electronic world map, surrounded by a dozen clocks showing the time in different parts of the world, was located on one wall. Here and there red, yellow, and green cursors blinked. These indicated the status of any project at a given time; red was the color for a dubious area, green represented a situation already in hand, yellow stood for those places where negotiations were under way. On the surfaces of the oceans white cursors tracked the movement of ships; presently one was located off the coast of Madagascar, another in the Caribbean some hundred miles from Cuba, still another in the Baltic, about seventy miles from Tallinn. A fourth was cruising the Adriatic. The direction of land traffic — trains, trucks — was indicated by orange cursors, which flickered in such places as South Africa, Guatemala, Angola, and Afghanistan.

Shelves were lined with computer equipment, video consoles, a couple of laser printers, three fax machines. He had rooms similar to this in all his other properties; machines interfaced with other machines, as if in some form of electronic polygamy. Barron's world was wired, and the wires carried all manner of information. He looked at the messages that had come in over the faxes.

These fell into four broad categories. Some were detailed accounts of incidents in various parts of the world — a mass grave of women and children freshly dug up in Bosnia, the resurgence of the Communist party in various parts of what had once been the Soviet Union, a bloody uprising of the People's Army in the Southern Philippines, the deaths of twelve blacks at the hands of right-wing extremists in Transvaal, two hundred dead during ethnic violence in Eastern Zaire; these reports might have come from an exceptionally well-informed wire service, except that the correspondents were not employed by Reuters or Associated Press. They were not from journalists accredited in any sense of the word.

The second category consisted of analyses created by experts paid by Barron; these were assessments of situations in an assortment of troubled countries and regions and computer-generated predictions concerning the possible outcomes of crises in places like Nigeria, the Lebanon, Bosnia, Somalia, Northern Ireland. Key figures involved in these disputes — politicians, dictators, potentates, warlords, gangsters and miscellaneous scum — were meticulously profiled. Barron always read these reports carefully.

The third category of messages was requests for assistance, sometimes in the form of money. The final classification concerned logistics, the movement of trains and trucks and ships, timetables.

Barron regarded all these messages for a while. As he did so, he was struck by the range of human dreams and aspirations. He considered his own role a moment. He was the man who provided the fuel for dreams. What did the nature of the dreams themselves matter? He saw himself sometimes as an illusionist, a magician whose art lay in imbuing dreams with substance, a shaper of other people's worlds. It was as if he were at the center of some enormous board game whose rules he'd devised himself. He brooded

over the board, shifted this or that piece, studied the consequences of each move; unlike other games, this one had no black
or white pieces, no forces set in opposition to each other, no sides
he favored.

He turned off the light, locked the antechamber. Inside the drawing room the woman was waiting for him. He went toward her, took
her hand and kissed it.

"You're cold," he said.

The woman smiled a little forlornly. He drew her toward a sofa
in front of the fireplace. The material of her blouse was icy to his
touch. He observed her beautiful face, which, already lightly
touched by the process of aging, had begun to show small lines —
but these contrived to add a dimension to her loveliness. Some
women were destined to spectacular maturity.

"Drink?" he asked.

She shook her head. "I think not. I'm not in the mood."

He finished his negroni. "What mood are you in?"

She shrugged. "Hard to say."

"Ambivalent."

"Call it that."

"You should never be ambivalent in Venice," he remarked. He
observed her briefly. What this room needed was genuine firelight,
flames that would enhance the woman's features. There was some
danger in her expression, a cutting brittle quality. He knew she was
in a state of withdrawal. She had these times in which she abandoned any known reality and retreated to a place of her own making. He could never quite follow her down these mazy trails. He
could never altogether imagine the inside of her head. She was beyond classification at times, a caller from another planet.

He mixed himself a second negroni — campari, a splash of ver-
mouth, a generous quantity of gin. The woman watched him and
thought: How typical of Barron to come out with a remark like that.
You should never be ambivalent in Venice. It had a quiet certitude to it.
It was the way he said so many things. He was so sure of himself.
Cocksure. She stood up, pressed the palms of her hands against her
thighs, felt the lamb's wool of her navy blue skirt create a friction

against her legs. She approached him, laid her face against his shoulder. The bronze of his skin seemed to emit a form of energy.

He put his hand against the side of her face. She always sent little depth charges through him. He wondered about the bizarre nature of chemistry, of human attraction, desire. He wondered about love, if it were merely a matter of musks that stimulated certain areas of the brain. Did he love this woman? The question was unanswerable. All he could ever truly admit was that she held a deep fascination for him, that when it came to her, he'd developed an uncharacteristic blind spot, that he experienced curious urges to protect her, both from the world and from herself.

"I'm not sure I'm enjoying your mood," he said. "You're too introspective. Too languid. If that's the word."

She wandered away from him, studied the pictures on the mantelpiece. "Why do you need these things?" she asked.

"My public persona needs them."

"And is there really such a difference between the public Barron and the private one?"

He stirred his drink. "You know that by this time."

"I'm not sure I really know anything."

He said nothing. She'd never asked about his life, his past, his origins. It was as if she wanted him to have no beginnings.

"I always think these photographs suggest a weakness," she said. "A defect of character."

"Are you going to tell me something obvious about my base need for recognition? If you are, skip it. I know what the pictures mean. There's no mystery about it. I have an ego, which likes being stroked."

"Yes," she said. "You have an ego."

He caught her hand and held it against his chest.

"As big as your own," he said.

"Maybe so."

"Except you're wayward. More theatrical."

"And you're not? What would you call these?" And she gestured toward the photographs. "You're a collector of famous people. What could be more theatrical?"

"My public image is useful to me," he said.

She broke free of him, strolled the room, then she paused at the foot of the spiral staircase that led to the large attic bedroom above. She gazed up along the intricate design of wrought iron to the shadows overhead. She thought of Barron's oversized bed, the silken canopy, the tapestry on the wall. Turning, she parted the curtains and opened the door to the balcony overlooking the canal.

Barron followed her. They stood together in silence for a time. A couple of tarpaulined gondolas shivered like glassy black coffins on water. The moon was flint, frosty. The night had an immeasurable density to it.

He kissed her. She turned her face to the side, gently pushed him away, shook her head.

"It's worse than ambivalent, I guess," he said.

"You taste of gin."

"Since when was that a problem?"

She ran her hand over the cold balcony rail. She peered out into the darkness. She sensed the night as one might sense nearby the presence of a large dangerous cat. Venice seemed to have a peculiarly feline quality just then, its passageways and darkened *campos* the hunting grounds of foraging leopards.

He took her hand, stroked it softly. "Let's go inside. Upstairs."

She hesitated before following him. She started up the spiral staircase, then stopped halfway. She turned to look down at him, at the impossibly tanned face, the exquisitely handsome features. The sheer perfection of him scared her in some way. Nobody had any right to look like Barron. His beauty was unreasonable. And how had he stopped his internal clocks from marking their passage?

She kept climbing. When she reached the bedroom she lay down, sprawled across the bed, one leg upraised. "I'm not in the mood, Barron."

"You keep saying so." He stood over the bed, gazing down at her. She looked vulnerable all at once. But the trouble with her vulnerability was how it could change and become hard-edged. She was in that sense like the weather. And he had no barometer for measuring her changes.

He lit a red candle on the bedside table, sat on the edge of the mattress, slid his hand up and down the lower part of her leg. "Tell me what you feel," he said.

"What I feel . . ."

He cupped his hand around her knee bone. With his other hand he picked up the candle and held it over her.

She turned to look up into his face. She knew she'd succumb to him, she understood the inevitability of it all. She watched the flame. She felt the first drip of red wax on her arm and then, as he moved the candle, the second fell across her knuckles. The wax burned, hardened on her skin as the heat dissipated. She drew the hand that held the candle closer to her face, and the shapeless hot wax slid against her cheeks, drip drip drip, each touch of heat bringing her momentary pain. She thought she felt some mild resistance in Barron, as if he wanted to set the candle aside.

"Nearer," she said. "Closer."

He drew her blouse away from her shoulders; hot waxy rivulets slithered toward her breasts. He worked the tips of his fingers along her inner thigh, back and forward, a gentle brushing motion. She shut her eyes and concentrated on his touch and the way wax spluttered upon her skin. She could still see the candle in her head, could still feel the heat against her face and neck.

"What I feel . . ." Her eyes were still shut. She was losing her breath. His hand moved across her stomach and rested in the smooth flat area below the navel. She brought her hand down so that it covered his and she maneuvered his fingers between her legs. She half-opened her eyes, drawn into the hypnotic shifting flame. She raised a hand, seized Barron's wrist, made him bring the candle closer to her nipples. She experienced the exquisite intensity of the flame's core, wax running and stiffening beneath her breasts, rolling and congealing on the surface of her stomach. The flame was searing, brilliant. She wanted to be sucked down into the explosive heart of it — but he set the candle back on the table and lowered his face toward her stomach. She felt his lips on her skin, his breath in her navel, and she caught his head between her hands, pushing him lower, down into herself, down into the secrets that were no longer secrets to him, but places so familiar he might have drawn maps of them from memory alone.

As if she were blind, robbed all at once of a sense, she guided his face between her legs, felt his mouth, his tongue, his teeth. It was freefall now, that loss of will and wisdom, balances upset, awareness no more than a series of fierce jolts to her nervous system. She drew herself up, her eyes still shut, and then she kneeled, pressing her face down into his groin, her fingers moving quickly, it was all haste, everything was grounded in the possibilities of the moment. Making a soft funnel of her tongue, she took him inside her mouth before he brought her face up with a mildly persistent gesture.

He gazed at the fine hair of her eyebrows, then he undid the buttons of her blouse more slowly than she liked, so she hurried him, helped him, then the room was shimmering away out of control, tilting on an unlikely axis, a contrary turning of the world outside her senses.

She felt him at the edge of entrance, that second before penetration. She heard herself say something, but the voice that emerged from her mouth wasn't her own, she was speaking as if for somebody else, a distinct entity that existed outside of who she was. She'd become a disconnected sequence of impulses and thrills, a thing fragmented like stained glass struck by a shotgun. She felt him enter her, the brute sweetness of it. A dark scented breeze blew through her mind.

She hung to him, held him, swayed with him, rocked furiously against him. She clawed his spine, dug, wanted him deeper inside her, to feel him in her womb. Indifferent to anything around her, she had the feeling she might suddenly rise and go on rising from the bed, uplifted by an enigmatic current of air. She spoke his name aloud, hearing the syllables break inside her mouth, listening to the crazy collision of vowels and consonants. But passion had no grammar, no logic, no meaning beyond itself. She drifted out over a dark promontory, a place of madness. The fall was long and heartbreaking and when it was over, she lay in the kind of silence that might be the aftermath of a dream, the juncture where waking thoughts trespass on the constructs of sleep.

She didn't move for a long time. She was aware of Barron staring at her. She edged slightly away from him now, dismayed by the disarray of her clothes, by the sight of his cock glistening against his thigh, the dark crown of hair in his groin. Her appetites devoured her; she had no escape from them.

She gazed at Barron, then looked into the flame of the candle. She ran her fingers through her hair. She'd never liked that look of content on Barron's impossible face. That satisfaction. It was as if she'd given him a gift she never intended. Rather, it was more as if he'd plundered it, seized it from her.

"Why do you make me behave like this?" she asked.

He said, "I've never made you do anything you didn't want to do."

She got up from the bed. "You have a hold over me and I don't understand it. But it makes me despise myself."

"What hold? You're a free agent," he said. "I don't own you."

She laughed at this one. A free agent. "All I am, Barron, is your dirty little secret. The woman who comes and goes after dark. We never walk together in the daylight. We don't go to restaurants. Theaters. What the hell. I don't think I give a shit. Not in the long run. You want to be the hotshot. You like to have people kissing your feet."

Barron said, "You're back in that weird mood again."

"How would you know anything about my moods?"

"From experience," he said. "From watching you. From caring."

"Caring," she said. She walked around the bed, heading toward the bathroom. "You can get inside me, Barron. But you can never get *inside* me."

She glanced toward the bathroom. Her image came back to her from the mirrored walls, strange angles, diminishing reflections. She didn't recognize herself in any of them. The hardened wax shapes on her flesh suggested fresh scars.

Barron smiled at her from the bed. His smile was like a fortress at times. You could scale the walls, you could climb to the turrets, but in the end you were defeated. She had times when she wanted to bring down the whole edifice that was Tobias Barron.

She locked the bathroom door, stepped inside the shower, ran scalding water over her flesh, soaped herself vigorously, cleansed herself of wax, of Barron's touch. But was it Barron she was trying to clean away — or was it that dark enjoyable aspect of herself he managed always to explore? She closed her eyes and listened to the drumming of water.

DUBLIN

5

Just after dawn, Frank Pagan bought a copy of the *London Times* at Dublin Airport. He found the story on the front page, together with a smoky photograph of what looked like the crushed and blackened remains of an Underground carriage. Without the accompanying caption it would have been difficult to tell. Rails, bent and uprooted by the blast, created pincers around the carriage, which had lost all shape and form. Firemen labored in the wreckage, their faces bleached of features by harsh lamps. The picture had the grainy feel of an old wartime photograph of atrocities.

Pagan stared at it for a long time; it defied understanding. It was painful and chaotic, brutal and tragic. It vibrated with loss. His eyes drifted across the story. He registered key words and phrases. *Rush hour. Underground. Piccadilly. The number of casualties has not been estimated. Nobody has claimed responsibility for the outrage, believed to have been caused by a sophisticated explosive device.*

Responsibility, he thought. He tried to imagine a bomb blast in the London Underground system during rush hour. Why would anyone want to claim *that* as their own work? He'd encountered many acts of terrorism before, too many, but he'd never been able to comprehend to his complete satisfaction the heart of them, not even when they came wrapped in tedious political dogma. Nor was he immune to the anger they induced in him. Did those lunatics

believe extreme violence brought sympathy for their cause, whatever it was? Did they think the massacre of innocents won them
some kind of bloodstained respectability? He knew he might have
had more composure, more professional detachment, but he'd
never achieved that state of disinterest.

He wandered around the terminal impatiently. He had half an
hour before his plane boarded. He bought a cup of coffee, spread
the newspaper out on his table, and looked at the photograph again.
So. He was going back to London to deal with this. This was why
Nimmo — Mr. Nimmo, as Foxworth pointedly called the upstart — had commanded him to return. My line of work, he
thought. My specialty. Blood and death. Carnage. Did he have the
heart for it? Did he have the protective armor it took to cope with
destruction? He was eager to get back into the stream of things, but
he wondered if his spell of recent inactivity, and the shabby way he'd
been treated during Nimmo's "reconstruction," might have diminished his appetite for dealing with terrorism.

He sighed, closed the newspaper, set it aside, and then picked it
up once more, drawn irresistibly back to the photograph. He was
sucked down into it, as though he were trapped inside the frame and
stood alongside the wreckage, a prisoner of violence. He imagined
he felt the heat of the lamps against his face and that if he were to
reach out a hand, his fingers would be scalded by molten metal.
Troubled, he folded the newspaper so that the photograph was no
longer visible. He pushed it aside and thought: I am going back to
a world where everything that moves does so in shadow.

London

Foxworth was waiting at Heathrow when Pagan's plane arrived before noon. He'd been Frank's assistant for years, give or take those
times when he'd been shuffled off into other areas of criminal investigation. He'd been in Art Fraud, that cut-price basement of police
activities, for a while. Once, briefly, he'd worked in Internal Affairs,
an unhappy interlude in his life; he didn't make a good spook. He
belonged with Pagan in counterterrorism, that nebulous zone populated by spurious little groups who bestowed acronyms upon

themselves as if these might impart dignity to motives that were often grubby.

"It's great to see you, Frank." He shook Pagan's hand and thought Frank looked fatigued, rather pale and sunken, although you could never quite douse the little light of determination in his gray eyes.

"Here. Make yourself useful. Take my bag."

"Always one to oblige," Foxie said. He grabbed Pagan's suitcase. "You travel light."

"What's the point of excess baggage? God knows, I carry enough of that as it is." He walked ahead of Foxie in the direction of the exit. The early sun over London was cold, drained of color, assailed by clouds. Pagan was struck by a longing to see a great blue sky.

"I have a car waiting," Foxie said.

They went toward the car park. Pagan said, "You look different, Foxie. I can't quite put my finger on it."

Foxie remarked that he'd had his hair cut, but Pagan saw only the usual gingery brush effect.

"Perhaps the new threads," Foxie said. He was wearing a pin-striped suit similar to all the other suits he owned. He favored the Savile Row thing, three-piecers, old school tie, a clubby appearance. Pagan liked more casual gear, jeans, bright shirts, linen suits he had made up for him by a tailor with basement premises on Greek Street. The Youthful Look. Keeping time at bay on a strict budget. Foxie at least had the benefit of income from a generous trust fund.

The car was a black Rover. Foxie stashed the suitcase on the back-seat and got behind the wheel.

"Bloody cold," Pagan said.

Foxie turned the heater on. "It's been the worst winter in twenty-five years, they say."

The weather, Pagan thought. Those poor bastards in the tube were beyond any weather. "Tell me what you know about the explosion, Foxie."

Straight to business, Foxie thought. Characteristic of the man. Small talk made him irritable. "What we know is that somebody put a bomb in the tube. We don't know yet what kind of device. The lab will come up with that information. The usual time-consuming reconstruction. I'll say this — I haven't seen anything quite like it in my life. The bodies are burned beyond recognition. It's an unholy mess down there."

"I can imagine." He thought of a tunnel, people trapped in fiery steel, the terrible claustrophobia of death.

"The truly puzzling thing is, we haven't had any of the usual phone calls. If it was the IRA, they'd have made one of their coded calls beforehand. But this is different. This isn't quite their style. It doesn't seem to be anybody's style, actually."

"I want to see the scene, Foxie."

"I'm under strict orders to deliver you to Nimmo before you do anything else. He wants to brief you himself."

Pagan looked from the window. The Rover was on the motorway to central London. "Tell me, Foxie. Why am I being resurrected?"

"Nimmo needs your experience."

"Suddenly." Pagan shoved his hands in the pockets of his coat. He was still cold, despite the heater.

Foxie said, "I suspect he's out of his depth and he wants somebody with experience to run the show. Look at it this way, Frank. He can't lose. If you make a success of it, he gets much glory. If you fudge it, he's got himself a whipping boy."

"I'm not whipping boy material. I bleed easily."

"It's politics," Foxie said.

"Fuck politics. I've never played politics. I don't have the skills. I'm short on turpitude. I prefer not to lie. I don't have the qualifications for politics."

Pagan stared out the window, brooding, silent, thinking of the explosion in the Underground. After a while he imagined he could hear the sound of people screaming in a dark tunnel. He shut the noise out of his head. Stand back. Keep your cool. If you allow it, you'll become submerged, drawn down into that place where you suffocate. Sometimes you imagine too much.

He turned to Foxie just as the car approached Hammersmith. "Have you heard anything about Martin Burr?"

"I understand he spends half his time down in Hampshire cultivating roses and the other half at his Knightsbridge place," Foxie said. "Enjoying his retirement by all accounts."

"The end of an era."

"On with the new," Foxie said.

"New doesn't necessarily mean better."

"How does one quantify better?"

"*How does one quantify better?* Who have you been reading recently, Foxie?"

"Thomas Aquinas. Does it show?"

Pagan sighed and folded his arms. "Thomas Aquinas. Stick with spy novels."

"They're not the same since the Berlin Wall came down."

Pagan was swept by a moment of fatigue. "Nothing's the same since the Wall came down."

Foxie stopped the Rover at a traffic light. There was something a little strange in Pagan's mood, he wasn't sure what. As an inveterate Pagan-watcher, he'd seen Frank in many phases. Arrogant. Brutal. Sympathetic. At times even softhearted. But now there was a difference about him, an alteration hard to define. He had a wearily defensive air. It was as if he'd come back from his enforced vacation disillusioned by the way he'd been cast aside in the first place, and now he felt vulnerable, bruised by the political shenanigans that had sent him into limbo. Maybe he was wary of his future. He had every right to be, Foxie thought.

He was at Nimmo's whim. And Nimmo's whim was no place to be.

■

The office was spartan, authoritarian. No family pictures; presumably George Nimmo didn't have a family, or if he did, he kept it tucked away in Berkshire or wherever he lived. No paintings on the walls. No pictures of Nimmo gabbing with the prime minister or the Home Secretary. No diplomas. No framed thank-you letters from grateful charities. Alone, waiting for Nimmo to appear, Pagan reflected on the strange blankness of the room. You could deduce nothing about the inhabitant from this place. It was a long cold box, a deep-freeze. It contained a plain desk, bookshelves of law volumes, a black leather swivel chair. An ascetic's room, a dedicated civil servant's room — where was the untidy array of papers, the stuffed In tray, the general dishevelment that had characterized Martin Burr's reign? He had a quiet surge of affection for Martin just then. Burr had been approachable, a friend. Burr had often put his neck on the guillotine for Pagan.

This place unnerved Pagan even as he tried to remain aloof from the prospect of seeing George Nimmo. Their last encounter had been marked by Nimmo's offhand hostility. We will try to find a place for you in the new scheme of things, Frank. I can't promise it will be easy or quick. Rhubarb rhubarb. The boot was the boot, Pagan thought, no matter what you called it. The swift kick in the anus.

Pagan drummed his fingers on the side of his chair and looked up at the ceiling. It was typical of Nimmo to keep you waiting. He wanted to give the impression that he'd squeezed you in between more urgent business.

When the door opened, Pagan didn't turn to look. He didn't get up from his chair. Nimmo walked past him to the desk and sat down. "How was your holiday, Frank?"

A holiday, Pagan thought. So that was what Nimmo was calling it. He looked at Nimmo, who was a big man with an air of blustery congeniality that might deceive an innocent into thinking he was not only human but quite affable besides. The soft round pink face, the pendulous lower lip, the high forehead. Nimmo's hair was unruly, curly, touching the collar of his jacket. Probably the hairstyle hadn't changed much since prep school. You could see on his face the ruins of childhood, a ghost of the boy he'd been, the kind of kid who tries to befriend everyone and yet somehow always fails, despite favors and gifts. He might have been cherubic in those days, with soft-cheeked choirboy features. This lapsed boyishness was altogether misleading, a useful disguise.

"My holiday was fine, Mr. Nimmo," Pagan said. He'd maintain an equilibrium here, a forced politeness. If he yielded to any other kind of behavior, if he loosed his cannons of complaint and anger, he'd drop points to Nimmo, and that was unthinkable.

"Come, Frank. Don't be so formal. George." Nimmo, who mistook light sarcasm for propriety, laughed. He had a professional laugh, one that was rooted not in mirth but in expediency. Some people fell for it. Some people thought the laugh contagious and were confused into thinking Nimmo a merry soul. "Europe, wasn't it? France? Switzerland?"

"Italy. Switzerland. Germany. Austria. Finally Ireland." Pagan wondered what would happen if he were to whip out a hundred holiday snapshots and flash them at George. *This is the center of Dijon, and that's me holding a pot of the local mustard. And this is the Floriani Wine Bar in the Hotel Weitzer in Graz. And here I am standing in front of the Bayerischer Hof in Lindau, freezing my arse.*

"Switzerland," said Nimmo, as if that was all he'd heard of Pagan's itinerary. "I have always admired the Swiss. Much to be said for neutrality, of course."

This was a very Nimmolike statement. He peppered his speech with unassailable *of courses*, and had the odd verbal mannerism of dropping the sound *yo* into his sentences the way some people might say *um* or *er*. Pagan supposed this was an affectation from public school or university. Perhaps Nimmo considered it an endearing little eccentricity.

"You wonder why I have had you returned to the fold," Nimmo said. He looked suddenly like a quizmaster awaiting a response.

"I saw the newspapers," Pagan said.

"We have a situation."

A situation? Pagan thought. Nimmo could have made Hiroshima sound like a fireworks display.

"A very bad situation. And I want you to handle it, Frank."

"Why me?"

"No need for false modesty. You have experience in this field."

"What field?"

Nimmo put the smile on again. "Are you trying to make this difficult for me?"

"On the contrary, George," Pagan said. He heard an edge of irritation in his own voice. "I'm asking a straightforward question. What field? My expertise is in counterterrorism. But I understand no group has come forward to take credit, if that's the word, for the explosion. And since that's the case, how can you be sure we're dealing with organized terrorism here?"

"Who else would bomb a bloody train, for God's sake? My money is squarely on this being the IRA, peacefire or no peacefire. And if it isn't the official IRA, then it's one of the die-hard splinter groups that refuse to accept the notion of peace."

"Maybe. But you could come up with a number of candidates for this one. A lone madman. A psychopath with some kind of bomb and a massive grudge against London Transport. There are some weirdly disaffected people in this world. They get very pissed off because fares are going up or trains don't run on time, or because they've been fired from their job as a ticket clerk. They begin to obsess and before long you've got a deranged person with a hugely destructive rage. There are some off-the-wall loonies in the quietest of suburbs. Strange men in string vests and combat jackets are patiently building tiny bombs in their garden sheds even as we sit here. You know that. I know that. So why do you assume this to be the act of the IRA or any other terrorist group?"

"Some assumptions *need* to be made. We cannot go around whistling in the dark, Frank."

"In my experience, organized terrorists always claim responsibility. There's hardly ever an exception. They're in the business of making statements, violent statements, and it does them no damn good to carry out the violence without claiming it. It doesn't fulfill them. It doesn't satisfy them."

Nimmo was quiet a moment. He clasped his fleshy hands on the desk and looked aggravated by Pagan's tone of voice. "Frank, Frank. Let's clear the air. I understand you think you've been wronged. I don't condemn you for your sense of injustice. I sympathize with it. You feel you were unjustly discarded. It was not an easy decision for us to make. Reorganization often entails difficult adjustment."

Difficult adjustment, Pagan thought. He stared at Nimmo. You'll never know, George.

"But what you perceive as exile was nothing more than, *yo*, a temporary business. We put you on hold, of course. I am not denying that. I admit it might have been done with more, shall we say, finesse. But it was not my decision alone, Frank. Contrary to popular belief, I don't make decisions in a vacuum. I consult. I inquire. I survey. That is the way business is done around here now."

"By consensus."

"As you say. Some of your colleagues, even those who express admiration for you, admit to a certain suspicion that you are not *entirely* a team player. I think you would agree with that assessment. And in a world of team players, the man who likes to carry the ball alone is sometimes suspect. You have an inclination to do things your own way. This tempered the decision to put you on hold. Keep that in mind, Frank. It was never the intention to discard you permanently. Far from it."

A world of team players, Pagan thought. He wondered if he wanted to live in it. It suggested drab conformity, a deadening of initiative. Men of little flair compensated for their failure of imagination by banding together in castrated herds that called themselves committees.

Nimmo said, "And now we have a situation that we believe will suit your talents." He opened a drawer absently, glanced inside, closed it again. "I think you are the best man to deal with this affair."

A little chilly flattery. Pagan wasn't buying it. It was too late in the day to be convinced that Nimmo felt even the smallest regret an injury had been done. Besides, with all his talk of team players, it was clear that Nimmo didn't accept total responsibility for the banishing order. He was too shifty for that, too cunning. He spread the blame around in a tidy fashion. But it was hard to shovel shit without some sticking to you.

"Isn't MI5 in on this?" Pagan asked. "I thought counterterrorism fell into their domain."

"They're sniffing around, of course. But as you just pointed out, there has been no terrorist claim. Consequently, no terrorist organization is as yet *officially* responsible. So our friends see it for the moment as, *yo, more or less* a police matter. We may have interference. They are not uninterested, naturally. They have an eye on the situation." Nimmo got up and walked to the bookshelves and gazed at the volumes. He plucked at his fleshy lower lip. Pagan thought there was an element of the fallen angel about Nimmo. He'd made commitments to a variety of devils.

"I have never subscribed to the idea that counterterrorist activity should be the exclusive domain of intelligence, Frank. And it isn't just MI5. You have a plethora of groups with their finger in the terrorist pie. The Defence Intelligence Staff. Army Intelligence Corps. Joint Intelligence Committee. The list goes on. I have always advocated that a single unit should be responsible for that area. Namely, Special Branch. We are just as well equipped as anyone else to handle everything. I have always said so. Mine has been, alas, a solitary voice in the clamor of Whitehall."

Ah. A light dawned on Pagan, a penny dropped. He understood now. Nimmo perceived this disaster as an opportunity for self-aggrandizement, a chance to show those who made major decisions along Whitehall that the police could cope as well as anyone, thank you. Nimmo saw this tragedy as a canvas on which he might, *yo*, inscribe his own florid signature. *George Nimmo. Look at me! I exist!* Why am I not surprised? Pagan wondered. The callous heart of the base human need for self-aggrandizement. The sorry desire for approbation, no matter what. He suspected Nimmo had been beaten up at school, bullied in the yard. Kids had a way of sniffing out a misfit in their midst. Now he was determined to show the boneheads of Whitehall that he'd been a visionary all along. It was political buccaneering.

"You will be answerable to me, of course. Any and all information you get comes to me. You make no significant decisions without consultation. Is that clear, Frank?"

It was ruthlessly clear. Nimmo wanted to get in before one of the intelligence agencies decided it was their business after all. He wanted his own foothold, his own encampment. And if the intelligence boys desired a piece of the action, Nimmo's investigation — conducted by Pagan, the old maestro — would be so deeply entrenched that they couldn't interfere without raising grave questions of jurisdiction. Sweet, if you liked that kind of brute sneaky ambition.

"And if this was a terrorist act? What then? Do the intelligence people take it over?" Pagan asked.

"Leave that to me, Frank. I rather think I'm more equipped to deal with the intricacies of the situation. Intelligence has to be handled in a certain way. And if you'll forgive me saying so, you are not the diplomatic type." Nimmo laughed, as if the idea of Pagan understanding the fragile balance of power between Special Branch and the intelligence agencies were too far-fetched for credibility. Pagan could never grasp what was discussed around green baize tables in locked rooms. He was the wrong sort of chap for that stratified area where matters of policy were determined. Good man in the field, of course, but hadn't gone to the right schools.

The laugh grated on Pagan. He said, "One thing. I want Foxworth with me."

"Take him. Call on anybody you like. Within reason."

"And I want my old office back."

"Why? I can have you accommodated here, Frank. Anyhow, your old stamping grounds are being used for storage, I believe."

Pagan was persistent. "Golden Square."

Nimmo, even if he looked mildly aggravated, put up no objection. "Golden Square it is."

"I'll get started immediately."

Nimmo wandered back to his desk. He sat in the swivel chair. Pagan was quiet a moment before he asked, "Is there any updated information about the kind of explosive device we're dealing with?"

"Not yet. But the explosives people have found promising signs. Don't ask me what promising means. I'm told we can expect the full picture soon." Nimmo stood up, looked at his wristwatch. "John Downey, Frank. Talk to him. He can bring you up to date. He's been at the scene since the beginning. He established an operations center down there. On the spot, as it were."

"I'll be in touch," Pagan said. He stepped out of the office and walked along the corridor. He pressed a button for the elevator. He considered John Downey. Downey down in the mines. Downey had always been an enemy, always hostile.

He entered the lift. The door slid shut. As he rode to the ground floor, he felt curiously lightheaded. He experienced a moment of displacement, as if everything around him were unreal.

"How did it go?" Foxie asked.

"Take me underground, Foxie," he said. "Take me to the pit."

BURGUNDY

6

For weeks now Jacob Streik had been driving with an automatic pistol in the glove compartment of his rented Saab. His big plump hands lay on the steering wheel like two plucked squabs. The French countryside drifting past was misty, stricken by wintry indifference. Streik, whose belly overhung the waist of his trousers with such prominence he might have been theatrically padded, was sweating. The heater blew out a relentless gust of hot air and no matter what dial Streik turned, he couldn't reduce the flow.

He looked in his rearview mirror. The road behind was empty. The symmetry of poplar trees had been eroded by foggy air. Streik had the radio turned on and was absently listening to a news bulletin. His French was very poor but he understood that some kind of explosion had happened in London.

London made him think of Bryce Harcourt. Bryce had a kind of Ivy League detachment, a nonchalance only old money and old schools could impart. Lucky Harcourt, Streik thought, born into privilege. Harcourt Senior had made his fortune growing oranges and pulping them for juice. Oranges, Christ's sake. How could you make a goddamn fortune out of things with *seeds?*

Streik didn't resent Bryce his upbringing. In his own way he was very fond of the guy, even if they came from different worlds. Streik had been born in the Bronx, abandoned by his vagabond father, brought up — if that was the expression to describe a childhood of broken-down playgrounds and decrepit tenements — by his mother, an ice pick of a woman who had a major chill factor in her voice. Jesus, what would she think of him now? He could practically hear her say, I knew you'd amount to nothing, Jake. Just like your father. Whine, whine.

The voice on the radio mentioned something about a number of casualties. Streik had never understood French arithmetic. Consequently the tally passed over his head. He pulled the Saab to the side of the road and fumbled beneath his seat for a bottle of wine he'd placed there a few hours ago, a cheap red he'd bought in one of the insignificant villages he'd spent the past few weeks driving through. A guy couldn't go on like this. Running, always running. It wrecked the system, frazzled the nerve endings. Maybe he should've stayed cool the way Harcourt had advised, maybe he should have remained in the States or the UK. Bryce had said, *There's no need to go into hiding yet. It probably isn't the way you think it is, Jake.* But Streik wasn't buying that. Harcourt was courting disaster by hanging around London and going through the everyday motions of a life. He was too attached to his world, the Court of St. James's, the parties, the whole social bit, the ladies. Especially the ladies. That was Bryce for you, Mister Cool. Thinking himself safe.

Streik knew otherwise. He'd been followed in Manhattan. He'd been hound-dogged in London. The guys watching him always had the same look of feigned indifference. But they weren't fooling him. He'd been around too long.

He took off the cork, raised the bottle to his mouth, drank. He was hung over, but that was a constant these days. He liked to take the brassy edge off reality. In his opinion reality was overrated.

He stepped out of the car. He moved in his usual cumbersome way. He stared into the mist, listened for the sound of traffic. He might have been standing in the heart of a void. No birds were singing. Winter had sucked life out of the landscape. He peered into the trees. Where will you spend the night, fat man? he wondered. Another half-assed pension? another greasy little room above some patisserie?

He looked this way and that. Visibility was about thirty yards. He finished the wine in one dazzling gulp and tossed the bottle into the trees. He didn't hear it fall. *They want me dead,* he thought. It was a numbing consideration. Killers in the mist.

He realized he was halfway buzzed again. When he moved toward the trees to urinate, his center of gravity was off. He listed to one side as he undid the buttons of his cavernous gray trousers. He relieved himself, then went back to the car.

He spread a map on the passenger seat. He stayed clear of the major highways and big towns. The idea was to keep losing himself in villages and hamlets, creating a pattern impossible to follow. A nomad in a Saab. It was one kind of future. Better a Saab than a coffin.

He ran a fingertip over the map. He had an old associate called Audrey Roczak in Lyon, but he wondered if old associates were reliable these days. They could have been forewarned. The whole world was uncertain. Audrey, though — there had always been a nice rapport with her. She'd always been kind to him. She had the knack of ignoring his gross appearance. She'd been warm and comforting and they might have amounted to something together, given a chance.

He started the car, steered down a twisting minor road that wasn't on his map. Before noon he found himself in a one-street hamlet. Post office, butcher's, a solitary café whose sidewalk tables were deserted. Parasols were folded for the dead season and resembled strange spooky birds with collapsed wings. Streik, raging with thirst, parked the car in an isolated lane behind the post office and made sure it was securely locked. In the trunk he had a quantity of documents rolled up and stuffed inside the sleeves of dirty shirts or crumpled in socks that needed to be laundered. These papers contained details of every transaction that had been made, the sums of money he'd collected from nefarious sources and shipped, by means of diplomatic pouches, to Bryce. A few times he'd been tempted to burn the records, but he had the vague notion they might one day be useful as bargaining chips. It cut both ways. They could save his life or end it.

He stuck the pistol in the inside pocket of his baggy jacket, and went into the café, a room of smoke-stained wood paneling and gas-lights that had been converted to electricity. The ceiling was so black as to suggest limitless space overhead. The patron looked at Jacob Streik with a certain Gallic surliness. They don't get many strangers here, Streik thought. He felt he was being dissected by the Frenchman, a small guy with a small bald head reminiscent of a pearl onion. And what did the Frenchman see? Streik wondered. An obese half-smashed American in a grubby gray suit, a bum who wheezed as he heaved his body into the room. He would notice the puffy cheeks, the eyes that were slitted and red, the way the white face seemed to sit on the shoulders with no neck to intervene. Blubber on the hoof. Well, Streik was used to that. He didn't suffer the burden of vanity. Take me as you find me, buddy.

"Vino," Streik said. He passed a hand over his thinning hair.

"*Rouge ou blanc?*"

"Red," said Streik. He used his English defiantly. Why try to pass himself off as something he wasn't? His French was so poor that whenever he tried it, he was treated with offhand contempt. Everybody could tell he was American, so why hide it?

A bottle and a glass were set down on the counter. Streik took them to a table at the window. He was the only customer. He drank two glasses quickly, folded his hands together, looked out at the street. Snatches of conversation came from a back room. Streik heard the words *poisson* and *mal*. A squabble in the kitchen. The French took their chow too seriously. When a soufflé collapsed, they acted like it was Armageddon.

The café had begun to smell of garlic suddenly. He realized he was hungry, but he'd never been one to believe there was a relationship between wine and food. Wine you drank, food you ate. He belched quietly and looked out the window. These small French burgs were always comatose. He poured a third glass, lit a cigarette, and thought: Fuck reality. A stooped woman came out of the butcher shop carrying a white package streaked with blood. Probably ox head or horse tongue, Streik thought. The French choked down anything.

He had the thought way at the back of his head that he ought to stay a little in touch with sobriety, but how was he supposed to deal with stress and fear without assistance? They had a contract out on him, for Christ's sake. Somewhere in the world executioners were hunting him. And when you lived with that fact, you were bound to get wigged-out now and then. He had a sudden image of Montgomery Rhodes, whose features might have been chiseled out of clay by an evil sculptor. He thought of the sinister dark shades Rhodes always wore. Rhodes really scared him shitless. Rhodes was a horror story. *Nice to be working with you again, Jake,* Rhodes had said in his weird sepulchral way. *Great to have you on board.*

Great, yeah, Streik thought. Fucking terrific. I need my head examined.

Out of nowhere a young man with a backpack materialized. Tall and blond with a fierce beard, your basic Viking, he eclipsed the gray light in the doorway when he stepped inside the café. Streik was at once as alert as he could be. Assassins came in different guises. They didn't all look like thugs. They didn't all carry violin cases. This hiker in the long black coat could be on the level, you never knew. Streik put his hand in the pocket containing the pistol and watched the young man go to the bar. In fluent French he asked for a beer and a packet of Disque Bleu. He exchanged a few words with the patron, then he sat down at a table facing Streik, who looked into the blue eyes briefly before turning his head away.

"*Français?*" the young man asked.

Streik said, "You talking to me?"

The young man smiled. "Ah. American."

Streik drank his wine, said nothing.

"Allow me to practice my English," said the young man.

"You think I look like some goddamn language instructor?" Streik said.

"Pardon?"

"Skip it." Gruffness had always come quite naturally to Streik. He was a true believer in defensive rudeness. If you were obese, you developed an abrasive shell. He turned away. His perceptions were askew. The window of the butcher shop was occupied by a lamb carcass and for a second Streik thought he saw it shimmer.

"I am learning English for seven years," said the young man in a stiff way that suggested arduous hours with English textbooks. "I am from Hamburg. Do you know it?"

Streik struck a match. He glanced at the young German, who was grinning benignly.

"I am a student in Holland. At Utrecht. I decided to take a little time to myself and hitchhike across Europe. The university is good. But I think there are other kinds of education, however. Perhaps I will go to Morocco. Have you been there?"

Jesus Christ, Streik thought. "Listen. No offense. I'm sitting here enjoying this, this *vinegar*, and I ain't in the mood for talking."

The German looked gloomy. "Everywhere I go, I find friendship."

"Yeah, well, that's terrific."

"People are kind, in general."

Streik thought there was a missionary quality to this kid. Maybe he was some sort of roving ambassador of German goodwill, a human travel poster. He looked at the backpack parked on the floor against the kid's chair. It was stitched with badges collected around Europe. Tallinn. St. Petersburg. Copenhagen. The boy got around.

Streik watched him light a Disque Bleu, the scent of which was offensive to him. Why the fuck had he chosen France as a place to hide, when he didn't like the food or the smokes or the language? Maybe he thought they wouldn't be looking for him here anyhow. They'd think he was still in America because it was bigger, there were more places to hide.

The young German, clearly imperturbable, said, "Are you here on business, may I ask?"

Streik picked up his glass. "I keep to myself, kid. I don't exactly ooze the milk of human kindness."

The German looked puzzled. "Milk?"

Streik said, "I'm a sociopath."

The kid stubbed out his cigarette. Jacob Streik seemed to represent some form of challenge for him, a conversational hurdle. "Ah. You have been drinking more than a little. I understand."

"Okay. So you understand. Leave it at that. You're overflowing with understanding. Fine. Great." Streik stared at the kid and wondered if those blue eyes concealed a murderous intent. They might. How could you be sure? He finished his wine. He needed something more fortifying, something with more bite than this rotgut.

He went to the bar, ordered a cognac, carried it back to his table. He was well down the road now. He was on his way. Soon he could become garrulous, even sentimental. When you had too much to drink, you couldn't predict the outcome. Morosity or good cheer — it was too close to call. He looked at the kid and heard himself say, "Listen. I got my worries."

"We all have our worries," said the German. He smiled at Jacob Streik and then, as if encouraged by the American's sudden slight softening of manner, moved closer to Streik's table. "Tomorrow is always another day, yes?"

"A philosopher," Streik remarked. "Heavy."

"I think a great deal."

"You and me both."

"What occupies your thoughts?"

"Death," Streik said. He heard the word coming out of his mouth, a sound ferried on a fissure of stale air, and he couldn't believe he'd embarked on a conversation with a stranger. But it happened, and it had happened before, and sometimes he was powerless to stop it. Drink was a slipstream and you were carried along on it and you had times when it made you babble. Haywire.

"The great mystery," said the German.

"Mystery, shit. You die and that's it. Welcome to the worm factory."

"There is no afterlife for you?"

"Who needs another life?"

Streik downed the cognac. He was dogged by the feeling he should get up and split. He looked inside his empty glass. Should he have another? The German answered the question for him by buying him a second cognac.

"Here's to you," Streik said, raising the glass.

"Tell me this. Why do you dwell on death when life is all around us?" The young man waved a hand airily. "So much is good. So much is worth living for. These are exciting times in Europe."

"Yeah? You tell me what's worth living for, kid. You got Serbs and Croats mutilating each other. You got Nazis in Germany. You got this ethnic group choking that ethnic group in the old Soviet Union, you got total corruption in Italy, you got the problems in Ireland." Streik ticked off each of these with a finger upon his sturdy thumb.

"There are problems, I admit," said the German. "But they will be overcome in time."

"Yeah. Onward to glory." Streik wondered if he was talking too loud. "You'll lose the Walt Disney outlook when you get older. When you look right in death's eye, you'll see it differently."

Streik was overwhelmed by the urge to get in touch with Bryce, Bryce understood things, Bryce would know the way he felt. Harcourt had that gift of making you pause and take an inventory. Jacob, he'd say. You're yielding to fear. There's too much fear around.

Streik stared at the young man, who was scratching his beard. His suspicions flared up afresh.

"Are you the one?"

"Sorry. I do not understand the question," the German said.

"Why not? It's simple enough. Have you been sent?"

"Sent by what?"

"You know what I'm talking about."

"No. I am sorry."

"Right. Skip it, skip it." Streik felt outside of himself again, as if there were two Jacobs, the one who drank too much, the other a phantom who saw things in a critical light. Stop drinking, the phantom would say. You need a clear head. This sober puritanical Streik, this vigilant doppelgänger, watched in absolute horror as the drunken wayward Jacob took out the pistol and showed it to the young German and said, "I carry this. Okay? If you get any funny thoughts. Okay?"

"Funny thoughts? I am sorry. I am not following you."

"I don't have to explain."

"Americans and their guns," the German said sadly. "It is a long destructive love affair." He appeared not to be shocked by the sight of the pistol, which Jacob Streik had already tucked back in his jacket.

"I just thought you should know, kid." Streik felt good about showing the weapon even as the voice in his head told him it was foolhardy.

"And am I meant to be impressed?"

"Yeah. You should be." Streik shut his eyes a second. There was some kind of discordant music going through his skull. The wine and cognac chorus. The shrieking sisters, the sirens.

"Very well. If you wish. Then I am impressed."

"Good." Streik felt he'd settled something, some vague dispute. Then, filled with thoughts of Bryce, good old Bryce, he wondered if there was a phone in this joint. Clumsily shoving his chair back, he stepped toward the bar. He looked at the patron and mimed somebody on a telephone, inscribing circles in the air with his index finger and holding a clenched fist to his ear.

"A telephone," said Streik. "You know?"

The man pointed to an alcove at the other side of the room. Streik clattered into a table on his way. He was aware of the patron and the German chatting in French behind his back. He caught a word here and there. They were saying something about Americans, and it didn't sound complimentary. They both laughed, and Streik wheeled around to look at them. They were staring at him.

"What's your problem?" he asked. He tried to make eye contact with the pair, but he was having visual difficulties. Eventually he managed to focus on the German. The kid smiled at him.

"There is no problem," the German said.

"Yeah, well." Jacob Streik let the matter drift. If they wanted to bad-mouth Americans, hey, that wasn't his worry. He could criticize Europeans just as well. But he had other things on his mind. He turned away, went into the alcove, picked up the telephone. He spoke to an operator who had a masterly command of English. He gave her two numbers — his credit card and Harcourt's number in London.

He heard Bryce Harcourt's voice. "At the sound of the tone, leave your name and number. Thank you."

Goddamn machines, Streik thought. "Bryce. This is Jake Streik. Listen. Listen. If you're there, pick up. Okay. I need to talk with you. How are things holding up at your end? I got problems. Listen. I'll get back to you later tonight if I can. You want my advice, get the fuck outta London. Get away from the Undertakers, unnerstand? Walk away from all that shit. If you don't, you're a dead man . . . Bryce? You there? Bryce?" He shrugged and put the receiver down. He was disappointed. You needed a human being and what did you get instead — a bunch of electronic impulses.

He didn't leave the alcove at once. He looked at the two men in the bar. The patron was idly staring out into the street. The German kid was doing the same. In a distorted kind of way, it struck Streik that they had the tense attitude of men waiting for something to happen. There was a conspiratorial quietness in their bearing.

Maybe the German *was* the one. Maybe the German had followed him here. And somehow the patron was involved, even though this was an association even Streik couldn't really make.

He moved out of the alcove. The kid was looking at him now. Streik heard something go off inside his head. A blown fuse. A firework. The kid was it. He had to be. All those questions. That superficial friendliness. None of that rang true. They'd sent a killer with a backpack.

He returned to his table with as much careful dignity as he could summon. He sat down, picked up the remains of his cognac, turned the glass around in his fingers. Get it straight, Jake. The German might be nothing more than a student doing Europe on the cheap. But why take chances? Why run risks you don't have to? He patted the pistol and felt its comforting weight against his chest. He'd get up, walk back to the Saab, drive away. If the German followed him outside, then that would prove his suspicion justified. He finished his drink and stood up. His balance was a delicate thing. He felt like an overweight stork one-legged on a tightrope.

"Right. I'm outta here," he said.

The German got up. "It has been interesting to talk."

Streik backed toward the door. Then he was out in the street. The mist had dissolved and a white sun hung behind gray clouds. It was cold, bitterly so. He walked past the post office. He was hurrying now. I can't trust anybody, he thought.

Just as he reached the corner of the lane where he'd left the Saab, he heard the kid coming behind him. He didn't look back, he kept going, and when he reached the car, the kid was coming up the lane toward him.

"You want something?" Streik said.

The German looked apologetic. "I am hesitant to ask this. You may find my request impolite. But I am wondering if there is a chance of a lift."

"Don't take this personally," Streik said. "I don't want company."

"I have not found the hitchhiking around here very easy," said the kid. He had his backpack hanging by a strap from one shoulder. "I was hopeful of hospitality. American hospitality. Forgive me."

"Yeah. You're forgiven."

The kid smiled and said, "I have the strange impression you think I am somebody else, yes?"

"Maybe," said Streik.

"Somebody you are in no hurry to meet."

Streik stared at the young man. He was confused. His mind was in a state of collapse.

"Allow me to reassure you," the kid said. He put a hand in the pocket of his coat. Streik had a rush of disconnected images, the kid's fine-boned fingers, the flight of a rook from a bare wintry tree, a broken stone wall some feet away, the tang of cognac in his mouth — everything was infused with menace. The kid plunged his hand into his pocket and Streik pulled out the pistol. The young German had an astonished look.

"There is no need," he said.

Streik fired once into the kid's chest. The German dropped to the ground and lay with his face pressed against the backpack, which had been dragged from his shoulder by the motion of his body. Streik looked at how the kid's open mouth touched a triangular cloth badge embroidered with the word COPENHAGEN, a strange kiss of sorts. Streik quickly unlocked the car. He had to get away from this place. Fast. But even as he moved, he had a feeling of slow motion, of suspension.

He opened the door on the driver's side, then looked down at the German. There was blood on the guy's blond beard. Something had spilled out of the coat pocket, a black eelskin wallet. Streik bent, picked it up, knowing at one level of awareness he didn't have time to go fishing through the contents of a wallet, but he was curious. He saw a laminated ID card with the name Mueller, W., and a bug-eyed mug shot of the kid. The card had been issued by the University of Utrecht. Streik dropped the wallet, got in the car, drove until the lane joined a narrow road where there were signs of place names that meant nothing to him. Just drive. Just drive and drive. Okay. So the kid had a student ID card. But that was plastic. And Streik knew you could make plastic say anything. Anything you liked.

When he'd driven twenty miles or so, he stopped the car and ran a hand across his clammy face and wondered what he'd done.

LONDON

7

Down in the tunnel, some hundred yards from the platform, arc lights had been rigged up, illuminating the ruins of the carriage. The photograph Pagan had seen in Dublin hadn't prepared him for the reality. The carriage, disengaged from the others that made up the train, lay on one side, crumpled, gashed, windowless. It might have been picked up and crushed in some massive iron fist. It resembled an insane sculpture, the work of a madman armed with blowtorches and dynamite. Rails, buckled in the blast, had been cut back by firemen; here and there you could see the stumps of twisted metal that remained.

Openings had been burned in the bodywork of the carriage, hatches through which the dead could be brought and carried back to the platform. Pagan had seen the body bags laid out in depressing rows. He'd seen men examining the remains. There was a distinctive smell he didn't want to identify: sickening and constant, deathly.

He put his hands in the pockets of his coat and shivered. It was cold and damp in the tunnel. He tried to picture the rush-hour crowd hurrying into the carriage, the suddenness of death. Would there have been an instant of recognition, a split second of shock? Or had the doomed passengers been engulfed before they realized anything? He shivered again. Forensic experts, those archaeologists of death, sifted the debris.

John Downey emerged from the shadows. "I understand all this is your baby now," Downey said.

Pagan looked at Downey, at the absurd little mustache. Downey was a clod in Pagan's book, a plodder with a nasty streak. He wore a drab overcoat and a dun scarf.

"How many dead?" Pagan asked.

"A hundred and seven."

"And no survivors."

Downey said, "Look at the bloody thing. How could anyone have lived through that?"

Pagan stepped closer to the carriage. "How's identification going?"

"Mainly we're relying on people who think they had relatives on this train. Otherwise ID would be practically impossible. We're talking about some serious burn victims. Also dismemberment."

Dismemberment, Pagan thought. He considered how Downey had added the word almost as an afterthought.

"Get me a list of the names so far," he said.

Downey took a handkerchief from his pocket. He blew his nose violently, then folded the handkerchief away. "Glad I'm out of it. Mind you, I don't see why Nimmo brought you back. I thought you'd been put out to pasture."

Pagan didn't have the energy to rise to Downey's bait. This animosity went back years, back to the time when Pagan, in pursuit of the man called Jig, had been given his own counterterrorist empire within Special Branch. Downey, overlooked, had been sullen and resentful. When the section had later been dismantled, Downey and his pals were the first to crow. They celebrated the demise of Pagan's dominion in a pub called the Sherlock Holmes near the Strand. They were said to have sung, just before closing time, "Hit the Road, Frank." Pagan's more recent diminishment at the hands of George Nimmo had been greeted with joy among Downey and his crowd. They disliked Pagan for a number of things — the way Martin Burr had favored him, the casual clothes he wore, his taste in colorful shirts, the Camaro he drove, his inclination to do things his own way. Fuck them all, Pagan thought. Who needs petty envies, the whole cumbersome structure of begrudgery and hostility?

Who needs the approval and acceptance of braying jackasses? This was no popularity contest. He had a job to do. The rest was bullshit.

Downey turned to look at Foxworth. He said to Pagan, "Hail hail, the gang's all here. The terrible twosome. Laurel and Hardy."

Foxie smiled thinly at Downey. "You're a prat, Downey," he said.

Downey seemed to enjoy the insult. He laughed, his shoulders shook, a hoarse rattle rose from his throat. He coughed and said, "Well, lads. Make sure you don't get your suits dirty. That wouldn't do. That wouldn't do at all." He wandered down the tunnel in the direction of the platform.

"Sad sort of bastard," Foxie said.

Pagan had already dismissed John Downey from his mind. He stared at the carriage. He hoisted himself up and peered inside through one of the openings that had been carved by firemen. The carriage was still warm to the touch despite the thousands of gallons of water that had been hosed over it.

He saw a shapeless tangle of black molten wires, seats that had dematerialized, melted plastic, bent metal, a single advertising card, an odd survivor of combustion, blackened and twisted, proclaiming the virtues of an employment agency. A charred garment of some kind was visible; you couldn't tell what it might have been. Puddles of water glistened in the bright lights. Formless ashes suggested the remains of briefcases, purses, handbags, all half-submerged in water. He wondered what insignificant things the bags and purses had contained, the personal articles that make up somebody's life, letters, hairpins, diaries, business cards, now scorched beyond reconstruction. The smell was harsher here; Pagan had a choking sensation. This place is a crematorium, he thought. Nobody could have lived through the smoke and flame, the unbearable intensity of heat.

He clambered down and stood alongside Foxie on the tracks. "Where the hell do we begin?"

Foxie watched the explosives experts for a moment. They worked with delicate concentration, fearful of destroying anything that might contain a clue. "I'd give anything for a passenger manifest," he remarked.

"Nothing's that simple." Pagan turned and walked back toward the platform. Foxie followed.

Downey was standing among the body bags, surveying them like a bureaucrat whose business is death. Tables had been set up against the wall, phone lines had been installed. Now and then one of the phones would ring and a uniformed policeman would pick up. The platform was brightly lit and busy — cops, more forensics people, explosives gurus, London Transport brass who were anxious to have the tunnel cleared and normal service resumed, although they had far deeper anxieties, such as the matter of security throughout the system, a problem of insuperable dimensions. Pagan thought the whole place resembled a ghoulish excavation site.

He glanced at the men who were going through the remains in their hideous search. He found himself looking at one of the dead. He hadn't intended to, but he was drawn down unwillingly into the sight. Blackened features, hair burned from flesh, clothes welded by heat to what was left of the corpse. Dear Christ, how could you even think of identifying anything like this?

"Sickening, isn't it?" Downey asked. "Human pudding."

Pagan said nothing.

"Hope you've got the stomach for it. Here." Downey gave Pagan a sheet of paper. "Sixty-three identified so far. Some of them have already been shipped to the morgue."

"Have you checked them?"

"Checked how?"

"Do we have anything on any of them?"

"I haven't got that far yet," Downey said. "It's bad enough dealing with all this, and the relatives, *and* the bloody press —"

"You should have done a run on the names," Pagan said. "Simple procedure."

"Nothing's simple in this inferno," said Downey, and fingered his mustache.

Pagan looked at the sheet. The names of the dead. Addresses. Why had they died? What unfathomable motive lay behind it? He felt sorrow. Lives snuffed out. He had an image of the carriage going into the tunnel. Very ordinary. People traveling home from work. A mundane Underground train moving as it did hundreds of times a day. But this time it was different, a coffin train.

"What about eyewitnesses?"

"During rush hour? Give me a break, Pagan. Nobody's come forward to say they saw a madman carrying a bomb, if that's what you mean. Hundreds of people, a mob — nobody sees anything in that situation."

"Somebody always sees something," Pagan said. "They just don't know it."

"We ran a press release anyway. Published a phone number. We've had calls, but you know how that goes."

"I know how it goes," Pagan said.

Downey rattled change in his coat pockets. "Tragedy brings out this burning desire to help the law. So they call in and say they saw a suspicious man on the platform. And what do you mean by suspicious, madam? Well, he had a black beard and a kind of bolshie look. It's thin soup."

"Sometimes you have to look very hard in that thin soup for a veggie," Pagan said.

"A veggie," Downey remarked disdainfully. "What you want, Pagan, is a smoking gun, not a bloody bit of cauliflower. Do you need me around here?"

"I doubt it."

Downey touched his forelock in a sarcastic way, then walked off. Pagan studied the list on the off chance that a name might yield up a meaning, an association, but he couldn't find any connections. They were just names. He handed it to Foxworth, who scanned it a couple of times.

"Sorry," he said.

Pagan took the paper back, folded it, put it in his pocket. He walked to one of the tables where a young policewoman was talking on a telephone. She looked weary. She'd probably been here for hours. She had several notepads in front of her, pages covered in meticulous handwriting.

Pagan waited until she'd hung up. "What's coming in?"

She tapped one of the notepads. "See for yourself, sir."

Pagan flicked the pages. The woman had dutifully written down every call she'd received, followed by a name and address to which was appended a brief summary of each message. *Saw long-haired man with a suitcase on the platform. Noticed unusual skinhead. Saw three*

Jamaicans talking suspiciously. These messages revealed more about the callers than anything else. Prejudices and fears. Phobic dross. Worthless. What dread did people entertain in their locked houses in the suburbs? Pagan put the notepad down. He was flooded all at once with the enormity of the task, paperwork, false sightings, information that was dud, voices babbling in the ether.

The policewoman said, "I keep thinking the next call's going to be something useful."

"I know the feeling," Pagan remarked. The numbing brutality of legwork. Putting together each tiny building block of information in the hope of a grand design.

A gray-haired man who walked with a limp approached Pagan. He carried an untidy sheaf of papers and a stuffed black briefcase. He gave an impression of disorder, spillage, preoccupation. "Frank Pagan," he said. "I heard they were bringing you in on this. Good to see you back."

The man was Dick McCluskey, an explosives expert. He had known Pagan for more than fifteen years. McCluskey was considered something of an anarchist who kept himself aloof from departmental politics. Pagan liked him for this alone. McCluskey had an intriguing hobby; he designed magical illusions. He constructed elaborate cabinets in which objects and people disappeared. Pagan wondered if he had a trick box that might spirit the wrecked carriage away.

"What do you think?" Pagan gestured toward the track, the lit mouth of the tunnel.

"A small device with enormous power, obviously. It had to be concealed inside some kind of container. You don't place anything that looks strange on a crowded tube. Too conspicuous."

"What kind of container?"

"Something routine. A briefcase. Somebody's bag. We've been running a few tests, so far not altogether conclusive. Remember, the initial explosion emitted an incredible blast of heat. If that didn't kill the people in the carriage, then fire and smoke did the rest. You know, the powers that be think I should have instant answers, but what they don't consider is how damned hard it is to keep up with technology. Destruction spawns extraordinary technical advances. It attracts oddballs and psychos who just happen to be electronic geniuses. If they applied themselves to other fields, who knows what they might accomplish?"

"Somebody placed the device in the carriage somewhere down the line, then got off —"

"Maybe. Maybe not. Consider another hypothesis."

"I know what you're going to say."

"A kamikaze sort."

Pagan nodded. "A human bomb. I don't need human bombs, Dick."

"Think about it. Say you're crazy, you're suicidal, you've built a compact high-explosive gizmo, you want to test it. More than that. Say you want to be at the suicidal epicenter of it. You want to *feel* it. Where's a good place to do it? In the tube. There's no security. No baggage check. People come and go at will."

"I can't stretch that far," Pagan said.

McCluskey moved away. "I'll get in touch when I have something definite. See you."

Pagan walked to the edge of the platform. A kamikaze. He didn't believe that. He was aware of Foxie at his side.

"Somebody blows up a carriage," Pagan said. "Why? Does he want to kill *everybody* inside? Does he have some kind of deranged grudge against a hundred people? I don't see that. I can't get my mind around that one."

Foxie heard a note of frustration in Pagan's voice. "Or was the bomber after just one person, Frank?"

"And everybody else just happened to be in the way?"

"It's a consideration."

Pagan pondered this a moment: it was the kind of idea that took you down inside an abyss of lunacy. What kind of mind would conjure such a scenario? A cold shadow crossed Pagan's brain. "It's not a consideration that appeals to me."

"Still. A possibility, Frank."

"Anything's possible." He took the list of names from his pocket and handed it to Foxworth.

"Is Billy Ewing available?" he asked. Ewing was an old associate, a Glaswegian with a permanent sinus problem. Sniffing Billy, reliable and loyal.

"I can get him."

"Have him run these names, Foxie. Tell him he's back on the team."

Pagan looked in the direction of the tunnel. It suggested a large maleficent eye, unblinking, relentless. He saw his future down there. And he didn't like it.

"I need a few hours to myself," he said. "Before the fray."

Foxie was not surprised by Pagan's statement. He was accustomed to the fact that Frank, who had only a passing acquaintance with police orthodoxy, needed moments of privacy and contemplation before he decided his next course of action. There was at times something of the monk in Pagan's character, Foxie thought — one a long way removed from Thomas Aquinas.

■

It was already dark by the time Pagan left the Underground station. He had Foxworth drive him home. He lived in a flat in Holland Park, nothing special, a couple of upstairs rooms that overlooked a square, a small park usually dense and green in summer but withered now, and uninviting. He unlocked the door and went inside, turned on the light. The air was stale, heavy with the trapped smell of a place that has lain unoccupied too long. He stepped into the living room, set his suitcase down, and poured himself a glass of Auchentoshan, a Lowland malt he favored. He sat in an armchair and looked around the room. On the mantelpiece were old photographs — himself and Roxanne on their wedding day, an artless black-and-white shot of Roxanne he'd taken one afternoon in Regent's Park, golden days, sunshine, wind in her hair, a puzzled smile on her lips. On the walls were posters from historic rock concerts. The Rolling Stones at Wembley. Fats Domino at the London Palladium.

He sipped his drink slowly. Something about the apartment bothered him. Silence. The place needed noise. Let's have sheer noise. Let's blow the cobwebs of quietness away. He sifted through his record collection — he hadn't succumbed to the compact disc, didn't believe in those smooth oily things, they lacked authenticity, they didn't have the necessary scratchy quality — and he put a long-playing record on the turntable of his stereo. It was vintage rock and roll, Little Richard singing "Good Golly Miss Molly." Pagan found the comfort of the familiar in these raucous old tunes. He refused to give up his passion for the music. He wasn't going to be swayed by new wave or rap or grunge or whatever the flavor of the month was called. More than mere nostalgia sustained Pagan's affection for the old rock. It was wild, liberating and it drove a stake through the heart of the silence he found intolerable.

Tracked by the hammering persistence of the music, he walked absently through the flat, bedroom, kitchen, bathroom. In the bathtub he found a dead mouse, a desiccated little corpse. He picked it up by its brittle tail and held it.

He heard somebody knocking on his front door. He knew at once that it was Miss Gabler from the flat below. He opened the door. She stood clutching the collar of her robe to her throat.

"You are playing your Negro music again," she said. She was fragile, seventyish, and had been raised in India, where her father had been some kind of colonial administrator. "I have had weeks of peace, Mr. Pagan. Blessed weeks. I really must protest. My nerves are bad enough. I have my angina to consider." She spoke of her heart condition as if it were a neurotic pet she had to nurse.

Pagan was apologetic. "I'll turn it down, Miss Gabler."

"I would understand it if you had less violent tastes, Mr. Pagan. Some soothing Haydn, a little Mozart. I would not object to these."

"I'll turn it down. Promise."

"Very well. See that you do." Miss Gabler still held her robe shut as if she thought there was some connection between "Negro music" and a menace to her chastity.

Pagan held up the mouse close to the woman's face. "Look what I found."

"Oh lord," said Miss Gabler, and stepped back, her mouth open.

"In the bathtub, no less. Poor little bastard."

"You have a cruel sense of humor." She flapped a hand, shuffled away. Her slippers flopped. "Some people," she remarked, more to herself than Pagan.

Smiling, Pagan shut the door. He liked Miss Gabler if only because she brought out a mischievous streak in him, a lightheartedness. He suspected she enjoyed their adversarial relationship as much as he did. He dumped the mouse in the garbage, then turned off the music. The silence rushed back in. He finished his drink just as his street-door buzzer made its customary rasping sound.

He went to the intercom and said, "Yeah?"

"Frank Pagan?" The voice that came up from the street was American. Pagan recognized the accent; the man was from one of the southern states, Alabama, Georgia. "My name's Al Quarterman. From the US embassy? I need to have a word."

The US embassy. Why? Pagan pressed the button that released the lock on the street door. He listened to his visitor climb the stairs. When he opened his apartment door, he saw a cadaverous man in his mid-forties. There was an air of ill health about Quarterman. He had dark mournful eyes and yellowy skin. In another age you might have said he was consumptive. He held out his hand, Pagan shook it. Quarterman's fingers felt like unfleshed bone.

"I don't want to intrude on your privacy. I tried your office first. Your associate Foxie was reluctant to give me your address. It was like getting a bone away from a Doberman. He relented only when I explained why I needed to see you." Quarterman glanced around the room, saw the rock posters. "Hey, an aficionado. I go way back. Bill Haley and the Comets. 'Rock Around the Clock.' When life was fun and games."

"I remember it," Pagan said. "Drink?"

"Don't mind if I do, Frank. Can I call you that?"

Pagan said he had no objection. He admired the easy familiarity of Americans. He poured two shots of Auchentoshan. He gave one to Quarterman, who said, "Here's to lost youth and rock and roll," and tossed the drink back, unforgivably, in one gulp.

"You ought to savor that, Al," Pagan said.

"Is that the proper way?"

"It is for me," Pagan said. He tasted the malt. It suggested peat, liquid smoke, heathery mysteries. "So. Why do you need to see me?"

Quarterman set his glass down on the coffee table. "One of our people is missing," he said. "He may have been on that tube."

"Are you sure?"

"No, we're not sure. And we hope to God we're completely wrong. But he didn't take his car to the embassy when he came to work. He said something to one of the typists about how he wasn't looking forward to going home on the tube. And he isn't answering his telephone. Consequently, it's a possibility we have to consider." There was an expression of sad uncertainty on Quarterman's face. "The ambassador considers this a matter of protocol. We need to nail this down before you publish a list of the casualties. We don't want Harcourt's family to just come across his name in the newspapers or on TV. If he was on the tube, the ambassador feels we should be the first to deliver the information to the next of kin."

"Harcourt, did you say?" Pagan asked.

"Bryce Harcourt."

Pagan found a pencil and wrote this down.

"If Bryce was on the train, naturally we'd want to ship his remains back. His family . . ." Quarterman looked at the bottle of Auchentoshan. "Do you mind?"

"Help yourself."

"Damn fine stuff." Quarterman poured himself a generous glass. "His family would want him interred in Florida. The Harcourts are old and influential. Plus they're personal friends of the president, which makes Harcourt's death all the more . . . significant. If we don't act as fast as we can and ship the body back — if there is a body — they're bound to bring some pressure to bear on us. I'm sure you understand."

"It's not going to be pleasant for them, I'm afraid."

"I figure that. Where are the victims being kept?"

"At the station. A few have already been removed."

"I'll send somebody around, see if we can't make an ID. We have his records, of course, if we need them. Medical. Dental. The usual. They might prove useful in the event . . ." Quarterman didn't finish the sentence. He sipped his drink as he'd been instructed. "How's the investigation going?"

"These are early days."

"You don't have any idea who perpetrated this?"

Perpetrated, Pagan thought. It was an antiseptic word. "Not yet." He drained his glass. His mind was foggy. He felt at one remove from his body. He longed for sleep, a couple of hours.

"I imagine it's a difficult operation," said Quarterman. "Do you have any leads? Anything valuable?"

Pagan shook his head. "We've hardly begun."

"I guess it's like a god-awful jigsaw puzzle."

"Except I don't have any idea of what the finished picture looks like," Pagan said. "What did Harcourt do at the embassy?"

"He prepared background papers. If the ambassador was to receive a visit from, let's say, a company in Norwich interested in building a microchip plant in Des Moines or wherever, Harcourt would work up profiles of the company just so Ambassador Caan had some grasp. A research position basically." Quarterman looked into his drink. "We were quite close. We played indoor squash together. He was a sociable kind of guy. A party animal. Poor bastard."

"Maybe he wasn't on the tube," Pagan suggested.

"Then where is he? He's not the type to stay out of the office without calling in to say he's sick. He's conscientious. Even a little driven. I can't imagine him going away without saying anything. His career was important to him."

"It's still a possibility."

"Maybe. Look. If I can help, or if the embassy can render any assistance, don't hesitate. You can reach me at the Security section. Thanks for the scotch."

Pagan walked Quarterman to the door and said good night. He heard Quarterman go down the stairs. Bryce Harcourt, possible victim. Another name for the list, for the roll call of the dead. Pagan went inside his bedroom, sat on the bed, tried to collect stray thoughts and impressions and see if they might be molded into a whole. But nothing came to him, he was empty; if he was blessed with a muse, it had abandoned him. As he stared up at the ceiling, he remembered Foxworth's unanswerable question: *Was the bomber after just one person, Frank?*

I t was just before nightfall when the contingent of Cuban forces entered the city of Santa Clara in a convoy of ten jeeps, most of which were in a state of disrepair. Palls of black exhaust hung in the air as the jeeps idled in the main square alongside the Leoncia Vidal Park. It was in this city that Castro's rebel army, under the command of Che Guevara, had won a decisive battle against counter-revolutionaries, armed with American weapons, in January 1959. Santa Clara had been absorbed into the myth of *Fidelismo*, complete with bullet-pocked walls and a number of exhibits showing how Che and his guerrillas had derailed a train carrying enemy troops more than forty years ago. The Revolution had been petrified here as in so many other places throughout Cuba; Fidel's triumph had been reduced to photographs and artifacts in what were no more than museums. Past glories coexisted with current deprivations. The place had the defeated look of unfulfilled dreams.

The young lieutenant in charge of the convoy, Rafael Mendoza, stepped down from his jeep and stood smoking a cigarette. He gazed at the park where, on benches under guasima and poinciana trees, old men sat in brooding contemplation of their chessboards, or simply dozed; here and there students from the Central University stood around in conversation that was seemingly casual. Everything appeared to Mendoza altogether normal, and yet he experienced tension. He had the habit of running the tips of his fingers through his mustache when he was anxious, and he was doing this now as he surveyed the square and the park.

He gazed at the soldiers in the jeeps, most of them younger than himself; none of them had known any form of government other than that of Fidel. They grumbled sometimes, especially when they looked at videos smuggled in from Florida, or when they received mail from relations in Miami, where the Good Life, *Yanqui*-style, was lived. Mendoza, although he'd been thoroughly indoctrinated and believed in the ultimate success of the Revolution, felt a certain sympathy toward his men. They'd come from poor backgrounds for the most part, they didn't get enough to eat, they were often obliquely critical when they spoke of food lines and rationing and shortages, and they were openly resentful of the tourists who came from Canada or Germany or Spain and had access to luxurious aspects of Cuba denied the ordinary citizen. Even when it came to artillery, there had been shortages since the dissolution of the Soviet Union. There was not enough ammunition, equipment was often outdated, and maintenance was slack. Fidel always said that things were changing, a better world was coming, patience was the greatest virtue of the revolutionary — but Mendoza knew the men in his charge regarded Fidel's words as so much meaningless noise, like the slapping sound made by fish dying in a barrel.

Mendoza's sergeant, a plump little man called Estevez, came toward him, hitching up his gunbelt as he walked. Estevez scratched his bald scalp and shrugged. "Nothing's happening," he said. Estevez was from Havana and considered Santa Clara strictly a provincial dump, a graveyard. So what if there were industrial plants and hospitals — it was still the sticks, compared to Havana.

Mendoza made no reply to his sergeant. He studied the square, the park, the idling jeeps. An old man on a bench raised his face from his chessboard and looked at the soldiers in a dispassionate way; he was accustomed to the fact that the military came and went at unusual times. He was stoic in the presence of soldiers. They were part of the landscape. Military decisions made in Havana had nothing to do with him.

Mendoza stepped on his cigarette.

Estevez asked, "What are we here for anyway?"

Mendoza listened to the song of a blackbird. He thought it a melancholy sound. A large orange sulphur butterfly floated against his face and he swatted it aside. *What are we here for anyway?* He pondered Estevez's question before he answered it. "There are rumors," he said.

"There are always rumors," Estevez said. "What is it this time? Rebels? Freedom fighters?"

"Freedom fighters?" Mendoza said. "That description is inappropriate, Estevez."

The sergeant belched into a folded hand. "Slip of the tongue," he said. "I meant counterrevolutionaries, of course."

"Of course."

Estevez looked slightly embarrassed by his faux pas. He needed to make amends, to ingratiate himself with Mendoza, whom he considered cold and aloof, a real Party hack. "Let them show their faces around here," and he patted his holstered gun. "That's all I say. Just let them show their faces."

"Your eagerness does you credit," Mendoza remarked in a dry way.

"We defend the Revolution, after all," said Estevez, and tried to remember some suitable phrase from one of the doctrinaire tracts he was supposed to have read. His mind blanked. He could never keep all that political dogma in his head anyway. It was convoluted, tedious, and seemed to have no relationship with the impoverished reality of Cuba.

"We defend the Revolution," Mendoza agreed. "It's worth remembering our function."

Estevez was silent. He looked down at his feet, his scuffed boots. His heels were chafed and caused him some discomfort. He'd asked for new boots two months ago, but nothing had happened to his request, presumably lost by this time under the standard avalanche of requisitions.

Mendoza wondered if he should move the convoy along, perhaps circle the square, drive past the Palacio Municipal, wheel around by the railway station; make the military presence felt, even if there were no counterrevolutionaries in the vicinity. His information had been vague at best. Anti-Castro groups had been reported near Remedios, fifty kilometers from Santa Clara — but this might have been rumor, although rumor had a way of being elevated to the status of gospel in the political climate of Cuba. An underground printing press had been seized a few weeks ago in the Escambray Mountains in the southern part of the province, that much Mendoza knew for certain. And a couple of AK–47 assault rifles had been confiscated from the suicidal students operating the press. But the rest . . .

He fingered his mustache, surveyed the square, glanced at Estevez, who was forever tugging at his belt. Mendoza decided to move. What was the point in hanging around?

"Let's go," he said to Estevez and stepped toward his jeep, which headed the convoy. He climbed in beside the driver, a scrawny young man from Camagüey whose expression was one of perpetual anxiety. The jeep moved forward; the others followed slowly. They passed the facade of the Santa Clara Libre Hotel, the Caridad Theater, a restaurant called El Pavito, and moved in the direction of the railway station near which the train captured by Che from Batista's forces was still on display, more a fixture than a tourist attraction these days.

Mendoza gazed at buildings, windows, archways. There were too many shadows for his liking. He was decidedly uneasy now; he touched the flap of his holster and turned his head to look at the jeeps in the rear. Estevez, who rode in the vehicle immediately behind, was rolling one of his pencil-thin cigarettes. It was a task that took almost all his concentration; his expression suggested a devout man at prayer. A little irritated by the sergeant's laxity, Mendoza turned away —

The first shot shattered his skull; the second, which he was beyond hearing, ripped into his heart. He was knocked half out of the jeep by the brutal force of the bullets. The driver, the young man from Camagüey, braked almost at once and ducked, but the firing continued, and although he reached for his gun, another shot destroyed the windshield and slivered glass flew into his eyes, blinding him. The jeeps at the back had ground to a halt in a series of minor collisions, and soldiers — led by the screaming Estevez — rushed for cover behind the vehicles. But the firing seemed to be coming from a variety of places now — rooftops, doorways, everywhere. Estevez pulled out his pistol, but before he could use it, his hand had been severed at the wrist, a fact he didn't quite register for a few seconds, the blood wasn't his, the pain wasn't his, he was dreaming, something terrible had fallen out of the sky. The gunfire rolled on, volley after volley directed at the unprotected jeeps and the vulnerable soldiers, windows shattered, tires exploded, flames spurted from engines. Estevez had fainted into the kind of deep dark blue swoon that is the harbinger of dying. He was conscious in a very vague sense of his soldiers trying to return fire, which they could only do in the most haphazard way because they were pinned by bullets and flame. There was choking smoke, burning oil and rubber. Men screamed and tossed their pistols and rifles aside and fled for such places of safety as they could find. But still the firing went on, round after round echoing sharply between buildings. The few pedestrians who hadn't managed to remove themselves from the line of fire lay here and there in the street in streaks and puddles of blood.

It was a long time before silence returned and the gunmen had slipped off mysteriously into the darkness. An hour later, when cautious policemen and officers of Cuban Intelligence, G-2, searched the scene, they found only one casualty among the attackers, a half-dead young man who'd been shot in the chest. He carried no papers of identification. He lay in an alley in a condition of shock, convulsing. The extraordinary weapon discovered a few feet from where he'd fallen was of a kind Intelligence hadn't encountered before — a bipod-supported Tejas .50-caliber, American-made, five feet in length and accurate up to a range of one mile.

VENICE

9

Barron spent several hours in the small room that was the heart of his various enterprises. He made phone calls to different parts of the world, to associates in Tbisili, Johannesburg, Havana, New York, Kiev. He read incoming faxes, arranging them in appropriate folders, each of which was labeled under specific code names he'd devised for his projects — Helix, Hibiscus, Jacaranda, Blackthorn. He had a fondness for poetic words, especially those relating to plants or flowers. He enjoyed the notion that there was an organic element to his business dealings: he planted seeds and, with a little care and attention, they flourished.

When he finally stepped out of the tiny cold room and locked the door behind him, he stood at the foot of the spiral staircase; the woman still slept in the attic bedroom at the top of the stairs. He thought about the sullen withdrawal she'd made from him last night, when, with her cold back to him, she'd fumed her way into a deep sleep. The strangeness of her moods, the swift way her passions changed, the shifting nature of her focus — a lovely irritating conundrum. He pondered the idea of climbing the stairs to wake her. Sometimes when he forced her out of sleep, there were unpredictable consequences.

He parted the curtains: Venice on a wintry morning. Blue smoke drifted across rooftops, pigeons clustered along the bank of the canal below. He let the curtain fall from his hand just as Schialli knocked and came inside the room, carrying the newspapers as he always did at this time of day. Schialli laid the papers on the table, then left the room without looking at Barron, who went inside the kitchen and prepared two cups of cappuccino and, with a large metal press, squeezed juice from blood oranges. If he was going to wake the woman, it was best to do so with domestic offerings — coffee and the dark red citrus juice she enjoyed.

He laid these out on a tray, tucked the newspapers under his arm, climbed the spiral staircase. He stepped inside the bedroom. He was surprised to see she was already awake, sitting up, a cigarette burning in her fingers. She looked at him without great interest, blowing a stream of smoke in his direction.

"Your wake-up call," Barron said, and laid the tray on the bedside table, then dumped the newspapers beside her.

She reached for the blood-orange juice, which she drank thirstily.

"Sleep well?" he asked.

"I had dreams."

"Good ones? Bad?" He laid his hand on her naked arm.

"Who remembers dreams," she said.

He looked at her, tried to assess her frame of mind, but sleep seemed to have drained expression from her face.

"I brought the papers," he said.

"I'm always suspicious when you're kind, Barron."

"Why?"

"I was under the impression you reserved all your good deeds for lepers in the Sahara desert or starving kids in Peru, wherever."

"You do me an injustice," he said. He lay alongside her a moment, enjoying her proximity, the smell of her skin, the way his flesh and hers fused at various points of contact — arms, fingers, thighs. A sense of tranquility descended on him. You could lie here all day like this, not moving, pretending nothing existed in the world beyond the house, that the planet was all your own. He kissed her on the forehead, then reached for one of the newspapers, the *Times*.

The front page displayed a photograph of a carriage that had been bombed in the London Underground system. He stared at the picture. The wrecked carriage was turned on its side; illuminated by strong lamps, smoke could be seen issuing from crushed metal. He set the paper down, picked up the others, scanned them. Each newspaper — French, Italian, German — carried the same story, the same wretched photograph. The stories all contained a reference to the possibility that the attack had been carried out by a renegade branch of the IRA, although this was speculation because nobody had claimed responsibility as yet.

"Look," he said.

She turned her face, examined the newspaper idly; a photograph, an ugly event in London, it didn't seem to hold her interest. Barron sat back, head propped against the pillow, and was quiet a moment. He was aware of a slight depression closing in on him. *A train in London, rush hour, casualties.*

She balanced herself on one elbow and swept a small lock of hair away from her brow. She set aside her empty glass; pulpy citrus strands clung to the inside. She reached for her coffee, sipped, leaving a pale line of milky froth on her upper lip. She licked it away.

He gazed at the photograph again. The murky shapes of figures could be seen in shadow alongside the carriage. Firemen, cops, investigators. "If it wasn't the IRA, who was it?" he asked. "Who else would stand to gain anything from this?"

"Oh, I can think of a few candidates. The Iranians. The Iraqis. Disenchanted Argentinians who never quite got over the Falklands fiasco. Any number of people with a grudge against the Brits."

He turned to face her. He watched her hand go out to touch the newspaper picture and he remembered how he'd met her during his first visit to Palestine seven years ago, the conversation with Arafat in which the little man had spoken of his persistent desire for peace in the Middle East even as he understood the urgent need for armed vigilance. He thought Barron some form of semi-official conduit for this information. Besides, it was a good photo opportunity for the Palestinian, who was a pragmatist above anything else. He knew Barron was fair gossip-column fodder. Later, at a large party Arafat had thrown, she'd materialized around midnight, lovely, seemingly indifferent to her surroundings. Arafat himself had made the introduction: *This is someone very special, Tobias.* Barron, unexpectedly enchanted, had kissed the back of her hand in a courteous way, and she'd seemed surprised by the gesture, which combined a certain boldness with old-fashioned manners.

She'd gone to bed with Barron that first night.

From the very start he'd understood there was something off-center about her. She was a hostage to her own moods. She could be gentle and vicious by turns. Her highs were scintillating, her lows manic. When she was up she tended to speak gunfire sentences. Down, she could be nasty, mean-spirited, sarcastic. You never knew which persona you were going to encounter, a situation Barron found both challenging and puzzling; she had dimensions he couldn't always map with certainty.

He'd learned very little about her upbringing save for the bare facts of her childhood in North Carolina, the oddball parents she sometimes referred to as a couple of monstrosities. She rarely spoke of her past, and only with distaste. But he knew enough. Over the years he'd carefully compiled a dossier on her, the existence of which she never suspected. He knew more about her than she could ever have guessed.

He rose from the bed, wandered around the room, clenching and unclenching his fists. He was still thinking of the incident in London.

"I'm going to make a few calls," he said. He descended the spiral staircase, unlocked the door of his office, picked up the telephone. He dialed a number in Belfast. His call was answered on the first ring. He pictured O'Neill in his small cluttered office situated over a drab tobacconist's shop behind the Smithfield Market.

Barron asked about London, about the Underground.

O'Neill, who had a raw Ulster accent, said, "Nobody here knows anything, Mr. B. And that's being honest with you now. We've been turning the city upside down and inside out, and there's not a bloody word. It wasn't done by us, I can tell you that much. And I don't believe it was done by the other side either. They'd be crowing if they were behind it. They'd be giving bloody press conferences by telephone. You have to ask yourself what the Loyalists would gain from doing a number on the London Underground anyway. I know they're stupid bastards, but not that stupid."

Barron was quiet a moment. "What about one of the splinter groups?" he asked.

O'Neill was heard to strike a match and inhale cigarette smoke. "No fucking chance. We'd know about them. We take some pride in our information network, Mr. B. It's a bloody puzzle. But I'm damn sure it didn't originate in the province."

"Keep me posted," Barron said.

"You'll be the first to know. Haven't we always worked in the spirit of true cooperation, after all?"

"Always," Barron said. "I'd like to keep it that way."

Barron put the receiver down. He lingered a second with his hand on the instrument, then he picked it up and dialed another number in Northern Ireland, this time in Derry. It rang for a long time before a woman answered. She had a soft mellow accent, quite unlike that of O'Neill. Barron knew her as Sophie McGuire, but that was a nom de guerre. A middle-aged widow with a couple of young grandchildren, she lived an ostensibly respectable life in a row of solid terraced houses near the city center. That she'd avoided the attentions of the Ulster Security Forces for years was a remarkable testimonial to the commonplace surface of her life. She paraded her grandchildren proudly on the streets, attended Presbyterian church unfailingly on Sundays, played bingo every Thursday, and made regular donations to pacifist enterprises. Once, she'd even ridden the Peace Train from Dublin to Belfast, clutching a wreath of flowers and looking sad. Her veneer, Barron thought, was immaculate.

"I thought I'd be hearing from you," she said. "I'll tell you straightaway, none of us was responsible for the business in London. If I knew otherwise, I'd say so. Usually I'd put my money on the Provos, because this is their kind of savagery. But not this time. Not this time. I don't know who the hell's behind this one because there isn't a word anywhere. Not a cheep. I don't think you'll find any answers in Ulster. After all, we're supposed to be at peace these days, aren't we?"

Barron gazed at the cursors on his wall map. He watched the flickering little beeps and was seized by a small sense of unease; if there was no Irish connection behind the Underground bomb, then it left him with the kind of puzzle he didn't like. He'd always enjoyed free access to a world of clandestine information from all manner of sources, and now something had happened that was beyond his range of knowledge, and he felt limited, excluded from events.

Sophie McGuire said, "I think you've got to look outside all the usual circles on this one. Somebody we don't know. That's about all I can tell you."

Barron sighed. Somebody outside all the usual circles. He thought how very fragile the situation was in Ulster; a massive dragnet conducted by Scotland Yard, the Royal Ulster Constabulary and British Army Intelligence could be upsetting. All kinds of people might be trawled in the nets of such an investigation. And who knew what they might say, what they might give away in the interests of self-preservation? Barron had worked hard and long in Ulster; his future business in the province depended upon a delicate balancing act. He knew the present ceasefire couldn't last forever. Sooner or later it would be undermined and broken because peace was ultimately unprofitable.

"It could be a one-off," the woman said. "Some murderous eedjit whose identity we'll never know. Some louse who'll crawl back in the woodwork and vanish."

"Maybe," Barron said. He severed the connection. He locked his office, went back up the staircase to the bedroom, where the woman — sprawled across the bed — was studying the newspapers. She looked up as Barron came in. "Well?" she asked.

Barron shrugged. "Nothing."

"Poor Tobias. You don't like states of ignorance, do you? You like to be well informed, don't you? You like to know everything in advance, don't you? You hate loose ends."

Barron sat on the bed. If, as Sophie had suggested, the destruction of the carriage had been a one-off carried out by a maniac, then the chances of ever discovering the identity of the bomber were slim — in which case he couldn't fault his network of information. It was some consolation. But still the thought of the train distressed him.

"According to the papers, a man called Frank Pagan is in charge of the bomb investigation," she said. She tossed one of the newspapers toward him.

He didn't pick it up. He said, "Frank Pagan. He has a reputation for being tenacious, I understand."

The woman said nothing. She rolled on her side, reached for her cigarette lighter, and struck it for flame, which she held toward the wick of the candle. Barron felt the tension drain out of his body and he leaned conspiratorially toward the woman, holding her face against his shoulder — hearing her sweep all the newspapers away from the bed, hearing them slither to the floor, the world turned aside, rejected, discarded, the bomb in the London Underground forgotten, leaving nothing but this room illuminated by the small steady flame of the candle.

LONDON

10

Afflicted by restlessness, haunted by visions of the tunnel, Pagan put on his overcoat and left the apartment. He took with him a bottle of Gordon's gin he'd bought at the duty-free shop in Dublin. He got inside the Camaro convertible. His infatuation with American cars went back to the time he'd seen Elvis driving a long-finned red Cadillac in a bad movie whose title he couldn't recall.

He turned the key in the ignition a couple of times before the car came to life and then he drove it through the streets of Holland Park. He traveled toward Battersea by a series of back roads, thinking how run-down certain neighborhoods had become. He gazed at the streets, the rows of handsome old houses carved into bed-sits, here and there a splash of graffiti, much of it incomprehensible to him; the spray-painters had an angry language of their own. Corner pubs looked shabby and unwelcoming, hostile. Houses had been abandoned, windows boarded up, front gardens overgrown with shrubbery, trash dumps. Groups of kids congregated in gloomy little parks that were nothing more than concrete slabs in which had been planted a few niggardly trees. Dear old London Town; what had become of her? A grubby broken-down old broad, an impecunious dowager in a tarnished tiara.

He parked in a littered cul-de-sac where a row of cottages had been transformed into a variety of business premises, some of them of a specious nature. A printshop that Pagan knew was a front for fake ID cards. A garage that had been raided at least twice in the past three years for doing paint jobs on stolen cars. Windows were barricaded behind steel shutters. He walked a few yards, skirting garbage cans and parked vehicles, until he came to a door on which was inscribed STAMP COLLECTIONS BOUGHT AND SOLD. He rang the bell, heard a shuffle of feet. The door was opened a few inches.

The woman before him was a thin wraith in a black cardigan and a kilt whose tartan was of uncertain provenance. She had pinched features and lips that were angled awkwardly, as if at some time in her life she'd suffered a stroke.

Pagan said, "Got any old Cayman Island stamps? Anything from Egypt showing King Farouk at the height of his fatness?"

The woman laughed. "I got some highly interesting examples from the Raj, Mr. Pagan."

Pagan stepped inside the room, which was filled with dirty glass display cabinets in which were enclosed cellophane packets of postage stamps, a riot of bright colors, butterflies and birds and beetles in red and yellow triangles issued by republics that had ceased to exist. Dead monarchs and deposed despots stared out of their plastic containers — the shah of Persia, General Franco, Stalin, Hitler. A half-drunk glass of stout stood on one of the cases.

"I was having my nightly," said the woman. She picked up the glass, sucked at the brown-white froth. "Want one, Mr. Pagan?"

Pagan produced the bottle of gin from his coat pocket. "Brought you a present."

"Aren't you a dear?" The woman picked up the bottle, opened it at once, poured two glasses. She gave one to Pagan, who took it reluctantly. Gin, especially straight, wasn't his drink. He sipped it anyway.

"Cheers," he said. "Is the other half around?"

"He's dossing in front of the telly, I expect." The woman went to a door, opened it, called out. "Freddie! Freddie! We got a visitor!"

A man appeared in the doorway. His slack trousers were held up by an old-fashioned leather belt. His thick hair rose in contrary clumps from his skull and he needed a shave. He had the appearance

of a man who has fallen asleep in one century only to waken, astonished, in the next. He blinked at Pagan. "I was having this dream
where I'd found the secret recipe of the alchemists. Happens a lot.
I get this close, *this* close," and here he clenched a fist slackly. "Then
I always wake up before the bearded bloke tells me how to turn lead
into gold."

"What bearded bloke?" Pagan asked.

"The All-Seeing One, I expect." Freddie tugged at his belt. He
wore an ancient V-necked pullover with no sleeves.

"He dreams a lot," the woman said, and drained her gin.

Freddie shuffled in Pagan's direction, then his attention was
drawn to the gin bottle. "I thought you was on leave of absence,
Mr. Pagan."

"Change of plan," Pagan said. He was oddly fond of this pair,
Freddie and Wilma Scarfe, despite their flirtation with the criminal
fringe. Maybe that was why he liked them; they made an improbable
pair of villains. Violence wasn't an integral part of their world.
When they committed a crime, it was always of a curiously innocent
kind, a minor embezzlement that was usually somebody else's fault,
an item of stolen property they'd come across in good faith, the sale
of allegedly rare stamps they had no idea were forgeries.

"Wasn't it nice of Mr. Pagan to bring us a bottle?" Wilma asked,
indicating the gin.

"You're a prince, Mr. Pagan," said Freddie and helped himself to
a generous glass. He knocked his glass against Pagan's and added,
"Don't tell me why you're here. See if I can guess."

"It wouldn't be hard," said Pagan.

Wilma Scarfe shook her head sadly. "Terrible bloody business,
Mr. Pagan. All those poor people on the tube. It's getting where you
can't go out these days."

Pagan walked around the room, examining the stamps. The air
smelled stuffy, as if it were infused with the stale saliva of everyone
who had ever licked any of these postage stamps. "How's business?"
he asked. He had another swallow of gin.

"Can't give stamps away," Freddie said, picking up the bottle and
screwing up his eyes to examine the label. "Dying hobby, you see,"
said Wilma. "Video games nowadays, if you don't mind. Beep beep.

Wankers looking at screens. Wonder they don't go blind before they're twelve."

"What have you heard?" Pagan asked.

Freddie scratched his chin. "Now now, Mr. Pagan. You know that's not my line. Not at all."

"I know you listen, Freddie." Pagan leaned against the wall, arms folded. "You keep your ear so close to the ground you should have chilblains in your lobes."

"Ha," Freddie said. "I don't keep up the way I used to." He reached for the bottle again, refilled Pagan's glass, then Wilma's, then his own.

"Come on, Freddie. Think. You're in the company of a desperate man. You heard of any movement? Anybody asking around for Semtex? Any kind of explosives? Detonators?"

Freddie poked around inside a display case and shuffled some packages of stamps. One fluttered in the air and fell to the floor. He bent, picked it up. "Southern Rhodesia," he said in a wistful manner. "The Princesses Elizabeth and Margaret. Royal tour of 1947. Lovely young girls they was then. Look at them now. Look at the whole bloody monarchy. Scandalous."

"I didn't come down here to talk about royalty," Pagan said. The Scarfes could go on about the monarchy for hours if you didn't intervene.

"Your generation doesn't feel the same way," Freddie said. "Doesn't mean the same to you at all."

Pagan said, "I don't give a shit about any of them, to be honest, Freddie. No offense."

"None taken." Freddie looked at Pagan for a long time as if all of a sudden he'd forgotten Frank's name and occupation. He had moments of wandering in and out of things. He finished his drink and moved in the direction of the bottle.

"Now," Wilma said, and frowned. "Don't be overdoing it, Freddie."

"What's a small drink between friends?" Freddie winked at Pagan. He was pouring gin again. Pagan, to his despair, saw his own glass filled to the rim.

"Cheers," Freddie said. "There was some fellow looking for Semtex about three weeks ago. That's what I heard. I can't say where I heard it. Some Arab, I believe it was."

"A Palestinian," said Wilma. "Least that's what I heard."

"Did he get it?" Pagan asked.

"I don't believe he did, Mr. Pagan. Mind you, I can't say for sure. Sometimes you hear the beginning of stories but you don't always hear the end of them. Know what I mean?"

"What about the Irish?" Pagan asked. "You hear anything on that front?"

"Ha," Freddie said. "The Irish don't need to be asking for Semtex in London, do they now? They have the stuff stockpiled."

"Have you heard anything else?" Pagan waited patiently because sometimes it took a long time for pennies to fall down the chutes of Freddie's memory. He looked inside his glass, realized he'd drunk a little more than he'd intended. Gin had a way of screeching directly to his brain.

"The word is that it's a foreign job, Mr. Pagan."

"What kind of foreign?"

Freddie shrugged. Pagan said, "Foreign can mean anything."

"I'm only saying that's the word," Freddie said. "And it's a quiet word too, Mr. Pagan. Barely a whisper."

"And that's it? That's all you've got?"

"That's it."

"You don't know anything else about this Arab?"

"Only that he was asking after explosives. That's all I heard. You know how it goes. Information's not always reliable."

Pagan was beset by a sense of people murmuring without purpose in a junkyard of rumor and gossip. A Palestinian asking about explosives. It was the sort of talk that might have originated in certain pubs just before closing time, somebody adrift on a raft of drunken bravado. *I'm looking for Semtex. Know anybody that can help?* Dreamers of angry dreams, men made belligerent by booze. It was an attitude that led more often to a battered wife and a hangover than an explosion.

He wandered among the display cases. "Nothing then," he said. He took another drink from his glass, then set it down. There was already a vague disturbance in his perceptions, nothing serious, a simple giddiness that would pass as soon as he had fresh air.

"I'll be listening," Freddie remarked. "You can be sure of that. Another drop?"

Wilma Scarfe reached for the bottle before Freddie and moved it away from his outstretched hand. "I think you've had enough, Freddie."

"One more," Freddie said.

Wilma shook her head. "You'd have the whole bleeding lot finished in no time."

Pagan looked around the room as he moved to the door. "Why don't you get a telephone installed in this place?"

"Don't believe in them," said Freddie. "Always safer to use a public phone."

Pagan shrugged and went outside, back to his car. He had other sources throughout London, but Freddie and Wilma Scarfe were usually the best-informed. What was the point in scouring half of the city only to encounter vague allusions to mysterious strangers looking for explosives? Besides, the nature of the device used in the tube hadn't yet been identified. How did he even know what he was looking for? It was as if he held in his hand a deck of cards evenly divided between blanks and jokers.

He drove to the Embankment, parked the car, got out. The wintry air helped clear his head somewhat, but he was still a little out of touch with himself. He found a call box, dialed the number in Golden Square, got through to Foxworth.

"Anything stirring?" he asked.

Foxie said there were no new developments.

"I'm going to do some work at home," Pagan said. "Pick me up at six A.M.. And if anything happens in the meantime, you know where to reach me."

"You okay?" Foxie asked.

"Why?"

"You sound funny."

Pagan said he didn't feel funny, and hung up. He walked a few yards. He looked at the Thames and watched the river flow sluggish and cold toward Tower Bridge and it seemed to him that the identity of the bomber was as elusive as any object that might be caught up and dragged by currents of black water toward the sea.

He turned, moving back in the direction of the Camaro — which was when he saw a small white car, traveling too quickly on the wrong side of the road, swing along the Embankment. The collision was inevitable, sudden, shocking. Pagan heard the scream of brakes, the roar of rubber on concrete as the driver of the white car tried to swerve — too late, too goddamn late. The car swiped into the back of Pagan's Camaro with the sorry sound of metal clanging on metal and glass breaking. *Sweet Christ.* Pagan broke run into an angry run, already trying to assess the damage to his vehicle. The passenger door of the white car opened, and a young woman stepped out and examined the collision with a gesture of dismay.

"Holy shit, holy shit," she said. She looked at Pagan, who was bending to scrutinize the point of contact. The Camaro's chrome fender was dented, the rear lights shattered, the lid of the trunk creased.

"Don't you look where you're bloody going?" Pagan asked. The license plate was crumpled, dangling from the body of the car. He picked up shards of broken red glass and rattled them in the palm of his hand. "You came around the corner like . . ." Exasperated, he got to his feet, stared at the girl, then looked back at the Camaro. He labored to repress his anger, thinking, *It's only a bloody car, it's not a human life, it's just a conglomeration of painted metal and rubber and wires* — but he'd been attached to this vehicle for years. He'd restored it, repaired it, bestowed attention on it, all of which affection he understood was slightly ridiculous in a sense, misplaced, a substitute for a genuine human fondness. *But still.*

The girl was shaking her head. "Look, I'm sorry, I took the corner too quickly and I'm not used to driving on the wrong side of the goddamn road anyway, I mean practically everybody else in the world drives on the right-hand side except in this country . . ." Her accent was American; Pagan couldn't place it exactly but guessed East Coast, possibly Connecticut. "In any case, I don't see tremendous damage. A few new lights, a little work on the fender. Some minor body work on the lid of your trunk. My car, on the other hand," and she gestured toward the Escort. Steam was pouring through the plastic grill, which was shattered. "I'd say my radiator has sprung a leak."

Pagan moved closer to the Escort. The hood was buckled slightly and the radiator was emitting an ominous hissing sound. Steam, tugged by the breeze from the Thames, swirled around the vehicle.

The girl said, "My insurance will take care of your car. You're not going to be out of pocket, if that's what's worrying you."

"That's not what worries me," he said. He looked at her, seeing her properly for the first time, even though the light was dim. She had a remarkable combination of very brown eyes and blond hair, a beguiling alliance of dark and light, a composition of opposites. The face, framed by wayward hair, which she kept pushing back, had a delicate bone structure of the kind you sometimes see on ballerinas. She wore almost no makeup or if she did it had been so skillfully applied it wasn't noticeable. Her only item of jewelry was a slender silver chain around her neck.

"I'm genuinely sorry. I am. Obviously the car means a lot to you. All I can say in my own defense is, I got confused when I turned the corner. I just kind of instinctively moved into the right lane instead of the left. Typical American tourist ditz, huh? They shouldn't let us loose in the world, should they?"

Pagan laid one hand on the side of the Camaro, the gesture of a man comforting a wounded horse. The girl moved a little closer to him, scanning the car. "What year? Seventy-one?"

"Seventy," Pagan said. "A collector's item."

"I'll give you my insurance details," she said. "The Ford's rented, but it's fully covered. I guess we should exchange names and addresses. Is that the routine here? Or do we have to call the cops and report the accident?"

Pagan took out his wallet, showed the girl his Special Branch identity card.

"Oh shit, no," she said. "You *are* a cop. Is this where you handcuff me and drag me in for reckless driving?"

"It's a temptation," Pagan said.

The girl was quiet for a time, looking beyond Pagan in the direction of the river. He was drawn into her features, the slight look of worry in her eyes. She brushed a gloved hand nervously against her lower lip and turned her face back to Pagan. "Well? What happens next? Do I need to get myself a lawyer?"

"A lawyer? God *forbid*," Pagan said. Lawyers, in Pagan's scheme of things, occupied the same oily rung as politicians. "We do just what you said. We exchange insurance information. I'll report the accident myself."

"And then what?"

"Then we let the insurance people sort it out."

"That's it? No arrest for dangerous driving?"

"You made a mistake, that's all."

"You're being generous —"

"Our economy needs tourists," Pagan said, trying to make light of the situation although his attention strayed back to the crease in the lid of the trunk, which resembled a scar. Flecks of red paint had peeled away from the undercoat. He thought, Tell yourself it's only a car, you've suffered more in your lifetime than a bloody dent in an automobile. You can restore cars; you can't resurrect people.

"You're going to need a mechanic," he said. "I don't think your car's going anywhere."

She turned to the Escort, which was still hissing madly. She shrugged. "I'll phone the car rental company. They'll fix me up with a replacement, I guess."

"That might take some time. And this isn't exactly the safest place in town to linger. Where were you headed before you decided to ram my Camaro?"

"I wouldn't phrase it quite like that," she remarked. "I'm staying at the Hilton. Park Lane."

"I'll drive you."

"You don't have to —"

Pagan opened the door, turned the key in the ignition. The Camaro started at once. The girl locked her Escort and stepped in on the passenger side of Pagan's car and said, "This only makes me feel more guilty, you know. Are you usually this tolerant and kind?"

"I'm usually a bastard," Pagan said.

"Yeah. Right." She laid her hands in her lap as the car started forward. "Are you what they call a bobby?"

"Not exactly. I was spared the indignity of a uniform. I specialize in counterterrorism. I track down deranged persons with bombs and sundry explosive devices. Your basic political madmen."

"Dangerous stuff."

"It has its moments."

He turned the car into Trafalgar Square, where a few drunks had clustered around Nelson's Column. They had the look of conspirators who had forgotten the basic reason for their assembly and were shuffling around aimlessly, as if in search of a lucid spokesman.

"What's your name, by the way?" the girl asked. "I didn't get to read it on your somewhat imposing ID."

"Frank Pagan." The interior of the car was filled with her perfume, which was fragile, a hint of cinnamon.

"Pagan. I'm Brennan."

"That's your first name?"

"It wasn't my choice. I got it at birth."

Pagan listened to the car as he drove. He thought he detected an unusual vibration from the area of the rear axle. *Terrific. Next thing the bloody wheels will fall off.* In Park Lane he parked as close to the Hilton as he could. The girl opened her door.

"The very least I can do is offer you a drink," she said.

Pagan hesitated. Maybe he needed company. Maybe he needed to slough off solitude, breathe air that wasn't tainted by the stench of the tunnel.

She got out of the car and said, "Come on," and Pagan followed, thinking of the unexpected twist the night had taken. He walked beside her into the lobby and they moved toward the bar. Inside, she took off her coat, scarf, and gloves, and placed them on a chair. She was wearing a short black silk dress.

"This is a hell of a way to meet somebody," she said.

"I can think of introductions involving less wreckage," Pagan said. He sat down, looked up into the girl's face, seeing in the muted light of the bar just how perfect the architecture of her bone structure was. The delicacy he'd noticed on the Embankment was gone; she had a surprisingly strong face. He saw layers there of determination, perhaps even a sedimentary stubbornness, but these were alleviated by a quiet mocking light in the eyes.

"What are you drinking?" she asked.

"Are you playing waitress?"

"I'm good at it."

"Scotch and soda. No ice."

He watched her walk to the bar. She moved with a lack of self-consciousness. With grace, he thought. He wondered how old she might be. Twenty? Twenty-one? That would make her slightly less than half his age. It was a sobering consideration, the kind that made you puzzle over where the years had gone and what you'd done with your time on the planet. Other people's youthfulness could be terrifying. He wondered what she saw when she looked at him. A tall lean man in a dark wool suit and blue shirt, steely hair brushed back across his scalp, gray eyes suggestive of a deep slightly cynical weariness with the human condition. He had an attractive vulnerability about his face that had drawn more than a few women to him in his time, usually strong-willed women who thought they could puncture the solitary air he emitted, who imagined they could enter his life and fill the hollows of what they saw as his loneliness. When he smiled, this aura of solitude seemed to alter, as if the act of smiling caused reactions beyond a simple motion of lips, the sudden release of tension, animated hand gestures, a brightness in the otherwise solemn eyes, and his posture, usually defensive, became one of relaxed attentiveness.

She returned with two drinks. She set the scotch and soda in front of him and sat down facing him, raising her glass of vodka. "Cheers," she said.

"What brings you to London?" he asked. He was useless when it came to small talk. He always felt clumsy with chatter. He hated parties, forced conversations.

"It was the last stop on my itinerary. All my life I've wanted to see Europe — the Doges' Palace in Venice, Notre Dame, Monte Carlo because I like to gamble. I'm usually lucky. Then I always wanted to see London."

"You travel alone."

"Is that so strange?"

He shook his head and was quiet a moment, fidgeting with his drink. "You're American," he said.

"New York. You know it?"

"A little."

"I run a catering company in Manhattan. Private parties for the most part. Bar mitzvahs. Weddings. I've got a few clients on Wall Street who still like to serve lavish lunches for their best customers. If there's a recession, they don't know about it."

"Chicken vol-au-vent and deviled eggs for the wealthy," Pagan said.

"And cocktail sausages on tiny sticks?" She laughed. It was a tuneful sound, a fragment of melody. "You've got it all wrong. Our customers are into American cuisine."

"What's that? Rattlesnake pâté? Cactus jam?"

"Quit teasing me. The stuff we do is for health-conscious Americans. Call it joggers' food. If there's meat, it has to be white and lean. Salads made from designer lettuces. Radicchio. Arugula. Mâche. Dandelion weeds are a big favorite. The good old iceberg has had its day. Why are you smiling? Does my occupation amuse you, Frank Pagan?"

Pagan shrugged. "I don't see you in a kitchen slicing greens. I can't imagine you in an apron, up to your elbows in stalks and leaves."

"Why not?"

"I'm not absolutely sure. The lovely young lady in the black silk dress at the tables in Monte Carlo, the woman in the apron. I don't know. Maybe it's the contrast."

She looked at him for a time, as if she were trying to classify him. "Let me see if I understand. You're an old-fashioned guy who likes easy categories, is that it? The kind of woman who's at home in a kitchen shouldn't be hanging out in European cities on her own, right?"

"I didn't say that."

"Then I'm not sure what you *are* saying, Frank."

"Maybe I'm just surprised."

"Surprised by what? I work, I play."

Pagan looked at her face and realized he was being quietly teased for his failure to fathom her. Dear God, he thought. Has my imagination atrophied after six weeks of my own company? What the hell is wrong with me anyway? An old-fashioned kind of guy: he wasn't like that. That implied premature senility, an arthritis of attitude. You need to get out more, Pagan. You need to live.

She looked down into her drink. "Anyway. I'm probably keeping you from something. You were probably rushing home when I smacked into you. Do you want to phone anyone?"

Pagan shook his head. "There's nobody," he remarked. He paused a second, then — without knowing why he felt the need to say more — added, "My wife's dead."

"Oh. I'm sorry."

"It was a long time ago. I don't dwell on it." He wondered if he'd carried off the lie. Lately, for reasons he didn't understand, he'd been thinking more and more of Roxanne. Maybe grief was something you never overcame; it was a lifelong series of absences that kept stalking you.

"I'm sorry I asked, Frank."

He sipped his drink. "She was killed near Harrods. A terrorist bomb. An IRA gift on Christmas Eve."

"Jesus," she said. The depth of sadness in her voice touched him.

He said, "It comes with the business of living. You take what comes along. Bad, good, whatever. Things happen. You can't do much about them. Life goes on . . . after a fashion."

She turned her face to one side. He couldn't see her expression. When she looked back at him, her eyes were damp.

"I didn't mean to upset you," he said.

"It's just," and she broke off her sentence, raised her glass to her mouth, sipped. "I have a sentimental streak *this* wide. I hate tragedies. I hate to hear about people dying for no reason. I go to weepie movies armed with wads of Kleenex and I cry when I hear the lines of certain songs. Call it a character flaw."

"I don't see it as a flaw," he said.

"Don't you?"

He shook his head and said, "There are enough hard characters in the world. What's so terrible about being sentimental?"

"Some people might consider it a weakness, that's all." She reached across the table and touched the back of his hand. "I'm sorry about your wife." The contact of skin lasted only a second but long enough for him to experience the vibrancy of unexpected intimacy. He couldn't remember the last time a woman had touched him. His passage through the world in recent years had been a solitary one. There had been a couple of liaisons, none entirely satisfactory in the end; it was as if each of these affairs, if that was the word, had contained the source of its own destruction from the very beginning.

She finished her drink. "Do you want a refill?"

"I really ought to be going," he said. He didn't have any great conviction in his voice and he wondered if she noticed. He was suddenly reluctant to be on his own; melancholy was rolling like a fog toward him. He looked at the girl, who was gazing at him. The connection of eyes seemed to diminish the physical space between them. He stared down into his drink and the connection was broken.

"Anyhow," she said. "You've been very understanding about the accident. I appreciate that. You've been nice."

Nice, he thought. It wasn't a word he would have applied to himself. He had a generous streak and he tried to bear no malice, but nice was for little old women in the Home Counties who sent money to needy children in Third World republics.

She rose from the table. "I better get some sleep."

"I just realized I don't know your last name," he said.

"It's Carberry."

"Brennan Carberry. It has a ring."

"You think so? I always thought it too masculine. I don't know. Too many *r* sounds. Harsh." She flicked a length of hair from the side of her face. Pagan set his glass down; he'd reached that point where he couldn't stall his departure. He got up from his chair. He felt a mild depression coming on, the sense of something crashing in his system.

"How much longer are you going to be in London?" he asked. Impetuous, he thought. But sometimes solitude, of which he'd had too many unbearable weeks, brought out a bold streak.

"Why?"

"I don't want a menace like you driving the streets of London on your own. If you're going to spend a few days in town, I'll give you a number where you can reach me — if you feel like it. Maybe we could find some time to do something together. On one condition. I drive."

"Sure," she said. "I'd like that."

He wrote his home number on a matchbook. She walked with him toward the door of the bar, where they both hesitated; for a moment he had the pleasing feeling she was about to raise her face and kiss his cheek but instead she took his hand and shook it briefly. A kiss, he thought. A heady notion, a possibility blown out of all proportion because his loneliness had been punctured briefly by the girl's company. In the foyer he plunged his hands into his pockets.

"Good night, Frank."

He walked in the direction of the doorway, paused, turned around. But she was already gone. Dematerialized. The lobby was empty. He went outside, glanced at the impenetrable expanses of Hyde Park, then strolled slowly to his damaged Camaro.

LONDON

11

Detective-Sergeant Scobie looked at the body on the bed. The wrists and ankles had been bound by a sheet torn into strips. The face had been lacerated, obviously by the blood-stained scissors that lay on the bedside rug. The sheet beneath the body was saturated, dark red turning brown. Scobie thought of the killer's sick frenzy, the brutality of repetition. It was hard to tell how many times the body had been stabbed.

He raised his face, gazed at the bedside lamp, stared at the blood-red hieroglyphics inscribed on the shade. The words were easy to decipher because they'd been written with obvious care, as if the killer knew he had all the time in the world to leave his mark. Scobie tried to imagine an index finger dipped in blood moving across the paper surface of the shade. But some things you couldn't envisage. Some things were just beyond your grasp.

He turned to the girl with the white makeup and eyelashes so black and thick they might have congealed. She was smoking a cigarette frantically.

"I came in and I found her like this," the girl said. "She was just lying there. Looking like that. Oh God."

"What's her name?" Scobie asked.

"Andrea Brown, I think." The girl spilled ash down the front of her coat.

"You think?"

"She used different names. I didn't know her that well."

"But you lived with her?" Scobie asked.

"Sort of, yeah."

Scobie stepped back from the bed. "Either you lived with her or you didn't. Which is it?"

"We shared, see. We weren't close, nothing like that."

"Does she have family?"

"I don't know."

Scobie, a cop for twenty-three years, looked at the girl's ashen makeup, which rendered her features masklike. She took a pack of Benson and Hedges from the pocket of her jeans and used the old cigarette to light the new. Her hand shook. She inhaled smoke with a tiny wheezing sound.

"Where's she from?" Scobie asked.

"She never said. Once she mentioned something about Hove, I don't remember what. She might've lived there, might not. Can't say, really."

"You're a right little encyclopedia," Scobie said.

"Well. I can't help it if I know nothing, can I? She never talked about family or boyfriends." The girl stared at the lamp shade and shuddered.

Scobie walked to the window and looked down into the street. This corner of Mayfair, confined by alleys located at the rear of business premises, was shabby. He gazed down into a lane where plastic bags of trash lay in a pile. He considered the fact that a mere half mile from this grubby room a bomb had exploded in an Underground station. There was too much violence in the world. When he was a boy, the worst that ever happened was that somebody got their lights punched out on a Saturday night outside a pub after a piss-up.

He returned to the bed. The dead girl was naked. Nakedness always shocked Scobie. Somehow he could handle the dead better when they were clothed. The naked dead had no dignity, especially when they were in the appalling condition of this poor girl. The whole room seemed to vibrate with the drumming reverberations of murder. Scobie imagined scissors rising and falling, tearing flesh, the savagery of it all.

He stared once again at the lamp shade, at the crazy writing. Odd — but you couldn't expect to find reason in this room. "That writing mean anything to you?" he asked.

The white-faced girl shook her head.

"Maybe one of her customers had a bad turn," Scobie suggested.

"Customers? What's that supposed to mean?"

"Don't play games with me, love."

"You insinuating something?"

Sometimes Scobie had an avuncular manner to which people responded. He put out a hand and touched the girl on the shoulder and said, "I'm not wet behind the ears, darling."

The girl blew smoke at him. "I've got a lawyer," she said.

"You and half the population."

"I'll call him."

"You do that."

The girl didn't move. Scobie took out his notebook. "Let's get it down on paper, shall we? What's your name?"

"Do you really need to know that?"

Scobie sighed. "This is a murder case. I need to know all there is to know."

"Sandra," the girl said reluctantly.

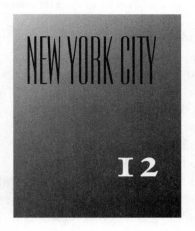

NEW YORK CITY

12

In Manhattan a thick swirling snow made hazy white funnels around streetlights. The storm blew from upstate, from Syracuse, Albany, Saratoga Springs. The General, stepping quickly from his Buick, turned up the collar of his coat and hurried inside a building in the Tribeca area. It had once housed a garment manufacturing company, but that sweatshop had gone under long ago and the place had lain derelict for years. The new owner had refurbished it entirely. Where once archaic machines had clacked and clattered and ill-paid seamstresses labored myopically over stitches, now there were walls of teal-colored ceramic tiles, genuine palm trees in great earthenware pots, a Southwestern conceit.

The General dusted snowflakes from his overcoat as he strode to the elevator. His mood was uncertain. For one thing, he wasn't altogether at ease in the United States, so long an enemy of his own country that old suspicions still lay close to the surface of his emotions. For another, the business on hand was not altogether pleasant, and the General, by nature a man of reasonably good humor, had no real heart for distasteful matters. In his long career he'd been obliged to make painful decisions that had condemned men and women to death because the system had demanded it of him. He had signed papers and issued decrees, though it sometimes seemed to him that the hand holding the pen wasn't his own but an instrument of the state. He'd been detached from the process of condemnation.

He rode up in the elevator to the top floor. A man greeted him when the doors opened, a cheerful fellow in a plaid suit and red necktie. He smelled so much of aftershave it was almost audible.

"General Schwarzenbach," the man said.

The General nodded.

"This way, General."

The General followed the man along a corridor, a long peach-colored passageway that led by means of a glass-enclosed walkway to an adjoining building. The General stopped to admire the view of the city. The scene was lovely, although it struck him as prodigal that any great city should be so brightly illuminated after dark. But much of this society was wasteful. It had a lot to learn in the ways of abstinence.

"Nice view, huh?" the man said.

"Unusual," said the General.

"Follow me," and the man continued to the end of the bridge, went through a door leading to a short flight of stairs. Pheasants and partridges had been hand-painted on the wall in elaborate detail. All this renovation, this reconstruction, the glass bridge, the ceramic tiles and the mural — how much had it cost?

The General had a lifetime of parsimony behind him. Even in the great days of his career in East Berlin, he'd spent hours pinching pennies, balancing budgets, imposing controls. He supposed he ought to let this old habit die, but it was difficult to change one's pattern of thinking. America — was it not the land of plenty? If so, it presented him with a paradox. Why were so many people sleeping in doorways and cardboard boxes? Why were so many killed by robbers for the sake of a few dollars, sometimes even cents?

"In here," said the man, smiling vaguely. He opened a door. The room beyond was white. A white canvas hung above the fireplace. The bright sterility of the room reminded the General of a Mormon film of the afterlife he'd seen in the Tabernacle during a tour of Salt Lake City. The man in the plaid suit shut the door and withdrew.

Another man sat on a white leather sofa. The General had met him before. He was called Saxon and he acted with an air of quiet self-importance. "Good evening, General." He rose from the sofa. He wore heavy eyeglasses of the kind that enlarge the eyes, giving them a constant startled expression.

The General said nothing, simply nodded. His fleshy eyelids imparted a certain hooded quality to his face.

Saxon said, "I'm afraid our friend would seem to know nothing after all. We've grilled him, if you follow my drift. It's very disappointing."

Saxon took off his glasses, held them to the light. He fogged the lenses with his breath, then wiped them in a fussy manner on the end of his necktie. "But see for yourself, General."

A door on the far side of the room opened in a flash of reflected white. A man dressed in plaid shirt and jeans was ushered in, his arm twisted by a muscular figure in a black T-shirt. The man in jeans was made to sit in a chair. His hair was disheveled. Under both eyes were blue-black bruises. The corner of his mouth was bleeding. He'd clearly been mistreated, though with a certain amount of expertise. The General had long experience of men whose talents lay in the kind of physical abuse that leaves only passing blemishes.

Saxon said, "Are you ready to tell us what you know about Jacob Streik, Charlie?"

Charlie said, "Jesus. I already told you and this goon everything I know. If Streik's gone, he sure didn't leave any forwarding address." Charlie dredged up a little defiance. "This is fucking absurd. You set this muscle on me, but what the hell good is it if I can't tell you anything?"

"We may not believe you, Charlie," said Saxon.

"Tough shit," said Charlie.

"Bad attitude," Saxon remarked. "You and Streik were close, as we understand it."

"All I know about Streik is, I married his sister, who happens to be a walking disaster. It's like being married to the San Andreas Fault. He never came around. Never visited."

"You were seen in his company about six weeks ago," Saxon said. He had something lawyerly about him, a courtroom bearing. The General understood that Saxon at one time had been with the Department of Justice, that he'd held a number of senior government positions of an advisory nature. Perhaps he still did.

"You were seen with him in HoJo's on Times Square. Enlighten us, Charlie. Give it a shot," Saxon said.

"Who the hell are you guys anyway?"

"What did he tell you, Charlie?"

"Nothing."

"A half hour in his company and he told you nothing? What did you talk about?"

"Horses."

"You and Streik talked about horses?"

"The track. The ponies. The only thing we got in common is an enthusiasm for losing money. It was an accidental meeting." Charlie rubbed his chest; an expression of pain crossed his face. "Listen. If you're through with me, I'd like to go home."

The General spoke now. "Charlie. We are perfectly serious here. It will be in your own best interest if you tell us where Streik has gone."

"How many times I gotta say it? If I knew, I'd tell you, Christ's sake. You think I'd protect Jake Streik? You think I'd risk my neck for that fat dickhead?"

Dickhead. The term was new to the General. He liked to learn something new every day. Dickhead was good.

"What's he supposed to have done anyway?" Charlie asked.

"That is not your concern," the General said. He sat on the arm of Charlie's chair, laid a hand on the man's shoulder; Charlie was shivering. All this trouble over Jacob Streik, who had never been anything more than a messenger. But he'd turned out to be a weakness, a liability.

"We simply want to know where he is, Charlie. Think of yourself. He is not worth protecting."

"I'm not protecting him. Why would I protect that lardass? He doesn't mean anything to me."

The General had a grizzled rather kindly face. People who looked at him might easily imagine him a retiree playing chess in Washington Square. He said, "Charlie. I am trying to help you."

"Yeah, right."

"Think, man. *Think.*"

"I'm *thinking*," said Charlie.

The General caught Charlie's ear and twisted it sharply, causing the unfortunate man to lower his face against the arm of the chair. The General smashed the back of Charlie's neck with his fist. "Do not protect the dickhead, Charlie. Save yourself. Now tell us. Where did he go?"

Charlie raised his face. Tears ran across his cheeks. "I don't know. I swear to God."

The General stood up. He suddenly grabbed Charlie, hauled him out of the chair, threw him against the wall. That an act of violence should come from somebody of the General's age and appearance made it all the more shocking for Charlie, who hit the wall and slithered to the floor. He wiped his tears with the cuff of the plaid shirt.

"You waste our time," said the General. Little outbreaks of violence fatigued and depressed him. They were such an effort these days. Once, his nickname had been the Bullock. His physical strength had been legendary in the old days. "I am too old to squander my time. Get rid of him," he said to the man in the black T-shirt. "Throw him from a high building. Do what you like with him. He bores me."

"Hey, wait," Charlie said.

"Why? Have you suddenly remembered something?"

Charlie stared at the General. "Streik might have mentioned he was going abroad. But he was always talking about trips he was going to take. I never paid attention. I never really listened to the guy. He always made out like he was some kind of big shot, somebody who had these great secrets. I had a way of tuning him out."

The General ran his hand across the top of Charlie's head in a gesture that might have been one of pity. "Abroad is vague, very vague."

"That's all I know."

"It's not enough, Charlie." The General gestured to the man in the black T-shirt. "Take him away."

"No," said Charlie.

"Take him now."

Charlie, protesting, struggling, was removed from the room. The General gazed at the closed door for a moment. He clasped his hands behind his back. He pondered the matter of Jacob Streik, whom he'd never met but whose face was familiar to him from photographs. He had a fat jowly face; ugly, but there was no denying the fact it concealed a certain animal cunning.

Saxon said, "Dead ends, I'm afraid. We also talked to Streik's sister. She knows nothing. He has a few acquaintances, but he doesn't keep in touch with them. A sorry life, by the look of it. He seemed to have befriended Bryce Harcourt, if I might stretch a definition. But that relationship by its very nature was subterranean. I doubt if they met more than five or six times. They came from two different worlds, General. A collision of circumstance."

The General said nothing. He stared at the walls. He wondered what the white canvas was meant to signify. Maybe some kind of mental condition, a spiritual breakdown. He remembered his office in East Berlin before it was seized during the unholy process called reunification. What had become of his paintings? His collection consisted mainly of pastoral scenes, farm laborers, horses, haystacks.

"Why was Harcourt not questioned?" he asked.

"There was no need," said Saxon. "His letters were read. His phone calls recorded. His apartment was examined. He was constantly followed. We have no evidence Streik told Harcourt he was taking a hike. What we do know is that Streik, seemingly very drunk, telephoned Harcourt a couple of days before his disappearance and rambled on about his life being in danger and how he should never have become involved in the first place and so on and so on. It was something of a drunkalogue."

The General spoke in a weary way. "I still say Harcourt ought to have been questioned —"

"It's beside the point now," Saxon said.

The General was unaccustomed to being interrupted. "Nothing is ever beside the point," he snapped. Restless, he rose. The white room beat inside his head like a nuisance of a child playing on a tin drum.

Saxon said, "Streik unfortunately lost his nerve and vanished. Harcourt did not. We know this much: Harcourt had begun to express his own misgivings. And misgivings are dangerous things . . ."

The General closed his eyes. He was drifting a little, remembering all that had once been his to control, the power he'd had. Old Honecker, in the good years before his shameful disgrace, had once said to him: *To have power is to live in a magnificent house that may not withstand bad weather.* Poor Honecker, maligned by history, condemned by an illegal new order, exiled in sickness, dead. The General felt restricted, obliged to work with people whose backgrounds were different from his own, whose ways of doing things were often strange to him. Men like Saxon had been raised without a knowledge of true fear, and so they lacked a dimension. They had no experience of midnight callers, no understanding of everyday terror, of the awesome reaches of state security. Sometimes it seemed to him that Americans considered themselves immortal, as if God had smiled on them.

Saxon said, "Anyhow. The book is now closed on Bryce Harcourt, as I understand it."

The General was suddenly frustrated. But what could he say or do? He wondered how the assassination had been arranged. In the old days, these were exactly the kinds of details he would have supervised himself. But now . . . now he was obliged to go along with the plans of other men. Ask no questions. Harcourt is dead. The book is closed and you are not expected to ask how.

The General beat the palms of his hands together. "Find Streik," he said. "I don't want to see Helix endangered in any way."

Saxon said, "We have a great many people looking for him in a number of countries. We're keeping tabs on anyone he's likely to contact. It isn't going to be difficult, General."

The General stared at Saxon a moment. "Just find him," he said, then walked toward the door. Saxon moved behind him, flapping an envelope he'd taken from his pocket.

"Your airline tickets, General. Mustn't forget them. First class, of course."

The General seized the envelope, folded it carefully in the inside pocket of his overcoat. He left the room, walked the glass bridge to the elevators. He rode to the ground floor. The snow was still heavy, collecting in mounds along the sidewalks. He got into his car and drove away.

A couple of blocks from the building two police cars were parked raggedly, roof lights flashing in the night. The General glanced as he passed. He saw briefly the shape of a man on the ground, the body already covered with a light layer of snow. Charlie, he thought. Your only misfortune lay in knowing too little about the wrong man.

■

The General drove through the illuminated grids of Manhattan, past sleeping figures in shop doorways, winos huddled cheerlessly on corners, bag ladies pushing shopping carts, the sorry detritus of the city. America, he thought. A land of the most astonishing contrasts. He enjoyed certain aspects of the diverse American scene. He was amazed by the unusual preponderance of seemingly useless consumer items such as toilet-roll holders that played "Yankee Doodle Dandy" when you tugged the tissue or some kitchen gadget that grated, pulverized, pulped, or sliced whatever was introduced into its maw. He admired the endless cartoons on morning TV, especially Magoo, whose blundering shortsightedness he thought symbolic of a certain national trait. At times the General pondered what his fate might have been — perhaps a mock trial, years of imprisonment, brutal treatment at the hands of misguided men who despised him. Ah, they had been so easily misled, he thought. They had discarded social order in favor of some amorphous notion of freedom, but what they had really encountered was a very old goddess, Chaos, whose handmaidens were unemployment, poverty, and crime.

He came to a brownstone on West Eighty-seventh. The Buick skidded slightly as he parked. He stepped out. The snow was ankle-deep. A figure shuffled out of shadow and approached the General, a black man in a ruined overcoat.

"Say, bro, got some spare change?"

The General shook his head. He never encouraged beggars. He stepped past the panhandler, who was persistent.

"I ain't asking for much. A buck or two ain't much. You look like a guy of substance, my man. Difference it gonna make to yo life?"

The General stared into the beggar's face. "Out of my way," he said quietly.

The panhandler, mistaken in the belief that he'd encountered a friendly old dude, an easy touch, seemed to perceive, with the instinct of the streets, an unexpected element of fortitude in the General's face. He raised both hands in a gesture that meant *Take it easy*, then he melted back into the shadows.

The General kept moving. New York, he thought. Beggars and thieves, cutthroats and madmen. A whole social order had broken down here.

He climbed the steps to the brownstone, rang a bell, heard a voice on the intercom. He spoke his name, a buzzer sounded, and he opened the big front door. He climbed a flight of stairs. The door on the second floor was already halfway open. He went inside the room. The air smelled of popcorn. A TV played *Fantasia* from a VCR. The General took off his overcoat, sat down, watched Mickey Mouse assailed by animated broomsticks. Remarkable.

He smiled when the young woman came in from the kitchen. She wore tight blue jeans and a dark red ribbon in her hair and carried a large glass bowl of popcorn, which she set before him. He dug into it at once. His fingertips became smeared with butter. The girl handed him a paper napkin.

"This is good," he said.

"I know you like *Fantasia*," she said. She sat beside him. "I think it's groovy."

"A work of art," said the General. Groovy, he thought. "The fusion of music and images — admirable. I had this videotape in Berlin." In his buttery hand, he held the girl's fingers. "I think of Berlin too often for my own good. I think of Europe, the way things were. I think of the way things are now. Is such nostalgia permissible at my age?"

"You're not old, General. You make out like you're prehistoric or something." She pushed his knee in a chiding way. "A brontosaurus. That how you see yourself?"

"Sixty-six is not old?"

"Age depends on what's in here." She tapped him on the chest. "In the heart."

The General supposed this was true enough in a metaphysical way. But the problem lay in an accurate reading of the signs in the heart. A moment of melancholy affected him. He was remembering old comrades, some of them dead at their own hands, some of them imprisoned, others disappeared. But they hadn't all lost the will to continue, they hadn't all just withered away in the greenhouse of history. He considered those who remained in the field, dedicated to the task, those who'd worked all their lives for the Staatssicherheit, STASI: Vanderwerker in Geneva, Bohl in Frankfurt, his name changed, a new identity assumed, daring Bohl. He thought of old KGB allies in other parts of Europe: Lisenko in Leningrad (the General would not give credence to the sacrilegious renaming of that city), Vassily, living in the very center of Moscow still, Sheshkin in Helsinki. In his mind he might have been studying a map of a fierce river into which countless powerful tributaries ran.

The girl looked at him brightly. "You seem down. Sad."

He shook his head. "Not sad, no. Perhaps a little anxious."

"Anxious how?"

The General thought a moment. "Perhaps anxious isn't altogether correct. Impatience is also involved."

She placed a hand on his knee in a comforting kind of way. "My mother always used to say tomorrow is another day. I used to think, shit, that was a real dumb thing to say. But now I kinda guess she had a good point."

The General stared at the TV. Tomorrow is another day. And all the tomorrows after that are other days too. He tried to see into the future. Clouds, here and there some flicker of sunshine. He thought of the man called Jacob Streik, worried over it a moment, then dismissed him from his mind — although it wasn't easy because Streik persisted in a corner of his brain like an ache. But where could Streik run to in the end? To whom could he go? He had to be very lonely wherever he was. And very scared. A scared man, the General knew, could also be a dangerous one. If Streik somehow talked to the wrong people, if he found somebody willing to listen to his stories concerning the movement of fabulous amounts of money, if he found somebody ready to believe him — who could predict the outcome?

"Are you hungry?" the girl asked.

"Hungry for what? I have many kinds of appetites."

The young woman dipped into the popcorn, stuck a few kernels in her mouth, and looked at the General. "So do I, General."

"This is what I call a happy coincidence."

"You're way too horny to be old," she said. She set aside the bowl of popcorn and, in a manner unmistakably suggestive, licked her fingers. The General watched her undo the buttons of her shirt and regarded her delightful breasts with pleasure; her nipples were the color of damsons. He wondered how much this lovely creature was reimbursed to keep him joyful. But some matters were beyond fiscal measure.

LONDON

13

In his apartment Frank Pagan spent until one A.M. making telephone calls from numbers listed in a small notebook that Foxie had often referred to as "Chairman Frank's Little Red Book." It contained the names of a variety of idiosyncratic characters connected with an assortment of causes, many of them lost ones, many pathetic, a few purely fictional. Frequently the kind of information Pagan extracted from these sources was worthless, but he worked on the principle that you left nothing to chance. Now and again he'd uncover something bright in the general dross of things.

The list, which had taken him years to build up, was constantly being changed, when people died, left the country, or simply vanished. It required patience and a form of dogged optimism — call it frail hope, Pagan thought — to labor through the names. He asked the same questions he'd asked Freddie and Wilma Scarfe and had to listen to a reformed West German terrorist called Ingrida extol the merits of vegetarianism, breast-feeding, and pacifism; a former Iranian diplomat who'd once allegedly tried to smuggle a hit squad into the UK and who had lately taken up bridge on a professional basis talk about how he'd played in the company of Omar Sharif, a very nice fellow; an old IRA hardliner called Charlie Locklin in Kilburn, slurring his words because he'd been ploughing through a bottle of Jameson's, swear the length of a hurling field that there had been no Irish involvement in the explosion.

Pagan spoke to more than a dozen people before he concluded that it was going to be one of those fruitless nights. Weary, he closed his little red book and walked around his apartment. He went inside the bedroom, lay down, shut his eyes. The voices he'd listened to on the phone fused into an incoherent chorus, a kind of bleak lament. *Nothing, Mr. Pagan. I know absolutely nothing.* He drifted into shallow sleep. He dreamed in a vague way of Brennan Carberry, a surreal bit of brain theater in which he was pursuing her through what appeared to be the opium dens of old Limehouse, although the Chinese clientele spoke pure Brooklynese. The madhouse of the unconscious: you bought your admission ticket, but you were never sure what you were going to get.

Still fully dressed, cramped from the angle of his body, he woke before dawn and made a cup of insufferably bad instant coffee which he drank black and strong. The apartment was chilly. Shivering, he showered quickly, put on a clean shirt and suit. From a shelf in his closet he took his handgun, a Bernardelli, which he stuck inside a holster located in the small of his back. He'd never found a truly comfortable place to carry the weapon, despite having tried a variety of holsters over the years. He wasn't even sure why he wanted to carry the gun; he supposed he felt a basic need for some form of reassurance.

Foxie, punctual as always, appeared in a Rover, banged the horn twice. Pagan got his coat and went downstairs. The street was treacherous with ice. A faint suggestion of fog hung around the lamps.

"Are we rested?" Foxworth asked.

"More or less," Pagan answered as he settled in the passenger seat. The gun pressed his spine. He rearranged his position.

"Golden Square?" Foxie asked.

"Of course."

"Like old times."

Pagan wasn't sure how like old times the Square would be, but at least the return to his former offices meant physical distance from

George Nimmo and an illusion of some independence. Illusion was the key word; Nimmo had made it clear he was ultimately in charge of matters, the lord of all he surveyed. We'll see about that, Pagan thought. The possibility of a struggle with George, a clash of authority, was something he looked forward to with relish. He had fire in him now, and steel, a feeling he'd returned to the land of the living.

"Anything new?" he asked.

Foxworth, who sensed Pagan's concentration, his focus, answered, "Nobody has called, Frank. Nobody has said a dicky-bird. Whoever did the business isn't talking."

Dicky-bird, Pagan thought. He hadn't heard that slang in years. Foxworth, whose background was public school, sometimes used phrases that were outmoded. He did so as if he'd only just learned them, a trait Pagan found endearing.

"We should have McCluskey's report soon," Foxie remarked. "Within an hour or two. So they tell me."

Pagan knew that such reports were frequently skeletons. They gave you bone structure but no idea of the flesh that had hung on it. Sometimes the skeleton was all you had. He mentioned the visit of Quarterman from the American embassy and the man, Harcourt, who might have been killed on the tube.

"I gave Quarterman your address, Frank. He pulled rank on me somewhat. Said he'd have the ambassador call Nimmo, et cetera." Foxie looked apologetic, and shrugged.

"It's not important," Pagan said.

"Could the death of this Harcourt have any significance?" Foxie asked.

"Doubt it," Pagan said. "He was some kind of researcher. I get the impression he wasn't important. Did Billy Ewing run the list of names?"

"He's at Golden Square right now, Frank. Complaining about overtime, of course."

"Good. Then he's in fine form. I'd worry if he wasn't grumbling."

Pagan thought of the tunnel, the way it bored into his imagination, as if it were a passageway through his own brain, something he'd created himself and in which he was now imprisoned. A hollow black place — and the only way out was to find the person or persons responsible. Maybe that's what all investigations came down to in the end, the pursuit of yourself, the hunt for your own identity, your liberty. Heavy stuff, Frank, he thought. Too heavy on an empty stomach.

He looked out. There were a few buses, taxicabs, some early morning delivery vans. The usual frantic commuter period hadn't started yet.

Foxie drove into Golden Square. The sky was still dark. Streetlamps burned. The square, small and undistinguished, was located at the edge of Soho. One end carried you into the narrow thoroughfares of the district, the other led you down into the sleazy neon of Piccadilly Circus, streets awash with discarded fast-food containers and newspapers. London as a whole had gone off, Pagan thought. Its familiarity was merely surface, a matter of geography. Its heart was absent without leave.

Foxie parked outside a building with no nameplate. Once it had been the offices of a company that manufactured bow ties. Before that, it had housed the London branch of a New York literary agency that had gone under in a scandal of unpaid royalties and creative accounting. It amused Pagan to envisage a group of authors laying siege to the building as they'd done, carrying placards and posters. DOWN WITH LITERARY AGENTS and other such subversive slogans.

Inside, Pagan and Foxworth rode the shaky iron cage of the elevator to the second floor, where it was clear that Nimmo had ordered some activity during the last few hours. Technicians were arranging computer consoles, men wired telephones, electricians installed fluorescent strips of light. An electric drill was being driven into plaster. Pagan tried to move along a narrow corridor to what had been his old office, but his way was blocked by cardboard cartons that contained files and folders.

"I understand this was being used as a storage facility," Foxworth said. "It has the icy charm of a bureaucrat's graveyard."

Pagan opened a carton, took out a folder, blew dust from it. The file contained yellowed case notes in the matter of the Crown *versus* one James Sixsmith, who had apparently been charged with murder in 1934.

"Prehistoric," Pagan said. He replaced the folder, clambered over the pile of cartons, made his way into his former office. The floor was covered with more boxes stuffed with files. His old desk was jammed back against the wall.

"An obstacle course," said Foxie.

"It smells like shit in here." Pagan sniffed the air, the stench of mildewed paper and damp cardboard. Under the window an old-fashioned iron radiator clanked and hissed. "Nimmo hasn't gone too far out of his way to accommodate us, has he? Obstructive bastard. He's had more than a few hours to get this place ready."

"It could be worse," Foxie suggested.

"Right. I suppose he might have forgotten to have the electricity turned on." Pagan made it to his desk eventually. In another incarnation, a huge silk screen of Buddy Holly had hung on the wall. Now there was a blank space, a sorry rectangle of faded beige paint.

He sat down, noticing he had two telephones on his desk and nothing else, no In tray, no notepad, no pencils or pens. It was almost as if Nimmo had deliberately peeled the operation down to a minimum. Which wouldn't make sense in the circumstances, unless you took into account Nimmo's sense of empire. Pagan could have his own facility, sure, but only up to a point. If he wanted any of life's luxuries — like pencil and paper — he'd probably have to requisition them through the Führer.

Hunched in his overcoat, scarf still around his neck, Pagan saw his own breath cloud the air. He rubbed his cold hands together, then undid the holstered gun and shoved it in a drawer of his desk. He made a small sound of relief.

"Armed, I see," Foxie commented.

"Do I detect disapproval, Foxie?"

"Not from me you don't. It's an uncertain world we inhabit."

Billy Ewing appeared in the doorway, sniffing, the tip of his nose scarlet. "Good to see you back, Frank."

"It's almost nice to be back."

"Is there any chance of getting the heat turned on?" Ewing asked. "My office upstairs is like a bloody morgue. I'm sitting there like a slab of meat." Ewing took an inhaler from the pocket of his coat and shoved it into his left nostril, sniffed, repeated the process on the right.

"Sinuses still playing up?" Pagan asked.

"They have a life of their own. I'm thinking of leaving them to science."

"Got anything for me?"

"Bumph." Ewing stepped as far into the room as he could before the cartons impeded his progress. He had dolorous eyes and a downcast mouth. He invariably reminded Pagan of a comedian whose stage persona is that of a man dominated by a harridan of a wife. He carried a hefty computer printout under his arm.

"So far, eighty-two have been positively ID'd, Frank. I've spent the last four hours running the names. No small chore."

"We're thankful, Billy. Believe me."

Billy Ewing glanced at Pagan and frowned. He sometimes had moments when he couldn't assess Pagan's tone of voice. The man had a kind of deadpan manner. You were never sure with Pagan.

"So. What's turned up?"

"Out of the total so far, twelve had some kind of police record."

Pagan beat his hands together for warmth. The radiator stuttered. Far away in the building pipes could be heard knocking. The electric drill kept buzzing. "Twelve out of eighty-two," he said.

"Aye," said Ewing. "Look for yourself," and he made to toss the computer-generated sheets onto Pagan's desk.

"Why don't you hold on to that, Billy? Just give me a summary."

"A summary," Ewing said, as if the word had the dead weight of a chore too terrible to contemplate. He fished inside his pocket, brought out the nasal inhaler, two handkerchiefs and a small notebook, everything jumbled together.

"You're organized, I see," Foxworth said.

"You'd be bloody organized if you were up all bloody night tapping a keyboard and staring at a screen. I didn't join the force to be a glorified typist. I could have stayed in Glasgow and gone to secretarial college for that, Christ." Ewing opened the notebook. "Right. Six had speeding violations. Two of the six hadn't paid up."

"Proper villains," Pagan said.

"Another two had forgery convictions. Bum checks."

"Two forgers on one train?"

"Maybe they were traveling together," Ewing said. "Maybe they were on their way to a forger's convention or something."

"Keep going," Pagan said.

"Another had been tried for the theft of a car and acquitted."

"That leaves one more."

"The last one's a nutter. A chap called Joseph Dracowitz, who'd done time for firing a water pistol at Margaret Thatcher."

"One wonders why that was considered a crime," Pagan said.

"A dim view was taken by Her Ladyship. Dracowitz got thirty days for his little jest. He was a radical of sorts. You know the type. Fighting at demonstrations. Scuffling with cops. The Thatcher incident was the last straw."

Pagan stood up. He felt a small admiration for the late Dracowitz, wondering if the water pistol had struck Maggie in the eye. "And that's it."

Ewing said, "That's it so far."

"Did Dracowitz belong to any odd political organizations that we know about?" Foxie asked. He was leaning against the wall, arms crossed. Pagan found it easy to imagine Robbie Foxworth lounging insouciantly in the drawing room of a country house, surrounded by men in pink hunting jackets, ladies in jodhpurs, glasses of hot whisky going the rounds. How had Foxworth survived his very genteel background intact? Depth of character, Pagan supposed. An element of iconoclasm.

Billy Ewing touched the tip of his nose and appeared on the edge of a mighty sneeze he fought back. "Dracowitz was something of a drifter. He went from one fringe outfit to another. Mostly harmless groups, the kind that tend to attract a membership of five and have the life span of an aphid. Squabblers. Ranters. Dunderheads."

Pagan pressed his fingertips against his eyelids. "Not the kind to make a kamikaze of himself in the London Underground?"

"I'd think not," Ewing said. "But you never know. There are some daft people about."

"Do you have an address for him?"

"Right here. Cricklewood." Ewing tore a page from the notebook, then clambered over cartons to give the page to Pagan, who looked at Ewing's scribble. Joseph Dracowitz's address was listed as number 38 Shoot-Up Hill.

George Nimmo suddenly appeared in the doorway. He wore a black cashmere coat and maroon scarf. "Settling in, Frank?"

Pagan gestured at the office. "We're making the best of it."

"Everything will be out of here in a matter of hours," Nimmo said. "Cartons. Boxes. All of it. A clean sweep."

"Glad to hear it."

Behind Nimmo stood two men Pagan vaguely recognized. One, fat and bald, had an enormous brow that gave him the fierce look of a mentally disturbed philosopher. The other was red-faced, dressed in a crumpled raincoat that hung open. The label was visible: Aquascutum.

"I believe you might have met Ted Wright," said Nimmo, indicating the bald man. Wright nodded once, rather severely. "And Joe Gladstone." The man in the raincoat stared at Pagan blankly.

"I'm giving them to you, Frank," said Nimmo.

"In what sense do you mean?" Pagan asked, although he knew.

"Beef up the team here. That sort of thing."

Beware of Nimmo bearing gifts, Pagan thought. So George was putting in a couple of his own boys, loyal servants to the regime. I cough and it gets back to Nimmo immediately. I shuffle some papers and Nimmo knows at once. That was the way these things worked. Men with empires to protect needed their own praetorian guards, their spies.

"We'll find them some office space upstairs," Pagan said. Banish them to the attic, he thought.

"That will be quite suitable," Nimmo remarked. He looked around the room. "Must be strange coming back here again."

"It brings back memories," Pagan said. He rose, made his way over the cartons. He handed Billy Ewing's slip of paper to Joe Gladstone. "Here, Joe. Take Ted and get over to this address. See what you can learn about a man called Dracowitz." That was how to deal with Nimmo's people: send them scurrying across London, a little tedious legwork.

Joe Gladstone looked at the paper, then glanced at Nimmo, as if he sought approval. Nimmo nodded in a fashion that was almost imperceptible. Pagan felt a small conspiratorial buzz in the air. You could read all the signs, you could feel the vibrations of the invisible threads that bound Gladstone and Wright to their Master.

"And who is Dracowitz, Frank?" Nimmo asked.

"Somebody I want checked out."

"Ah. A lead?" Nimmo looked optimistic.

Right, Pagan thought. Only a man like George Nimmo would live in a world of sudden leads, big breaks, culprits nailed to the masthead within a few hours of a crime. Dream on. "You never can tell," he said. Then he looked at Gladstone. "You know how to find Cricklewood? You have an *A to Z?*"

Joe Gladstone had a Yorkshire accent. "I'm familiar with Cricklewood," he said in a dry way.

Pagan turned to Nimmo. "By the way, we need a good plumber."

"A plumber?" Nimmo asked.

"A plumber. Somebody with experience in boiler rooms. It's damned cold in this place. We need heat."

"We'll work something out," Nimmo said, and smiled in a stressed manner. You could see behind the expression a reprimand taking shape, a repressed urge to trim some of the brazen wind from Pagan's sails.

Pagan stepped out into the hallway. Nimmo, lightly laying a hand on Pagan's arm, said, "I'll be in touch." He wandered off along the corridor, followed by Wright and Gladstone. Gladstone clutched the slip of paper as if it were suspect.

Pagan leaned against the wall and sighed, watching the three men leave. He was strangely out of balance all at once, assailed by pressures both small and large, the ridiculous cardboard boxes, the intolerable cold, the whine of the electric drill, the sudden addition of Nimmo's lackeys. How the fuck could he work like this? How could he work impeded on all sides? And then he was plunged back inside the tunnel, he was gazing into the wreckage of the carriage, smelling death. You'll work in any conditions, he thought. Because you have to. Because you believe in what you have to do. Because that's the way you are.

Billy Ewing shook his head. "I know Gladstone. In my book he's a right arsehole. I never met Wright before, but . . ." Ewing changed the subject. "Incidentally, I've got all the messages from the emergency number upstairs in my office. If you want to sift them —"

"Not yet," Pagan answered.

"They're a disappointing collection," Ewing said.

"I've seen a few of them." Pagan remembered the young police-woman in the tube station, the telephone and notebook. He had an urge to get out of the building for a while, to walk, think. All this clutter was suffocating. He told Foxie he'd be back in a few minutes. Foxie appeared slightly concerned, as if disturbed by Pagan's sudden decision to leave.

"Is there anything you need, Frank?"

"Look through the messages," Pagan said. "See if there's anything even remotely interesting." He took the elevator to the ground floor, conscious of how Foxie had been frowning. Foxie, guard dog, sentry over Pagan's moods. Now he'd be fretting in Pagan's absence.

Outside, the darkness had begun to yield to streaks of gray that hung in the form of drab canopies over Soho. He crossed Golden Square, where the first of the morning's office workers were coming up from the Piccadilly Circus tube. On Beak Street he turned left, walking quickly past Carnaby Street, a carnival during that period of history when London had been a mercurial mecca of fashion — the Beatles, Union Jack boxers, hairstyles by Mary Quant. The narrow street felt tawdry to him as he glanced at it. The bright pageant had left long ago and now only tourists or disoriented nostalgia freaks came this way, like people checking for a pulse they would never find.

When he reached Regent Street, he paused. Buses came raging down from Oxford Circus, pouring exhaust into the air, where it hung trapped. He waited for a traffic light to change, then he crossed Regent Street and made his way by an indirect route through back streets toward Piccadilly. He realized he was heading for the tunnel, although that hadn't been his purpose in leaving Golden Square, at least on a conscious level. Drawn back to the scene, he thought. Looking for something. Any old hook on which to hang a thought.

On Piccadilly he paused. He had the curious instinct he was being followed. It was nothing very definite, a formless sensation, a feeling of somebody shadowing him. He didn't look around. Besides, how could he tell? The streets were busier now, clerks hurrying to offices, shops opening, lights going on, buses disgorging their passengers.

He continued to walk, stopped at a newsstand, looked at headlines. POLICE CLUELESS IN TUBE BOMBING, one of them read. Clueless, he thought. What did these scribblers want from the police? A quick salve for the public? He scanned the page, read George Nimmo's name, and some way beneath it his own. He was identified as the officer delegated by Nimmo to administer the investigation. Administer: he liked that one.

He gazed at a headline in the *Sun*. I SURVIVED TUBE HORROR. This was allegedly the first-person narrative of a woman who'd been riding in the carriage behind the one that had exploded. Pagan ran an eye over it rapidly; overcharged with sweaty clichés.

He walked on. The odd feeling of being watched persisted. He paused outside a pharmacy. He wondered if the bomber had come this very way. If he'd strolled the route to the station Pagan was now taking. He had a ghostly little sensation, a quick shiver, almost as if he expected to turn his face and see the bomber a few steps behind.

He looked inside the pharmacy window, absently gazing at cylinders of lipsticks, eyeliner displays, rainbows of eyeshadow. He glanced to the side, saw crowds of people hurrying to their places of employment. Then he turned and continued in the direction of the tube station.

Across from the Ritz, he pretended to study the menu in the window of a Lebanese restaurant. Somebody is following me. The damned feeling was stronger now, ringing in his skull.

He didn't notice the woman until she was alongside him.

"Pretend I'm not here," she said.

Pagan didn't look at her. "Okay. I'm pretending."

"You're Frank Pagan?"

He nodded, still examining the menu.

"I need to talk to you. But not here. Not like this." Her accent was Home Counties, her vowels expansive. "It isn't safe. Go to the

Atheneum Hotel. Ask for me at the desk. I'm registered under the name of Canningsby. Give me fifteen minutes or so."

She walked away from him and only then did he look at her. Tall, dressed in wintry elegance, fur coat, leather boots, a bright silk headscarf. She walked with brisk purpose, hurried and yet seemingly unpressured, as if her time were entirely her own, like a woman on her way to an appointment with somebody she didn't consider very important.

Canningsby, he thought. The name didn't mean a thing to him. She vanished out of sight after she'd passed the tube station, where various uniformed policemen lingered behind the tape: guardians of the dead. *It isn't safe*, she'd said. Why isn't it safe? he wondered. If she wanted to talk, why hadn't she come to the office? Puzzled, he continued to stroll, pausing when he reached the station.

"Good morning, Mr. Pagan," one of the constables said. "Cold enough for you, sir?"

Pagan, still pondering the woman, merely nodded. He went inside the empty station, rode the escalator down to the platform. He thought: the bomber must have come this way, must have traveled on this same escalator — unless, of course, the device had been placed inside the carriage at another station along the line. Why did he get the feeling that this wasn't the case, that the killer had come here to this station, the device concealed on his body? Instincts were frequently groundless affairs, formed in a place beyond reason, but he usually went with them. So. The killer had traveled on this escalator, walked onto the platform — and then what? Then what?

Pagan looked the length of the platform. There were two uniformed constables manning the telephones. The young policewoman had been replaced. London Transport officials spoke quietly together, smoking, drinking tea from mugs. A score or so of body bags remained in the place where they'd been before.

A plainclothes cop Pagan recognized as Detective-Sergeant Benny Banforth was standing on the edge of the platform, gazing down the tunnel. He turned when Pagan approached. "Fucking depressing this, Frank," he said. He gestured to the body bags. "Those poor sods haven't been identified yet."

Pagan watched Banforth light a cigarette.

"Some guy came from the US embassy a couple of hours ago," Banforth said. "It seems one of their people was on the tube."

"Positive ID?"

"Positive. Dead man's name was Harcourt."

Pagan looked at the mouth of the tunnel. Black and uninviting, it nevertheless drew him toward it. He touched Banforth on the arm, then walked the length of the platform. He lowered himself onto the track and gazed at the ruined carriage, where lamps still illuminated the wreckage. Something flashed in the distance, a buzz of light and sparks flying out of a welding tool. The carriage would have to be removed sooner or later, which involved cutting it into manageable pieces that could be hauled off the broken track by machines.

He stared at the shower of sparks and thought: *The killer stands on the platform. The train comes in, stops, doors open, crowds get on and off, the regular hurly-burly of rush hour. And then what? Is the device placed inside the carriage unnoticed? Is it stashed inside a briefcase, as McCluskey had suggested?* Pagan tried to imagine this, as if from some mystical source inside himself he might conjure the face and body of the bomber. A sixth sense was what he needed, something beyond mere instinct alone. Get well soon, Frank. Crystal balls, tarot cards, casting the runes — none of this abracadabra had a role to play in the routine drudgery of police work.

He walked toward the carriage, stopped, studied the ruin. The wreck had an immediacy to it, a clarity it hadn't had some hours before. He contemplated the inside of the killer's head, trying to catch on to a mood, but it was slippery and eddied away from him. Tension? Surely. Even if this had been done by a professional, there would be nervousness and strain. Only a deranged amateur might feel absolutely nothing. Only somebody far gone down the avenues of madness might have transcended normal anxiety.

Amateur or pro, it was a hell of a way to make a statement. But if this *was* meant to be a statement, why hadn't there been a follow-up? This came back to puzzle Pagan yet again as he gazed at sparks and lights and the crushed outline of the carriage. Frustrated, he turned and walked in the direction of the platform. The burst of heat in the tunnel had been so intense it had seared the advertising posters on the wall across the track. The faces of lipsticked models peeled from brick.

He wandered toward the exit, rode the escalator up to the street, then walked in the direction of the Atheneum Hotel. The wind blowing off Green Park had a cruel intensity. He was glad to step inside the warmth of the hotel.

At the reception desk he asked for Miss Canningsby. He wasn't sure if it was Mrs. or Ms. The receptionist punched some buttons on her computer and shook her head. "We don't have anyone registered by that name."

"You sure?"

"I'll check again." She did so. "Sorry. Nothing. Do you have the right name, sir?"

Pagan tapped his fingers impatiently on the reception desk. "I believe so."

"Are you sure you have the right hotel?"

Pagan looked into the girl's pleasant face. "I thought I had." He turned away from the desk and made his way past a group of elderly American tourists doing Europe in the dead season. An old pink-cheeked geezer from the Midwest was grumbling about the weather. Pagan moved toward the doorway.

The woman appeared suddenly at his right. "You have to forgive me," she said. "I need to be sure, you see."

"Sure of what?" Pagan asked.

The woman was in her middle forties, immaculately made-up, good-looking if you went in for a slightly arrogant beauty.

"I want to be certain we are not being followed."

"Miss Canningsby, if that's your name, I'm in the middle of a bloody troublesome investigation. I don't have time for fun and games."

"We need to talk," she said. "It might be useful."

"If it's useful, I'll listen."

"There's a Turkish coffee shop around the corner. Meet me there in five minutes."

Pagan sighed. "Give me one good reason why I should bother."

"Does the name Bryce Harcourt mean anything to you?" The woman smiled in a manner both condescending and polite. You

could imagine this one holding court in a fine drawing room, surrounded by her cronies and dishing the dirt over tea in china cups
and dainty plates of petits fours.

"I've heard it," Pagan said.

The woman walked out of the hotel. The door was opened for
her by a top-hatted flunky. Pagan saw his own reflection flash in the
movement of glass. He thought he looked ectoplasmic, as if he'd
entered the world by the dubious means of a medium's power, by
some psychic back door.

■

He waited in the lobby of the hotel for ten minutes, then went outside, walked to the corner, turned. He reached the coffee shop,
which was a dark little place you might not have noticed if you
hadn't been looking for it.

Inside, the light was dim, the room quiet and shadowy. The
woman sat in a corner, studying her face in a compact mirror. Pagan
moved to the table, sat opposite her, ordered a cup of Turkish
coffee.

"I am sorry for the subterfuge," the woman said. She held one
hand out rather limply to be shaken. Her perfume was rich, over-
powering. If you were too long in this woman's company, you'd
need an oxygen mask. "My name is Victoria Canningsby."

"You said something about Bryce Harcourt," Pagan remarked.
He sipped the thick coffee; his heart did a slight jump.

"You don't stand on ceremony, do you?" she asked.

"I was never big on pomp. It takes too much time, Miss Canningsby."

"Mrs., actually."

Pagan set his cup down. "Bryce Harcourt," he reminded her.

"I wanted to come to your office," she said, and here she drifted
a little, changing a mental gear and floating off into the distance.
Her blue eyes seemed to scan some inner region, perhaps a memory.
"But I wouldn't have felt safe, you see."

"I don't really see, Mrs. Canningsby."

"Bear with me, if you will." She came back into focus and smiled
at him and all at once the apparent brittle quality about her ap-

peared to defrost in the smile. There was a seductive little edge to the expression, directed not at Pagan specifically but executed as if by habit. He had a feeling that men much younger than herself had shared her bed.

"I have known Bryce for two years," she said. "Let us say we were well acquainted, and leave it at that. I find disclosures of a very personal nature tiresome. But we were close."

Pagan looked into his coffee. The woman opened her purse, took out a cigarette, and slid her lighter across the table to him. He struck the flame for her, wondering at his own response. Mrs. Victoria Canningsby was accustomed to having her cigarettes lit for her, to a world of willing doormen and obliging cabbies. In the presence of imperious women, Pagan found an odd reservoir of good manners in himself.

"He was on that tube," she said.

"How do you know?"

"I know a good deal about Bryce. I correct myself. I *did* know a good deal."

"Okay. But how do you know he was on that tube?"

She tilted her chin, blew a fine line of smoke upward. Only when she raised her face in this way could you see a certain puckering of her neck. She would have a few bad moments in front of mirrors, Pagan thought.

"I have sources inside the embassy where he worked, Mr. Pagan. It only took a telephone call to one of his associates to have my fears confirmed."

"So he was on the tube and that's a tragedy. But why all this secrecy? What are you afraid of?"

"Some fears cannot be specified," she remarked.

"Christ, I hate mystification."

"Really? I would have thought it was part and parcel of your profession, Mr. Pagan."

"It doesn't mean I have to like it."

She put out her cigarette. "Bryce Harcourt was a charming man. He had a weakness for the fairer sex, as we're sometimes called. I won't say he was a sexual predator. Far from it. He knew how to treat a woman. He had a certain grace about him."

"Where is this leading, Mrs. Canningsby?"

"Call this background if it makes you a little less impatient. I'm coming to the point." She raised her coffee and sipped, leaving along the rim of the cup the dark rosy stain of her lipstick. "I saw Bryce three or four times in the last couple of weeks. Something was troubling him deeply."

A jukebox kicked into life all at once, a female singing a Turkish version of "Smoke Gets in Your Eyes." Pagan worked at tuning it out of his head.

"What exactly?" he asked.

"He said he thought he was being followed. I think I'm correct in saying he'd begun to fear for his life. He was not the kind of man who might usually yield to such anxieties. He was carefree by nature. He'd try to be flippant about his worries. He'd try to make light of them. But he never fooled me."

"Why would people be following him?"

She shrugged, a delicate little motion of shoulders. "I don't have an answer for that. My impression is that it had something to do with his work. Beyond that . . ." She shrugged again.

"My understanding is, he was a researcher of some sort," Pagan said.

Victoria Canningsby laughed. A small clock might have chimed in her throat. "Bryce? A researcher?"

"Why is that so funny?"

"The only thing Bryce might have researched was the female anatomy. Any other kind of research would have been far too *plodding* for him."

"Then what did he do at the embassy?"

"He was never entirely clear about that, Mr. Pagan. I had the impression he was doing work he didn't altogether care for. It didn't come up to his own expectations. If somebody has given you to believe that he was some kind of researcher, I think you've been . . . misled. Sometimes an innocuous job description can cover a multitude of sins."

Pagan thought of Quarterman. If Victoria Canningsby was correct, then Quarterman had lied about Harcourt's line of work. It was a concrete wall, though, a curtain of hard steel. What went on inside the American fortress in Grosvenor Square was beyond Pagan's reach, far beyond his authority. Diplomatic personnel enjoyed all the immunity of cows wandering the banks of the Ganges. Quarterman would have had reasons of his own for misleading Pagan — if indeed that was what he'd done. Maybe Harcourt operated in a sensitive area, something Quarterman was neither authorized nor inclined to reveal.

"Why were you afraid to come to my office, Mrs. Canningsby?"

"For the simple reason that lately I believe I have been followed myself. Strange cars passing my house. One or two unexplained phone calls."

People following people, Pagan thought. Shadows after shadows. The world was out of joint. Things were unhinged wherever you looked. "Because of your connection with Bryce."

"I imagine so."

"You felt it would be unhealthy to be seen in my company."

"Even as we sit here, I feel unhealthy, Mr. Pagan. The feeling isn't going to go away."

Pagan was quiet for a time. "Let me ask you this. Do you think the explosion on the tube had a direct connection to Harcourt's presence?"

"How could I possibly make a connection like that?"

"Then all you're really telling me is that Harcourt was a worried man," he said. "The world is full of worried men, Mrs. Canningsby."

She pushed her chair back. "I'm telling you that he lived in fear of his life, Mr. Pagan. You can do what you like with the information. I happen to find it strange that somebody with Bryce's apprehensions should be killed in an explosion. That's all. You're the detective, not me."

"Coincidence," Pagan said. He remembered Foxie's question: *Was the bomber after just one person, Frank?*

"As you say." She rose, drawing her fur coat around her shoulders. "Coincidences happen, after all."

"The alternative to coincidence in this case is very hard to accept, Mrs. Canningsby." He looked up into her face. She was staring down at him rather coldly, brittle again, regal.

"How would I get in touch with you if I had to?" he asked.

"Look in the telephone book, Mr. Pagan. Wivelsfield, Sussex. I caution you though. I don't want a certain party to be involved in any of this."

A husband, Pagan thought. Some hardworking cuckold in the City who doesn't know about Madame's infidelities. "I can be discreet," he said.

"I'm sure you can. When you need to be." She walked to the door and, without a backward look, went out into the street. Pagan waited for several minutes and left only when the jukebox began to play a constipated version of "My Way" in Turkish.

He took a taxi back to Golden Square, where a cleaning crew was busy hauling the cardboard boxes away. His own office had already been emptied; a woman with her hair in a makeshift turban was running a vacuum over the floor. She switched it off as soon as he entered the room.

"Can't hear meself think," she said. "Just about done, dear." She turned the machine back on. Pagan listened to it roar across the ancient rug, raising clouds and spirals of dust from worn fiber. He sat behind his desk and forced a look of patience. He needed quiet in which to think about Victoria Canningsby's information. Did it clarify anything? Or was it just another isolated item in an investigation that hadn't yet become airborne? Among the roll call of the dead there had to be a hundred secrets, and presumably Bryce Harcourt had a few of his own.

"Right, dear. Done now." The woman unplugged the vacuum and wheeled it out of the room.

"I'm grateful," said Pagan. On his desk was a pile of telephone messages gathered by Ewing or one of the uniforms on the upper floor. He scanned them quickly. Nothing riveting.

Foxie came into the room, accompanied by a man Pagan had never seen before.

"Frank," Foxworth said eagerly. "Do you know Detective-Sergeant Andrew Scobie? He has something rather interesting to tell you."

"I could use something interesting," Pagan said, shaking the hand of the man called Scobie, who was built like a safe and had the grip of a longshoreman. Scobie had a rather kindly face. He was a cop of an older generation, close to retirement, a man who'd probably begun his career on a neighborhood beat when the world was a simpler place and the local police knew by name all the villains in their parish. A time before handguns, before mindless violence, before the current climate of brutishness had descended on the land.

"A prostitute was murdered in Mayfair, Mr. Pagan. A particularly ugly killing by any standards. Scissors. A royal mess."

Pagan listened, wondering what this had to do with his own investigation. "And?"

Scobie looked slightly embarrassed. In an awkward way, he shifted his weight. "I don't know quite how to say this, Mr. Pagan."

"Say it any way you like, Scobie."

"Well, your name's attached to it."

"Attached? How? I'm not following you."

"I think you better see for yourself."

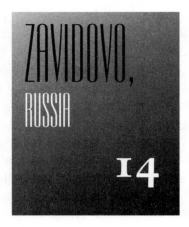

ZAVIDOVO, RUSSIA

14

Three horsemen in heavy overcoats came over a rise between pine trees. Snowdrifts lay thick under a cold, sunny sky. The horses sank to their flanks in the brilliant drifts and labored, breath crystallizing on the frozen air; the landscape was stark and secretive. A wind came and went in forceful flurries, shaking snow from pine branches, creating tiny pockets of greenery in an otherwise unbroken expanse of white.

The front rider carried an automatic rifle strapped to his shoulder. He rode some yards in advance of the other two. He surveyed the landscape; the presidential security force, six white-uniformed men spread here and there between the trees, was invisible to his eye. He reined his horse, a big black brute of an animal, and brought it to a stop.

He turned, looked back, seeing Gurenko on the bay mare; Gurenko's companion, Budenny, was in the saddle of a chestnut gelding. Both men were lighting cigarettes.

Gurenko, in his late fifties, often had the slightly bewildered look of a poet decayed by drink. As a young man in Kazan critical of the inadequacies of Soviet Marxism, he'd tried his hand at a few allegorical verses that, with hindsight, were embarrassing in their naïveté. He was also something of an authority on the work of Tintoretto; when he was a student he'd published a slim monograph on the artist's work. Apparently nobody had read it. This artistic sensibility had been eclipsed during the rugged years of his political life, which had been dedicated at first to the complex matter of survival after the collapse of the Union, and then later to the arduous struggle for the presidency, an unseemly armed conflict — a squalid bloody business in the center of Moscow — that had resulted in his opponents being tried and jailed for acts of treason against the state.

Despite the occasional appearance of bemusement and self-absorbed gloom, there was iron in Gurenko, and ambition. He'd fought hard and long for his supremacy and guarded it avidly, even though he had sentimental moments when he thought of his earlier lost self, a dimly remembered state of innocence. Innocence, alas, was a perishable commodity. It had no place in the brutality of politics.

Budenny, chief of state security, was older than the president, a smooth-shaven individual whose cologne could be smelled at a distance and whose lust for young girls was reputed to be insatiable. Budenny, who favored Armani suits and hand-painted silk ties, had a dacha at Zavidovo. So did Gurenko. Even in post-Union Russia, political power retained its old advantages.

Gurenko exhaled blue smoke and patted his horse in an absent-minded way. Budenny was gazing through the trees. Having smoked his cigarette with the raw exuberance he brought to all his appetites, he flicked the butt away and it sizzled in the snow.

Gurenko looked up at the sunlit skies. The wind had died and the stillness of the landscape was exquisite. It caused a pleasant flutter of melancholy to descend on him. "Magnificent," he said, and he gestured at the white stretches. He'd always had an affinity with wild landscapes. He found romance in desolation.

Humbug. Budenny didn't think the place was magnificent at all. He was cold and miserable. His horse whinnied, as if spooked by some invisible menace. He rapped the animal sharply with his whip. Unlike Gurenko, he had no love of the great outdoors. Horses and trees and up to your fucking ass in snow — none of that was his scene. He preferred bars, brothels, warm fires, the company of soft pliant perfumed girls.

He said, "I'd like to go over the security arrangements with you."

Gurenko didn't want to think about business, although he knew this was the only reason Budenny had agreed to accompany him on this ride, which he clearly hated; but there was privacy in this place, which was an obsession with the man. No eavesdroppers.

"I leave all that to you. I have every confidence," Gurenko said.

Budenny said, "I'd like to see more security than normal. Consequently, I'd recommend an increase in manpower."

Gurenko laughed. "Can we afford more airline tickets and hotel rooms? We're supposed to be in the poorhouse, after all." Budenny's paranoia was sometimes excessive.

"It's not a question of money," said Budenny, who didn't like the way Gurenko sometimes treated important matters with such flippancy. "It's a question of safety."

Gurenko's face was fleshy and pink. He rubbed his nose with the back of a glove and was quiet for a few seconds. "Do what you feel is necessary. You know I find all this talk of security very dull." He breathed the sharp clear air deeply into his lungs. He didn't need to be encumbered with Budenny's worries. He watched a winter hawk soar from the uppermost branches of a tree, its awesome wing movements powdering the air with snowflakes.

Budenny said, "Of course it's dull. But when it comes to your security, I can't take anything for granted. The world has a surplus of loonies."

Gurenko spurred his horse on. Budenny, uncomfortable in the saddle, his buttocks already sore from friction, his balls itching, trotted after the president. He detested this wretched place. Birdsong drove him frantic, and as for flowers and plants — these were the domain of grubby-fingered gardeners. He wished this bloody long ride was over, this whole day behind him.

He caught up with Gurenko, who had the blissful look of a man in his element. Gurenko tended to live in a dreamworld as far as Budenny was concerned. No grip on reality, or at best a tenuous one. He was a wonderful orator, and sometimes his inspirational words compensated for the inadequacies of Russian life, but the truth was that the country, depleted by Gurenko's own so-called reforms, crippled by lawlessness and a lack of patriotic spirit, was on a greased slipway to hell. Certainly, Gurenko had subdued many of his opponents and reined in the military and most of the generals were as obedient as lapdogs, but out there in the heart of Russia was a discontent, a black murmuring he appeared not to hear.

Budenny set the thought aside. He had a superb little number lined up for the evening; Latvian, but he wouldn't hold that against her. He projected himself into the immediate future. He contemplated a sauna, sparkling wine, the Latvian girl's tits. He supposed she'd pretend she knew no Russian and speak to him in that funny language of hers. What the hell. It wasn't her voice he was interested in anyway.

Gurenko stopped his horse again. He studied the landscape for a time. Budenny lit another cigarette rather clumsily with one hand. The horse under him, perhaps alarmed by the sight of flame, shuddered and snorted, nostrils flared. Christ, horses were such ugly fuckers.

Gurenko looked forlorn for a moment, as if a passing thought had saddened him. "I have moments when I wonder . . ." He left the sentence unfinished. Budenny, who sensed one of Gurenko's occasional confessionals looming up, was quietly embarrassed.

"What do you wonder?" Budenny felt obliged to ask. He didn't want to hear a speech. He didn't want to sit through one of Gurenko's rambling discourses on the nature of self. It was almost a form of punishment. He liked Gurenko well enough on a personal level, but there were limits.

Gurenko shrugged. "I've given my entire life to one thing. And sometimes it crosses my mind that I might have taken another path, something more . . . placid, shall we say? Something less demanding. A professor, perhaps. A teacher . . ."

Christ, Budenny thought. Gurenko was beyond the age for mid-life crises. This was the man's weakness, though. He entertained frivolous yearnings to revisit crossroads where he'd made decisions long ago. He didn't understand a simple fact: you couldn't go back and change the maps of your past.

"The basic trouble with politics is how it demands total ruthlessness," Gurenko said.

"It isn't a quality you lack," said Budenny.

"I may not lack it. But it didn't come naturally to me. I had to learn it early on. I had to develop an instinct for hearing the sound of knives being sharpened in the darkness. A man has to protect himself. Develop a hard shell. You don't have any friends in the game of politics, Budenny. Every smiling face conceals a hidden agenda, an ambition. The question I ask myself is, What has it done to me? What has it done to the inner man?" Gurenko gazed at Budenny and smiled. "Perhaps there isn't an inner man, Budenny, eh? Perhaps that kind of conceit has been extinguished long ago."

Budenny disliked self-examination in himself; when he encountered it in others, especially Gurenko, he always felt ill at ease. What was he? Some kind of fucking priest that he had to listen to Gurenko jabber on about his soul? Budenny's view of life was simple. You made a decision and you acted on it. You didn't get your shorts in a twist along the way. You didn't sit around contemplating doubts, entertaining anxieties. Christ, no, you did what you had to do. You got on with things.

Gurenko said, "You think I'm talking nonsense, don't you?"

Budenny shook his head. "Of course not."

"You're a bad liar. You think — here goes Gurenko again on one of his soul-searching moments. What a bore. What drivel." Gurenko slackened his hold on the reins of his horse. The animal flicked its great powerful head. "At least you pretend to listen, Budenny. And for that I thank you."

Melting snow, having fallen from a branch, trickled under Budenny's collar and slithered down his spine, an icy fingertip. He said, "You want to look into your heart, that's your affair. If it gets to the point where you think you're having a nervous breakdown, let me know so that I can make alternative arrangements for running the country."

Gurenko laughed. "There's something about your attitude that amuses me, Budenny. Your self-assurance, I suspect."

"It comes from my peasant background," Budenny said. "When a cow's about to calf, you don't sit around on your ass and ponder the miracle of birth. When the corn has to come in, you don't fart about contemplating the wonder of a seed."

Gurenko said, "I'll remember that next time I have one of my futile moments of introspection." He spurred his horse on through the drifts and Budenny, whose buttocks felt like thin-sliced raw meat, sluggishly followed.

Gurenko turned. "Time for a drink," he said. "Time to get out of these damp clothes."

"You won't find me arguing with that," Budenny said. He tapped his horse with the whip and thought of the Latvian number, trying to remember her name, a task that eluded him in the end. Besides, he had other things in his mind, things of a less diversionary nature than some carnal heave-ho, some fleshy gallop with a sixteen-year-old bonbon from Riga.

■

Svetlana rubbed Gurenko's shoulders dry with a hot towel as soon as he stepped from the bath. They had been married, it seemed to Gurenko, forever; she knew his moods, his expressions, even his thoughts before he uttered them. Marriage was the core of Gurenko's life; Svetlana — grown plump over the years, her crow-black hair turned gray but worn long, was to him still beautiful. She avoided the limelight, she was rarely photographed, she usually found some excuse to miss state functions, but she was Gurenko's full partner, counsel, confidante. He made no decisions without her; it would never have occurred to him to do so. He sometimes wondered how he'd cope with a solitary life if Svetlana were to die before him. The notion withered him.

Now, as he stood dripping bathwater on the tiled floor, he enjoyed the penetrating rub of the towel under her fingers. She sang quietly to herself as she worked down, shoulders, back, thighs. Then she dropped the towel and draped a robe over him.

"There," she said. "Done."

Once, too many years ago to remember, he'd written poems for her. They were naive and romantic and he'd asked her to burn them, but she'd tied them with ribbon and locked them in a small mahogany box, the key to which she wore on a chain around her neck. This was her secret, Gurenko wasn't supposed to know. But they had no secrets from each other. He reached for her hands, held them between his, smiled at her. She looked a little sad; her eyes were darker than usual.

"You've never liked Budenny, have you?" he asked.

"He's crude. He treats young women badly. He has too much raw energy. He likes to overwhelm people."

"He's protected me for years," Gurenko said. "Are you questioning his loyalty? His efficiency?"

She shook her head. "No. I wouldn't question those. It's just . . ." She sat, wrapped in a thick green robe, on the edge of the huge bathtub. "I'll tell you what it is. It isn't Budenny. It's this trip. It's the idea of your going away."

"For three short days —"

"I know, I know —"

"It isn't the first time I've been away," he said. "What's different about this?"

She was silent now, frowning. "You're trying to do too much," she said after a time. "Five countries in three days. God knows how many meetings. How many awful dinners and speeches. You'll burn out."

He laughed. He sat perched alongside her and raised one of her hands, noticing how age had glazed the skin. "It's a question of reassuring people about our country. It's a matter of settling certain doubts and anxieties about our stability. I have to do it. I look around, I see how delicate our situation is, I try to understand the viewpoints of the English, the Germans, the French — they feel very uneasy about us. I have to convince them otherwise."

"Like a salesman," she said.

"You might say that."

"You want to reassure them about your product."

"Yes," he said.

"Who's going to reassure *me* when you're gone?" she asked.

He patted her hand now. He didn't intend the gesture to be construed as patronizing, but he knew she'd see it that way. "Three short days," he said.

"Three *long* days."

She stood up, walked to the mirror, looked at her face. Without makeup, she could see the lines, the erosions of age, the way the eyelids sagged, the downturned lips. She turned to her husband, thinking it best to introduce a touch of flippancy; he didn't need to be worried about her misgivings, did he? He had enough on his mind.

"You know what I think?" she asked. "The whole trip's an excuse to see your beloved Tintorettos. Am I right? Am I?"

"You see straight through me," he complained.

"As always." She hugged him, a little harder than usual. And she held him a little longer than she normally did. "When you're away, don't forget to take your vitamins."

"I promise," Gurenko said.

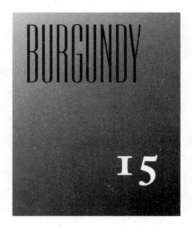

BURGUNDY

15

Jacob Streik was confused, didn't know how many hours had passed since he'd shot the kid. A wicked weariness was clawing away at him. Twice he stopped the car and was sick by the side of the road. The second time he'd had to throw up and the fierce headlights of a passing truck had picked him out and he thought he must have looked ghostly and stupid retching into a grassy bank.

He hadn't a clue where he was, hadn't looked at the map in hours, he could only think of driving, just on and on, mile after bleary mile. At some points he was bugged by a weird loneliness. He wanted to park in a tiny French burg and jaw with the locals, talk about soccer and whether Paris Saint-Germain was good enough to win the league or whatever it was, maybe drink some more of the red dreck, but he wasn't sure if the cops were after him now as well. The lane where he'd shot the kid was lonely enough, but who could tell? Somebody might have seen him drive away, noted the registration number of the Saab, called in the gendarmerie. Everybody and his brother could be hunting in this region of France for an overweight American. A good disguise would help — yeah, if he could magically lose about eighty pounds, he wouldn't feel so goddamn conspicuous, but they hadn't invented that kind of diet yet. So he kept going, eyelids heavy, stomach churning, a fat man running nowhere through the hours before daybreak.

He didn't realize he'd hit anything until he heard a thud against the front of his car and even then he swerved, although he knew it was too late. He braked, got out, stumbled back down the darkened road. The dog was a black mongrel. The Saab had knocked it about twenty feet from the point of collision and it lay awkwardly, hind legs broken, head twisted sorrowfully to one side. Its pink mouth hung open and bloody. Appalled, Streik bent down over the wretched creature, which turned its eyes toward him.

Streik thought: This thing pities me, this dying dog actually *pities* me. You're going out of control, Jake, you're beginning to imagine absolution in the eyes of a dying animal.

He put his hand on the dog's head a moment. The fur was sticky with blood. You can't leave it lying here, he thought. You can't just leave it in the road for a truck to mangle. He raised the animal in his arms, carried it with grunting effort to the verge, and set it down among long stalks of grass, then he hurried back to his car. He didn't move for a while. Dense shadows of sleep were congregating inside his head. If he didn't cop a few zzzs damn soon, he'd be a zombie.

He peered at the first light of morning, visible through barren trees. It was then he realized his jacket was covered with the dog's blood. How the hell could he turn up at some pension streaked with blood? *Bienvenu*, sign the register, here's your key, room ten second floor — and they'd be on the blower to the gendarmes before your head hit the pillow.

He stepped out of the car, opened the trunk, fished around in the piles of clothing for something to wear. He found a crumpled black blazer and a pair of old flannel pants and a gray shirt. He went into the trees and, shuddering in the cold air, discarded the bloodied suit. He stood in his mustard-colored boxer shorts like a frightened man on the edge of a high diving board. He put on the shirt and struggled into the flannels — they were too tight — and then the blazer with the silly Ralph Lauren badge. He tucked his pistol in the inside pocket of the blazer. He picked up the soiled clothes and wandered farther into the trees, where he buried the useless suit under a heap of brittle leaves. Then he went back to the car and drove away.

Eventually, when he couldn't hack any more mileage, when his eyes had begun to pop and his vision fail, he came to a small village where a café in the tiny central square was the only place open. He had to stop, take the chance, rest somewhere, eat. He parked the Saab at the side of the square and waddled inside the café. Sit, have a sandwich, something to wash it down with. Relax.

But when he entered, he was jumpy, couldn't stand the sullen early-morning peasant faces that turned to look at him. He wondered if he was already on wanted posters and TV screens. His imagination did a tricky little dance. What were all these guys doing in a café at this ungodly hour?

He walked to the bar, ordered a ham sandwich in his bad French, *jambon sur le pain*, then asked for a cold lager. He had a killing thirst. He waited for the old woman in the hair net to serve him. A TV played in the room. Two guys in khaki suits were digging carefully in some ruins. They had unearthed shattered bits of pottery. Very engrossing, Streik thought. If all I had to worry about were the shards of old Greek vases, wouldn't life be hunky-dory?

His order came, he carried it to a table in the corner, munched the sandwich down quickly. The beer was a gaseous joy and went speeding at once to his brain along the same slick track wine and cognac had taken earlier. He rose, ordered a second lager. Slow now, he thought. Speak to nobody. Do your thing and get the hell out.

The lager was beginning to make him drowsy. He wondered if they had accommodation here, but maybe that was risky. For a minute or so he floated off into a light sleep, waking with a start when he realized his head was sinking down to the table.

He thought: I'll go to Audrey Roczak, I'll find her, she always had good advice. What the hell was the name of the place where she lived? Memory was a flawed fishing net now, slippery images and recollections dripped through it like silvery cod. He could see her face and remember the big hooped earrings she'd always worn in the old days in Prague and East Berlin, back when the cold war hadn't begun to thaw — so why couldn't he remember where the hell she lived?

Then it popped back into his head: Lyon. That was the place. Lyon. How far away was he from Lyon?

The door of the café flashed open and a uniformed cop came in. He walked straight to the bar, ordered coffee, and with his elbow propped on the counter glanced around the room. He greeted a few people, a bit of cheerful banter was exchanged, and then he turned his face in Streik's direction.

Streik thought of the German kid in the lane. He thought about the gun he carried tucked in the back of his pants and for which he had no permit, no papers of any kind, a gun he'd purchased illicitly in Montmartre from a small-time hood in a bar. He blinked, laid his hands on the table, caught the cop's eye, then stared at the TV. The cop finished his coffee, then said his good-byes and walked out.

Streik thought: He's probably waiting for you on the street, Jake. Doesn't want to make a scene arresting you in front of everybody. Dear Christ. It was a mess, a fucking mess, but it had been a mess from the very start, he'd sensed it months ago when he'd first agreed to do a little bag work for Montgomery Rhodes, he'd felt a nonspecific doom about the whole business, he'd vaguely *known* it couldn't come to any good in the long run. Why hadn't he listened to his inner self back then? Why hadn't he paid attention to the wise old fart that occupied a limited space at the back of his brain?

There were all the usual reasons. Good money. A sense of adventure. Activity. Involvement. Some of the old tingle, the pizzazz. He could still hear Rhodes saying: *All you gotta do is pick up some bags now and again and deliver them to an address in New York City, that's it. Nothing could be simpler. Plus we'll fix you up with some nice shiny brand-new diplomatic credentials.* He could still remember the smoky little bar on Mulberry Street where he'd talked with Rhodes in a quiet corner booth and the way Rhodes had grinned in that skull-like way of his and how the black glasses had glinted in the red light of a Wurlitzer jukebox that kept playing old Al Martino songs. He remembered Montgomery Rhodes patting the back of his hand with his icy palm and saying, *Keep your nose clean, your eyes open, and keep your cool, and you'll do just fine, Jake . . . And stay off the booze, you understand me.*

Keep your cool. Stay off the booze. Sure. Now everything was shit soup. He knew too much. He'd lost his nerve, he'd snapped like a cheap rubber band and he'd run and he'd keep on running until . . .

He got up from the table, paid his bill, walked slowly outside. The square was empty and a couple of lamps still burned against the remnants of darkness. Streik went in the direction of the Saab, unlocked the door and was about to get inside, when the cop appeared seemingly out of nowhere and Streik's heart, already an overburdened organ, was filled with a rushing fizz of terror.

"*Bonjour,*" the gendarme said. He was smiling and seemingly friendly, but Streik knew that when it came to the cops you couldn't tell anything from their appearance.

"Tourist?" the cop asked.

"American," Streik said, as if a declaration of his national identity were protection against the law and order of foreign countries.

"Ah," said the policeman. "I have some little English."

"Hey, all right," Streik said enthusiastically. What now? Do I confess to killing a fucking dog in the hope that I'll divert him from any other line of inquiry? Did somebody see me change my suit in the woods? Was I observed shivering in my boxers?

"And your destination, where is she?"

"She?"

"Yes."

Streik thought about genders in the French language. Everything was either male or female, a fact that had to do a number on your brain if you were French. How were you supposed to remember if an envelope or a bicycle was a guy or a woman?

"Marseille," he answered, still smiling. It was the first name that popped into his head.

"Marseille. Ah."

He studied Streik's face with some curiosity and then asked to see a driver's license. This request startled Streik, who fumbled for his wallet, produced his New York state license, which the cop examined with more attention than Streik needed.

The cop didn't give back the license. Instead he said, "Passport, please."

Passport, Streik thought. What is this? What's going down here? He took his passport from his blazer and the gendarme flipped through the pages.

The cop, whose red neck was nicked from a recent shave, compared the passport photograph with Streik's face, as if he might stumble upon a discrepancy between the picture and reality. Streik held his hand out for the return of the document, but the cop was in no great hurry to oblige. He flicked the pages in a leisurely way. Streik grew agitated; he imagined a small panicked bird in his throat. He suspects me, Streik thought. He knows something.

The gendarme said, "It is not the best time of the year for the touring."

"Yeah, but it's quiet." Streik kept the smile going, even as he wondered if this cop meant to detain him deliberately while reinforcements were on their way. "Like, it's cheaper. Hotels. Restaurants. Cheaper all around and less crowded." He had an urge to babble.

The gendarme shrugged. Maybe he thought Streik odd to be driving around in freezing weather. Streik, trying to restrain his impatience, jiggled the keys in his hand.

"I have questions," the cop said.

"Questions?"

The cop held up a hand. "How long are you in this country?"

"Coupla weeks."

"And where have you been?"

Streik laughed and sounded totally manic. "Here. There. You know how it is. Say, is something wrong? My brake lights not working or something?"

The cop seemed not to understand this. "I will need you to come with me —"

"What?"

"I have other questions."

"Hold on," Streik said. "I'm a US citizen. I'm only passing through. Gimme the passport. Gimme the license."

The cop tucked both documents in the pocket of his jacket. "Later. Now, please. Come with me."

The fuck, Streik thought. Panic throbbed inside him. Had the cop been notified about the German's death? Had a bulletin been circulated? His mind was filled with wanted posters. DEAD OR ALIVE. He looked up and down the square. This was bad. This was sour. There was no way he was going anywhere with this goon. But what would happen if he refused? He looked at the car, wondered if he could make it inside, turn the key, drive the hell away; the element of surprise offered only the most slender of margins. He listened to a mournful wind blow across the square, the quiet rattle of crisp dead leaves.

"Let's be reasonable," he said. "I gotta right to know what you want to detain me for. Correct?"

"I have questions," the gendarme said.

"Questions, yeah. You already said that. So ask. Ask them right here. I don't mind answering anything."

The cop stubbornly shook his head. "Come. Come with me. My car," and he pointed to the other side of the square.

Streik hesitated. He had to act, act quickly. If this uniformed asshole thought he was going to get a medal for bringing in a killer, he was barking up all the wrong trees. Streik moved his arm with an alacrity that belied his bulk. He whipped out the gun and pointed it directly at the cop, who took one step back, his expression fearful.

"I'll blow you the fuck away," Streik said.

"Put the gun down," the cop said.

"Yeah. Right. You take me for a complete moron?"

Streik, his pistol still pointed at the cop, clambered inside the Saab, stuffed the key in the ignition, rolled down the window, drew the door shut; how far am I going to get, for Christ's sake? For a moment he considered surrendering to the cop, undergoing the ordeal of imprisonment in some French jail — but he'd be trapped behind bars, and one day somebody would get to him, somebody would smoke him: end of Jacob Streik. Even if he didn't go to jail, a trial would expose him and the American embassy would be informed, and Streik wanted absolutely no involvement with any embassy. No goddamn way. He had no such thing as a death wish.

He thought about shooting the cop, but a dead cop would bring all kinds of shit down on him. He stuck his foot hard on the gas pedal. He drove out of the square, compelled by the need to get as far away from the cop as he could. In his rearview mirror he watched the gendarme rush across the square to his own car.

Streik hit the open road, which was narrow and twisted treacherously. He forced himself to concentrate. He'd always been a good driver. That was one thing he could say for himself. He had an affinity with cars. He'd been hot-wiring and driving them since he was thirteen years old in the Bronx.

He swung into bends, an eye on the rearview mirror. He saw the cop car half a mile behind him. He gave the Saab more gas. He heard his tires scream on concrete and felt the car bounce when it struck potholes and ruts. He imagined the cop jabbering into his car phone, *I've got a suspect in the German murder case, he may be heading in the direction of Route 89, erect roadblocks, send in the cavalry.* Jacob Streik, marked man, a target. A fugitive in a foreign country with neither driver's license nor passport, but what the hell. Let's go for it, he thought. Let's take this sonofabitch for a trip. And he gassed the car as hard as he could, but the cop was still on his tail, bend after bend.

The road was straight for a couple of miles. The speedometer was reading ninety-seven miles an hour and the Saab was beginning to vibrate under pressure. Streik struggled for more speed, pushed the pedal into the floor. Come on, come on, gimme something extra! Another bend, another swing of the wheel, another peek in the rearview mirror. The cop was about a hundred yards back and gaining and Streik strained, *strained* to get more juice out of his car. His hands were tensed on the wheel, his throat was as parched as prairie grass in a season of drought.

The cop was coming up fast. Streik realized he couldn't outdrive the French car. The Saab didn't have the balls. The cop's Renault was some souped-up affair. Okay. What now? Pull over? Give up? He kept going. The landscape was a series of absurd impressions, a goat chained to a fence, swarms of pink pigs lathered in mud, an abandoned château with broken windows and slats nailed across the front door. None of it made sense. Animals and trees and houses all seemed to be spinning off the face of the earth because gravity no longer applied.

The cop car was alongside him now on the narrow road. Streik glanced at the stressed face of the gendarme, who was waving one hand in a gesture that meant, *Pull over to the side*, but Streik swung the car and heard metal grind on metal as wheel touched wheel and a hubcap flew off with a clanging noise. Yahoo! Keep going!

The cop dropped back, came again, and Streik wondered about the possibility of shooting the man. He had the automatic in his lap, he could pick it up, try his luck through the window, but accuracy was unlikely at this speed. He twisted the steering wheel and the Saab struck the Renault; the cop skidded to the side but didn't lose control. Tenacious fuck, Streik thought. You aren't going to shake this character. He picked up the pistol and, trying to steer one-handed, fired a shot in the general direction of the other car, but it went whining off harmlessly into trees.

The Renault came alongside him again. The cop was screaming what Streik took to be obscenities. *Up yours too, Frère Jacques.*

Desperate, Streik fired the gun again and this time he scored a hit on the French car, puncturing the hood, which immediately re-leased a fireworks display of sparks. *Gotcha*, Streik thought. The wiring, the electric connections, something had been disabled. The Renault slowed, the cop's face receded, and Streik watched in the rearview mirror as the French car slithered miserably into a clump of trees at the side of the road, where it sent up a delicious column of black smoke.

Streik didn't lose speed, didn't pause to ponder this small accidental victory, didn't dwell on his good luck, no, no, he kept trucking, he had to get as far away from the cop as possible, to which end he began seeking out ever more obscure side roads that invariably passed through somnolent hamlets or tracts of barren agricultural terrain where an occasional farmer could be seen pottering mysteriously in a dismal field.

Go go go. Keep going.

When he reached that state of mind where he knew he didn't have the adrenaline to drive any farther and total inner collapse threatened him, he pulled over into a field, parked under dead trees, reclined his seat, and, hideously cramped, fell into a light sleep.

He dreamed of Audrey Roczak, who was dressed in her customary gypsy threads and who, in the quiet comfort of the dream, was hugging him and saying, *You're safe with me, Jake. Safe as houses.* But the dream, which began so peacefully, took a nasty turn in the course of which Streik had the distinct feeling that Audrey had stolen his passport and driver's license. *You're a man without a country now, Jake. How does that feel?*

LONDON

16

he room smelled of death and cigarette ends. Bedsheets had been drawn over the girl's body. They were streaked with blood already turning from scarlet to a dark funereal brown. Pagan drew the top sheet back, looked into the pale drained face. The young girl's dull eyes were open; the indifference of death. He stared at the thin lips, the smudged mascara. A tooth was missing. He experienced a small sadness; what he needed was a vaccination of sorts to render him immune to violent death. Confrontations with murder, which seemed to harden some cops and induce in others a sense of black humor, still threw him off balance, plunged him into pessimistic reflection on the general malaise of the species.

He replaced the sheet, turned to look at Scobie, who was standing at the window. Foxworth lingered at the foot of the bed, tapping one shoe on the floor, as if he were anxious to be gone from this room. Pagan moved toward the bedside lamp, studied the shade, then wandered to the other side of the room, where he propped himself against the wall, arms folded.

The message on the shade was legible: a fingerpainting in blood. He listened to an odd throbbing pulse at the side of his forehead.

Scobie nodded toward the lamp and said, "You see what I mean."

"Clearly," Pagan remarked. He gazed at the shade, glanced at Foxie, who was making a humming sound of mystification through closed lips.

"So," Foxie said. "What does it mean? Any ideas?"

Pagan walked back to the bed. On the surface of the bedside table were traces of powder left behind by the fingerprint people. The room had been dusted, photographed, a file opened, a computer entry made; murder created its own bureaucracy. Scobie had already said that the room was an illegible chart of prints — the girl's, her flatmate's, those of customers drifting in and out. Scores of people had left their marks here. Some were fragmentary, others complete, it was going to take time to run them all.

"The writing on the shade was done by somebody wearing gloves," Scobie said. "We checked that immediately. Black silk gloves, to be precise."

The gloved hand writes, Pagan thought. But whose hand was in the damned thing? He stared at the shade. A message in blood, a greeting, a puzzle, whatever you wanted to call it; it was legible, undeniable. He touched the shade. Cheap, papery, the kind you could buy in any cut-price lighting supply shop. What surprised him about the writing was its neatness, the precision of the letters. *Been a long while since Heathrow, Mr. Pagan. Are you still smoking?* He tried to imagine a gloved index finger going back time and again to the palette of the dead girl's body for more blood, a sick dipping motion.

Foxie asked his question again. "What does it mean, Frank?"

Pagan let his thoughts drift a second to the encounter last night with Brennan Carberry as if, despite the damage to his car, that brief meeting was the only bright thing that had happened to him in months. He thought about the foolishness of expecting the girl to kiss him. A phantom touch of lips. Folly. A light-headedness. He shook his head and said, "I don't know, Foxie."

Scobie cleared his throat and looked glumly at Pagan. "One thing. The killer knows you."

"My name anyway," said Pagan. The atmosphere in the room was making him queasy. He longed to wrench the window open and gulp cold air into his lungs. He thought of the girl's killer out there in the chill, a shadow, a shadow who happened to have left behind a personal message. The notion was unsettling, spooky.

"What's the reference to Heathrow, Frank?" Foxie asked.

"I'm not sure," he replied.

"And this stuff about smoking —"

"I'm not sure about that either." Pagan heard an angry raw note in his voice, directed not at Foxie's questions but at his own inability to make sense of the message. He was too tense; the room was too small, the walls drab, the proximity of the dead girl upsetting.

"Somebody you met before," Foxie suggested quietly. He studied the handwriting and added, "Fastidious, I'd say. An orderly mind — at least on one level. Who do you know that might fit the bill, Frank?"

Pagan drew a hand across his face. His mind was unoccupied space. He heard Scobie move slightly, the rub of his overcoat against the wall.

"Whoever killed the girl wanted you to know," Scobie said.

"Apparently," Pagan remarked.

"Odd sort of business," said Scobie.

Odd, Pagan thought. Odd wasn't quite the word. Somebody commits a murder and leaves behind a calling card. Because because because . . . He walked around the room, shaking his head. Think, Frank. Sometimes when you rummaged your memories, you came up with nothing, not even elusive little shadows. He went to the door, opened it, looked across a narrow landing to a staircase. A uniformed constable stood at the top of the stairs. The landing was cold.

Killers, alas, came in a bewildering variety of forms. Mild-mannered, meek; awesomely deranged, wild-eyed, babbling; they could be ugly or beautiful, they could be cunning game players, lovers of problems, writers of confessional letters, makers of anonymous phone calls — there was no distinct pattern. If they walked around with a tattoo in the center of their forehead, catching them would be altogether a simple proposition. But the world, unfortunately, hadn't been arranged that way.

Are you still smoking?

He wished he had a cigarette just then, something to play with, nicotine to take into his system. He stepped back into the room, shut the door, stared at the message. *Mr. Pagan.* He wondered about the form of this address — sarcastic? a jibe? Why not simply *Pagan?* Come to that, why not *Frank?* He loosened the shade from the lamp and held it between his hands as if it were the skull of some long-dead creature that defied identification.

Heathrow. The middle *h* was faint because the writer had run out of writing material. He'd gone back for more blood at that point, because the rest of the word — *row* — was distinct. You could study this message all day, you could map the killer's hand movements, but none of that would ferry you any closer to a solution.

"I have one suggestion," Foxie said. "You might show the writing to Gunderson."

Hans Gunderson was a handwriting analyst who had worked in the past for the Yard on a freelance basis. Pagan had very little faith in Gunderson's expertise. Graphology seemed to him a quasi science, quirky, speculative. Besides, he found Gunderson at times arrogant, assertive, too unquestioning of his craft. A person's handwriting, Gunderson had once said with outrageous seriousness, is more a true mirror of the soul than the eyes. You talked to Gunderson, you were obliged to listen to that kind of pomposity. Handwriting analysts, phrenologists, numerologists — Pagan considered them all quacks to one degree or another.

He said, "You know what I think of Gunderson."

Foxie shrugged. "Worth a try."

"It's a bit like going to your local chiropodist and asking him to operate on a brain tumor, Foxie."

"Perhaps. But you've got nothing to lose, Frank."

"Except time." Pagan sighed. He strolled to the window, looked down into the alley below. The thought occurred to him that this room was located less than a mile from the tunnel where the explosion had taken place — and for a moment he wondered if there might be a connection between the murder of the girl and the bomb in the tube. A cop's mind, he thought. Always looking for connections, always searching for the adhesive that would bind one event to another — as if in the middle of mayhem there might be logic.

"You never know. Gunderson might shed some light, Frank. Can you come up with a better alternative?"

Pagan was stalled, his memory banks down. With a great show of reluctance he agreed to Foxie's suggestion. They would take the writing to Gunderson and see what the Guru had to say. He gave the shade to Foxie, who held it tenuously.

"If it's a waste of time, Foxie, I know who to blame."

"Isn't that why you keep me around, Frank?" Foxie asked. "I'm somebody to kick."

Pagan looked at his associate and wondered if he detected an edge in the younger man's voice. It was true, he supposed, that Foxie often felt the sharp end of his frustrations. But it came with the territory. It was part of the job. And Foxie knew that. Maybe, in his own headstrong fashion, he sometimes underestimated Foxworth's sensitivity. He reached out, touched Foxie on the shoulder a second. "I always thought my bark was worse than my bite," he said.

"Sometimes it's vice versa," Foxie replied.

"You want me to say I'm sorry?"

"It would be out of character, Frank."

■

They left Scobie in the flat and went down into the street, where the car was parked. Foxie placed the shade delicately on the backseat, switched on the engine, and started to drive in the direction of Regent's Park. Pagan stared ahead numbly, urging his mind into activity. He was missing something, something submerged in the drifts of memory. He was also impatient, seeing this new complication as a diversion from the business of the bomb. Once, he turned to look at the lamp shade and thought how absurd it seemed, like another passenger in the car. It was almost as if the killer had foreseen the fact that this stupid commonplace shade would have to be moved and transported and studied as carefully as if it were a Dead

Sea Scroll; an enjoyable little joke, if your mind had that kind of black turn.

On Baker Street Foxie stopped at a traffic light and turned to Pagan. "Well? Anything new come to mind?"

Pagan tapped his fingers on his knees. "I'll tell you what I feel, Foxie. I feel stupid carrying this bloody thing across London. Why wasn't the message left on something less ridiculous? A scrap of paper would have been perfectly acceptable. A lamp shade, for Christ's sake."

Foxie drove on up Baker Street toward Regent's Park. When he reached the street where Gunderson lived in the basement flat of an old Regency house, he parked the car. He took the shade from the backseat and, following Pagan, made his way down the crumbling, slippery steps that led to Gunderson's front door. Pagan rang the doorbell, waited. Gunderson, a small bald man with an expression of perpetual grumpiness, appeared. He was dressed in an old fisherman's sweater, elbows darned; baggy corduroy trousers, ancient slippers. He smelled, curiously, of marzipan.

"I don't remember ordering a new lamp shade," he said.

"Bloody funny." Pagan turned, grabbed the shade from Foxie, shoved it into Gunderson's arms.

"You better come in," Gunderson said, clutching the shade. He led them along a dark corridor to his study, a dimly lit room stacked with books — many of them Gunderson's own, which he'd had published by a vanity press.

"Still well stocked, I see," Pagan remarked.

"My time will come around," Gunderson said in his high-pitched voice. "The wheel always turns, Pagan. Always turns. Today's cranks are tomorrow's scientific pioneers."

Pagan glanced at a title: *My Years in Handwriting Analysis* by Hans Gunderson. Hot stuff. You could see the public gobbling it up. *I'll have three, terrific Christmas stocking stuffers.*

Gunderson put on a pair of glasses and set the shade down on his desk, pushing aside coffee mugs, an open can of alphabet soup in which was stuck a spoon, and a bunch of unopened envelopes of the windowed variety. "Now. What have we here? What have we here?"

"What does it look like?" Pagan asked.

Foxie, anxious to defuse Pagan's abruptness, deferred to Gunderson in a quiet voice. "We need some advice on the handwriting, Hans."

"Mmmmmmm." Gunderson peered at the letters.

Heathrow, Pagan thought. *Smoking.* Why the hell leave any kind of message unless you liked risky games? Was the idea to leave little arrows pointing to your identity? And if that was your goal, why? Pagan's mind floated away, out of this room, back toward the tunnel. He was restless, disturbed.

"Written in blood," Gunderson said.

"That's an expert observation," Pagan remarked.

Gunderson pushed his glasses up his forehead. "Look. You want my opinion or not, Pagan?"

Foxie said, "We want your opinion, Hans."

"I was asking Pagan, not you." Gunderson squinted at Pagan. "Well?"

Pagan nodded his head slowly.

Gunderson said, "I didn't hear you, Pagan."

"Yes. Yes, we want your opinion, Hans."

Gunderson, having scored a small victory, smiled. He had tiny chipped teeth, like those of an aged rodent. "I know you think I'm a crank, Pagan. But handwriting analysis is respectable. I wouldn't expect you to believe that, of course. But consider: somebody writes something, they shape their letters in a certain way, they apply different pressures at times — all of which suggests some internal state of mind. Anxiety. Insecurity. Fear. There are those in your own Scotland Yard who consider me most reliable, Pagan. And insightful. But why should I waste my time justifying myself in front of you, for God's sake?"

Pagan had it in mind to mention a case two years ago when Gunderson had blundered in a matter of forgery, attributing handwriting to quite the wrong person. But he said nothing; what was the point? He watched Gunderson shuffle around the shade, then reach inside a drawer for a magnifying glass. The old man peered through it, his face close to the handwriting. Every now and then he whistled snatches of something tuneless or issued his drawn-out characteristic *mmmmmmmm* sound.

"Interesting loops," said Gunderson. "This was written with enormous care by somebody who felt no pressure. Somebody un-hurried. Very neat."

Expert analysis indeed, Pagan thought. He glanced at Foxie, who was listening to old Hans with a look of concern. Often Foxie's man-ners were just a little too good. He belonged, Pagan thought, in the diplomatic service, taking tea with unpredictable warlords in dry tropical places and trying to explain, in plain reasonable English, the position of Her Majesty's government.

"Notice the alignment," Gunderson said. "Notice how straight it is, despite the curvature of the writing surface. The writer has envisaged invisible lines, such as you see in a child's exercise book. This is an imaginative person. Given the medium in which the letters have been written, this imagination is also capable of great cruelty."

Pagan frowned, wandered the room, passing the stacks of books, looking at framed diplomas on the walls, each attesting to Gunder-son's proficiency. He'd never heard of any of the institutes named on these certificates. On the bookshelves were several glass jars con-taining old-fashioned candies, which presumably explained the per-fume of marzipan that hung around Gunderson.

Pagan listened to Gunderson whistle; sometimes the old fellow sighed or clucked, but it was impossible to tell what these sounds meant. Little discoveries? *Insights?* Pagan paused by the curtained window, turned, saw Hans's bloodshot right eye enlarged by the lens of the magnifying glass.

"Whoever wrote this has an ambivalent attitude toward you, Pa-gan," Gunderson said.

"How do you figure that out?" Pagan asked.

"It would take too long to explain to a sceptic such as yourself," Gunderson said. "But sometimes letters — how shall I put this in a way you might grasp — emit sounds, tones. You can almost *hear* the words. You can hear the way in which they might have been spoken. It's like reading a poem. You get a feel for the tone of the writer's voice. The attitude behind the language. The person who wrote this, Pagan, appears on one level to respect you. But on another level the writer means mischief toward you."

"Mischief?" Pagan asked.

"The writer wants to stir you up, to goad you. Call it nose-thumbing."

"And you can tell all that from a few words?"

"That's only the beginning," said Gunderson. "I've barely begun. Keep this in mind. I've been doing this for more than thirty years. I like to think I've learned a few things along the way."

Pagan tried to ponder Gunderson's statement without prejudice, which wasn't easy. *Somebody who respects me but who also means me mischief.* It wasn't exactly helpful in establishing the identity of the writer. Gunderson's description could cover a number of people, criminals he'd caught, terrorists he'd outwitted. Pagan found an armchair, sat down, crossed his legs, closed his eyes; he felt the real solution lay in the recesses of his memory, not in Hans Gunderson's speculations. *Been a long while since Heathrow, Mr. Pagan.* He sensed an echo, a whisper from a faraway place, but it faded out on him before he could grasp it. He got out of the chair, walked to the desk, stood directly behind Gunderson.

"I'd say the writer isn't British," Gunderson said.

"How do you arrive at that one?" Pagan asked.

"A British native would be more inclined to say *time* instead of *while. While* suggests an American."

Pagan wasn't sure he agreed with this judgment, but didn't say so. He didn't want to get involved in a prolonged discussion about American usage of the English language with Hans. He watched as Gunderson, in a hunched position, continued to scan the message.

"The two els in 'still' are almost twins," the old man said in an enthusiastic manner. "Same height, same range. You don't often see that kind of exactitude."

"Does it mean anything?" Foxie asked.

"Oh, it can mean a number of things," Gunderson answered. Pagan could have predicted this uninformative reply but again chose to refrain from comment.

Gunderson said, "It could indicate a desire for emotional balance in the writer, for one thing. It could suggest that the writer likes to weigh opposing elements in the personality — a search for symmetry that may be lacking in the writer's life. Careful writing isn't necessarily the work of a balanced individual. It may be quite the opposite, in fact. I have personally seen the finest copperplate style produced by psychotic personalities."

A pontifical note had come into Gunderson's voice. He had the bearing of a man about to launch himself into a lecture. Pagan fretted around the desk, watching Gunderson lower his face once again to the writing. After a few minutes, the old man stepped back from the lamp shade and put down his magnifying glass.

"I'll need to spend more time on it, of course," he said. "Give me a day, I'll write you up a full analysis."

Pagan, yielding to a fresh burst of impatience, reached for the lamp shade, picked it up, held it against his side. "Sorry, Hans. I can't leave police evidence lying around unsecured. This isn't my case anyway."

"That's your prerogative, Pagan."

In Pagan's scheme of things, the explosion in the tunnel had priority over a mystifying message and the unhappy death of a young prostitute in Mayfair. He'd give the lamp shade back to Scobie; it was Scobie's business. Let him deal with it. Let him handle the evidence.

"All I can say is, I hope you find her," Gunderson remarked.

"Her?" Pagan asked.

"The handwriting was done by a woman," Gunderson said. "Didn't I mention that?"

"You're sure of that?"

"One hundred and one per cent."

Pagan stared at the old man. "You'd swear on the family Bible, would you?"

"On a stack of them."

Pagan went out into the corridor, moving toward the front door. Foxie came after him. Together, they left the basement flat and climbed the steps to the street, where a vicious wind, creating a dolorous sound, blew long-dead leaves from the direction of Regent's Park. A woman, Pagan thought.

The turbulence in his mind cleared a second, a tide receded. He felt as if a tuning fork were reverberating in his skull.

A woman.

But it couldn't be, he thought.

Not after ten years, it couldn't be.

AMSTERDAM

17

The General left his luggage in a locker and walked through the Amsterdam airport, passing a variety of glittering stores in which were displayed jewels, expensive clothing, the very latest in electronic gadgetry. He paused here and there to study a wristwatch, a ring, the latest computer. He had the thought that the basic human lust for such items had brought down an empire. For the sake of a new VCR, societies had dissolved, histories had been eroded, dynasties shattered. It was a strange consideration. In faraway Tokyo or Seoul, electronics experts had inadvertently caused the death of a political system almost eighty years old.

He kept moving in his rather straight-backed fashion. He needed to sneeze and drew from his coat pocket a Kleenex, which he thrust toward his nose. The coat, made out of vicuña by an exclusive tailor in Milan, had been bought for him in New York City. Here were other strange considerations and connections of the kind the General liked to ponder — an animal raised in South America had been shorn of its wool by some Peruvian shepherd and the fleece shipped to a tailor in Italy so that a coat could be purchased in a shop on Fifth Avenue. One could not help but be amazed by such global correlations.

He left the airport at eleven A.M. and took a taxicab into the city, where a variety of drugged-out young people, seemingly immune to the weather, lolled on frigid benches. They passed dope back and forth and looked generally blissed. A few slept on the frosty grass of small park areas, where every so often a policeman would try to wake them. Berlin, the General understood, had gone in much the same direction, kids smoking grass on the streets, shooting themselves up with heroin, white-faced young people in leather and earrings whose only known goal in life was to find a way to get high. It was a depressing phenomenon, this lack of direction and discipline. The behavior of youth — ah, well, it was only a symptom of a more serious condition.

"A fine sight," the cabdriver said. He was a polite Dutch-African with dreadlocks. He spoke good English.

The General nodded, said nothing.

"Is this your first visit?" the driver asked.

"No." The General preferred to be uncommunicative when it came to taxi drivers. He didn't want to be remembered later.

"Drugs," the driver said. "A criminal element is always involved in drugs."

"Of course," said the General. He gazed at an outsized pizza sign which hung in the morning light like a scabrous moon.

The General noticed a lovely teenage girl in torn black leggings and short black skirt weave along the sidewalk, a tragic angel. He understood that holes in leggings were fashionable, but so were safety pins in earlobes, hatpins in nipples, and gothic tattoos. A whole generation seemed intent on lacerating itself. This desire to disfigure oneself was further evidence of moral decline. He studied the girl as the cab passed, turning his head to see the sad hollow beauty of her young face.

He stepped out of the cab by the Herengracht. A group of tourists, wrapped up against the elements, passed in a barge along the canal; their faces peered out miserably from windows. He turned away from the sight, walking quickly toward his destination, a small pastry shop.

He entered, took a table against the wall, looked at his wristwatch. He was some eight minutes early for his appointment. He ordered coffee and a concoction of light pastry and strawberries, a taste of summer and sunlight in the core of this wintry city. An obsessive checker of time, he glanced again at his watch after five minutes had passed. He was due back at the airport in two hours for his connecting flight. Exactly eight minutes after he'd arrived, the door opened and a man in a black fur coat came inside.

Although Vassily looked different from the old days, although his silvery hair had been layered and blow-dried and his eyebrows plucked and the pouches under his eyes surgically removed, the General would have recognized him anywhere. Nothing had changed in the way Vassily moved, certainly not that sense of volcanic energy held in check. There was no physical space that seemed capable of containing him. It was as if he were in constant combat with the limitations of his environment. He came in swift strides to the table, sat down, laid his hand on the General's wrist and patted it two or three times with a vigor that was almost painful.

"My friend Erich, how very good to see you," Vassily said, and dragged his chair close to the table.

"Likewise," said the General.

"America is good to you, I see." Vassily fingered the cuff of the General's coat.

"Materially. Which isn't everything."

Vassily raised a finger to the side of his face. The General noticed that where once there had been a magnificent hairy wart, there was now only a small, unremarkable blemish. So Vassily had had more than his eyebags removed.

"And yourself?" the General asked.

"Moscow is changed." Vassily looked vaguely forlorn but such expressions never remained for long on his face. "We have a new class of entrepreneurs, which is in reality the old class except they've come out from the shadows. We have more criminals, of course. And they're armed with every weapon known to man. Rocket launchers, anti-tank guns, automatic weapons. We even have our own neo-Nazis. But that is to be expected in the present climate. People are discontented. Gurenko leads them into mazes with trapdoors. He doesn't see things the way they are. Now he's about to play the role of international statesman, shaking hands with the mighty of Europe, reassuring them. Blah blah blah."

The General couldn't resist a little humor. "Among all your other social changes, I see you also have new cosmetic surgeons."

"Ah. You notice. Vanity is good for the soul. I'm a vain bastard, Erich. Always have been."

The General looked around the pastry shop. What did they see, those Dutch matrons sipping coffee and eating cream cakes? A couple of retirees with nothing better to do than meet for coffee and pastries? How deceptive appearances could be, he thought. You could never trust surfaces. He suddenly thought about the missing man, Jacob Streik, and wondered if Streik, like Vassily, had managed to alter his appearance in some way. Even though he'd been reassured by Saxon, the matter of Streik still dogged him.

"But we didn't meet to lament Gurenko, did we?" Vassily asked. "How are things in America?"

The General shrugged. "The Americans are proud of their efficiency. I suspect this pride is largely unfounded. They go about business briskly, but sometimes their very haste leads to oversights, lapses, errors."

"New World energy," said Vassily, and turned to summon a waitress. "I prefer Old World thoroughness. Less speed, of course, but we always had an eye for detail. A great eye, if I may say so."

"Indeed," said the General. "But the times demand strange bedfellows."

"That doesn't mean we have to think like whores."

The General forked a sliver of pastry between his lips. "I sometimes despair, Vassily. I have moments when all I see are black clouds on the horizon. Then I feel useless. One of yesterday's men."

Vassily laughed in his staccato way. "You overstate, my friend."

"Do I? Do I really? I wonder."

Vassily ate the pastry the waitress set before him. He scrutinized the girl's big hips in his practiced way, then he chopped and chewed as if he hadn't eaten in years. He drank his coffee in one quick gulp. He drew a napkin across his mouth. "Think of it like this, Erich. We are simply using the Americans. They are not controlling us."

"Perhaps. But they write the rules, Vassily. We play by their regulations."

"A temporary business," Vassily said.

"I'm not so sure. They may make demands later that we can't meet. They may create impossible impositions."

Vassily said, "You were always too much of a worrier. Look. The Americans want only one thing — and you know what that is, don't you, Erich? Profit. In a word. If they profit, they're delighted. They're happy as pigs in shit. Their whole society turns on an axis of profit."

The General thought this too simplistic. There was more to this than turning a buck, as the Americans were so fond of saying. Admittedly, profit was a motive, but he'd found other stimuli among the Americans with whom he'd had to deal. There was a hard core of belief in what they were doing, a certain self-righteousness that could only come into being when there was an identifiable enemy. Without such an enemy, America was forced to turn inward, to look into its own heart, where there were more failings, more inadequacies than any Congress could deal with. Drug wars, the escalation of home violations, the rising murder rate, social inequities. In the General's view, Americans — certainly those he worked with — were better at looking outward than they were at examining their own flaws. Vassily, who had no experience of the United States, saw only a surface.

The General said, "But —"

"But but but. Forget buts!" Vassily punched the General on the shoulder, a playful gesture delivered with more force than was necessary. "We are on the move, Erich. Hardly a day goes by when there isn't some new crisis or an old one that has worsened. The Georgians are at the throats of the Abkhazians. The Chechens are shooting the Ingushetians. The Moldovans don't know if they're coming or going. As for Yugoslavia . . ." Vassily rattled his coffee cup in its saucer. "Germany's reunification is a damned rat's nest. The country's practically bankrupt. They got East Germany, but they inherited more than they imagined. And the Baltic nations aren't exactly prospering. The list is a long one. We're prepared, Erich. We're ready."

"I know, I know," said the General.

"In big cities, in small towns, in various organizations — we have people of enormous influence. With due modesty, I have to include myself in that category. We didn't vanish off the face of the earth, Erich. We didn't go the way of the dinosaurs, you know. Some of us went to ground, but only to hibernate. Not to sleep the sleep of the dead. We're alive and we're kicking. Don't forget that."

"I try to keep it in mind." The General sat back in his chair. He looked at his watch.

"Then don't be discouraged."

"Discouraged? That isn't it." The General thought of the young girl in the Manhattan apartment and how far away she seemed. What had she said to him? *Tomorrow is another day?* Something like that. He wondered how many tomorrows were left to him. He leaned forward across the table. "I worry more than is good for me, Vassily."

Vassily laughed once again and punched the General's shoulder a second time. "Worry is for old women. Everything will go the way it is planned to go. I have taken the appropriate steps at my end. And if it is going well at your end — how can it turn out badly?"

The General forced a small smile and gazed around the pastry shop, thinking it was time to go back to the airport. But he was reluctant to rise; after so many months in the company of Americans it was good to sit with somebody whose ideological background was much the same as his own, whose goals and ideals resembled his, it was comforting. Even if there had been past differences between STASI and the KGB, these had been buried by circumstance.

And he thought again of Streik, an abysmal shadow falling across his private landscape. Vassily knew nothing of Streik, nothing of Harcourt. He knew only of the big picture, as the Americans might say.

Vassily said, "Now! Why don't we find ourselves a couple of little whores and have some fun?"

"I have a plane to catch, Vassily."

"The beauty of planes is if you miss one you can always catch another. Forget planes! There are other kinds of flying much more interesting."

"You haven't lost the appetite, I see."

"The day I lose that will be the day they shovel earth on my face."
Vassily was already standing up, tugging at the General's sleeve.

They stepped out of the pastry shop and Vassily put an arm
around the General's shoulder. The General looked toward the
still dark water of the Herengracht. A wind blew up suddenly,
fracturing the surface. A duck flew under a bridge, a rich streak
of white.

"We'll take a taxi to the red-light district, Erich. We'll window-
shop until you see something that takes your fancy."

The General relented. "I can always catch a later plane." He
walked alongside the canal with a certain buoyancy in his step. It
was only when he passed two drugged teenage boys, both red-
eyed and laughing hysterically, that his mood underwent a change.
He looked at the boys. Their laughter was crazed. As his young
lady in Manhattan might have said, they were airheads. Space
cadets.

"Look, Vassily. Look."

Vassily pawed the air in a gesture of dismissal. "Kids on drugs.
So what?"

"It's the same in Berlin. In Moscow. The same all over Europe. Is
this the generation for which we're working?"

"They've lost their way, that's all."

The General put a hand on Vassily's sleeve. "Are they worth it?
Are they worth the effort?"

"Erich, Erich. They have lost their gods. They have no heroes.
How are they supposed to find commitment? Where is the structure for them? We need to give them structure. Think of it that
way."

"It's hard." The General looked dejectedly into the water.

"For God's sake! Have faith!"

The General sighed and reminded himself he should be hurrying
to the airport and not into the arms of some whore. He looked away
from the Herengracht and into his comrade's eyes, which had lost
none of their liveliness. In Vassily's eyes you could see a whole world
of possibilities.

Vassily put his hand in the inside pocket of his coat and took out a plain brown sealed envelope. "Before I forget," and he handed it to the General.

"Ah, yes. Of course." The General slipped the envelope into his coat.

Business concluded, both men went, in the manner of two sprightly elderly satyrs, in search of a taxi.

The General said, "You're a bad influence, Vassily Budenny."

"The worst," Budenny answered.

LONDON

18

Two hours after leaving Gunderson, Pagan went up into the attic at Golden Square, a chilly space filled with a complex arrangement of pipes that ran between floors down to the ill-tempered boiler in the basement. It was in the attic that Foxie, unable to find a suitable space elsewhere in the building, had set up an old-fashioned slide projector and a makeshift screen fashioned from an old dustcover.

I can call you Frank, can't I? If we're going to spend hours in each other's company, why bother with formalities? Or do you prefer Mr. Pagan? Pagan remembered this now: fine hands, fine long fingers slightly spatulated, slender wrists. Her fingernails are varnished a secretive black. She crosses her long legs, her very short black suede skirt rides her thigh, her legs are bare, Pagan looks away. She knows her power. She knows exactly. She knows how to hold, how to captivate. *You smoke too much, you know. You should really cut down. Think of your lungs. Have you ever seen pictures of cancerous lungs?*

Foxworth fidgeted with the projector and a beam of white light created a circle on the screen. "Give me a minute before I get this thing running properly."

"Why isn't this material on computer?" Pagan asked.

Foxie said, "Actually it is. But we can't access it yet."

"We're not linked up, is that it?"

"Interfaced is the word, Frank. We're not one hundred percent interfaced with the mainframe."

Pagan loathed these computer terms. He understood the need for the new technology, the way facts could explode on screens before your eyes, the hours of slog from which you were liberated, the information that could be summoned from a thousand sources at the press of a couple of buttons, but the language — pixels, batch processing, fact allocation files — made him feel he belonged to a new class of illiterates.

He shut his eyes, waited. *Perhaps I'll join you in a cigarette, Frank. I like one from time to time. It's one of my lesser vices. Do you want to know what the others are? Some of them are amusing. Shall I tell you? Shall I confess the things I like to do? Are you blushing, Frank?* He remembers: he reaches across the table, a struck match held in one hand. He tries to light her cigarette but she pulls her face back and the flame burns his fingertip. He realizes she has done this deliberately. *Let's try that again, Frank. I don't understand why your hand is shaking. Am I having a bad effect on you?* He offers a second match, applies it to her cigarette. She doesn't inhale. She blows a stream of blue smoke straight at him and smiles and his eyes are caught in hers and he has the feeling he's a fleck of iron drawn into a magnetic field, can't resist it, the pull, the energy, the sheer dazzling fact of her beauty. To her, beauty is power. Beauty is what you inflict on other people. A punishment, a surgical instrument.

Pagan said, "She's been inactive for years. *Years.* Why make a comeback now? It doesn't make any sense."

"We're not even sure this *is* the woman, Frank," Foxie said. "We don't have fingerprints. We don't have evidence. All we've got is Gunderson's hypothesis that the message was left by a female — that, plus your memory. And memory isn't always reliable."

It's reliable in this case, Foxie, Pagan thought. Believe me. The attic made him feel claustrophobic. Ten years ago the windowless interrogation room he'd shared with the woman had made him feel the same, but even more so, because she dominated the space, she controlled the mood, she played on his tensions as if they were keys on a clarinet. *I unsettle you, don't I? I can't think why I should bring that response out of you. Why don't we relax, try to make this easier?* Her voice had a sultry quality, sometimes a low-pitched whisper, sometimes the half-hoarse cadence of a torch singer. He remembers: she crushes her cigarette on the floor and reaches across the table to touch his hand, a moment of intimacy unnerving in its unexpectedness; her flesh is soft and warm and her fingertips slide across the ridges of his knuckles, *and he doesn't pull back his hand, doesn't move, he simply lets her skin remain in contact with his, because he likes it, because he enjoys the feeling, because for a few crucial seconds he's completely lost in the woman's force field. And he recognizes in himself the unmistakable warm sensation of desire.* She says: *It might have been fun to meet under other circumstances, don't you agree? I think we might have had a fine old time of it.* He turns his face to the side, embarrassed because she's intuited his desire. And then he feels her foot under the table, she's kicked off a shoe and is stroking his leg with her toes —

Foxie pressed a button. Pagan opened his eyes. The image on the screen was almost black, lacking contrast. "I need to adjust this gizmo, Frank. A minute."

Pagan leaned against the wall, a web touched his forehead, he brushed it aside. From tunnels to attics, he thought. This investigation was all over the place, which he certainly didn't like. Give me form. Shapes. He felt like a man puzzling over an abacus on which somebody of malice had rearranged all the beads. And one of those beads was a woman he hadn't seen in ten years, hadn't thought about in a long time, somebody shipwrecked in his memory.

"Ah," Foxie said. "There we are."

On the screen was a photograph of a long-haired woman of about twenty-three. It had clearly been taken without the woman's knowledge. Her face was turned to one side; a good profile, beautiful and strong and determined. She was dressed in the style of the seventies, beaded jacket, flared jeans. A ribbon flowed from her hair. The background was that of a European city, evidenced by the kinds of cars and license-plate numbers that were also in the shot.

Foxie said, "Nineteen seventy-three. Athens."

Yes, Pagan thought. "Keep going."

"Click," said Foxworth.

The second image was ostensibly that of the same woman, but the difference between the pictures was remarkable. Her hair was shorn in an irregular way and she appeared boyish. She wore a two-piece suit that might have been tailored for a man. She had a necktie loosely knotted at her throat. Androgynously lovely. There was even an element, altogether misleading, of vulnerability about her in this shot. Behind the woman was another figure, shadowy, slightly out of focus. Whether he was in her company or merely a pedestrian who'd come into range, it was hard to tell.

Pagan moved, took a closer look.

Foxie said, "Taken in nineteen eighty-eight, Rio de Janeiro. Photo courtesy of Brazilian police surveillance. I'm not quite sure how we came by it."

"Who's the fellow just behind her? The one with the shades?"

Foxie shook his head. "Can't say he looks familiar, Frank. Not even sure he's in her company."

Pagan went directly to the screen. He studied the man's features. He had an irritating sense of familiarity, a murmur at the back of his mind, but it slipped away from him before he could define it. "He reminds me of somebody."

Foxie scrutinized the shot. The man in the picture was blurred. The photograph had clearly been taken with a long-distance lens. Pagan snapped his fingers, a measure of frustration. He'd seen the face before, he was sure of that, but where in his memory did it belong? He played with vague associations in his head — was the man connected in some way with the fashion industry? cosmetics? movies? — but these produced nothing fruitful. Why had he come up with these areas of activity? What random linkage was floating free in his mind? He had the distinct impression, based on no observation in particular, that the man was definitely in the woman's company.

"Skip it. Keep going," he said. But the man's face nagged him.

"This is the last one, Frank."

A police mug shot appeared on the screen, a picture sliced in two: one side showed only the profile, the other was full face. She looked defiantly pale in these images, contemptuous of the police photographer. It was a marvelous face, filled with cavalier resonance, a flare of sexuality that would initially incite a man and then ultimately undermine him. You could imagine that the business of being her lover would be an endless war fought on terrain of her own making. There would be skirmishes, battles, frail unreliable truces, blood in the trenches. The depths in the eyes were a little scary. But she could do anything with those eyes, he remembered. They could be ice, they could be alluring, they could be incongruously innocent, childlike.

"Nineteen eighty-four," Foxie said. "New York City. Arrested on charges of sedition. Plotting the overthrow of the US government."

Pagan stared at the face. "Then she escaped. Went underground."

"Correct." Foxie flicked through the pages of a manila folder. "She belonged to an organization — some splinter group of the Weathermen — responsible for planting bombs in Washington. One was discovered close to the Washington Monument, another was defused in a parking garage next to the House of Representatives. She was sent to the federal penitentiary in Danbury and managed to disappear within a matter of a few weeks. Thin air. Reported sightings include Los Angeles nineteen eighty-seven, Frankfurt the same year. She had an apparently close call in a hotel in Deauville in nineteen ninety-one, where she was recognized by a retired FBI agent on vacation. The hotel was promptly surrounded by the local heat. But the lady had vanished. She'd registered under the name of Charlotte Pike. She appears to have a fondness for aliases involving creatures. God knows why, but she's called herself Caroline Starling, Cara Raven, Carola Fox."

Pagan stepped in front of the projector beam. "Carlotta. That's what we always called her. That's what the press always called her." *Carlotta*, he thought. The name had the timbre of a bell rung in a far-off steeple, a puzzling summons.

Foxie was quiet for a moment. "Do you want to fill me in on the personal background, Frank? What makes you certain it was Carlotta who left you the message?"

"I have to go back a bit, Foxie. Ten years. Nineteen eighty-five. There was a tip from Belfast. She was supposed to be jobbing for a fringe of the IRA. She was suspected of trying to smuggle explosives into the UK. We had everybody watching the ports, railway terminals, airports. I'd just begun working with Martin Burr then. I spent six days behind a one-way mirror at Heathrow watching everybody coming through customs. A yawn of a job. But the tip was supposed to be the genuine article. Carlotta was coming to England to finalize the details of the smuggling. I had her photograph in front of me for a week." He looked at the mug shot on the makeshift screen. "That does her absolutely no justice. She was — the word is gorgeous, I suppose. But that's not quite right either."

He pressed his hands together. He could recall obsessing over the woman's picture. He'd lived and breathed Carlotta for days, establishing a queer kind of intimacy with her image even before he'd met her.

"What happened?" Foxie asked.

"I intercepted her at Heathrow on the sixth day of my surveillance."

"And?"

"I took her in for questioning. Keep in mind the fact that everybody wanted her. Everybody wanted the glory of capturing Carlotta. Special Branch. The CID. The FBI was waiting in the wings. Careers would have been made overnight. I had this bright idea I'd be an instant hero. Instant promotion. Watch my jet stream." Pagan laughed at himself; the brashness of old ambitions, of youth.

"What happened?"

"I don't exactly know how to describe her. She projected — I can only call it a kind of bewitching sexuality, Foxie. Okay. Like a spell. I was stuck with her in an interrogation room for two days. She had an answer for everything. She was in London to visit a dying aunt. That story checked out nicely. The strange thing is, it was damn difficult to imagine anyone with *her* looks being involved in the sordid business of terrorism. When I spoke to her, I had the unsettling sense of interrogating an angel. A sexy angel, admittedly. But that's how she looked. She charmed us all. She seduced us. Even Martin Burr, who knew his way around an interrogation. I think she fluttered old Martin's heart. I know she did a small number on mine." He was editing his story for Foxie, sanitizing it. Her hand on his, the heat in his blood, the abrupt fissure of lust she'd released in him — how could he tell Foxie any of this? Ten years ago he'd been a different person. Ten years ago he'd been married only five or six months, in love with his wife — and Carlotta, like a messenger from the abyss, had forced him to recognize that he was capable of entertaining notions of infidelity and betrayal. *Is this a wedding band, Frank? Tell me about your wife. Is she smart? pretty? Is she faithful? Are you true to her?* He remembers her fingertips closing over the thin gold ring, the palm of the hand clasping the finger in an undeniably suggestive way. He remembers the feel of her palm on bone, his reluctance to have her stop. *You have to learn to relax, Frank. You have to learn a whole lot of things, don't you? But then you're what — thirty-three, four? You haven't really begun to live.*

"We couldn't hold her," he said. "We had no reason. So we decided to turn her over to the FBI, who had more positive reasons for wanting her." Pagan paused. "They sent a couple of agents from Washington."

"And?"

"We put her in a hotel under guard while our friends from Washington were on their way to fetch her. Nobody knows exactly how she got away. There was some speculation she dressed as a maid and just walked out. Another story has her bribing a room-service waiter into helping her. Who can say for sure? A few days after she vanished, there was an explosion at an RAF base in Norfolk. Was she behind it? Nobody ever knew."

He remembered the hotel room, the corridor where half a dozen uniforms kept watch, he remembered ushering Carlotta inside the room. She sits on the bed and says: *This feels fine, Frank. Not too soft, not too hard, just right.* She raises her eyes, looks at him, stretches a hand out toward him, fingers stretched. The short skirt reveals the softness of thigh; he looks at the breasts under the white silk blouse. A bad moment, time turned upside down, the turbulence of feelings. *Why don't you lock the door, Frank? Sit down beside me, have a cigarette. Nobody's going to disturb us.* He takes a couple of steps toward her, fevered, emboldened by his desire, unthinking, career jettisoned, wife forgotten, all his responsibilities tossed into a bonfire of amnesia, and he watches her hand stroke the quilt, watches the way she spreads her legs, stretches them, sees how one hand moves to her own thigh, fingertips caressing her own flesh. And then her hand disappears under the hem of the skirt into darkness. She tosses back her head, lips parted, eyes still focused on Pagan as if she sees straight through him, divining the nature of his arousal. He knows it's a game, but it's a desperate one, and reckless, because he can't see the consequences of it, and he takes another step toward her, a step closer to the edge. Her hand, invisible to him, moves between her legs, and she says his name a couple of times in a breathless way. She keeps watching his face. *What is this doing to you, Frank? Is this turning you on? Is this getting to you?* In somebody else the whole thing might have been crude and tawdry, but she carries it off. *What are you waiting for, Frank? Come on, what the hell are you waiting for? Lock the door.* And then he's standing over the bed, looking down at her, gazing into her face and going out of control, yielding to berserk notions, watching the rise and fall of her breasts, the tantalizingly slow movements of her hand, the shadows in her thighs.

Then she reaches out toward him. *Frank, Frank.*

He had no way of knowing what might have happened next because Martin Burr chose that moment to come inside the room, and if the old man sensed anything sexually conspiratorial, any charge in the air, he made no remark. *Must keep the prisoner comfortable* was what he said. *She's going back to Washington in the morning.* Carlotta smiled and smoothed her hands on her legs, Pagan stared uncomfortably from the window, and Burr surveyed the room, as if assessing the security of the place. Then, locking the door, Pagan and Burr had left.

If no physical contact had taken place, the realization that he'd betrayed Roxanne — at least in his intentions, his yearnings — altered his perceptions of himself for a time, depressed him. He'd wanted this woman, this Carlotta; he'd wanted, for lack of a better expression, the debasement of indulging himself in an infidelity. Lust — commonplace, banal — was finally inexplicable; and it was demeaning to realize you could surrender to it so easily. Everything you held in esteem — marriage, career, loyalty — had flown like crazed birds from open cages. He recalled returning the woman's photograph to the files, and thinking at the time that it had been a tiny act of exorcism. But the face had lingered for weeks in his head. The touch had remained on his hand. And he'd been unsettlingly aware of a hitherto unknown side of himself, a destructive urge in his character.

Pagan moved away from the projector. The attic had a small oval window directly overlooking Golden Square. He peered down into the early afternoon activity. Office workers buzzed to or from lunch. A solitary eccentric in a raincoat sat with a thermos flask on a cold bench.

"Carlotta," Pagan said, as if to himself. There was a time when her name had been synonymous with terrorism, like Baader-Meinhoff. Or Danny the Red. Or Jig. Nothing had been heard of her in years, if you didn't count the various sightings that were always reported when it came to enigmatic terrorist figures who'd somehow captivated the public. She was said to have been working with Khaddafi, organizing training camps for potential terrorists in the desert. She was reported to be "counseling" the IRA in County Armagh. Nothing had come of these allegations. Legends flourished around people like Carlotta; notorious terrorists were sighted like UFOs, strange configurations in the sky.

Foxie said, "She's quite a piece of work, Frank. This file contains stuff from the prison shrink in Danbury. Our girl was born into a family of considerable wealth, ran away from boarding school at the tender age of ten after stabbing a friend with a kitchen knife. You wouldn't want to be *her* chum, would you? More boarding schools, more unhappily violent incidents. She drifted into the radical underground when she was sixteen. She did the rounds. A bombing in Denver. A bank job in Des Moines. The sabotage of a train carrying a shipment of arms to a naval base in San Diego. According to the shrink's report, she has an extraordinary IQ. Fluent in French, Russian, and German. She has — and I quote — a penchant for violence. Which is to say she doesn't always have to be politically motivated to do her thing. She's probably not even interested in politics as such. They're merely a pretext for her acts of violence."

"And now she turns up in London," Pagan said in a flat tone.

"We don't know that for sure," Foxie said.

"The reference to Heathrow. The thing about smoking. She kept telling me I smoked too much, which was true in those days. She kept saying it was bad for my health, I ought to give it up. Foxie, nobody else fits. Nobody."

Weary, he gazed down into Golden Square. He'd relegated Carlotta into a forbidden zone of recollection; a crypt of memory he never visited. It was damp and unpleasant down there.

"I get the impression . . ." Foxie started to say.

"What impression?"

"You're not telling me everything. You're holding something back."

Pagan was silent. What was he supposed to say? Look, I wanted the woman, I wanted to fuck her, I wanted to play her game.

"I think you got to know this woman better than you're prepared to say," Foxie suggested.

"You spend forty-eight hours almost nonstop in somebody's company, you learn a few things," Pagan said. "Why don't we leave it at that?"

"As you wish." Foxie fidgeted with the projector in a slightly sullen way. Pagan's heart: an impenetrable shield. "Let's say Carlotta killed the girl. Let's go with that for a moment. Let's take the speculation a little further. On the very day of the girl's murder, a bomb goes off in a tube station no more than a mile away from the girl's flat. Given Carlotta's terrorist background, is that coincidence?"

"I seriously doubt it." Pagan walked away from the window, gazed at the mug shot again. He remembered the scent of the hotel room, the furniture polish, the smell of apples in a wicker basket. The encounter with Carlotta was a bleak episode in his life — so why was there still some relish in the memory? A shiver of pleasure, a frisson of self-dislike?

Foxie said, "She puts a bomb in the Underground, then walks a few blocks, picks up this wretched girl, goes back to her flat and stabs her to death with a pair of scissors. Why? A hundred or so people aren't *enough* for her. Is that it? She needs another kind of satisfaction. Hands-on stuff. She needs to see the blood and the suffering. She needs personal involvement."

Pagan said, "Maybe you're right. She's unfulfilled because she can't get to watch the faces of her victims in the tube. So she wants a bigger and better rush. She wants to look right into the eyes of somebody dying." Hands in his pockets, he strolled around the attic. "If she put the device on the tube, it doesn't tell us a damn thing about the purpose behind it. So what are we looking at, Foxie? An unmotivated piece of destruction? I don't buy into that one. I don't see Carlotta placing the device on the tube because she was having a bad day. She had some reason. And then to leave the message . . ."

"What did Gunderson call it? Nose-thumbing? Maybe he's right. Perhaps she wants to goad you. She wants to say, Come on, Frank, catch me. Let's see how bloody good you are. Find me."

Pagan was drawn into the circle of light on the white screen. If you looked long enough, you might imagine yourself hypnotized. Sleep, Frank. Relax. Everything's going to be warm and comfortable. The central-heating pipes knocked and moaned and vibrated for a few seconds. "Let's get out of here."

They went down from the attic and entered Pagan's office. He sat behind his desk, banged his hands together. "Okay. First we need to find out how she entered the country. And then how she left, assuming she didn't want to hang around. Put Billy Ewing on that. Airline companies. Trains. The usual. Tell him the kind of aliases she likes to use."

"Will do," Foxie said.

Pagan drifted a second, trying to imagine Carlotta descending into the Underground station, moving through rush-hour crowds to the platform — but he couldn't force the vision along. It lay in his mind ill formed, a Polaroid picture eaten around the edges by acid. He got up, walked the room.

"If she did the train, who instructed her?" he asked. "Who's the paymaster, Foxie? I don't see her randomly blowing up a train. I don't imagine she woke up one morning and said, Hey, what a bloody good idea to put a bomb in the tube. No, somebody contracted her services. And the reason she didn't call and leave a fake message blaming the business on the IRA or some other terrorist outfit is because she wants *me* to know that *she's* the one responsible. She knew I'd see her message. She knew I'd make the connection." He thought: A game, another of her games. This one especially deadly. This one beyond a simple, if persuasive, attempt at seduction. This one in an altogether different category.

Billy Ewing suddenly appeared in the doorway. "We've got full identification of the victims now. I've run all the names. They're clean. Nothing strange. Except for one small thing, which probably doesn't have any connection with our business."

"And what's that, Billy?"

"There was an American in the carriage. Name of Harcourt. Bryce Harcourt."

Pagan experienced a certain quickening, an alertness. "What about him?"

"Nothing really. It just so happened he made out a complaint to the Hampstead police about his car a few days before the explosion. Seems somebody slashed all four tires. The usual mindless vandalism. Expensive tires, I'd say. The car's a Mercedes, top-of-the-line job."

Pagan glanced at Foxie, who said, "Isn't he the chap from the US embassy?"

Pagan nodded. "Is there an address for Harcourt?"

"There is."

"Let me have it, Billy."

Ewing wrote it down, handed Pagan a sheet of paper torn from his notebook. The address was in Hampstead, a street close to the Heath.

■

They drove through St. John's Wood and Swiss Cottage. On Finchley Road Pagan watched hapless shoppers scurry around beneath umbrellas. He told Foxie about his meeting with Victoria Canningsby and her description of Harcourt as a frightened man.

"Harcourt's name comes up once. Fine," he said. "I don't pay it much attention. It comes up a second time, I get interested. Three times now. Three times intrigues me, Foxie."

"This Quarterman fellow led you to understand Harcourt was a researcher of sorts —"

"Which caused Mrs. Canningsby a moment of amazement."

"Why would Quarterman mislead you?"

"I can only think of one reason. Harcourt was working in a sensitive area. Grosvenor Square has its share of spooks. We all know that. If Harcourt was one of them, Quarterman wasn't going to announce it. So he wants to defuse any intrigue instantly by calling on me and telling me poor Bryce was low on the totem at the embassy."

Pagan turned his face from the sight of the rainy street. "It's going to be damn hard to get to the bottom of it anyway. Grosvenor Square's like the Kremlin. You just can't start poking around the place. The marines would have you in front of a firing squad in no time."

Foxie turned the Rover in the direction of Hampstead Heath. "Consider this," he said. "What if Harcourt, because of his job, was the target? What if he was the only target?"

"You keep coming back to this notion of a single victim, Foxie, which throws my head into turmoil. Somebody — we'll assume Carlotta — goes to the trouble of wiping out more than a hundred lives to get one man. Why, for Christ's sake? There are more economical ways to dispose of an individual. A single bullet in the skull on a dark night would be infinitely easier." He had the urge to light a cigarette but then remembered he'd left them in his apartment. He tapped the pockets of his coat in the hope of finding a stray that might have fallen from the packet. Nothing.

He turned to look at Foxie. "Okay. Let's say for the sake of argument your hypothesis has some plausibility. Then it's a short simple step to the idea that somebody deliberately hobbled Harcourt's car —"

"So that he was obliged to travel by tube."

"Exactly. He's obliged to take the tube because that's where he's going to be killed. Where does that leave us?"

"One thought does occur, Frank. And it isn't altogether pleasant. The whole thing's a diversion. A show. A bit of the old legerdemain."

"It's a bloody awful diversion. We're supposed to think it's an act of terrorism — when what we're *really* dealing with is the murder of a single man. Harcourt's just another name on the list. Another number. We don't pay him too much attention because we don't have the time, the manpower, et cetera. Everybody's in a state of shock. The nation is outraged. So the death of one American isn't going to attract attention — that's what you're saying."

"It's only a suggestion," Foxie said.

A diversion, Pagan thought. A smokescreen. A massacre in the tunnel because one man had to be eliminated. He had to stretch for this concept.

Foxie parked the Rover outside a Victorian house, a well-maintained structure of solid yellowy brick that extolled the imperial virtues of another time, when the world wasn't jerrybuilt and bricklayers knew their game and waistcoated businessmen listened to their daughters play the pianoforte on Sunday afternoons and wives arranged lilacs and lilies in vases.

Pagan got out of the car. He stared in the direction of the Heath, where wind and rain rubbed raggedly against trees. He stepped toward the house, followed by Foxie, whose coat was caught by the wind and whipped back. In the driveway was a silver Mercedes 450SL with flat tires. Pagan bent down, examined the slashes in the rubber. A pretty thorough job, done with enthusiastic malice.

He moved up the driveway. The house had been split into two separate flats. Harcourt's name was on the upper bell. The lower nameplate said Gilman. Pagan pressed Gilman's buzzer and within moments the front door was opened by a thin barefoot man who wore a white silk robe and black glasses. Pagan showed his ID. The man, who said his name was Victor Gilman, swayed slightly in the doorway; there was a whiff of booze on his breath. He was about five cocktails down, Pagan thought.

"And what can I do for dear old Scotland Yard?" Gilman asked. "What can I do for London's finest, eh?"

"We want to talk about Bryce Harcourt. Your upstairs neighbor."

"A gentleman from head to toe," said Gilman. "Altogether delightful."

"We need access to his apartment," Pagan said.

Gilman lost his balance a second, slipped against the door frame, laughed. "Pardon my equilibrium. I had a bad night. And I was obliged to take the cure today. Naughty of me."

"Very naughty," Pagan said, and stepped past Gilman into the hallway, followed by Foxie.

"Have you got a warrant?" Gilman asked.

"I don't have time for niceties, friend," Pagan said. "Harcourt has been killed."

"Killed?"

"Believed murdered."

"Murdered? Dear God. Murdered?" Gilman's silk robe parted, revealing a pair of red briefs and thin white hairless legs. "*Murdered?*"

"Do you have a key to Harcourt's apartment?"

Gilman took off his dark glasses. His eyes were bloodshot. "Who would murder a sweet fellow like Bryce, for heaven's sake?"

Pagan moved along the hallway to the foot of the stairs. Gilman, robe flapping, followed.

"I don't have a key," Gilman said.

"It doesn't matter." Pagan was already halfway up the stairs and Gilman, with the lurching movements of the drunk, was following.

Pagan reached the landing. The door to Harcourt's apartment was sturdy. The lock was a simple business, though, a Yale. He looked at Foxie. "Do your thing," he said.

Foxworth said, "It's been a while, Frank. I may be rusty." He studied the lock a second, then took from his pocket a Swiss Army knife. He inserted a thin blade into the Yale and twisted it a couple of times. Gilman was still bemoaning Harcourt's murder.

Foxworth withdrew the knife. "I must have lost my touch, Frank. I can't shift it."

Pagan stepped back. "We'll do it my way." He lunged, kicked the door hard, heard the wood around the lock splinter as the door shuddered and sprang open.

Gilman was making retching sounds. "Murdered. I can't believe it." He was sick all at once; a sticky substance bubbled from his lips.

"Why don't you go back to your flat and lie down," Pagan said.

"Great idea." Gilman stumbled across the landing. "Lie down. Yes. Indeed. Will do." He made more retching sounds and clutched his stomach as he descended in his clumsy manner.

Pagan and Foxworth went inside Harcourt's apartment. It was furnished sparsely but with a certain taste, if you enjoyed the minimalist look. Chrome and black leather, a coffee table that was some kind of transparent Perspex cube. Harcourt clearly hadn't liked clutter. The dining room contained only a glass-topped table and four simple chairs. No pictures on the walls. The bedroom was simple enough — large unmade double bed, burgundy silk sheets, bedside lamp.

Pagan glanced around the bedroom, looked inside the bathroom, tiles and mirrors and recessed lights, everything tidy, toothbrush in place, razor placed neatly on a tub of shaving soap, clean towels hung in precise arrangements. He wandered inside the living room, which contained a leather sofa and a single armchair; shelves of books, mainly classics in cheap paperback editions. Harcourt's desk was situated beneath the shelves. A telephone, an answering machine, a small stack of bills. Pagan had that curious sense of trespass he always felt in the apartments of the dead. Harcourt's life had been cut off abruptly and his possessions had the aura of objects displayed in a museum.

He sifted the bills. Harcourt used an American Express Platinum card extensively; his bill consisted mainly of restaurant charges, expensive ones, but there were also three charges from florists. Flowers for his girlfriends, Pagan thought. Also an electricity bill, and a letter written by a young woman called Louise who lived in Chicago. *It's bitterly cold here right now. I wish the summer would come. I wish we could be together.*

He opened the desk drawers. There was more correspondence from women, affectionate letters written by lovers or former lovers. Harcourt had obviously been the kind of man who knew how to break off an affair without acrimony. Quite a gift, Pagan thought.

In another drawer he found some unused stationery from the American embassy. There was also a predictable collection of rubber bands, paperclips, and a stapler. Nothing unusual. There was no sign of a diary, an appointment book.

Foxie came in from the bedroom. "He bought expensive shirts and suits," he said. "He also had a goodly supply of rubbers in the drawer of the bedside table."

"Busy man," Pagan said. He closed the desk drawers. "Funny. I don't get much of an impression of this person. I know he was fond of women, but what else? There's something absent from this place.

It's as if he didn't really live here. Or if he did, he didn't leave any marks behind." He thought of his own apartment in Holland Park, a place of clutter, scarred and scuffed and crumpled. There was no *crumple* in Bryce Harcourt's flat.

"Maybe he was just tidy," Foxie said.

Pagan sat on the sofa. "He doesn't have a music collection. There's a radio but no turntable, no CD player, nothing like that. A seducer of women who doesn't play music. I find that odd."

"There isn't a TV either," said Foxie.

"That's to his credit," Pagan said.

Foxie looked at the bookshelves, removed a copy of *Lady Chatterley's Lover*, skimmed the pages, then returned the book. "He obviously preferred books to telly."

Pagan strolled inside the kitchen. Pots and pans hung on the walls. The tiled work surfaces were spotless. The cabinets contained an array of Baxter's soups. Scotch Broth. Cream of Pheasant. The refrigerator was practically empty; a carton of milk, an apple shriveled to the size of a walnut, two jars of spaghetti sauce, a single brown egg to which a fleck of feather adhered. There were no notes pinned to walls or magnetized to the refrigerator. No reminders, no shopping lists, no telephone numbers. Inside a closet Pagan found a half-drunk bottle of Remy Martin and a couple of prescription bottles. One contained sleeping pills, the other antibiotics. The antibiotics hadn't been used, but the sleeping pills had. So Bryce needed a little help dozing off at night.

Pagan went back into the living room. Foxie was standing at the desk, gazing at the answering machine, whose red light was blinking.

"Let's hear the messages," Pagan said.

Foxie pushed the playback button, the tape whirred a second. A woman's voice said, *Bryce, sweetheart, why don't you give me a call? You know my number. Have you made any decision about Robin's party?* The message ended. The voice hadn't been Mrs. Canningsby's. The next message was from another woman. *Bryce? This is DeeDee Gauge. Are you interested in making up the numbers at a dinner party next Friday night? It's at Daxen's place and I suppose it will be a bit of a bloody bore because they always are, but a promise is a promise is a promise. Anyway.*

Do let me know, will you? Love and kisses. There was a sucking sound and then the message ended.

"He had women coming out of the woodwork," Foxie said. "Maybe he suffered from satyriasis. If suffered is the correct word in that context."

The machine was silent a second before the third and final message played. This time it was a man's voice. *Bryce. This is Jake Streik. Listen. Listen. If you're there, pick up. Okay. I need to talk with you. How are things holding up at your end? I got problems. Listen. I'll get back to you later tonight if I can. You want my advice, get the fuck outta London. Get away from the Undertakers, unnerstand? Walk away from all that shit. If you don't, you're a dead man . . . Bryce? You there? Bryce?*

Pagan listened attentively. "Play that one again, Foxie."

Foxie rewound the tape, turned up the volume because the sound was faint, distant, as if the call had originated in another country. Pagan listened to the message a second time. When it was over, he walked to the window and looked out at the rainswept Heath. He remembered Victoria Canningsby's words. *I believe I'm correct in saying Bryce feared for his life.* And now this Streik: *If you don't, you're a dead man.*

"He sounds desperate," Foxie said.

"Panic-stricken. I wonder what his problems are and how they're connected to Bryce Harcourt. Why was he urging Harcourt to get out of London?"

"And who are the undertakers?" Foxie asked. "Is Streik using a euphemism along the lines of Grim Reaper?"

Pagan turned from the window. Something was shifting in his head, a gear changing, as if all at once this investigation was drawing him in directions he didn't want to go. Foxie's suggestion that Harcourt's presence on the train was the only reason for the bomb — this suddenly shed its outer skin of implausibility. He wasn't prepared to accept it completely just yet, but it had taken shape at the back of his mind as a possibility, a small fungus in a cellar. What the hell was there in Harcourt's life that had made him a victim, that had Jake Streik so worried about him? Why had he lived in fear? *Get away from the undertakers.*

Pagan didn't like how his thoughts were becoming fractured, webby little strands that billowed this and that way.

"Okay. Let's say Carlotta planted the device. Let's imagine Bryce was the only target. What the hell did he do to deserve to be killed? Why would somebody hire Carlotta to kill him?" He sat on the sofa and looked around the room in a stricken manner. "What I want to know is the connection between Streik and Harcourt. I want to know what kind of trouble Harcourt and Streik were in."

"Exactly how do you propose to achieve that?"

Pagan rose, picked up the telephone directory, looked up the number for the American embassy. "The logical place to start would be with a certain Al Quarterman. Maybe he can throw some light on the matter."

He dialed the number. The phone rang for a long time before it was picked up by a woman who said, "United States embassy."

Pagan asked to speak with Quarterman.

"Can I say who's calling?"

"Frank Pagan."

Pagan waited. There was a certain amount of clicking on the line. Then he heard Al Quarterman's voice.

"Frank. What can I do for you?"

"I'd like a meeting."

"Has something come up?"

"You might say that."

"I don't have anything on this afternoon so far as I can see."

"You know Brown's Hotel?"

"I can find it."

"Meet me there in an hour."

"Fine." Quarterman hung up.

Pagan looked a moment at the answering machine. He slipped the cassette out of the machine and put it in his pocket.

■

Traffic in Mayfair was congested. Buses slugged through heavy rain, taxis idled in eclipses of their own pollution. Foxie traveled side streets, but even these were clogged with delivery vans and cars. He managed to find a parking space a block from Brown's. Al Quarterman was already waiting for them in the lobby.

"I suggest the bar," Pagan said. He introduced Foxie, who shook Quarterman's rather clammy hand with his usual good-natured vigor.

The bar was empty. Quarterman sniffed the air of the hotel, as if he thought old English authenticity might have a scent all its own. Pagan had found that most Americans were afflicted by an exaggerated affection for anything that suggested antiquity. They were like rather amiable vultures feasting with great fascination on old bones. He found this trait touching.

Pagan ordered three lagers, which the waiter brought to a corner table. Quarterman sipped his, then smacked his thin lips. His jaundiced complexion seemed even more pronounced than it had before.

"So, Frank. What's on your mind?"

"Bryce Harcourt."

Quarterman looked into his lager. "Poor Bryce. What a way to die."

"I need some information. Such as — what did he actually do at the embassy?"

"I thought I'd covered that ground before."

"Look. I don't want to trespass on anything remotely sensitive —"

"Sensitive?"

"But Harcourt was in some kind of trouble, and I want to know if it was connected with anything he might have done at the embassy. If it's within your authority to tell me —"

"He was a researcher. That's it. I'm not sure what direction you're taking, Frank. I don't know anything about deep trouble. He seemed okay to me. If he had problems, I would have known about them. Here's a guy I knew socially, a guy I saw every working day of my life."

"Does the name Jake Streik mean anything to you?"

"You come out of left field, don't you?" Quarterman looked thoughtful.

"Streik left a bizarre message on Harcourt's answering machine. A warning."

"Why this flurry of interest in Harcourt anyhow? Where did all this suddenly come from? What led you to Harcourt's apartment? The guy died in the goddamn explosion, Frank. He was the unfortunate victim of some kind of terrorist attack. He was in the wrong place at the wrong time. Why are you probing into his life?"

"Because it's my job."

Quarterman smiled his somber smile and set down his lager. "You're not saying, right?"

"Let's get back to Streik. Does it ring any bells?"

"I can't say it does, Frank. Sorry."

Pagan sat back. "Streik mentioned something about undertakers, which was presumably a reference Harcourt would have understood. What does that mean to you?"

"Undertakers," Quarterman said. "Doesn't mean a thing." He reached for his glass. As he did so, an expression of pained surprise crossed his face. His features contorted, his mouth dropped open, and he slumped back in his chair, his arms dangling at his sides. For a second Pagan thought the man had suffered a sudden heart attack, but then he saw blood flow from Quarterman's chest and he got up, kicking aside his chair and turning to the door in time to see a man in a dark green overcoat hurry toward the street exit.

Pagan dashed across the bar, reached the lobby, saw the man rush into the street. He charged after him, mindless of pedestrians in his way, scattering aside two fur-coated old women who swore viciously at him from under their shared umbrella. The man was swift, swifter than Pagan, younger, fitter, but Pagan kept going anyway, pushing as hard as he could even as he realized that the man who'd shot Quarterman was drawing away from him. Breathing heavily, lungs aching, he sprinted up the street, thinking of his own gun stuck uselessly in his office desk.

The gunman had already turned a corner and was probably more than a hundred yards away by this time. But Pagan kept at it, blood thundering in his head. He saw the gunman turn another corner and still he chased. The man was pulling further away with every step; he gave the impression of a dark green blur. His long sandy hair bounced against his collar as he fled. Puffing, Pagan forced himself through space, conscious of his blurred reflection in the windows of shops. He looked crazed, coat flying, face flushed, a half-wit in the rain.

The gunman turned yet another corner.

Why doesn't somebody stop him, whatever happened to citizens' arrests, doesn't anybody have a conscience these days?

Pagan reached the corner — but there was no sight of the man, who might have gone in one of several directions or even into one of the buildings. How could you tell? He collapsed against a wall; a monstrous pressure rose in his throat. Fireflies buzzed in his eyes. This isn't good enough, Frank. This is ignominious. It will say on your epitaph: *Ran Himself into the Ground.* He was sweating heavily.

He remained motionless for a long time and when he'd recovered his strength he walked slowly back to the hotel. Inside the bar Foxworth was standing over Quarterman. He'd unbuttoned the American's shirt. He raised his face, looked at Pagan, shook his head.

An assortment of hotel staff were fussing around, clucking. "Clear the room," Pagan said. "Everybody out. Now!"

"I don't think he knew what hit him," Foxworth said when the room was empty.

Pagan looked down at the dead man. Then he sagged into a chair and shook his head. He drew a hand wearily across his damp face.

"What are we not supposed to find out about Bryce Harcourt and Jake Streik?" Foxie asked. A muscle in his neck strained, a dark knotted cord. "What is so bloody important that a gunman takes the risk of shooting a man in the middle of Mayfair in broad bloody daylight, for God's sake?"

Pagan licked his dry lips.

He had a sensation of being lost in the Underground tunnel, that he'd taken a wrong turning somewhere and wandered into abandoned passageways where trains no longer ran and rails had rusted long ago, secret shafts where the air was unbreathable and no light ever fell and everything was shrouded by the dank bloom of mystery.

VENICE

19

Tobias Barron had scheduled a brief meeting before his evening meal. His visitor was an Afrikaner named Rolfe Van den Kamp, a leather-faced man with hard blue eyes who looked uncomfortable in the wintry climate of Venice. Barron offered sherry; the Afrikaner said he'd prefer something with a kick, and accepted a Wild Turkey straight. The two men sat facing each other in the drawing room and Van den Kamp threw the drink back in one swallow. He emitted an air of quiet nervousness. "I'm glad you could see me at such short notice," he said.

Barron shrugged. "I'm just sorry we didn't have more time together in South Africa." He'd met Van den Kamp briefly at a cocktail reception held in a Durban hotel, one of those affairs that by their very nature limit conversation to the most superficial level. They had briefly discussed the political changes in South Africa, which Van den Kamp of course thought calamitous. Though he hadn't said so, Barron was of the opinion that the ascendancy of the blacks was a matter of historical inevitability, and people such as Van den Kamp were dinosaurs struggling to hold back an impossible tide. You could build dikes, stash sandbags against the swell, but in the end Rolfe and those like him were going to be swept away like so many twigs.

Barron said, "You know how those receptions are, Rolfe. In and out. Sign a couple of documents, talk to bankers, see a few government officials, make a speech, fly out."

Rolfe Van den Kamp looked sympathetic. "'Course, 'course. I know how busy it gets. I'll help myself to another drink, you don't mind?" He filled his glass to the brim with Wild Turkey. "You're not the only one spreading a little light on the Dark Continent, Tobias. Christ, *we* do it all the time. Been doing it for years. Some of our blacks have gone on to vocational schools. Colleges. 'Course, we footed the bills when necessary."

Some of our blacks, Barron thought. Van den Kamp couldn't help the proprietorial note in his voice. His was a world of ownership and patronage; the lords of creation. It was easy to imagine him, a descendant of the Dutch who'd made the Great Trek, standing feet apart and hands on hips and surveying a great expanse of veldt his family owned that was now menaced by black nationalism and democracy.

"When you're in a position to help those less fortunate . . ." Barron remarked, and airily waved a hand. "I'm interested in a number of charitable causes, not just in South Africa, of course."

Van den Kamp turned his acid-blue eyes on Barron. You could read in those eyes a number of things — fear, anxiety, the need for self-preservation. The Afrikaner smiled, a frugal little movement of lips. "You occupy an unusual position. You come and go as you please in the townships because you're the white man who brings good cheer. You don't have a political ax to grind. You can go places in South Africa where any other white would be shot on sight." Van den Kamp turned his glass around in his big hands. "I sometimes wonder . . . if you ever hear anything."

"Hear anything?" Barron asked. "Such as?"

"This, that. Tidbits. Information that might be useful to me and my people."

Barron smiled. "What are you fishing for, Rolfe? Perhaps if you came to the point . . ." He leaned forward in his chair.

Van den Kamp gazed into his drink in a brooding manner. When he spoke next he talked of the need to protect his family. Barron understood that he was referring to something more extensive than his immediate blood relations; he was talking about a way of life.

The Afrikaner sipped his Wild Turkey. "It's my understanding that some of the more militant blacks, the ones that don't have any faith in the African National Congress and who see Mandela and his crew as a bunch of time-servers — which is basically what they are — have been stockpiling AK–47s and Uzis. We don't know where they're coming from, but Christ, we know they're getting them somewhere. We'd like to know their source."

"And you think I might have access to that kind of knowledge?"

"I think you might."

Barron said, "The world is filled with arms merchants, Rolfe. We both know that. In any event, do you imagine militants take me into their confidence? All I ever meet are mayors and tribal chiefs and pols. I don't think I'd recognize a militant if I saw one." He permitted himself a small laugh, as if the very idea that he might be associated with radicals were ridiculous.

Van den Kamp rose from his chair. He was a massive, well-muscled man. He wandered the room, picked out the first few bars of "Pack Up Your Troubles" on the spinet in a cackhanded way. "Strange old instrument." When he stepped back from the keyboard, he said, "We need to balance the situation in our favor."

"What have you got in mind?" Barron asked. He wondered about the Afrikaner's logic; how could a situation be *balanced* in somebody's favor? It was a perverse use of language. Van den Kamp's perception of balance meant that he wanted the scales tipped decisively to his benefit.

"My people have certain urgent requirements."

"Such as?"

Van den Kamp didn't answer the question directly. "I got the impression in Durban you might be of assistance. Correct me if I'm wrong."

"I'm not sure what impression I gave you, Rolfe."

"You seemed to have, ah, a wide range of connections."

"I know a great many people, if that's what you mean. I have associates in a number of fields. Medicine. Agriculture. Education. All kinds of useful friends and allies. I have projects of different kinds all over the place. Crop rotation in Cuba. Medical aid in Ethiopia. Irrigation schemes in Angola."

Van den Kamp shook his head. "I think you know I'm driving at something else, Tobias."

Barron said nothing. He had a sense of the delicacy of the situation. He might have helped Van den Kamp along, might have urged him to speak his mind, but he enjoyed the waiting game. He walked to the mantelpiece, where the photographs of his famous friends provided a striking backdrop. It was a piece of theater intended to impress upon the Afrikaner that he was fortunate to have been granted an audience.

"I'll put it another way," Van den Kamp said. "I had the feeling in Durban that you were sympathetic to the plight of the Afrikaners in view of recent political changes."

"Did I give that impression?"

"'Course, I may have misunderstood you . . ."

"I try to stay detached, Rolfe. If I said anything to mislead you, I'm sorry."

Van den Kamp looked down at the keyboard of the spinet. His expression was one of disappointment. "I hope I haven't come all this way for nothing."

"Perhaps if you said what's on your mind," Barron suggested.

Van den Kamp, who was not by nature a circumspect man, enjoyed frank exchanges. In his world men spoke brute facts over ice-cold lagers. "Okay. I'm not good at games, Tobias. I like the deck face up. In Durban I got the feeling that among your associates there were those who might be in a position to help us."

Barron stared at the Afrikaner. "It depends on the kind of help you're looking for, Rolfe. Clearly, you're not talking about irrigation technicians or AIDS experts, are you?"

"I think you know what I'm talking about. Do I need to spell it out for you?"

"I don't like fumbling in the dark any more than you do," Barron said.

"Okay. For purely defensive purposes, we're in the market for armored Range Rovers. Kevlar body armor. Stun grenades. Our way of life is under threat, Tobias. Obviously, this is a source of great concern to us."

Barron listened. He knew Van den Kamp was the kind of man who would first of all mention his defensive needs. He didn't want to be perceived as the aggressor. That role could be attributed to the blacks.

"To defend yourself," Barron said, "you also need to be able to attack."

"If it comes to that."

"And . . . ?"

"We're looking for Webley gas-grenade launchers. HK93s. MP5Ks. Remington 870s 12 bore. Glock 9 millimeter automatics. Tejas .50 caliber rifles. All the necessary ammo. It's a long list."

Barron pressed his fingertips to his lips, remembering Nofometo coming to his hotel in Durban. Van den Kamp and Nofometo, a study in contrasts, in attitudes; and yet when you reached the bottom line, both men had a similar desire — the right of possession.

"I can always pass along a message, Rolfe. But the final decision, you must understand, would have absolutely nothing to do with me." Barron experienced a feeling of distance from the conversation. It was a way of protecting himself, a shell of sorts. "Assuming I happen to know some people who *might* be helpful — and I'm not saying I do — you're talking about a considerable amount of money, Rolfe."

"Money's the least of our problems."

Barron studied the Afrikaner, on whom he'd compiled a dossier. Rolfe Van den Kamp, whose personal fortune was estimated to be in the region of five million pounds sterling, was the leader of a white right-wing movement that considered its future in the new South Africa tenuous. They wanted to fly the tattered defiant flag of white supremacy. But flags without weapons were useless symbols. Consequently, Van den Kamp and his people needed strike power.

Barron said, "Let's get one thing straight from the beginning. I'm not in a position to promise you anything. All I can do is put certain people in touch with you. And if they want to do business, that's their affair. It's nothing to do with me. Frankly, I shouldn't even be listening to any of this."

"I understand." Van den Kamp finished his drink, put the empty glass down on the polished wood of the spinet.

Barron picked up the glass before it could leave a ring in the wood. "I find the whole subject of guns distasteful."

"But you'll see the message gets to its destination?"

Barron nodded. He changed the subject abruptly. "Are you doing a little sightseeing while you're in Venice?"

"I don't have the time."

"A pity. The city in winter has certain charms." Barron looked at his watch. "You must excuse me. I'm expecting company."

"Sure."

He walked Rolfe Van den Kamp to the door and shook his hand briefly. When the Afrikaner had gone, Schialli entered the drawing room to announce that the dinner guests had arrived.

"All," Schialli added, "save the old one."

■

Barron twisted a length of fettucini around his fork and raised it to his mouth. It tasted of anchovy and Parmesan. He picked up his wineglass and sipped the Sardinian Vermentino, then held the glass up to the light as if seeking impurities in the liquid. Satisfied, he set the wine down and looked across the table at his companions, his eye passing over the place set for the missing guest.

On his right sat Henry Saxon in his hideously thick glasses; despite what manners he might have learned in prep schools and at Harvard, Henry was never entirely at ease at dinner tables, as if he were constantly afraid of a faux pas in the area of etiquette. Henry tended to sweat; the palms of his hands were moist. He was forever wiping them in the folds of a handkerchief.

Next to Henry was Leo Kinsella, dressed in an expensive three-piece charcoal gray suit. He wore decorative leather boots made to his own specifications by a craftsman in Taos, New Mexico. His expression was flinty, austere. He spoke in an accent designed to remind others of his impoverished childhood in the dirt hills of Oklahoma. Leo was proud of his origins and how he'd transcended them: the embodiment, Barron supposed, of the American Dream, every immigrant's fantasy — streets of gold, arid deserts out of which oil gushed.

Beside Leo was Montgomery Rhodes, a taciturn figure in dark shades. Rhodes was dressed in the kind of sharp black suit that suggested the garb of an upscale funeral-parlor director. He'd once been attached to a clandestine section of the Defense Intelligence Agency. There was a quality of brutality about Monty Rhodes, a manic intensity in his silences and the way he scribbled in his little notebook. Barron wasn't fond of Rhodes because the man suggested a human black hole. He drained light out of any room in which he sat. He dragged menace around with him like a rancid dead animal.

Barron raised his wineglass. "Welcome to Venice, gentlemen."

Leo Kinsella, who didn't like eye-tie food or wine, and whose tastes ran no further than charbroiled steaks of Texan dimensions, pushed his plate aside. "Let's get down to the business, Tobias. I don't have time to wait for our absent guest."

Barron looked at Saxon and said, "Henry?"

Saxon produced a set of folders. He began to flick through the messages. "A few of these are requests for money and matériel," he said in his intoning way.

"Summarize for the sake of brevity," said Kinsella. "I know how you can go on at times, Henry. Goddamn lawyers too fond of their own voices."

Henry Saxon cleared his throat and glanced at Barron, who smiled in cheerful indulgence of Kinsella's manner. "The sum of one million US dollars is requested by Lotus."

"I thought we'd taken care of all the money business. I was of the opinion, Tobias, that we'd laid out all the bread we were ever going to. I'm not sure we can approve that request." Kinsella glanced at Rhodes, who took out a notebook, jotted something down with his maroon Waterman fountain pen, the nib of which scratched the surface of the paper.

Kinsella continued. "Lotus is a goddamn bottomless pit. If we give him the go-ahead, and that's a mighty big if, it's going to take time. We have to find alternative routes for money now. You can't move that kind of cash without somebody asking questions. We don't want anybody sticking their noses in. Most of all we don't want people who have a habit of developing sudden *qualms*, do we? We don't want anybody likely to be stricken by an abrupt attack of conscience. If you know what I mean."

Barron asked, "Who can predict a man's conscience, Leo?"

"Yeah," Rhodes said. "Who indeed? Myself, I happen to think conscience a goddamn expensive item, as some people find out too late."

There was a short silence before Saxon continued. "Orchid needs one point three million in Warsaw."

"I bet he does," said Kinsella. He stared at Tobias Barron. "You wonder about these guys sometimes. My people Stateside ask a lot of questions, Tobias. They see a whole lot going out and nothing much coming in so far. They think they've contributed enough."

"I'm sure the money is well spent," Barron answered.

Kinsella raised his dense gray eyebrows. "Jesus Christ, how much can it cost to buy votes in Poland anyway? What's he paying people per head to mark their ballots for Communists?"

"I gather it's an expensive business," Barron remarked.

Montgomery Rhodes said in his quiet nasal way, "There's going to be an accounting at the end of all this, Tobias. And it better be goddamn accurate."

"Indeed," said Barron. He stared a second at Rhodes. The darkness of the man's shades was decidedly sinister. You could never tell if Rhodes was looking at you or not. And if he was, you couldn't read his expression. Barron sighed. He thought money a grubby topic. What truly interested him about these meetings was his sense of being the *epicenter* of things. Even if Barron was finally apolitical, even if he found politics an unsightly game played by scoundrels, the idea that he was the adhesive holding everything together narcoticized him, jangled his system like speed. He brought together diverse people in unlikely partnerships. He found the resources. He sat at the heart of a great web he'd created himself.

Kinsella, Rhodes, the others throughout Europe and the United States — they would never have come together had it not been for the influence and connections of Tobias Barron. Whether he approved of their individual aims was of no ultimate concern to him.

His mind drifted away from this room a moment, it floated up and beyond Venice, beyond the confines of Europe, it became a kind of satellite high above the planet, monitoring events, digesting information, analyzing and assessing, scouring the world for opportunities. He was suddenly seized by a sharp sense of self, as if he were outlined by a supernatural current of electricity. If you turned out the lights in the room, he might be phosphorescent.

"Dandelion wants weaponry," Saxon said, turning over a new sheet of paper.

"Does he specify?" Rhodes asked.

"The same as before," Saxon answered.

Rhodes rapped his pen on his notebook. "Seven hundred and fifty thousand rounds of ammunition for Uzis."

"What do they do, these guys? Eat the goddamn bullets?" Kinsella asked. "These guys kill me. They make demands like it's some kind of supermarket we're working here. They don't think logistics. Okay, some places are easy. They're wide-open barn doors. But others are real tough. Last time we sent ammo into Yugoslavia or whatever it calls itself these days, we had to smuggle the shit inside UN convoys. Bullets in bags of flour. Machine guns in crates of antibiotics."

Tobias Barron poured himself another glass of wine and said, "I don't think in this case there are overwhelming problems, Monty. Angola isn't Bosnia. In any case, logistics are my concern."

Barron turned to see Henry Saxon, formerly of the Department of State, formerly an adviser on Eastern European matters to the Pentagon, flick over another sheet of paper. As he did so, the door opened, and Barron looked around to watch the latecomer enter. The man had a rather kindly face that belied his history. A kid with some imagination might have envisaged him in the role of a department store Santa Claus.

"Forgive me, forgive me, I was delayed, this weather plays havoc with airline timetables."

"Take off your coat and sit down," Barron said. "We were just beginning to go through the agenda."

Barron observed the old man walk to his place at the table, where he removed his coat, hung it over the back of his chair, and sat.

"Hungry?" Barron asked.

The old man shook his head. "I had a meal of sorts on the flight. It has unsettled me a little," and he patted his stomach.

"Wine?"

"It might help my digestive system."

Barron pushed the bottle across the table and watched the General pour himself an ample glass, which he raised to his lips and sipped. He shut his eyes appreciatively. "Fine. Very fine, Tobias." He looked around the table at the other faces and added, "Please. Continue with business."

"Thanks for your permission," Rhodes said. He had a jagged little line in sarcasm that Barron found unpleasant. But if the old man noticed, he paid no attention to it. Sometimes the nuances of spoken English seemed to elude him.

Henry Saxon said, "This is a report written by Nightshade in Berlin."

The General set his glass down and leaned forward, his interest quickened. He thought these code names Barron had come up with were absurd. Flowers and plants, for God's sake. What did Barron think: this was all some kind of botanical gathering?

Nightshade was the code name of a West Berliner who'd been a secret servant of both STASI and the KGB in the old days of the divided Germanies, a reliable Party member who, even after the reunification process — the *Wende* as it was called, the bastard Germany that had been dragged into existence by the forceps of greed and expediency — had managed to conceal his past allegiance to the East. He'd been a good servant to the General. His position of authority had allowed him to pass important information to East Berlin and Moscow. The General was very fond of the man Barron had christened Nightshade.

"According to this, the arrangements are made, the business in Berlin will proceed without interference," Saxon said.

Barron caught the old man's eye and saw there a small gleam of pleasure.

Saxon went on with the next report. "From Sesame in Prague. The arrangements are in progress. Expect success in a matter of hours."

The old man sat back, folding his hands on his stomach. Nightshade in Berlin, Sesame in Prague; he experienced a moment of quiet satisfaction.

Saxon closed the folder. "Those are the main items on this agenda."

Kinsella tucked his thumbs in the pockets of his waistcoat and said, "Which leaves us with the matter of Helix," and he looked at Barron, who drained his wineglass and ran a fingertip around the rim.

The General spoke. "I have assurances that there will be no difficulties."

"I don't need to tell you my people are anxious," Kinsella said. He had a large projecting jaw which gave him the appearance of a retired prizefighter.

Barron smiled. "It's a sure thing. You know that. I know that." He wiped his lips with a linen napkin. Schialli came into the room with coffee, set it out on the table, then retreated in his quietly fastidious way.

Barron poured from the cafetiere and for a time there was a subdued quiet in which he thought of the assorted concerns and ambitions in the room. There was the General, of course, with his yearnings for a vanished world; he was impaled upon his need for vengeance and restitution. He and his cronies — and there were many of them across Europe — genuinely believed that clocks could be turned backward, upstart nations dismantled, a return to the old ways.

There was Henry Saxon, probably uneasy with his role of Barron's gofer, Henry, who'd been to the best schools and held down important positions in government, and who now found himself working for Barron. What did Henry Saxon really feel? Barron always thought Henry required status, proximity to power, the urge to leave his mark, however small and illegible, upon the world. In one way, there was something of the leech about Henry Saxon; he sucked the blood of men bigger than himself.

There was Kinsella, who had parlayed a fortune in Oklahoma crude into a spectral political machine with many covert sympathizers in America, quietly influential men whose financial aspirations were threatened by changes in the world order; they'd seen their outrageous profits dwindle over the last few years and they didn't like the plunge in their graphs. They weren't used to disappointing balance sheets; they were suffering from a case of the financial bends. They liked to live in cathedrals of great wealth, places where profit was the only known divinity. But now they were beginning to notice cracks in the stained glass.

And then there was Rhodes, who, for what was no doubt a considerable commission, gathered obscene amounts of money from Kinsella's sources and filtered it through an organization which concealed its existence behind the impeccably official facade of diplomatic privilege.

Barron picked up his coffee and thought: They are all, in one way or other, merchants of chaos. They all stand to profit from calamity. Kinsella and his associates, the General and his old friends, and Rhodes, that creature of the dark places.

Saxon coughed into his hand and quietly said, "There's still the business with our fugitive friend."

Barron made a dismissive gesture with his hand. "I wouldn't worry about him."

Rhodes said, "Guy lost his nerve, that's all. He just reared up and bolted. Maybe it was all too much for him. Maybe he realized he was coming to the end of his usefulness. So he took a hike. We'll find him. Anyhow, what does the sonofabitch really know, huh? You think he's gonna blow us out of the water or something, Saxon?" Rhodes had a strange laugh, like the high strings of a harp plucked.

Saxon fidgeted with his fork, lapsed into silence. He looked like a schoolboy who has spoken out of turn.

"He's a loose end, Henry," Barron said. "Even if he knows what's going on, what can he authenticate? Who is there to back up his claims?"

"It's only a matter of time before we pick him up." Rhodes sucked air deeply into his mouth, a sound of irritation. "I'm not going to work myself up into a goddamn lather because of the Weed."

The General, who had been listening carefully, said, "The Weed, as you have so aptly code-named him, is a mistake. Who hired him? Who is responsible for him?"

"I'm not blaming anyone but myself," Barron said. He infused his voice with the appropriate contrition; a consummate actor. "We needed somebody with his experience. None of us imagined he'd act the way he did."

"Error of judgment," the old man said in a solemn voice. "On your part."

Montgomery Rhodes took off his shades to reveal odd-colored eyes, one green, the other blue. He clicked the stems of his dark glasses shut. "Look. You want the truth, I was the one hired the Weed. If there's been an error of judgment, then it was mine. He had very vague connections with the Central Intelligence Agency for the past fifteen years. He's what they call in the jargon of the spook trade 'a reliable deniable.' His affiliations were loose ones. He was a floater. A loner. That's why I chose him." Rhodes spoke quietly, as if his real purpose was not so much to inform this thick-skulled old Kraut as to hypnotize him. "But he's no big deal. We've got a net out for him. And by God he'll walk straight into it. He isn't the smartest kid on the block. You relax. Take it easy."

Barron thought of the Weed, whose life — according to Rhodes — had been spent in that shapeless hinterland populated by those claiming nebulous associations with the CIA, with Mossad or MI6 or any number of secret organizations; fantasists, failed poets, jobless politicians, petty crooks with vainglorious notions, soldiers of fortune, that whole set of drifting international flotsam who deluded themselves that they were adventurers, romantics, spies. How was anyone to know the Weed would blow a fuse? You couldn't predict people.

Bryce Harcourt was a perfect example of that.

The room was quiet for a time, the atmosphere weighted. Everyone present knew that disagreements at this stage were dangerous. Helix had its own momentum. Leo Kinsella broke the silence. "Well. I guess that covers everything for now. You need to contact me, I'll be at the Grunwald until everything's over."

When the Americans had gone, only the old man lingered. He removed two items from his pocket, one a brown envelope, the other a small cylindrical object wrapped in childish gift paper —

clowns, seals balancing colored balls, elephants. Barron didn't open the gift-wrapped object, but he looked inside the brown envelope and saw the ID card, glanced at the blank space where a photograph was meant to be inserted.

"This Weed. This I do not like," the General said.

"Scores of people are looking for him."

"Just the same."

"Put him out of your mind. Pretend he doesn't exist. Pretend Streik never existed."

"Easy to say."

Barron smiled confidently and escorted the German to the door, a hand on the old fellow's elbow. "Everything will be fine, Erich," he said. "I promise you," and he closed the door slowly as his visitor departed.

Sometimes, Barron thought, it was hard to believe that Erich Schwarzenbach had once been the highest-ranking officer in one of the most efficient state security systems in the world, STASI, the man who had kept the keys to the files, who had stored in his head the secret computer passwords that allowed him access to the histories of almost every citizen in East Germany.

When the General had gone, Barron spent some time in his office. He studied the movement of ships, following the cursors on the wall map; the *Falcon* was already cruising close to Madagascar, an ideal location when it came to Van den Kamp's request. The cargo ship, which flew a Nicaraguan flag, was due to lay anchor thirty miles west of the island, where it would take on board consignments delivered by ferry from Tambohorano. These shipments, intended to meet some of Nofometo's needs, wouldn't bring the vessel up to capacity. There would also be room for at least some of the matériel required by Van den Kamp. It was a matter of logistics; and there was a neatness, a sense of economy, Barron liked about using the *Falcon* to deliver two consignments. Nofometo's would be brought ashore under darkness near Port Shepstone; a further arrangement could be made for the *Falcon* to continue south in the Indian Ocean and deliver Van den Kamp's matériel offshore between East London and Umzimvubu.

He sent a couple of faxes, one to the captain of the *Falcon*, the other to an airstrip hacked from swampland beyond Jacksonville, Florida, where the transport planes were regularly loaded. Then he opened the General's envelope and let the ID card slide out onto the table. Tilting an anglepoise lamp, he examined the card beneath the bulb. Perfect, he thought. Just so.

He was about to leave the room when he received a fax from Cuba, signed by a man called Hector Camocondo, the deputy minister of defense. He read the message. Camocondo's bureaucratic turn of phrase invited you to read between the lines. The gist was that Barron's projected agricultural research center in the Guantanamo Province had received "preliminary approval" — whatever that meant — and could now go into committee. There were, however, "certain conditions" attached to these discussions, which would involve Barron's making a visit to Havana within the next two weeks. Barron smiled; in Cuba's labyrinthine bureaucracy, it was not at all surprising that the deputy minister of defense should be interested in an agricultural project — if you read the hidden message in the spaces.

Barron fingered the fax. By this time, Deputy Minister Camocondo would have discovered the lethal weaponry accumulated by the anti-Castro movement inside Cuba — in particular the so-called super-rifle, the sniper's dream, the Tejas. The balance would have to be redressed; the army had to stay a step ahead of the underground movement. It was always this way. One side trying to outstrip the other, to be better armed, better prepared, to be more efficient in the business of death.

Barron left his office, locked the door. From the bedroom overhead he could hear the woman singing softly to herself, a sound that was melancholic and strangely moving. He walked to the foot of the stairs and listened.

George Nimmo said, "You haven't been keeping me abreast of things, Frank. You've been going along in your usual wayward fashion, which is precisely what I asked you not to do. Why wasn't I told about this Harcourt chap? And now we have this wretched business with Quarterman. Two US embassy employees are dead. I have to face some hard questions, Frank. The Home Secretary is not happy. He's under pressure to do something about the situation."

Pagan sat in Nimmo's pristine office. He'd summarized the events of the investigation, but what he'd given Nimmo was an edited version; too many details might flood George's brain. He folded his hands in his lap and remembered the way Quarterman had been shot. A gunman, a silenced pistol in a sedate hotel bar, the ridiculous chase through the streets of Mayfair. What had Quarterman known that had caused a gunman to undertake such a risky assassination? What had he been privy to? You didn't shoot a man down in daylight in the heart of a city unless you were scared beyond reason of what he might reveal. You waited for a dark place, the right situation. Whoever wanted Quarterman dead didn't want to take the chance that Al, in a moment of weakness or flash of self-preservation, might become a little too chummy with a couple of London cops.

Pagan felt exhausted, perplexed, harried by devils more important than George Nimmo's exasperation and the Home Secretary's un-happiness. He had the feeling of being locked in a box of tricks, or studying one of those join-the-dots puzzles whose ultimate solution would have all the coherence of a blot of spilled milk.

"Harcourt had been involved in some form of, *yo*, illegality," Nimmo said. "Is that what you're telling me?"

"Let's just say the message on the answering machine suggested such a possibility. I can't be more explicit. Not yet."

Nimmo had a sour expression, as if he'd found a dead cockroach in his sherry trifle. "And so you contacted Quarterman in the hope of assistance. And now Quarterman is also dead. Before he could tell you anything." He rubbed his jowls. "We will soon have the streets of London littered with our dead American friends, I don't doubt. Charming. See London and die."

"Look, this is a bloody investigation into a calamity, I'm not working for the tourist board," Pagan said, his voice rising. Blood coursed to his head. "I go where the investigation takes me. I didn't arrange for Quarterman to be shot, for Christ's sake. It was the last damn thing I expected. I wanted some answers, I thought he might supply them, the next thing he's a corpse."

Nimmo stood up. "Don't rage at me, Pagan. I will not have that."

Pagan gazed at the windows. He was frazzled, his edges were un-raveling, but he wasn't going to apologize to Nimmo for the out-burst. Such outbreaks served a useful psychic purpose. Balm to the troubled soul. In any case, Nimmo sounded like an overbearing schoolteacher chastising a guilty pupil. And Pagan didn't feel guilty about anything.

"Understand one thing," Nimmo said. "Your position is fragile here. You hang by the proverbial thread. At a snap of my fingers I can have it cut. Bear that in mind, Pagan."

Nimmo sat down again, his face flushed. He had a gift, essential to all politicians, of easing from one mood to another, of readjusting his emotions without blinking. Quite a knack.

"The Home Secretary is going to meet the US ambassador, Mr. William J. Caan. I will be present, of course. There may be further questions you will have to answer to the satisfaction of both these eminent men."

"I'll be only too happy," Pagan said.

"Now. This woman. This Carlotta."

"We're checking her," Pagan said. "She's presumably left the country. If she departed by any of the usual ways, there's got to be some kind of record."

"She's a nasty piece of goods," said Nimmo. "I've been reading her file. And you think she might be behind the attack?"

"I can't say that for certain. There's always a chance." *And that's all you're going to get out of me, George.*

Nimmo was quiet a second. "One other thing. I don't like the way you handled Gladstone and Wright. They're experienced men, they could be very useful to you, but what do you do with them? Send them off to Cricklewood on some fool's errand." He looked in his In tray, fished out a slip of paper, stared at it. "This chap Dracowitz. He turns out to have been a harmless idiot who lived in some dreary basement filled with a mildewed paperback collection of Lenin and a score of mousetraps, which he seemed unwilling to empty."

"I thought he was worth looking into," Pagan said. So Gladstone and Wright send their reports to Nimmo directly. I ought not to be utterly astonished.

"When it comes to that kind of boring legwork, use a uniform, for God's sake. Gladstone and Wright don't need to be scurrying halfway across London for nothing."

Pagan nodded in a gesture that might have passed for agreement. He rose from his chair and as he did so Nimmo smiled; it was a fake affair intended to be conciliatory. "This investigation is above personality, Frank. You're a professional. You should know that. Conflicts of style and attitude have no place in any of this. We're a team. I don't have to remind you, do I?"

Pagan muttered something inaudible. There were times in his life when he couldn't muster politeness, when he couldn't force what he didn't feel. Sometimes it cost too much to be falsely agreeable. Sometimes the price was too high in terms of what you valued, such as your integrity, your sense of self-worth.

"Have we an understanding?" Nimmo asked.

"Yes," Pagan said in a dry way. "We have an understanding."

"Then I expect you to behave accordingly. When you have any news of this Carlotta, let me know at once. In the meantime, I think we should refrain from publicizing her name in any way. Keep it out of the press. I don't want any putative connection bruited about the place. Do you agree? I don't want her forewarned, as it were."

"Fine," Pagan said.

"By the way. Here's McCluskey's analysis for you." And Nimmo took from the surface of his desk a thin folder he handed to Pagan. Even McCluskey had been ordered to submit his reports here before they reached Pagan; Pagan couldn't blame McCluskey, couldn't accuse him of betrayal, he was only following Nimmo's directions.

He left Nimmo's office and went downstairs. Foxie was waiting outside in the car. The rain had ceased, but the day had the allure of a threadbare coat.

Pagan got in the car on the passenger side.

"Well?" Foxie asked. "Or shouldn't I ask?"

"You shouldn't ask, Foxie."

"He was on his high horse."

"Saddled and bridled."

Foxie started the car. "Golden Square?"

Pagan nodded. He gazed at the rainy streets as Foxie drove. Give me bright sunshine and explanations, he thought. Tell me why Quarterman was shot. Tell me what Bryce Harcourt was up to that Carlotta killed him — if indeed it was Carlotta who did the business. Speak to me about Jake Streik.

His inspiration was as numb as the season.

He looked at Dick McCluskey's folder but didn't have the urge to open it just then, almost as if the fact that Nimmo had perused it beforehand had contaminated whatever it might contain. Be forgiving, Frank, he thought. Try to like George Nimmo. Try to fit in. After all: *We're a team*. My arse we're a team. What we are is antagonists, George Nimmo. We don't breathe the same air.

He turned to look at Foxie. "You have a friend in MI6, don't you?"

"McLaren? I wouldn't say he's a friend exactly. We went to school together."

"Contact him. Run this Jake Streik past him. See if he has anything on file. It's worth a shot."

"That means I'll have to take him out for drinks. He only opens up when he's pissed as a newt."

In Soho Foxie parked and both men went inside the building on Golden Square and rode in silence in the cranky elevator. They stepped from the lift and walked inside Pagan's office.

"Somebody didn't like the kind of company Al Quarterman was keeping. So Al was a potential threat and had to be removed."

"And the grave, they say, is an awfully silent place," Foxworth observed.

"So what did Al Quarterman know about Harcourt's activities," Pagan said, thinking aloud. "One thing's pretty clear. Harcourt was no innocent researcher. Whatever he was up to, Quarterman knew about it."

"Something is rotten in Grosvenor Square," Foxworth said.

"Sure. But how do we find the source of the stench? There are boundaries here, Foxie. There are serious limitations to what we can do without causing a diplomatic incident." Pagan got up, wandered the room. He couldn't get out of his mind the image of Quarterman's death, the brute suddenness of it.

He picked up Dick McCluskey's report, read it. It was highly technical. The material used was a plastique called C-4, Czech-made, triggered by a nonelectric detonator. McCluskey described fragments of a spring discovered at the scene; he'd attached a drawing of the explosive to his report. It looked like a tampon inside which compartments had been constructed. One contained the spring, another a primer; acid had been used to erode a retaining device which freed the spring which in turn activated a plunger that provided the spark. Pagan studied McCluskey's drawing, admired its meticulous quality, and wondered how anything so innocuous in appearance as this tampon-shaped object could cause such devastation.

He imagined hands shaping this device, fingers constructing it; he tried to picture Carlotta in a room somewhere, building this compact monster. Maybe she hadn't. Maybe she'd purchased it ready-made.

Billy Ewing came inside the room, closing the door behind him. He made a grunt of exasperation. "Frank. For Christ's sake, I can't blow my nose without Gladstone and Wright watching me. Can't you do something about them?"

"They're with us for the duration, Billy. Nimmo's directive. What we know, they know. What they know, Nimmo knows. They're in-house spies."

"Can't you send them on a bloody mission?" Ewing asked. "Don't we have leads they can follow in North Wales or somewhere bracing like that?"

"I'll see what I can come up with." He'd plunge them into the tunnel, he thought. They could liaise between the tunnel and Golden Square, although Pagan wasn't sure what that might involve. But it would sound good to Wright and Gladstone: liaison officers. It had a ring of importance to it. Consign them to the depths.

"In the meantime," Ewing said, "you might be interested to know that a certain Karen Lamb, carrying a US passport, left Heathrow on the night the prostitute was murdered in Mayfair. She caught a late Air France flight to Paris. Does she sound like your woman?"

Karen Lamb. Caroline Starling. Charlotte Pike. Pagan considered the permutations of aliases. Karen Lamb was a strong contender.

"According to Air France, she had a connecting flight to Nice. For some reason she never made that plane. It could be the usual diversionary tactic. She might have stayed in Paris. Or hired a car and gone on elsewhere. None of the other airlines operating out of Paris have a record of a passenger under that name. But she could have changed it anyway, assuming she has access to a set of passports, which I'd say is a given. I've got a call into the French police. But I'm not optimistic, Frank. They're helpful, but only up to a point. And if they get an inkling they have Carlotta on their territory, they'd like nothing better than to nab her. Consider the kudos."

Pagan had a connection in the Sûreté, Claude Quistrebert, who'd been mildly helpful a few years ago in the search for a German terrorist known as Gunther Ruhr, but he wasn't about to ask the rather unapproachable Quistrebert for help — unless it became absolutely essential.

"Effectively she's disappeared," Ewing remarked. "Unless our French friends can come up with something."

Quarterman dead. Carlotta vanished. Blind alleys. "Did you turn up anything on Jake Streik?" Pagan asked.

"Zero," Ewing answered.

Pagan envisaged the embassy on Grosvenor Square, the US flag, the great stone eagle that hovered over the building, the lines of would-be emigrants seeking visas that would enable them to exchange one kind of recession for another. The doorway to democracy and two hundred million handguns. *Here's your green card, sir. Do remember to buy yourself a pistol first chance you get. We generally recommend a Colt for newcomers.*

How to get inside the mysterious fortress? he wondered. In the unlikely event of gaining access to the place, where would you look? Where would you even begin? What he needed was somebody with knowledge. On an impulse, he picked up his telephone and dialed Martin Burr's number in Knightsbridge. Burr answered on the second ring.

"Frank," he said. "Heard you were back in harness. Working you hard, are they?"

"Hard enough," Pagan replied.

"It's good for you, Frank. What can I do for you?"

"I need a few minutes of your time."

"Come over in an hour."

"Perfect."

Pagan hung up the phone. An hour. That gave him time to grab a sandwich somewhere; he was hungry, couldn't remember when he'd last eaten. He put on his coat and as he moved toward the hallway, Foxie asked, "If I need to reach you, where will you be?"

"I'm going to the oracle," Pagan answered. "I'll be back as soon as I can."

Foxworth frowned. Pagan could be infuriatingly mystifying at times. How were you supposed to keep up with him? He was too fond of wandering labyrinths alone.

∎

Pagan stepped out into Golden Square, where he turned up the collar of his coat against the wind. He walked in the direction of a nearby sandwich bar. He was unaware of the girl approaching until she came within inches.

"Miles away, were you?" Brennan Carberry asked.

Surprised, he looked into her face.

"Well, I called the number you gave me, didn't get an answer. So I used some of that famed Yankee initiative and called Scotland Yard, and after some persistence on my part they told me where you could be found." She smiled at him, touched his sleeve. The smile was smart, knowing, as if she had an unerring capacity for looking directly inside him.

She linked her arm through his, a gesture that pleased and surprised him. He walked with her to the end of the square, where it flowed into a narrow street leading down to Piccadilly Circus. He had the feeling that some of the chill had just been sucked out of the afternoon; behind the barren density of cloud cover a sun was shining somewhere.

∎

He bit into an egg salad sandwich. The girl sipped coffee and watched him, seemingly amused by the speed at which he ate.

"You don't waste much time on food, do you?" she asked.

"I don't have time to waste," Pagan said. "Anyway, my attitude to food's pathetically basic. It's fuel. Keeps the body going. That would be sacrilege to somebody in your occupation, I suppose."

"Worse," she said. "Do you know you're supposed to chew each morsel of food at least fifteen times?"

"Christ, I'd be here forever," he said. "I'd never get anything done."

She propped an elbow on the table, placed her chin in the palm of her hand. She had, Pagan thought, a way of looking at him that was just a little unsettling. The brown eyes probed, certainly, but it was the small light of mischief behind them he found the unnervingly attractive factor. He was pleased to be in her unexpected company; he kept receiving tiny waves of enjoyment — the old-time word *vibes* came into his head — but under her gaze he was conscious of a strange awkwardness in himself, a clumsiness. A glob of egg salad slid from his sandwich and dropped in the middle of his plate and he was embarrassed. He made flurries with his paper napkin, which disintegrated between his fingers. He wasn't doing very well and he wasn't sure why.

He looked at his watch. He still had thirty minutes before he was due to meet Martin Burr.

"I'm keeping you from something," she said.

"I have an appointment."

"You sound apologetic. Don't. You don't have to drop everything just because I'm here. And that includes your egg salad."

She pushed a lock of hair from her forehead. Pagan thought this gesture endearing. Endearing: now there was a fresh discovery for him. All of a sudden. He looked at her face. She had a fine mouth which, when she smiled, created an impression of honesty and directness. He could detect nothing false or hidden in her and wondered why he even took the trouble to think about quarrying faults out of her. Old habits. He had a turn of mind, stoked by years of seeking concealed motives and foraging in the darker territories of the human heart, that led him into foggy areas. He sometimes found it impossible to accept things at their face value. It was cop mentality. After years, it was a tough habit to break.

He pushed aside his plate, covering the stray dab of egg salad with the ruin of his napkin.

She said, "I saw your name in the morning paper. I read you're working on this explosion business in the Underground. I couldn't cope with anything like that, Frank. I guess you need a shield around you when that kind of shit happens."

"I'm not sure how good my shield is," Pagan replied. "You get older, death gets harder to take. Funny. I always thought the opposite would happen." He looked down at the shredded napkin, seeing how moisture from the egg salad had seeped through the paper. He raised his face and thought: You could look into her eyes and believe no such thing as the tunnel existed, nobody had died, there were no mysteries, like Quarterman, Bryce Harcourt, Streik, Carlotta. These were unconnected shadows from another dimension.

Brennan Carberry represented a simpler world, a sunny place where birds sang and every night brought a full moon. *Jesus Christ.* Get real, Frank. Next thing you'll be thinking nightingales in Berkeley Square. He withdrew into silence. You couldn't make the world go away just because you found a good-looking young woman sympathetic.

"Have you any idea who planted the bomb?" she asked. Then she shook her head, held up one hand. "No. Forget I asked that. It's none of my business. And you've had it up to here anyhow. I can tell. You don't look so good. Stressed out."

"It must be the light. I never look my best under fluorescence."

"Sure. And I bet you don't get enough sleep. I bet you don't look after yourself properly. You don't eat what's good for you."

"Yes, mother," he said.

"You've got circles under your eyes. You're pale."

Pagan wanted a cigarette, a jolt of nicotine. Instead he tapped his fingertips on the Formica table. He noticed the half-moons of his nails were practically invisible. Wasn't that a sign of poor nutrition and vitamin deficiency? He said, "I probably need freshly squeezed orange juice. Raw carrots. Some of that posh lettuce you mentioned."

"You need more than posh lettuce," she said. She drank some coffee, gazing at him over the rim of her cup.

Was there a hint of flirtation in her manner? It was nothing so blatant as a fluttering of eyelashes; it was the clarity of her look, the way she focused on him.

"And what would you recommend?" he asked.

"A week in a health spa. Daily workouts. Massages. Sleep. All the stuff you don't have time for right now."

"It sounds like bloody torture anyway." He was not overweight — in fact his weight hadn't changed in years and he still looked lean — but under the surface was another matter. Under the surface was some slight deterioration. He'd been sedentary for too long, weeks behind the wheel of a car, too many cigarettes smoked on dreary highways.

The girl reached across the table and momentarily touched his hand. He was abruptly shuttled back to the Hilton, the expectation of her kiss, the electricity of the moment.

"How long are you staying in London?" he asked.

"It depends."

"Depends on what?"

She shrugged. "This and that. If I like the place . . . I'm getting kind've attached to the Hilton. You keep running into nice old folks from Idaho who want to show you photographs of their grandkids. It's all very American. Like a club. We Americans don't travel too well, Frank. One foot is always back in the States." She had a good line in self-mockery he enjoyed.

"I suppose you want to see Buckingham Palace and the changing of the guards and the Houses of Parliament and all the rest of this great city's sights."

She was quiet a moment. "Actually, I was kind of hoping to take you up on your offer of showing me around. Obviously I could have picked a better time."

Pagan had the sudden urge to take the girl by the hand and walk her through those parts of the city that still had elements of enchantment for him, Pall Mall, Regent's Park. He had a lingering fondness for the Serpentine, parts of Chelsea, the leafy walks of Harrow-on-the-Hill, Kew.

"You're right about your timing," he said. He looked at his watch again. He had fifteen minutes to get to Martin Burr, and the old man liked punctuality. "Look. I'll call you at the Hilton. I can't say when. I wish I could, but I just don't know."

"Frank, you don't have to feel any obligation. I mean that. I don't want to get in your way."

"*You're* not in my way."

"Next time you're hungry and want to take time out to eat, get in touch with me. If I'm not in my room, leave a message." She touched his hand again. She let her palm rest against his knuckles. He was reluctant to get up and go. What was happening here? What was going on between himself and this girl he barely knew? The perplexities of feeling. The quicksands of emotions. He wanted her; a quick shadow of desire stirred inside him.

He gazed a second at the window of the sandwich bar, where slanting rain struck glass and created intricate rivulets. How much easier it would be to sit here with Brennan Carberry than to go into the world. He sighed and stood up. "I'm sorry. I hate to leave you so abruptly." Pagan moved away from her. He turned, looked back at her as he went toward the door. "I'll be really disappointed if you don't call, Frank."

The smile, he thought. Something in the smile: a suggestion of joy. He went out into the drab wet street in search of a taxi. When he found one, he settled in the backseat, head inclined, thinking about the girl. She's too young for you, he thought. She's a generation removed from yours. What common element could bind you? Her apparent affection was undeniably flattering. It stroked the dormant beast of his ego. But his mind, that murmuring insomniac nuisance in his head, raised a question of its own: *What can she possibly see in you, Frank?* The question bothered him all the way to Knightsbridge, gathering an uneasy kind of density with each mile the taxi traveled.

■

Martin Burr's flat was located in a quiet square. It was a gracious nineteenth-century place, high ceilings, marble fireplaces, but the sense of space had been diminished by the amazing clutter of furniture. Too many chairs, tables, couches; there was a kind of obstacle course in each of the rooms. Burr, who walked with a walnut cane and wore a dark green eye patch over his missing right eye — a consequence of World War II, when he'd served in the navy — greeted Pagan effusively, a prolonged tight handshake, a smile, a slap across the shoulder.

"Herself," he said, and frowned as he waved his cane at the furnishings. "Marcia considers this a storage unit. Sell some of the bloody stuff, I tell her. Get rid of it. Says she doesn't know what she needs down in the country cottage. Hasn't decided yet. Meanwhile, everything stays here until that strange entity known as a woman's mind goes through the decision-making business. Like a bloody auction room in here."

Pagan had a moment in which he realized how much he missed Burr, even if in the past they'd had their differences. But Burr, unlike George Nimmo, had understood police work and stayed as far away from politics as any commissioner could. Burr wasn't a control freak. He allowed his men to get on with their work. He rarely interfered unless he found it essential.

"Step into my office." Burr hobbled ahead of Pagan along the hallway. They went inside a long narrow room stuffed with books; a word processor hummed on a desk strewn with sheets of paper. Burr, who used his cane as a means of expression, waved it toward the desk. "Predictably, I'm writing the old memoirs, Frank. Publisher chap called me up when I retired. Had a bit of a chat. Next thing I know, I'm signing a contract. I was never one for putting words on paper. Damned hard. Don't know how those writer fellows do it, frankly."

Pagan walked toward the window, which overlooked a barren back garden, a greenhouse against which rain hammered. It was a desolate scene; the crux of winter, decay, corruption. Spring might have been a thousand seasons away.

"Find a pew," Burr said. "Just toss the papers on the floor."

Pagan moved some papers from a chair and sat down. He regarded Burr a moment, thinking how retirement had diminished him. The gray wool cardigan, the baggy old flannels, carpet slippers. He also needed a shave. During his term of office, Martin Burr had always dressed in immaculate conservative suits.

"I know what's on your mind, Frank. I don't look like my old self. Right?"

Pagan began to dispute this, but Burr jabbed him gently in the stomach with the walnut stick. "Don't deny it, Frank. One thing about you. You were always a bloody poor liar. Good policeman. If too headstrong. But damn awful liar. You're looking at me and you're thinking: Poor old sod's gone to seed. Writing his memoirs like some superannuated general or something."

Pagan smiled. "I've never seen you in anything but a suit," he remarked quietly.

"Suits. Not much use to me these days." Burr sighed, glanced at the word processor as if it had materialized on his desk from another galaxy, an object of unknown function. "Still. Retirement has its advantages. Provided you keep in touch. That's the secret, Frank. Be informed. Don't hibernate. What's the term the Americans use? Be with it?"

Pagan wasn't going to comment on Burr's misuse of slang. He watched Burr adjust his eye patch, which he did periodically.

"I keep an ear to the old wall," Burr said. "I hear about our man Nimmo. Not my style. George always strikes me as the sort of fellow who'd be better off doing something nasty in the City. Shark at heart. Doesn't have a way with people. Look how he treated you. Banishment. No tact." Burr shook his head in a sorrowful way. "Still. He's got the job and that's it. No good moaning and bitching about the old faits accomplis. Place has changed, I would say."

"That would be an understatement," Pagan said.

"They brought you back for this appalling Underground business, correct? Ghastly all around. Any progress?"

"The name of Carlotta has cropped up."

"Carlotta?" The old man rubbed his chin. "Well, now there's a sharp echo. Is there evidence?"

"Not yet. She killed a young prostitute the night of the explosion. Not far from the tube station. We know that much."

"Carlotta, Carlotta," Burr said, as if to himself. "I always had the sense she was the sort who liked the limelight. She had to work in the dark, naturally, but I always had the impression she wanted more, somehow. She wanted . . . how shall I say it? Recognition? Admiration for her destructive abilities? A round of applause? That's the feeling she gave me. I do, however, recall being more than a touch staggered by her audacious beauty . . . as you were, Frank."

Nothing escaped Martin Burr, Pagan thought.

"I thought she'd retired," Burr said.

"Didn't we all?"

"They never really retire, do they?" Burr said, looking thoughtful. "Something keeps bringing them back. In the blood, I daresay. Inactivity makes them restless. Bored. They need a high."

A hell of a high, Pagan thought. He gazed at Martin Burr a moment, noticing how the elbows of his cardigan were frayed. He rose from his chair, gazed down at the greenhouse in the rain. His thoughts strayed momentarily toward Brennan Carberry. Why had she chosen such a god-awful time to come to London? Why hadn't she come when he was free?

"There's a complication. Which is why I'm here." He turned to look at Martin Burr.

"Good. Love complications. Speak."

"I need information on the American embassy."

"Ah. And I assume it isn't entirely the kind of information you can just pop in and get from any old consular official, Frank, is it?"

"Right."

"You want inside the machine, so to speak."

"Right again."

"And this is connected to the explosion?"

"It appears so."

Martin Burr juggled his cane from one hand to the other in a deft little movement. "Speak to me, Frank. Tell me what you have and what you want."

Pagan quickly related the story of Bryce Harcourt, the death of Quarterman, Streik's message. In his pocket he had the cassette he'd purloined from Harcourt's answering machine, but decided against playing it for the moment, as if doing so might slow his hurried narrative down.

Burr looked suddenly cheerful, animated, as if Pagan's request were a passage of high excitement in a retirement more dreary than Burr was prepared to admit. He hobbled around the narrow room, humming to himself, avoiding boxes and chairs and an empty old-fashioned birdcage on an iron stand. "The American embassy," he remarked. "That font of mystery."

"I was hoping you might know something," Pagan said.

Burr leaned on his cane. "The names you mentioned. Streik doesn't mean anything to me. Nor Harcourt. Sorry. Quarterman, though. He was one of William Caan's boys."

"One of his boys in what way?"

"What do you know about Caan?"

"I'm not famous for mixing in ambassadorial circles," Pagan said drily.

"He's been ambassador for — what — two years now? Made his fortune in electronics, weapons systems, computer support for long-range missiles, that sort of thing. He gave liberally to the president's election campaign and was consequently rewarded with a nice diplomatic posting. A peach." Burr wandered to his desk, leaned against it. "Politics being what they are, the president — haunted by the horror of the budget deficit — decides to slash away at the Pentagon's profligate spending. Easier said than done. Consider the vested interests pitted against him. Consider the fellows in the Pentagon who're accustomed to a continuing supply of new toys. Suddenly, Santa's a skinflint. The stockings aren't filled quite so liberally. A whole industry suffers and some very powerful people with it. And all the subindustries, all the subcontractors, all the research and development boys start to hurt as well. The old domino effect. Scrap a new missile, you also scrap everything that goes with it. Suddenly billionaires are reduced to mere millionaires overnight."

Burr shrugged. "I'm not saying Caan is hurting personally. But the future for that whole industry isn't quite so rose-colored these days. . . . Anyway, that's a little background for you on William J. Caan. I've met him a few times socially. He's big on law and order, but he's no cowboy. Quite the contrary, he's as smooth as they come. A little flashy, perhaps, from my staid English point of view. But civilized with it. Spent a year at Cambridge. Some time at the Sorbonne."

Pagan wondered where this portrait of Caan was leading. But he knew better than to interrupt Martin Burr. "An ambassador always sets the tone for his embassy. Or so they say. In Caan's case, it seems to be true enough." Burr raised an index finger in the manner of a man testing the direction of the wind. "It's been common knowledge for ages that the embassy has, shall we say, a darker aspect?"

"Spooks," Pagan said.

Burr looked at the tip of his finger, engrossed in a callus. "If you like. Now, under the supervision of Caan, more electronic equipment has come in, more sophisticated stuff than Grosvenor Square had before. Her Majesty's government can only look the other way. If the Americans want to haul state-of-the-art spook equipment into their own embassy — that's nobody's business but their own. But these weren't the only changes. Out went most of the old staff and in came a new brigade. Maybe that's par for the course. The ambassador's new broom, so to speak . . ."

Burr hesitated, turned his good eye toward Pagan, who experienced a moment of slight tension, even if he wasn't sure why. "You're trying to tell me something," he said.

Burr smiled in a slightly secretive manner. "We're not supposed to know the inner business of the US embassy, Frank. That's the protocol. The embassy might lie in the heart of London and all, but it's American territory as surely as Kentucky — with this significant difference: you can wander around Kentucky. Just the same . . . You hear things. You pick things up. It's unavoidable. There's a rumor mill. Only human nature."

"And what are these rumor mills grinding out?" Pagan asked.

"Some of the new people . . . how do I phrase this? Caan's gone outside the usual pool of young career diplomats to fish in strange waters. And he's landed some oddities altogether."

"Such as?"

"Quarterman, for one. He was a career officer in the US Marines. Did a couple of tours of duty in Vietnam. A hard man, as I understand it. Not what you'd call ideal background for a diplomatic posting. But Caan — or quite possibly somebody acting on his behalf, I don't discount the idea he may not have made the appointment *directly* — plucks him out of limbo and gives him the wonderfully nebulous title of special projects officer."

"Special projects. That can mean anything," Pagan said.

"The Americans have raised job titles to an art form. As I understand it, Caan also brought on board a couple of retired colonels, also old Vietnam hands, career officers whose careers since that unfortunate war have been less than exemplary. Political chicanery, as I hear it. Dirty tricks, that kind of thing. These are men with blood on their hands. Figuratively, for sure. Perhaps even literally. They weren't in Vietnam playing croquet, we may be sure of that."

"Special projects officers, like Quarterman?"

"I daresay. In addition, Caan's added a few characters with past experience in a variety of financial transactions. Money markets. Wall Street, et cetera. Don't ask me *their* job titles, because I don't know."

Pagan pondered this information a moment. "The Vietnam veterans — they could just be part of the spook pool."

"That's a possibility."

"And the financial people . . ." Pagan shrugged. "Maybe they're here to drum up business investors. Who knows?"

"Who indeed." Burr moved across the room, edging forward with his cane. "All I can say is that some odd bods are gathered under the roof of Grosvenor Square. Makes you wonder." The old man smiled and turned to Pagan. "I don't have the names of these people, Frank. Quarterman I knew, because I met him at some function in the company of Caan. The rest is rumor, and it's fuzzy around the edges, because that's the nature of the beast."

Pagan was silent, turning over in his mind this assembly of characters Martin had called a rough crew. He had the feeling of being caught up in a maelstrom of gossip and fable. He slipped his hand in his pocket and took out Harcourt's cassette. "I'd like you to listen to this," he said.

Burr indicated an answering machine stuffed behind the word processor on his cluttered desk, where there was a knot of wires. "Try that."

Pagan inserted the cassette, pressed the playback button. He turned up the volume and Streik's demented voice filled the narrow room. *Bryce. This is Jake Streik. Listen. Listen. If you're there, pick up. Okay. I need to talk with you. How are things holding up at your end? I got problems. Listen. I'll get back to you later tonight if I can. You want my advice, get the fuck outta London. Get away from the Undertakers, unnerstand? Walk away from all that shit. If you don't, you're a dead man . . . Bryce? You there? Bryce?*

The message ended. Burr stood looking directly down at the machine. He pressed rewind and replayed the tape. When it ended, he turned to look at Pagan. "'Get away from the Undertakers,'" he said rather quietly. "That's interesting. That's very interesting indeed."

"Tell me why," Pagan said.

"Some years back, two, three, there was some talk about a group inside the embassy that called itself the Undertakers. Uppercase U, Frank. They apparently specialized in such jolly pastimes as character assassination. Blackmail. They laundered money when it needed to be done. They were not above dipping their fingers in the waters of British politics either, when it served their purpose. I heard of one government minister — and perhaps this is apocryphal — whose taste for small boys led to his being coerced by the Undertakers into seeking certain *highly* favorable tax concessions for American corporations doing business on these shores. There were said to be rather delicate photographs." Burr paused, coughed into his hand. "There's more, of course. Rumors have a way of spawning themselves and multiplying. The Undertakers, when necessary, would *arrange* accidents. They would make people *disappear*. They were reported to be very good at this kind of thing. Distance no obstacle. Anti-American radicals in Europe, fugitives from US justice, and so forth."

Pagan was jolted into the realization he'd been thinking wrongly, he'd gone along with Foxie's quite reasonable assumption that "the Undertakers" was Streik's euphemism for people intent on killing Harcourt. But Burr's information had turned this supposition upside down. "Do you believe such a group existed?" Pagan asked. "That it still exists?"

"Frank, it was never more than one of those whispers that just breeze across your desk and pass on into oblivion. Nobody really knows how the story got started, but it went the rounds, then faded away, and I hadn't even thought about it until I heard this tape. Never take scuttlebutt as gospel, Frank."

"But if they exist, it's possible that the oddball embassy personnel you mentioned are part of them."

"Possible, of course. In the sense that *anything's* possible. But even if they exist, what in the world can *you* do about it? What can anyone do? The embassy isn't going to come out and admit it. Caan certainly isn't going to sit you down and say, *Well, Frank, what do you want to know about the Undertakers?*" Burr shook his head emphatically from side to side. "Besides, Caan's position would certainly be one of official ignorance. There might be dirty work going on inside the embassy — but it's down in the basement, so to speak. Caan breathes a more rarefied air, I'm sure. It's even possible that he doesn't *know* what's happening in his own cellar. Or he turns a blind eye to it. He's the ambassador, after all. How can he *possibly* be associated with illicit activity? You see the problem, Frank. Where do you point the finger? Where do you place culpability? You don't, because you can't."

Pagan let an echo of Streik's message play inside his head. The only conclusion he could draw from it was that Harcourt and Streik had somehow crossed the Undertakers. Really useful. True progress.

"Here's what I don't understand," he said. "If the Undertakers wanted Harcourt out of the way — how does Carlotta fit into the scheme of things? Did they hire her on a freelance basis to blow up the train?"

Burr emitted a long sigh. "Frank. I couldn't even begin to answer that one. I couldn't begin to fathom the connections involved. For starters, you'd have to prove the Undertakers exist . . ."

Burr was correct, of course. The Undertakers were eminently deniable, a fiction, a myth created by those people — and there were more than a few in the world — whose principal occupation was to disparage all things American. Where did this leave him? Fistfuls of sand, grainy particles of information that seeped through his fingers. Frustration, sheer and bloody.

"Herself wants us to hie off to bloody Tangiers for a holiday," Burr said. The subject had been changed. The old man clapped his hand on Pagan's shoulder. "Wants sunlight. Do the bazaars. Eat kebabs or whatever. I'm disinclined."

"Why?"

Burr smiled. "Because I'm a funny old codger, Frank. I actually like England in the winter. It touches something in my heart. An expectation of spring. Renewal." He laughed, then tapped his cane on the floor with a gesture of finality. "Well. Come and see me again when it isn't business."

"I will," Pagan said.

"And tread carefully, Frank. Do you hear me?"

"I hear you."

Outside it was already dark. Pagan walked almost as far as Harrod's before he found a taxi to return him to Golden Square. He was lost in contemplation, and the more he thought, the more his reckonings diminished. When he stepped out of the taxi, his brain felt like an airless chamber.

LONDON

2 I

The British Home Secretary, Arthur Wesker, did not like the American ambassador. This hostility was rooted in the relationship between Britain and the United States; while the former had shrunk in worldly significance, Wesker thought the latter imagined itself a strutting global policeman, the planet's bullyboy. The Home Secretary, a man with a Lancashire accent and horn-rimmed glasses, tried to suppress an assortment of resentments. His working-class background, the way he pronounced his vowels, the fact he felt drab in contrast to the well-dressed William Caan — these matters grieved him.

George Nimmo, who sat facing the two men at the table in the Home Secretary's club — an oak-paneled room festooned with art-less oil paintings of former members — seemed totally at ease with the ambassador, a fact Wesker ascribed rather grudgingly to Nimmo's expensive education. George would be comfortable around men of power, of course. It was a class thing.

The Home Secretary scratched his head and flakes of dandruff showered the shoulders of his jacket. His suit was creased, another source of rancor, because Caan was fastidious in appearance, look-ing as if he were freshly shaved and showered. The American's thick silver hair had been blow-dried. He wore a gold wristwatch, which the Home Secretary considered brassy.

Caan had an easy kind of charm, though. You had to give him that. He spoke very gently and without any visible evidence of annoyance. "It's my understanding," he said, "that your police had questions to ask of Al Quarterman."

The Home Secretary, passing the leaden buck, looked at Nimmo. Nimmo said, "As part of the ongoing investigation into the explosion, yes."

"And this ongoing investigation is a license for your man Pagan to kick down the door of Bryce Harcourt's apartment and rummage among the dead man's effects?"

Nimmo had known nothing of doors being kicked down. The information rattled him. He said, "Pagan is sometimes a little crude, I'm afraid."

Caan smiled. "I am not criticizing you personally, Mr. Nimmo. George, isn't it? Do you mind? Call me William. God knows, cops can be overenthusiastic at times, George. Zealous. They have a difficult job to do. Our own policemen sometimes act with too much fervor. Or react. It's a common fact, undeniable. I'm thinking of certain events that were videotaped in Los Angeles not so long ago. These things happen in the heat of the moment. And you can't always oversee the behavior of those under you." Caan adjusted his shirt cuffs, and more gold glinted.

The Home Secretary looked at George Nimmo. First-name terms already, George and William. Wesker felt as if he were the nonmember here, when in fact George and William were *his* guests at *his* club. "I think the ambassador is being very agreeable, George."

"And why not? Allies shouldn't squabble," Caan remarked amiably. He looked at George Nimmo. "I simply wonder why it was necessary to question Quarterman. Al had already gone to see your man Pagan to say that he thought Harcourt was killed in the miserable tube business. The next thing, Pagan goes over to Hampstead, enters Harcourt's apartment without a warrant, then arranges a meeting with Al. The tragic outcome . . ." The ambassador lit a small black cheroot. "Anyone mind?"

Nobody minded. The ambassador could have rolled himself a joint of Acapulco Gold and nobody would have minded. He sucked in smoke, exhaled a pale blue stream.

Nimmo said, "Pagan suspected Harcourt was involved in some kind of abnormal activity."

"Abnormal. Do you mean Bryce was trying to solicit sexual favors in the men's room at Victoria Station? Or do you mean his tastes ran to bondage and handcuffs?"

The Home Secretary smiled dutifully. Nimmo laughed in the brayingly jolly way he sometimes used.

"By abnormal, of course you mean illegal?" Caan asked.

"Illegal, yes."

"What laws did Bryce break?"

"I'm not absolutely sure. I don't presume to intrude on my senior officers' investigations. Frank Pagan obviously had a reason for thinking Bryce Harcourt had been involved in illegal activity. I have faith in his judgment, although I often question his approach. But in general, I do not disrupt the inquiries of any senior officer."

The Home Secretary looked away. Nimmo was amazing when it came to barefaced lying. A waiter glided past with a silver tray and the Home Secretary ordered three glasses of port.

Caan smoked his cheroot. "Gentlemen, look," he said. "It is not within my jurisdiction to interfere with the operations of the British police. Quite the opposite. I simply represent my country's interests in the UK. That's as far as I go. That's my job description. But when it comes to my own personnel, clearly I have an obligation. I'll look into Harcourt's affairs in the office. If I find anything, I'll let you know."

The Home Secretary leaned forward, took out his shabby old briar pipe, and filled it with tobacco. Shreds from the leather pouch spilled across his trousers. He'd begun to feel detached from the situation around him. His motto in life was to sit back and let other people take care of business. Nimmo and Caan could deal with this between themselves. They seemed to talk each other's language. Besides, he wouldn't have been here in the first place if it hadn't been for the fact that Her Majesty's government took a dim view of dead

American diplomats. He wished he were back in Lancashire walking his Labradors on the moors, throwing sticks for them to fetch, his favorite mode of recreation.

Nimmo looked at the ambassador. "I propose that we keep you informed of any further investigation that might involve embassy personnel. With the Home Secretary's permission, of course."

"Permission granted," said Wesker. "No question."

"The spirit of cooperation," Caan said.

"Exactly." Nimmo stared down into his glass of port a moment. "When our interests trespass on yours, you'll be the first to know. You'll have advance warning."

"That's all I want to hear," the ambassador said. "Now my mind's at rest. I can enjoy this fine port. Cheers." He sipped from his glass; the port was utterly wretched, but he swallowed some of it anyway. He set the drink down and gazed at Nimmo. "As a matter of interest, how is the investigation going?"

Nimmo said, "We know the kind of explosive used. And a certain name has popped up in connection with the incident, but there's no certainty."

"May I ask what name?" Caan stubbed out his cheroot. "Or am I out of line?"

"Carlotta," Nimmo said quietly.

Caan looked off into the middle distance in a slightly glazed manner. "Carlotta? Are you sure? She hasn't surfaced in years."

Nimmo said, "Maybe Pagan's barking up the wrong tree. I don't know."

"Carlotta belongs to the era of bell-bottom jeans and hashish and toke pipes," said Caan. He forced a little smile that seemed to Wesker — who wondered what a toke pipe was and decided it had to be a form of American slang — altogether insincere. "I think of Carlotta and I smell incense."

"I think of Carlotta," said the Home Secretary, "and I smell blood."

Caan was quiet for a time. He looked at his watch, then stood up. "Well, gentlemen. Sorry this had to be so brief. I must run." He shook Wesker's hand and then Nimmo's and said, "We'll talk again soon, George."

"Of course," Nimmo agreed.

When Caan had gone, Wesker said, "Bugger didn't finish his port. Oh, well," and he reached for Caan's glass, wiped the rim with a paper napkin, and drained the drink himself. "Waste not want not, George."

LYON

22

Jacob Streik pulled his car to the side of the road. He looked at the road sign blearily. LYON 36KM. What was that — about twenty miles? He'd never been at ease in the metrical world in spite of the years he'd spent going in and out of eastern Europe. It was as if he wanted to retain a part of himself that was just plain old American, a guy happy with ounces and yards and pints. Yessiree.

Okay. He'd find a phone book somewhere. He'd look up Audrey's number. He'd call. But he'd be circumspect, he'd use one of their old codes. And if there was any kind of problem, she'd let him know. That was Audrey. Loyal. Consistent. She wouldn't let him down.

He continued to drive. Fifteen kilometers from the city limits he parked at a filling station. The afternoon had turned to dark, a cold wind blew across the narrow highway, the stripped branches of trees roared in a field where a lonesome horse stared at him with a frigid baleful look.

He hurried inside the public callbox. There was no directory. No goddamn directory! He dashed across the forecourt, battered by the wind. A squeaking gasoline sign swung back and forth overhead. He hesitated for a while before he decided to risk going inside the station. What if? What if his face was famous, notorious all across France? Shit, he needed to get to a phone book.

Sucking air deeply, he went into the building, a concrete box, where an old geezer with an oxygen bottle attached by plastic tubes to his nose was writing in a ledger. He raised his face at Streik. The bottle, fixed by a harness to his side, made a slight hissing sound, like a bad lung.

"*Monsieur?*" he asked in a raw voice.

"You speak English?"

"*Anglais? Non. Pas anglais. Je regrette.*"

"Okay. Watch my hands." Streik mimed making a phone call. The old guy smiled and pointed across the forecourt to the callbox.

Streik sighed and tried to be patient. "Look. There's no directory. Unnerstand? No phone book. No . . . Christ, no *livre*."

"*Livre?*"

"*Livre des nombres?*" Streik asked hopefully. "*Nombres du téléphone?*"

"Ah ah ah." The old guy opened a drawer and produced a phone directory. Streik said mairsy bocoo and began to thumb the pages. He flicked quickly to the Rs. What if she'd married, changed her name? What if she was unlisted? He thumbed through the flimsy sheets. Audrey Audrey, where are you?

R R R. He ran his index finger down the names — and there, mercifully, it was. *Rozcak, Audrey.* He took out a ballpoint pen and scribbled the number on the back of his hand, then dumped the book on the counter and hurried outside into the black howling wind, which tugged at his jacket, yanked at his pants, threatened to blow him off the face of the earth like a dirigible in a storm. *Jacob Streik, lost in space.*

Inside the callbox he fumbled with coins, dialed the number, listened to the ringing tone for a long time. She isn't home, he thought. She's out. Shopping. Dinner. Possibilities tumbled down the chute of his brain like silver dollars from slot machines. And then, praise Jesus, praise *Jesus*, she answered.

"Hallo." The voice was unmistakable, hoarse and smoky.

Streik took a deep breath and asked, "I wonder if they have any vacancies at the Adria?"

There was a long pause. Streik tried to picture Audrey's face and wondered how long it had been since they'd last met. Eight years? Nine?

She said in a whisper, "Do you mean the Adria in Wenceslas Square?"

"Is there any other?"

"Where the hell are you?"

"Close. Meet me. I want you to meet me. Name a place, I'll find it."

"You know the area?"

"Like the backside of the moon."

"Rue du Plat. There's a bookshop. The Eton. Do you think you can find it?"

Streik was assailed by a feeling of being hopelessly lost. Lyon could have been Rio or Adelaide for all he knew. He might venture into the unknown and roam forever down one-way streets and become trapped in endless grids and never find the Rue du Plat and this Eton bookshop.

She said, "Ask anybody for the Place Bellecour if you get lost. Rue du Plat's right alongside it."

"Bellecour."

"Right. I'll wait for you inside the bookshop. There's underground parking at the Place, if that's any help." She hung up.

Streik stepped out of the callbox and hurried to his car. The horse in the field was gazing at him as if they were comrades in adversity, man and horse against the fiendish elements. Streik wished he could saddle the beast and ride off to far horizons. Hi-ho, Silver.

He got in his car. Paralysis gripped him. He shut his eyes and laid his damp forehead against the steering wheel and saw with great clarity the eager young face of the German hitchhiker; suddenly he was consumed by sorrow and guilt. He remembered firing the pistol and seeing the kid fall, remembered the ID card in the wallet; he felt sick to his heart. All this was strange to him, this struggle with conscience. Nerves, that was it. I don't have time for this, this is too much of a luxury, this *wallowing*. He heard the wind whip around the car, watched the gasoline sign swing, a metal disc brutalized by the weather.

The Adria in Wenceslas Square. Old passwords, old keys. Often they were different. Would you recommend the Koruna Hotel at Opatovicka 16? How's the grub at the Restaurace V. Krakovske? Krak. Kracking up.

He rolled down his window and let the biting air have his face. The wind stung his eyes, clawed his nose and lips. What if Audrey was being followed? What if she was being watched? No. She'd have said something on the phone. Most assuredly she'd have found a way of warning him. That was Audrey. She wouldn't let him walk into a trap. Unless. Unless she didn't *know* she was being watched. No way. She had terrific instincts about such things. She had a brain like a goddamn satellite dish, always picking things up out of the clear blue nowhere.

He closed the window, studied his crumpled map. Downtown Lyon looked like a maze of streets surrounded by two rivers, the Rhône and the Saône. On a long skinny peninsula he located the Place Bellecour. Orientation time. Okay. It's simple. Just concentrate, follow the signs.

He started the car, headed along the highway. The wind was so strong the Saab swayed and shook. Streik had the feeling he was riding inside a paper jet.

The countryside disappeared. Buildings rose on either side of him. He was traveling a freeway, three lanes, cars whizzing past him with complete disregard. He had a moment in which he felt the security of anonymity, surrounded as he was by industrial buildings, billboards, apartment towers. This was a big city, he was just another prole lost in the great slipstream of things. This was a comfort.

He came off the motorway at a sign that read CENTRE VILLE. There was a sudden proliferation of signposts. He picked out one that simply said BELLECOUR and he headed that way. He found himself driving along a riverbank, but he wasn't sure now if it was the Rhône or the Saône. If it was the Saône, then did he turn left or right? If it was the Rhône, what did he do? He was aware of terraced buildings rising into trees on the far bank of the river, and some kind of illuminated church seemingly floating in the murky light of late afternoon. But landmarks meant nothing if you were lost.

He braked and tried to glance at the map on the passenger seat, causing impatient drivers behind him to lean on their horns. He was disconcerted, impatient, flustered. He wanted to roll down his window and tell them to go fuck off, but instead he took a quick right and found himself in a narrow street. Pedestrians strolled nonchalantly along. A couple of lovers picked at food from a McDonald's bag, and Streik felt a twinge of homesickness. He yearned for an Egg McMuffin, something that tasted truly chemical, unblemished by garlic.

He came to a no-entry sign. A pedestrian precinct. Shit. Now he'd have to back up, which complicated everything. He thought of simply abandoning the goddamn Saab and taking off on foot, but there were his clothes in the trunk, and all the documents he'd collected, and he couldn't just walk away from that stuff. Keep cool, he thought. Take your time. Look at the map. Get your bearings.

Something thudded against the back window of the car and instinctively he ducked his head down. He saw a bunch of kids gather up a soccer ball alongside the car. They looked at him regretfully. A ball, he thought. It was only a ball. But it might have been a bullet, a grenade, anything. He felt vulnerable. He listened to the ricochet of the ball as the kids knocked it against the wall of an old church and he thought of an automatic weapon being fired. Get the hell out of here, Jake.

He glanced at the church. A sign informed him that it was the church of Saint-Martin d'Aimay. According to his map, Place Bellecour was only a few blocks away. He put the Saab in reverse, turned it in a tight circle, drove back the way he'd come. He saw frozen boozers passing a bottle of purple wine back and forth in the Square JanMot on the corner of the Quai Tilsitt, a bleak little wintry cameo. He stared at the runny eyes of one of the alkies and felt an affinity for people who find the world too much for them.

He traveled the Quai Tilsitt, saw a sign for Bellecour, and took a right which led him directly to a large open square hemmed by trees. The center of the Place Bellecour was dominated by a statue of some dude on a horse, some kind of general or king sculpted out of greenish metal. Streik steered the car around the square, looking for a place to park.

When he reached the corner of the Place Poncet, he found a space and slid into it clumsily. He got out, grabbed his map, locked the car. Okay, he didn't have far to go now. He had only to find the Rue du Plat. The Eton Bookshop. Don't look like you're panicky, like your head is about to explode, just go gently.

He studied the map discreetly, kept walking, nerves tingling, throat held in a tight lasso. He looked this way and that, as if he might just spot anyone tracking him. A man was lingering with a newspaper outside the Yves San Laurent shop and raised his face and seemed to stare at Streik a moment — but they didn't do that kind of thing, they didn't hide behind newspapers or hang out on street corners smoking pipes, that was all myth. If they found you, they swooped, and that was the end of it.

He came to a corner of the Place Bellecour. Along the next block was the entrance to the Rue du Plat. He paused. How could he go directly to this bookshop where Audrey waited? Now he was convinced she'd been bugged and followed. It was a fact of nature, indisputable. To imagine anything else was a violation of reality. He had a sense of being suspended, held aloft by thin silvery strands that couldn't bear his weight. They'd just snap and he'd fall and go on falling and when he hit the ground he'd be hamburger. He didn't move. Here, in the big sand-colored heart of a city totally strange to him, he stood indecisively while traffic zoomed past him into the dark and the smell of frying onions floated from the doorway of the Café Bellecour — and he thought of his life all coming down to this pinpoint, this cruelly sharp angle, this place where the air was scented with onions and exhaust fumes. He was, he thought, trapped. Cornered. Onions and gasoline and death.

Instead of heading for the Rue du Plat, he walked to the Café Bellecour. He went inside, sat at a table near the door, asked the waitress for a glass of wine. Her English was excellent. He didn't have to plummet into his awful French. He tapped his fingers on the table, felt very cold far inside. When the waitress brought him his drink, he asked if he could use the telephone. She led him toward the counter by the cash desk, picked up the receiver, held it toward him. Something in his manner must have been obvious to her because she gave him a look of pity and asked, "Who do you wish to call, *monsieur?*"

He told her the name of the bookshop. She looked up the number, dialed it for him, handed him the phone. He thanked her.

"Eton Bookshop," a man's voice said.

"You speak English?" Streik asked.

"This is an English bookshop, *monsieur*," the man answered.

"Do me a favor. Look around. Is there a woman in your shop? A customer?"

"There is."

"Is she late fortyish?"

"Fortyish? *Monsieur*, I would not presume to guess a woman's age."

"Lemme speak to her, please."

There was a silence. Then he heard Audrey's voice.

"I'm in a place called the Café Bellecour," he said.

"I know it."

"Make sure, make goddamn sure you're not being followed. Okay? If you feel good, meet me here. If you have any reservations, *any*, walk away. Go home." He put the phone down, smiled at the waitress, went back to his table. He waited. Audrey would walk a few blocks, window-shop, glance in reflections, wander — and only when she was sure everything was safe would she come to the café.

Streik bit his lower lip. He waited. He downed the wine, called for another, drank it fast. It did nothing for him, didn't blunt the edges. He stared into the street and thought: What if Audrey is rusty these days? What if she doesn't have the old knack? What if — you could lose yourself in a quagmire of what-ifs. He smoked a cigarette. When he was on his third glass of wine he saw her enter the café and smile at him and suddenly everything was just fine, just dandy.

She came to his table, sat down, opened her large purse, took out a gold cigarette case. "Jake, what kind of shit are you in?" And she put her hand across the back of his.

"Good old Audrey," he said. "Straight to the point, huh? No screwing around."

She lit a Gitane, blew smoke away from his face by distending her lip. She had marvelous blue eyes and a froth of deep red hair. She wore a long tweedy overcoat and under it a gypsy-style skirt to her ankles; it was a look she'd always favored. There was still something of the sixties hippie bit about Audrey, evidenced by the great dangling half-moon earrings, the new-age crystal choker at the throat, the blouse that looked as if it had been smeared with pastel paints. Her fingers were long, nails glossy plum.

"It's good to see you. No, it's great, that's the word I want," Streik said. He thought of Prague and Warsaw and East Berlin and all the good old places, the good old days. "Why did they have to go and fuck with our world, Audrey?"

"Times change," she said. "Progress, Jake."

"Progress. We had a fine time until Gorbachev came along with some downright funny notions, didn't we?"

"The best of times," and she stroked his hand. "But it's a new world, Jake. And you have to adapt. Nothing stands still."

"Yeah. Adapt. I tried that." He had a sense of security all at once. His heart, that sluggish ship so close to capsizing, had become calm. This was a good sensation. He gazed at Audrey. There was a mellow light in her eyes.

She crushed her cigarette half smoked and asked the waitress for a *citron pressé*. "So, Jake. What the hell is going on with you? What are you running from?"

"I made the mistake of getting involved with Monty Rhodes, the Undertakers."

She shook her head, puffed her cheeks. "The Undertakers? More than a mistake, Jake. Way more. And Rhodes. Jesus, Rhodes is like Satan's PA on planet Earth."

"Listen. I was bored. I needed action. I needed bread. I wanted the taste of the old business."

"The business is changed, Jake. Face it. Me, I just accepted the fact you can't stand in the way of history. So I stepped aside. I don't miss the old days. And I don't miss guys like Rhodes, always hatching schemes. I mean, there's a whole other world out there to be enjoyed."

He liked the way she was making circles with her fingertips on his hands. Her touch lulled him. He felt his eyelids become heavy. He needed to sleep in a warm safe place.

"You happy?" he asked.

"I'm doing all right, Jake. I have a small apartment on the Rue de Marseille. I share it with my cats. I do some translating. I took up oil painting, but I haven't lifted a brush in ages. I get by. It's not a thrilling life. But it suits me." She withdrew her hand, gazed out the window a second, then turned her attention back to him. "How deep is the shit?"

"Deep," he said.

"What kind of scam was it?"

"A bagman routine."

"And you wanted out."

"Let's say it was starting to get too fucking hot, Audrey. I was moving vast amounts of cash, and that was making me nervous."

"You drink too much when you're nervous, Jake. And when you drink you have this unfortunate tendency to indiscretion."

"Yeah, yeah."

"You knew too much. And you didn't like what you knew."

"Yeah. But you know those guys. They operate in dark places. Then they get the idea you might be a liability instead of an asset and that makes them anxious. The Undertakers don't take prisoners."

"So you're running."

He nodded. "On empty."

"Talk to me about the bagman angle," she said.

"The money was being filtered into some pretty weird areas via the Undertakers. My connection inside, a guy called Harcourt, wasn't happy about it. And I wasn't over the moon about it either. I saw a whole lotta trouble coming down on me. I mean, it was no skin off my nose where the fucking cash went, I wasn't about to go out and shout it from the rooftops, but I guess the Undertakers got a tad edgy about me. So they bug my phone and maybe they heard me call Harcourt one time and maybe I talked a little too openly about my misgivings. I dunno. Anyway they start trailing me around. I begin to feel highly insecure. They don't have a reputation for charity, those guys. So it came down to did I want to sit around and wait for the hand of fate or did I want to run?" He laughed in an unconvincing way. "I'm a survivor."

"You've always been that," Audrey said.

"I kept records," he said. "I kept notes on every delivery. Every transaction. I wrote it all down."

"Dangerous paper, man."

"Yeah. Dangerous paper is right."

"These records," Audrey said. "What do you intend to do with them?"

Streik shrugged. "I had some notion I could show them to somebody in authority."

Audrey laughed at this in her bronchial manner. "Lotsa luck, Jake. Where do you find somebody in authority you can trust?"

"That's the Big One, ain't it," Streik said. "I played with the vague idea — don't laugh at this, Audrey — of getting them eventually to the White House, into the president's hands."

"Excuse me." Audrey covered her mouth with her hand.

"Jesus, I asked you not to laugh."

"Streik, even if the president was a guy in a ten-gallon white hat, even if he rode some great white steed and was the offspring of Mother Teresa by John Wayne, how could he help you? You wouldn't get within a mile of him. Your papers would cross the desk of some shit-hot assistant, who'd do one of two things. Either he'd turn them over to Langley, or else he'd have you removed and placed in Straitjacket Hall. Either way, you're a dead man . . . After all this time, Jake, you still believe in America, don't you? You still think wrongs can be put right by presidential fiat. Send me your poor, your huddled masses crap."

"Yeah. Well. I guess it's ingrained."

Audrey was quiet a moment. "What do you want me to do? Help you find a hiding place? Is that it?"

"The thought popped into my mind, Audrey. I need some space, some time to think. Jesus, I really need to think."

She sipped her drink. "Maybe I *could* stash you away, Jake. But obviously not at my apartment."

"I don't want you running risks," he said. "Meeting me like this is bad enough. These guys have watchers, Audrey. You know they're good at it." He looked out into the street a second. "You sure you weren't followed?"

"Sure as I can be."

"And you haven't seen anyone strange around? Haven't had anything out of the ordinary happen?"

She shook her head. "As far as I know."

He sat forward over the table, nervy again. His head was fogged. "They gotta know about your connection with me, Audrey. There's no way they couldn't know. These guys have files like you wouldn't believe. They've got computers that can tell them your blood type and when you last took a piss. That's what bothers me. Why they haven't been on your ass."

Audrey shrugged, smiled. "Unless I've lost my touch, Jake."

Streik looked back into the street. Insecurity dogged him afresh; he was assaulted by dread. He heard off-key notes in his brain.

"Where's your car?" she asked.

"Other side of the square there."

She got up. She was a big woman, leaning toward stoutness. She tapped him on the shoulder. "Let's go."

He didn't want to leave the café. Outside, he was going to be exposed again. But he rose reluctantly, followed Audrey to the door. The air was freezing. His breath came in small clouds. His lips felt like marble. He followed her across the Place Bellecour, passing under dead trees through which streetlamps pierced. The square was enormous, scary. Despite the chill, he was sweating heavily under his coat.

"Keep moving," she said. She was scanning the Place, looking from side to side in a practiced manner. She had a way of doing this that suggested an inner calm. She wasn't nervous, wasn't obvious. They might have been two people simply strolling through a French city, maybe heading for a cinema, a theater. She took his arm, and the illusion of the commonplace was bolstered by this intimacy.

"There's the car." He pointed to the Saab.

"Give me the keys," she said.

He did so. She unlocked the door, got in behind the wheel. He sat uncomfortably in the passenger seat. His throat was ash dry. His tongue was like a dead lizard in his mouth. He watched her place the key in the ignition. He had the alarming thought that as soon as she turned the key the car would explode, a bomb had been attached to the vehicle, something that would go off when the engine fired up. Click. She twisted the key. The motor hummed. Life goes on, he thought, in a series of sentences and reprieves. He tried to relax.

The windshield shattered. Streik' flinched and cried aloud in shock.

His first thought was that a kid had thrown a stone or some other missile. Audrey snapped her head back. Streik ducked down, grabbing for her arm at the same time, as if he needed something solid to hold on to. *O Audrey Audrey, have you ever lost your touch.*

"Jesus," she said. She backed the car directly into the BMW behind, spun the steering wheel, edged forward. Streik peered through the splintered windshield. The figure that had fired the shot stood about twenty feet away, face concealed by upraised coat collar, a perception barely registered by Streik. The gunman fired a second time and Streik felt something yield in his chest. The pain was brutal, and he gasped, pitched forward. He had the weird druggy sense that he was floating out across the rooftops of Lyon. He was a kite set free.

"I'm bleeding, Audrey. I'm bleeding like fuck."

But the voice wasn't his own. It came from another region altogether. He was dimly aware of motion, of the car lurching forward through a series of explosions, the deadening rattle of gunfire on metal, more glass breaking. Then Lyon was flowing past in a bright sequence of sparkling lights, neon, flashes. The pain was crippling; he'd never felt anything this severe in his life. It was so bad it seemed to spawn a malignant existence of its own. Like a cancer. Like a pulsating fiery fungus. He heard Audrey say something like *Hang in there, Jake, hang in.* But he couldn't be sure, everything was misted with uncertainty. Streets, traffic signals, buildings, everything was a string on which senseless little knots of perception had been tied at irregular intervals. In the extremities of his pain he forgot his name and why he was traveling inside a car with a shot-out windshield through the streets of a city that surely only existed in his fancy.

"Hang on, Jake. Just don't give in. I'll get us out of this."

They seemed to be crossing a bridge, Streik couldn't be sure. He glanced sideways at the woman. He uttered the unthinkable. "I'm dying, I'm fucking dying."

"No, Jake. You're going to be okay."

Okay, he thought. He tipped his head back against the seat. Pain was rampant in him, pain triumphed over him. He shut his eyes.

"Jake, for Christ's sake. Stay awake. Don't drift."

But Streik had already drifted, down and down into some whirl-pooling dream, into caverns under roiling surfaces of water, a world of green tendrils and silver floating things — and there, swimming toward him, hair swept back by currents, eyes open and knowing, was Bryce Harcourt, good old Bryce.

Hi, Jake.

Streik's last puzzle before he lost consciousness was how anyone could talk under water without drowning.

VENICE

23

Gazing at the ceiling, the woman kicked aside the bedsheets, ran her fingertips around her nipples in a gesture of lazy interest that might amount in the end to self-arousal, then drew the palm of her hand down across the flat of her stomach. A while ago, the rumble of voices from the room below had silenced. She knew Barron's little group had been talking about Helix, a word she found strange and mysterious. She'd looked it up in a dictionary and found a plethora of meanings, but the one she liked best was its original Latin derivation — a kind of ivy. She considered spirals, vines, the shells of molluscs. Her thoughts took an abstract turn, shapes formed and disintegrated in her mind; she had the feeling that her internal gyroscope had gone out of control.

She tried to force her imagination in more specific directions, the body of a Norwegian girl she'd once met on the Cherbourg ferry, say, or Barron's tanned flesh as it glistened against her own white skin. She stroked her fibrous pubic hair in a detached way. Then she pulled her hand aside and let it linger against her hip. No memory inspired her. Nothing particular materialized. Faces, bodies, moments of brief passion; nothing.

She sat up, ran her fingers across her eyelids, closed her eyes. She was thinking of her father suddenly, that old stiff-faced cripple whose only interest in life was his estate outside Raleigh, North

Carolina. Surrounded by servants, half-crazy, he tended to speak in creepy racist monologues about the family history, about slavery, the old days, the sexual misadventures of his ancestors. *Goddamn mulattoes everywhere. Every shade of skin known to man.*

He laughed at inappropriate things. He found merriment in malice. He had a psychotic hatred of Roman Catholics for reasons he'd never specified. One time he'd said to her that he suffered from papaphobia. In the presence of a priest he found it hard to swallow and his muscles became locked. When he passed a Catholic church he always shuddered, shut his eyes.

She hadn't thought about him in years. Nor about her mother, a Southern belle in the fabulous tradition, a vague, lacy figure given to drunken speeches on the state of the nation, the way blacks and Hispanics were taking over everything and pretty darn soon whites would be a minority, just like in South Africa. Her mother was a transparency with pale glassy hands who floated ghostlike across the memory. She could still hear her say, in that zombie voice of hers, *Darling, your daddy and myself, well, we're thinking of putting you into Doctor Lannigan's clinic, he's a wonder-worker, he can perform miracles for people with problems, honey.* Problems, she thought. Honey. She wondered what had become of her parents, if they were still alive. What did it matter? She'd severed herself from her own history. She'd amputated her past.

She went inside the bathroom, closed the door carefully. Under recessed lights her shadow fell across the tiled floor. She turned on the water and stepped into the shower. She heard Barron enter. Through opaque glass she watched him undress. He slid the shower door open, stepped in naked beside her.

"Everybody's gone," he said. "We have the place to ourselves."

Ourselves, she thought. Just you and me, Barron. She wiped water from her eyes and gazed at him. She wanted him, but the yearning was in some way detached from her. She had these times in which she became a spectator at her own life.

"You were talking about Helix," she said.

"And you were eavesdropping."

"I don't understand why you can't tell me more."

"Patience."

"Not one of my virtues, Barron."

She adjusted the balance between hot and cold, let the stream run directly into her face and hair. Barron drew her closer to his body, she lowered her hand between his legs, directed him inside her. She tilted her head back against the tiled wall, opened her mouth, let water splash against her lips and teeth. Barron thrust against her hips. Unlike other men she'd known, he had a sense of rhythm attuned to her needs; he was capable of intuiting her physical impulses, as if he were listening to the measure of her inner metronome. She stared into his eyes. He was looking at her, his expression one of intensity, concentration; what she wanted to see in his eyes was something else — tenderness, compassion, sympathy. Maybe these qualities were there and she didn't have the capacity to recognize them. How could she know for sure? Everything was tainted by uncertainty, even identity.

She came with surprising quickness and was at once flooded with an unexpected loneliness. She slid away from Barron, went down on her knees. He reached down and caught her by the elbows and helped her to her feet. He opened the shower door, draped a large white towel around her shoulders, then led her inside the bedroom. Damp, she lay across the bed. He held her hand, studied her face. He stroked her fingers, touched her wet hair.

"I'm not some fucking invalid," she said. "You don't have to treat me like one."

"Was I doing that?" he asked. She was gone again, drifting off into that territory of self he had no way of charting.

"Stroking my hair. Like I'm lying on my deathbed, Barron."

Barron stretched out alongside her. He reached for her hand. Her fingers lay unresponsive in his palm.

She said, "Take me out, Barron. I want to go out. I want to walk on the Rialto. Or take me to Harry's Bar. I want to do something normal. Something ordinary. I don't care what it is. I want air. I need air. I feel so goddamned *confined* here."

He swung his legs over the side of the bed. It was growing dark outside.

"We'll take the launch," she said. "We'll go to Burano. To the trattoria. The Pescatori."

He stared into her face, thinking how difficult it was to deny her anything. This weakness for her was beyond his comprehension. Her life might have been some perplexing scented maze in which he was doomed to wander. Her expression was focused and hard. He'd seen that look before; she was keeping her temper in check. She could explode any time. Or she could slide off into one of those defiantly brooding silences that might last for days. He found those worse than anything else.

He thought for a moment. "Okay. This is what we'll do. When it's dark, we'll take the launch. We'll go as far as Burano. But we won't get off. No restaurants. No bars. No public appearances. Just a quiet trip to Burano and back by the Porto di Lido."

She looked at him and said, "We're always waiting for nightfall, aren't we, Barron? I'm the fucking dark lady of your sonnets." She rose from the bed.

"We don't live ordinary lives," he replied.

"Tell me about it." Ordinary lives, she thought. What were ordinary lives? People going through the motions of everyday business, working, raising children, paying bills, falling in and out of love. People carrying credit cards, drivers' licenses, social security numbers, all these things that hooked you into the quotidian world, that made you feel as if you knew who you were and where you belonged. She had no affinity with that dull reality. She had no sense of belonging anywhere.

■

The launch, driven by Schialli, ploughed the cold black waters of the Grand Canal in the direction of the Bacino di San Marco. Barron and the woman stood at the stern. They wore heavy overcoats, scarves, gloves. The night sky was clear, starry. There were lights in the palaces along the canal. A *motoscafi* churned past and its wake caused the launch to rise and fall slightly. Barron put his arm around the woman's shoulder. The sky, the sound of water knocking upon the launch, the extraordinary buildings along the banks — these things combined to make him feel expansive, talkative.

He kissed her forehead and said, "You never ask me about myself. Where I come from. My background. In all the years we've known each other — why?"

"Should I be interested?" Her face, wrapped in a headscarf, caught a passing light. She looked suddenly very young, breathtakingly so.

"Interested or not, I'm going to tell you. Tobias Barron's secret background. I was that creature known, perhaps rather quaintly, as a foundling. My dear mother, whoever she was, left me on the doorstep of a convent in Poughkeepsie, New York. The Sisters of Mercy." He was plunged back suddenly into a world of catechisms, confessions, the stale smell of nuns' habits. He remembered it as a man might recall years in a dungeon.

For a moment the woman seemed attentive. "I don't see you in that setting, Barron."

"I got out as fast as I could. Sixteen years of age, I ran away. I went to New York City. I found I had some talent for acting. A little Off-Broadway stuff."

"Oh, you're a good actor," she remarked. The Grand Canal opened into the Bacino di San Marco, the lights of the city receded.

"What I didn't like was waiting tables between jobs," he said. "So I took myself off to California. Where I found I had other talents."

"Let me guess. Women flocked to you. Rich women."

"Rich and lonely."

"And so you became a gigolo and they made you wealthy."

"There was one woman in particular. Amanda Gardner. She lived in La Jolla. When she died, I discovered I was her sole beneficiary. Armed with two million dollars I didn't expect, where could I go wrong? Those were the good old days in America, when you could invest money and be assured of a return. I developed market fever. Real estate. Stocks. Bonds. The market was very kind." He laughed suddenly, and the woman, surprised by the sound, stared at him.

"You might find this amusing. I used to keep changing my name back then. The nuns called me Paul Smith. I never wanted to be this Paul Smith person. Some of my pseudonyms were absurd. I had my pretentious French phase. Michel Leclaire. Then I wanted something vaguely British-sounding. For a while I called myself

Roger Dickinson-Brown. I liked the hyphenation." He was quiet a moment, thinking of the years of his reinvention, the way he'd smoothed his way through those clear blue waters where wealthy women in Palm Springs and Beverly Hills needed playthings, emotional flotation devices against drowning in solitude.

"By fucking sad middle-aged women, you reached your present elevated state," she said. "Houses everywhere. Cars. Boats. Planes. You're another American success story, Barron. Thanks for sharing." Barron's past depressed her, mainly because it afforded her an insight into how much she resembled him, how she'd rearranged her own identity the way he'd done. The idea that she was like Barron irked her. Were she and Barron twinned in some ungodly way? Was it more — was she imprisoned in Barron, as if he were a mirror and she a reflection of his desires? Maybe she'd done far more than reassemble her identity. Maybe she'd lost any sense of self she might ever have had; maybe her only definition was whatever Barron bestowed on her. It was the kind of niggling thought that could flower into a profound resentment.

She shivered in the cold air. "And now you've succeeded in changing yourself, you're changing the world next. It's quite a step, Barron."

"Changing the world? I wouldn't go that far. I'm only helping certain people get what they want," he remarked. "I'm a provider. That's all."

"Oh? Like one of your charities? Is that it? Get real. Barron, you get your kicks out of the power bit. You get off on being the center of your own little planet. See Tobias Barron pull the strings. Watch the puppets jump. How clever Toby is. That's how you get off, Barron."

"Is that what you think?"

"Sometimes. Sometimes I don't think at all. My mind goes gloriously blank."

He considered the woman's remarks. *How clever Toby is. Watch the puppets jump.* Perhaps she was close to the truth. He pulled strings and people danced. He made phone calls that had consequences in places he'd never been, places he'd never go. He sent ships and trains on journeys he'd never undertake himself.

"The trouble with power," she said, "is how it insulates you. You're all wrapped up in a big protective Band-Aid. Nothing touches you. You're in control . . ." She thought: *At least you like to believe you are. But it isn't that simple, Tobias. It isn't as straightforward as you want it to be.*

He said nothing. He looked out over the darkened water. The launch was heading toward the Porto di Lido. Clouds, blown in from the Gulf of Venice, obscured the stars.

"Have you ever loved?" she asked.

A question characteristic of the woman, he thought. Out of nowhere. "I have feelings for you," he said. He considered this statement, fumbled toward articulation, but he wasn't sure how to say what he truly felt.

"I don't know anything about feelings," she said. "What they are. Where they come from. How you identify them. I think of them as weaknesses. Blind spots. Things that make you vulnerable."

He turned her face toward him, put his arms around her. She said *feelings* as though it were a word from a dead language. This saddened him; he experienced a tiny jab in his heart.

"These feelings you say you have for me . . . How do you define them?" she asked.

He sidestepped the matter of clarification. He wasn't sure he knew where to begin in any case. "That's far too complex a question. I've had too many complicated things recently. I'd like more . . . simplicity. I can foresee a day when Tobias Barron will have to reinvent himself from scratch."

"Another incarnation."

"Why not?"

"And do I figure in this scheme of things?"

"Yes. Yes, you do."

She wasn't sure she wanted to participate in Barron's future. Some days she did, others she didn't. Moods were trapdoors through which she kept falling. She'd managed on her own before Barron, she could do so again quite easily. It was a matter of recognizing your needs, that was all. She'd been in Barron's life for seven years — lover, collaborator, always close to the core of his conspiracies, at least as close as he wanted her to be. But did she need him?

Or was the relationship — with its elaborate sequence of emotional pulleys being tugged in too many directions at once — a kind of locked box in which she'd come to feel trapped? He tired her, he exhilarated her, a see-saw that rocked endlessly back and forth. Identify your needs, she thought. Was Barron one of them? She wasn't sure she had a frame of reference that would allow her to answer the question. She fluctuated. Her expectations kept changing. Her needs were different from one day to the next. Know yourself, she thought. She felt curiously splintered all at once. *Yourself.* That was the key word. That was the impenetrable heart of everything. Yourself: but if you had no self to turn to, what then?

Barron put his hand in the inside pocket of his overcoat. He took out a small flat laminated card. "Here. I have something for you."

"A present?"

"Of a kind."

She held it under the pale light that burned on the stern. She saw an ID card issued by the Russian intelligence service, the successor to the KGB, in the name of a certain Alyssia Baranova, thirty-seven years of age, height five feet seven inches, hair brown, distinguishing features none. The photograph inserted in the center of the card was of herself.

Carlotta's identity had been reinvented yet again.

Karl-Heinz Buchboden watched the first demonstration, which began at ten o'clock in the evening outside the Palast der Republik on the Marx-Engels-Platz. It was an unexpectedly muted gathering of about five thousand people intent on expressing their frustration and disappointment and fear. Muffled in scarves and heavy overcoats, a few of them masked to avoid identification on account of the fear of some vague retribution — a hangover from their conditioned pasts, from the days of STASI and the Wall — the demonstrators saw themselves as the victims of reunification. The point behind the march was evident from the placards and posters they carried. They'd lost their homes, their jobs, and the security once afforded them by the socialist state had dissipated. They were third-class citizens in a new Germany they'd at first embraced with enthusiasm because it promised freedom and opportunity, but it had become a country in which they were misfits, a place they didn't understand and where they were misunderstood.

Lost souls, Karl-Heinz Buchboden thought. Their leader, Heinrich Gebhart, a fierce white-haired figure whose bearing suggested that of a prophet coming out of the wilderness, walked in front of the procession toward the Unter den Linden. Buchboden followed at some distance.

The marchers moved in a rather eerie silence along the Unter den Linden. Some carried flashlights, others held candles aloft, flames fluttering in the chill breeze. A police helicopter, blades slicing the night, hovered above them. A cavalcade of police cars followed the marchers warily; any form of demonstration had the potential to turn sour and violent. Buchboden noticed how some onlookers shook their fists in derision, how some jeered, while others watched warily, the oldest among them perhaps remembering different kinds of parades along the Unter den Linden in the 1930s.

The Ossis, the former East Germans, paid no attention to their detractors. It was as if the five thousand or so individuals had a single will, a blind purpose they shared. Traffic snarled around them, horns blaring, headlights flashing angrily. Now and then the marchers broke ranks whenever a car or truck threatened to run them over, but for the most part they managed to maintain a semblance of order. They were dissatisfied, but Gebhart's key word was dignity. Dignity at all times.

Karl-Heinz Buchboden continued to follow. Every now and then he beat his gloved hands together against the cold. He passed the stand of a vendor selling frankfurters and a faint wave of heat embraced him momentarily.

The vendor, a man of Turkish extraction, remarked, "Lazy fuckers. Always looking for a handout from the state. That's all they've ever been used to, I suppose. But why should we support them? Why should we support the Ossis? Let them work."

Buchboden gestured in agreement, but without any enthusiasm.

The vendor commented, "I never thought I'd hear myself saying this. But the Wall served a purpose. They should have left the damn thing in place." He looked angrily at Buchboden, who merely nodded his head. All the euphoria of the *Wende* had long since evaporated, hot air rushing from a balloon. Now there was discontent and resentment; the initial joy of a united Germany had disintegrated in a series of grudges and raw resentment. Buchboden knew that when you had resentment, you had at least one of the ingredients for turmoil, because it had a way of festering.

He kept moving. The marchers reached the junction of Friedrichstrasse and headed toward the Brandenburg Gate, by which time traffic had become chaotic around them, and the number of spectators, many of them howling in a hostile way, a few amused, had grown along the sidewalks. Ossis would always be Ossis. Who needed these people and their problems? They'd lived under a different system all their lives, and that system had collapsed; if they couldn't adapt, too bad.

The march came to a stop at the Brandenburg Gate. From somewhere a small platform was produced and Heinrich Gebhart clambered up on it, loudspeaker in hand. His message was lost in the sound of traffic horns from buses and taxicabs. Its gist was direct, though, for those close enough to hear him: Germany reunified was nothing more than a shoddy piece of political carpentry. Politicians had made wondrous promises, none of which had come to pass. Property had been seized from the East Germans by prewar claimants from the West. There were no jobs. There was no future. The Ossis were as much misfits as any guestworkers, any *Gastarbeiter*. Gebhart had an orator's flair, an actor's presence.

Standing at the rear of the crowd, Buchboden looked at his watch. Gebhart was still ranting, waving his arms, even if his words weren't carrying far. Buchboden moved away from the crowd. He gazed up at the helicopter that hovered now directly over the Brandenburg Gate before it swung toward the Tiergarten and came back again, droning.

Buchboden stopped near a parked police car occupied by two grim-faced uniformed cops. Across the backseat lay assault rifles, riot visors, bullet-proof shields. He ran his fingers over his mustache, a nervous little gesture.

Nobody knew who fired the first bullet. Nobody knew from which direction it came. It struck Gebhart in the neck and he fell back from the small platform, still clutching his loudspeaker. The automatic gunfire that followed was short and intense and appeared to originate from a place beyond the Brandenburg Gate, perhaps from the edges of the Tiergarten.

"Jesus Christ!" A young cop jumped out of the car and grabbed his rifle. With less speed his overweight partner, who was chewing gum, also got out. Buchboden watched the demonstrators spread in sudden chaos, throwing themselves to the ground, covering their heads with their hands. Police, pouring from their cars all over the place, had their passage toward the source of gunfire blocked by the mob.

Screaming, confusion, bewilderment; it was impossible to know how many had been struck by bullets, how many were dead. The gunfire stopped as abruptly as it had begun. The police who managed to make their way beyond the Gate were too late to apprehend the gunmen, who had vanished into darkness. The officers in the helicopter, scouring the sky over the Tiergarten, later reported that they'd seen nothing.

Karl-Heinz Buchboden walked away. He'd parked his car earlier in a street behind the Russian embassy. He unlocked it, got in, and drove away from the vicinity of the Unter den Linden. He went in the direction of Kreuzburg, a district inhabited by Turkish immigrants where the air smelled of Eastern spices and the windows of small kebab restaurants were lit long into the night.

He listened to police bulletins as he drove. The coded messages were urgent, panicky. Every patrol car within a three-mile radius was being despatched to the Brandenburg Gate.

He tuned the radio to a local news station. Already there were reports of the night's events, most of them garbled, exaggerated, poorly informed. Broadcasters liked that heightened sense of reality, they enjoyed tragic immediacy, the speedy communication of unexpected occurrences. Reporters, cameramen, the whole jabbering squadron of media would be rushing toward the Brandenburg Gate.

He parked in a side street off the Orienstrasse, beyond Moritzplatz. He locked the car, then began to walk. He went inside a small Turkish café, drank two cups of sweet thick coffee, smoked a couple of cigarettes. He studied the waitress for a while, a girl whose mix of Turk and Nord appealed to him. She wore her dark hair plaited, and she bustled around the place, cleaning tables, emptying ashtrays. Buchboden looked at the clock on the wall. It was more than an hour since Gebhart had been shot. In another fifteen minutes he'd get up, leave the café, and stroll slowly in the direction of the Kortbusser Tor.

From the kitchen somebody spoke in Turkish. The girl vanished for a while inside the kitchen. When she came back, she propped her elbows on the counter of the bar and looked at Buchboden. "Have you heard?"

"Heard?" he asked.

"They say twenty-five people are dead at the Brandenburg Gate. There was gunfire. Nobody knows who did it. Nobody knows why."

Buchboden shook his head. "I hadn't heard."

"They were marchers. Some kind of demonstration. I don't know. Then they started shooting. This city . . ." She shrugged, turned from the counter, poured herself a glass of orange juice.

Buchboden said, "What is the world coming to."

He got up, left some coins on the table, said good night. He stepped into the street and walked toward the Kortbusser Tor. This was an exotic, uneasy vicinity, filled with kebab vendors, nightclubs that had a certain seedy quality, gay bars, Yugoslavian restaurants, a few Greek joints. Buchboden had always been intrigued by this part of Kreuzburg because it had a nefarious quality, an air of criminality; you knew drug deals were going down behind closed doors.

Clothing stores were open late, funky little places selling cut-price jeans, Doc Martins, punk gear. A scent of spices and roasting lamb floated from doorways. In spite of the bitter night the streets were thronged, people window-gazing, studying menus, hurrying to assignations. Buchboden enjoyed all this hustle, the life of the place, the swarm. He looked at his watch. He was tense all at once.

He heard them before he saw them, the sound of chanting, of boots clattering on concrete, the noise of glass being smashed, of baseball bats struck against walls and cars. He slipped into a narrow side street. He heard angry voices raised, more chanting.

They came seemingly out of nowhere, three, maybe four hundred of them, as if brought together by a command only they could hear. They wore the insignia of their prejudices, swastika armbands on their leather jackets, swastika headbands across their brows. There were skinheads, tattoo freaks, black-booted, chain-carrying, knife-flashing, and they were compelled by rage beyond reason. They strutted down the street, breaking shop windows, tearing down signs, chanting as they moved.

Then somebody threw a Molotov cocktail into a kebab joint, which seemed to be the signal for the mob to step up their activities.

More fiery bottles were thrown into restaurants, bars, through the windows of apartments or cars. Whenever they encountered resistance from store owners, who had armed themselves during the years of ethnic tensions, they responded with knives, chains, sharpened steel combs, spiked leather belts, baseball bats. Shotguns, revolvers, semi-automatic weapons. Buchboden, concealed in darkness, held his breath. He watched them work through the neighborhood in their apocalyptic fashion, leaving behind a maze of flame and death. They worked thoroughly too, as if whatever urge drove them was of no random nature. A few buildings began to burn in the night, rafters collapsing in flame, cars exploding; the neighborhood might have been kindling. The air was rich with the stench of burning rubber, blackened meat, cinders. The whole business took maybe five or six minutes.

And then, as if in response to an order from an unknown source, the mob dispersed, some disappearing in the direction of the Gorlitzer Station, others hurrying toward the Reichenberger Strasse or vanishing along side streets off the Orienstrasse. They split into small groups, discarding their swastika accoutrements as they went.

Buchboden stepped out of the alley. All around him in the reflections of fire, people lay on the sidewalks, women clutched each other and wept, a child went screaming past, clothes aflame. The scene was chaotic, insane; all sense of order had disintegrated for a few frenzied minutes, as if some mass craziness had possessed those young men and women briefly, a collective hallucination of savage brevity. Buchboden wandered across the street, avoiding a burning car, seeing three men gathered around a woman who was clearly dead, hearing cries, angry curses, noticing firelight glisten from broken shards of plateglass. He gazed at sparks rising from the roof of a building, a swift orange lick of flame whipping up into the wintry sky.

They had done their job well.

Buchboden walked to a corner, stepping past the injured, the dead. A Greek woman lay against a wall, the side of her face bloodied, her skull battered. A man, presumably her husband, hovered around her in panicky concern and helplessness. He looked at Buchboden imploringly. Help me, do something, help me. Buchboden continued to move. He couldn't help. He couldn't do anything. He made a gesture of sympathy — what more was expected of him? He heard sirens, ambulances, fire engines. The night was filled with noise. The sounds of law and order and sanity; too late. Too late again.

Buchboden saw a patrol car draw up a few yards away. Three uniformed cops came out, armed with rifles. Buchboden stepped toward them. He recognized none of them. He showed them his ID and they were immediately deferential.

"Skinheads," Buchboden said. "Our young Nazi friends. They scattered all over the place. You'll probably round up a few if you can get through this mess," and he gestured along the street, where another car suddenly exploded, blowing out the window of a bookshop. Somebody screamed.

The cops hurried away on foot even as more patrol cars arrived. A fire engine rumbled along the street, men unraveling hoses hurriedly. Two ambulances appeared, medics emerged, stretchers ready. Nurses and doctors wandered along the sidewalks, wondering where to start. Buchboden lit a cigarette in his gloved hand. Madness on a cold night; an asylum might have released its incurable in this part of the city. Fires raged. The street was an inferno.

There had to be twenty cop cars on the scene now. Another fire engine appeared, more ambulances. Somebody strolled toward Buchboden. It was Grunwald, who worked out of the same office as Buchboden at the Platz der Luftbrucke. Grunwald was young, naive, one of life's optimists.

"It's hard to grasp," he said. He shook his head slowly. It was the gesture of a man whose basic nature was generous, an incorruptible man. "I just don't see any point to this . . ." He gazed the length of the street. "When did you get here?"

"I just arrived," Buchboden said.

"You heard about the other business with the Ossis?"

Buchboden said he hadn't.

"Twenty-three dead at the Brandenburg Gate. For what? For what?" Grunwald looked bewildered, as if he'd just seen a rampaging beast that defied any zoological category.

"That's a mystery a little too profound for me to unravel," Buchboden answered. "The human savage."

"The human savage," said Grunwald, whose cleanshaven face was illuminated by flame and looked glossy. "It's fucking satanic."

Buchboden pondered this description a moment. Satanic: no, it wasn't quite right. He laid a hand on Grunwald's sleeve. Grunwald looked despairingly at him. "First the killings at the Brandenburg Gate. And now this. I'd call that satanic," he said.

Buchboden said, "I don't believe in supernatural agencies, Gerhardt. Only human ones."

Grunwald seemed not to have heard. He said, "What's going on? What the *fuck* is going on?"

Buchboden shrugged. He could already see the next day's newspapers, the analyses of events. Columnists, editorial writers, would be speculating on whether the second demonstration of the night had been planned in advance or if it had spawned itself out of the violence around the Brandenburg Gate. They would contemplate the possibility of a connection between the two outrages and wonder if it were some mad coincidence of rage and destruction. There would be laments, the beating of breasts, deep concerns expressed over the state of the German nation; since World War II, Germans had become accustomed to analyzing their collective psyche in print. Buchboden could see it all. He wouldn't even have to read the goddamn papers. A nation at war with itself. The primitive animal rises again. The specter over the land. All that and more.

His attention was drawn by the appearance of two uniformed policemen who were dragging a young man along the sidewalk. The kid, maybe eighteen, wore a black leather jacket, the customary boots, and on the back of his hand was a gothic tattoo, perhaps a bat, Buchboden couldn't tell. The kid had blood running from a wound on his forehead. He blinked at Buchboden. He had a glazed, druggy expression.

"We caught him in an alley," one of the uniforms said. "Trying to hide. The fucker."

"I had nothing to do with this," the kid said. He was all defiance and hardness. "Go ahead. Got any eyewitnesses?"

Buchboden pushed the kid against the wall. "How come you're bleeding?"

"I don't know. Somebody hit me. I was minding my own fucking business. Walking along. That's all."

"Sing me another song," Buchboden said. He turned to one of the uniforms. "Take him to my office. I'll talk to him there. And anybody else you might round up. Bring them along. It might be quite a party."

Buchboden released the kid, who raised a hand to his wound. "I wasn't involved in any of this," he said.

Buchboden turned away. He knew there would be a long night ahead of him, interrogations, taciturn kids with nothing much to say, nothing much to offer by way of explanation. They'd regard the incident as some kind of happening, as if that were justification enough. Part of the *Szene*, nothing else. Beyond that, they'd be sullen and indifferent.

Even Karl-Heinz Buchboden, notorious for his interrogative expertise, wouldn't get anything out of them. As Nightshade, he wouldn't be trying too hard in any event.

LONDON

2 5

In his office Pagan found a memo from Nimmo. *Further to my meeting with the American ambassador, I demand that in future any aspect of the investigation that involves the American embassy or its personnel must be cleared by me, personally, in advance. Under no circumstances will you disregard this. In addition, I await your progress report.*

Pagan pushed the sheet aside.

He imagined Nimmo and the Home Secretary having a little chat with Caan. He thought of the undercurrents of such a conversation, the ambassador talking in his most cordial manner, the Home Secretary listening with his customary doped expression, Nimmo into his appeasement mode.

Pagan wasn't sure how to respond to the memo. He could report his conversation with Burr, but he reckoned that Nimmo would consider it the gossip of an old man who was either resentful or demented. Willie Caan involved in skulduggery? Unthinkable, out of the question. Caan was beyond reach, unassailable. He was A Good Guy, he took HIV-positive kids from the decrepit inner cities of England to Disneyland. He did Good Deeds. Besides, he represented a country from which, in ways to complex too unravel, the United Kingdom had come to expect patronage and support.

A shadow had been nagging Pagan ever since the meeting with Burr. If the Undertakers existed, and Caan knew about them, then the ambassador was involved — however remotely — with the death of Bryce Harcourt; which meant there had to be some link, even at many very careful removes, between the ambassador and Carlotta. And if Caan was being kept abreast of the investigation by Nimmo or the Home Secretary, what did that imply? *Everything Pagan passed to George Nimmo would go ultimately to Grosvenor Square. Nothing was secret. Confidentiality was a joke.*

And Caan had an inside track, a fast track.

Pagan wandered the room, worrying over this consideration. He could hardly go to George and tell him to give Caan absolutely nothing. Nimmo wouldn't entertain such a notion. The alternative was simple. He'd be very selective about what he reported to Nimmo. And if George felt he was being ignored or sidetracked, screw it. It was no time to show George Nimmo, *yo*, a whole deck of cards.

Billy Ewing entered Pagan's office. "This just came in." He laid a fax on Pagan's desk. The message was from the Sûreté in Paris and had been signed by Claude Quistrebert. It was addressed to Pagan and stated that somebody using the name Karen Lamb had rented a car from Hertz in Paris. She'd given her destination as Marseille. The car had been found, seemingly abandoned, in the town of Chartres. Karen Lamb had apparently disappeared.

End of message, end of trail, Pagan thought.

"She's playing games," Ewing said. "Rents a car, informs the Hertz people where she's going, then dumps it. At which point she either gets picked up by somebody else, probably by prearrangement, or she finds another means of transport out of Chartres. She's making a maze, Frank. But it doesn't tell us where the hell she is, does it?"

Pagan sat back in his chair. He thought about Carlotta and wondered if she'd changed her appearance. She might be unrecognizable. Plastic surgery. Disguises. Even if he were to issue a photograph of her to the press, what good could come of it? There would be the usual series of false sightings and reports from cranks and crackpots. He didn't need that clamor.

Pagan closed his eyes. He was thinking of the photograph that had been taken of Carlotta in Rio, the shadowy male figure in the

background, that little stroke of familiarity he'd felt. But it led nowhere. It faded out in the blunt recesses of memory. Who was the
guy?

He looked at Ewing. "Is Foxie around?"

"Told me to tell you he'd gone out hunting for somebody called
McLaren. Said you'd know."

Pagan massaged his eyelids in a weary way. "If he needs me, he
can call me at home."

■

He went back to Holland Park and sat for a time listening to the
silences of the apartment. Familiar sounds — the buzz of the refrigerator, the click of the thermostat in the water heater — struck him
as strange for some reason. Perhaps he'd been gone too long; perhaps he needed a change in his life. He pondered the alleged existence of the Undertakers, considered the complicity of Ambassador
Caan, thought about Jake Streik. He was restless, pacing the apartment. In the kitchen he unwrapped a ham sandwich he'd bought at
the deli down the street. Bland. Brennan Carberry would probably
have suggested mustard, Dijon or an exotic brand he'd never heard
of. He chewed as he wandered through the rooms. He put the half-
eaten sandwich down on the bedside table. He wasn't in the mood
for fodder. His head was buzzing. He was juggling names, possibilities, connections; gridlock in his skull.

The apartment was confining. He had to get out. He changed his
clothes, put on a clean overcoat, and went downstairs. He got into
the Camaro and drove without any sense of direction, without conscious purpose. But he knew in his heart where he was headed. Why
deny it? He passed the black wind-shaken expanse of Hyde Park,
and then he was in Park Lane. He parked the car in a narrow street
near the Hilton. He went into the lobby, approached the desk, and
asked for Brennan Carberry. He was directed to the house telephone. He dialed her room number. She picked up and said,
"Hello, Frank."

"How did you know it was me? You psychic?"

"Who else do I know in London? Where are you?"

"In the lobby."

"Well? Come on up."

He walked to the elevators, rode to the ninth floor, wondered what he was doing here. It was an easy question to answer on one level: the girl attracts you. You're lonely. Perplexed. But other levels were more difficult to reach. Did he want involvement? Was he looking for something *meaningful?* God help me, he thought. No, this was surely something else: infatuation, say. Or simple need.

She was standing in the doorway of her room when he stepped out of the elevator. She smiled, raised a hand; she was barefoot and wearing a black velvet robe, knee-length.

"Enter," she said.

He stepped into the room, she shut the door.

"I hope I'm not disturbing you," he said.

"It depends on your definition. You can disturb people in different ways. It doesn't always have to be unpleasant."

He gazed at her face. There was an air of expectancy in her expression.

Pagan scanned the room, looked at the newspapers and magazines strewn across the bed, an open box of chocolates on the bedside table. A single lamp was lit; the shadows were calming, but he felt awkward and wondered why she kept having this effect on him. He recalled the egg salad sandwich, the shredded mess he'd made of his paper napkin. He had the feeling that if he were to embrace her, he'd somehow manage to break her spine or bring about some kind of calamity.

"I should go," he said. He looked at his watch.

"Don't be ridiculous. You've only just arrived. Sit. Relax. Get comfortable. Have a chocolate. Here."

She held the box toward him.

"I'm trying to give them up," he said.

Was his desire for her a means of dismissing the variety of problems that confronted him? Easy to deal with on that level: Brennan Carberry as a rocket leaving planet Earth. Up up and away. No more conundrums, perplexities. The desire was suddenly strong; it had intensified, opened out into other possibilities. A mysterious kind of flowering had gone on. He remembered the way she'd touched him in the sandwich shop in Soho. He recalled the feel of her skin. He wanted to touch her even now — so why was he restraining himself?

"Look," he started to say. He didn't know where the sentence was going. Probably into a series of self-imposed objections and excuses. I'm old enough to be your father. You're going back to the States. I won't see you again. On and on.

"No. *You* look," she said, and her voice was firm. "There's something between us. Or am I way off beam?"

"There's something. Yes."

"It happened almost from the start. In this very hotel. When you were leaving, I shook your hand. But what I wanted to do was kiss you. Call it some kind of chemistry. No, that's not the word I want. That's too clinical."

"Attraction," he suggested.

She shook her head. "Uh-uh. Too shallow somehow." She reached out, laid her fingertips on his wrist, then let her hand fall away. "Whatever it is, here we are, Frank. You and me. This bedroom. What next? What do we do about this . . . thing?"

Pagan didn't move. There were particles of energy shooting aimlessly around him. The longing he felt was overwhelming but he made no effort to reach for her. She took the first step, in a manner both bold and wary, raising his hand and drawing it toward her breasts and for a long time he left it there, as if this were enough, this contact of his hand against velvet. Then she slid his fingers under her robe, placed them against a naked breast. Her skin was delightful, silken; he could feel the beating of her heart. He thought of blood running in her veins, the flow of life rushing through her.

She was gazing at him in a questioning way.

He laid her slowly across the bed; she swept aside the newspapers and magazines. She looked into his eyes and smiled. She placed a fingertip against his lips. He was drawn down, mouth upon mouth, breath on breath, a mutual yielding. She shifted her body slightly, undid her robe, letting it fall away from her shoulders. Fair hair on black velvet, brown eyes, scent of flesh: Pagan imagined he could live in this moment for a long time.

She whispered his name in his ear. He remembered how seashells contained the sounds of tides. He heard that same oceanic murmur in his head. He placed his face between her breasts and for a time lay without moving. There was no hurry, clocks had collapsed. He was aware of an onslaught of perceptions — the hardening of her nipple against his lip, the veins running under the surface of her breasts, a tiny mole just beneath her ear, a blemish he found enchanting. He was conscious of the chocolates on the bedside table and the way they glistened darkly in lamplight. She pushed his overcoat from his shoulders, then his jacket, and undid the buttons of his shirt, and ran her hands along his chest. He caught his breath as she reached for the buckle of his belt. Her palm was cool on his skin. He had a sense of being cut free from ancient shackles. This girl was his liberator.

"Frank," she said. "Frank."

Whispers, the hush of breath, the touch of her tongue upon his upper lip, his teeth. When had he last felt this alive? Just when you thought solitude was the condition of your life, something happens, something changes, and behold: a whole new panorama appears before you. He buried his face in her hair, tasted the blond strands in his mouth. He felt her hips pressed against his.

"I want you inside me," she said.

Yes, he thought. There was no other destination. He looked into her eyes; she was gazing back at him. What passed between them in that contact was a moment of such truth and frankness, Pagan had the feeling that all his life since Roxanne had been nothing more than treading water. He didn't think of his marriage, old grief, past pains. He had a sense of resurrection. How easy it seemed, how natural. When he entered her, he experienced, under the surface of his excitement, an unexpected tranquillity.

She held him tightly, raising her knees on either side of him. "Come for me, Frank. Come inside me."

Pagan was stunned by the fusion, the passionate interlocking, and yet nothing was hurried. He had the sensation they might have been lovers for a long time, because of the ease, the mutual understanding of each other's bodies, the concern. He was profoundly touched by this insight, by the gentle way she said his name when he came, how she drew him deeper into her and clasped him as if his satisfaction were the only event of importance in history. She came with him, took the same trip, shivering. Even then, when it was over, they were reluctant to move away from each other. They were silent for a long time, enclosed in a private sphere. They might have been two people seeking retreat from the brutally indifferent world that existed beyond the window.

She ran her hand across the side of his face. "Frank," she said.

He thought he'd never heard his name pronounced in quite that way before. She uttered it as if it were precious, a form of code only they understood. Wasn't that what lovers did? Re-created language to please themselves? Gave it new sounds, fresh descriptions? Lovers, he thought. Love, lovers.

"I want to ask you a strange question. Promise you won't laugh."

"I won't laugh."

"Do you believe in . . . past lives?"

"Past lives?"

"I'm out of my mind. But I have a feeling I must have met you before."

He smiled. "Maybe you did," he said.

Her expression was serious. "Really. I think I believe in reincarnation. Something weird and wonderful is going on, and I can't explain it."

"Neither can I." And he couldn't. Past lives, reincarnation, dead souls linked through eternities? He was in the mood to accept anything. He might have been dancing on the moon in defiance of gravity. Love! For God's sake, what was he thinking? He wasn't a kid any more, didn't believe in lightning striking the heart, the old bolt from the blue. He was surely immune to all that.

She moved out from under him, propped herself up on one elbow. He lay on his back and she looked down into his face. "Explain it. How come it was like that. What's going on between us, Frank?"

"I don't know. And I don't want to analyze it either. Analysis is bad. It reduces things."

"Other men . . ." She hesitated. "I've never known this . . . closeness with anyone else," she said. She looked puzzled, as if suddenly perplexed by a metaphysical problem.

Other men. The phrase created a shadow across his mind. Was it a sign of a new condition, this envy of other men? Adolescent of you, Frank. Of course there have been other men before you. What did you expect?

She said, "I didn't plan on anything like this. It just seemed to blow in out of nowhere. I don't know. I've never felt like this before. Are we crazy or what?"

He turned his face, looked up at the ceiling. He experienced an aftershock of orgasm. She reached out, clasped her hand around his penis, stroked it, and he was hard again. She took him inside her mouth for a few seconds, then raised her face, pushed hair from her forehead.

"I wanted the taste of you," she said. He watched her; she had all that shining honesty, that astounding curiosity, of youth.

She straddled him, hair fell into her eyes, she tilted back her head, thrust herself against him. He was astonished by his own capacity. He watched the muscles in her neck strain, the motion of her small breasts, the mysterious little oval of her navel. Where did his reserves of desire come from? he wondered. Where this incomprehensible stamina? He couldn't stop watching her, couldn't refrain from marveling at her, the closed eyelids, the slightly parted lips, the sculpted curve of hip. When he came again, it was from a place far back inside himself. She fell flat against him, motionless, breathing hard. He enjoyed the feel of her face upon his shoulder.

She was silent for a long time.

"Tell me about your world," she said. "Tell me how you live."

"What do you want to know?"

"Anything. Everything. Just speak to me."

He talked; as soon as he started he couldn't stop, he talked in the way of a man making a confession many years too late, he spoke of his marriage, the emptiness of his life after, the various women who had drifted in and out, he spoke of his work, he traveled down with her into the Underground tunnel, described the devastation, he spoke of terrorism — a process of unburdening himself. And she listened. She looked into his face and listened with great concentration.

"My life seems so dull by comparison," she said at one point. "I think of all the characters you've met, the people you've been involved with — and what have I done in my lifetime?"

"Your lifetime has been considerably shorter than mine," he said. He heard this statement echo in his head, and it depressed him slightly. This lovely girl — why had she chosen *him?* Why give herself to *him?* Maybe it was something uncomplicated: she didn't like men her own age, she found them immature, boring. But why me? he wondered. A cop in his mid-forties is no great catch, is he, Frank?

She ran a fingertip across his lips. "These people you hunt — are they always bad?"

Bad. The word struck Pagan as innocent in a fashion. "Most of them are psychotics you wouldn't want to meet in an alley on a dark night. But some are just misguided zealots. Others are loners suckered into violence because they need to belong to a cause of some kind, any kind. It's hard to categorize them."

She continued to stroke his lips. "Have you ever met one you admired? One you liked?"

Pagan was quiet for a time. "Only Cairney."

"Cairney?"

"Patrick Cairney. He called himself Jig. He was IRA."

"Why did you admire him?"

"He was different from the others. Basically, I don't believe he liked violence. He was above crude, unfocused terrorism. He was good at what he did — but he always went to great lengths to make sure nobody except the intended target was hurt. Discretionary terrorism, I suppose you'd call it. He had dignity. I think that's the word. I spent months running him down. All the way to America."

"What happened to him?"

"He was killed." Pagan didn't want to elaborate on this clipped sentence. He didn't want to dwell on Jig. He remembered the final confrontation in a mansion in upstate New York, the treachery of relationships in that great gray mausoleum of a house that Cairney's father, a United States senator, an old IRA fund-raiser, had christened Roscommon out of nostalgia for his upbringing in Ireland.

"How was he killed?"

"Does it matter?"

"Not really." She pushed hair from her forehead. "I'm just curious."

"He was shot by his stepmother, a nasty character called Celestine who was playing too many roles for her own good. She professed sympathy for the IRA because her husband was a misguided old Republican who raised funds in the States for the Cause. In reality, she was an Ulster Loyalist of a particularly vicious kind."

"I get confused about the different sides in the Irish conflict," she said, frowning.

"You're not alone in that."

She was quiet for a time. "What became of Jig's father?"

"The stepmother took a gun to him. Father and son — she shot them both."

"Classy lady."

"Oh, Celestine had class all right. The wrong kind."

She moved her hand from his face. "Tell me about some of the others."

"Do you really want to hear all this?"

"I want to know you," she said. "I want to know all there is to know."

All there is to know. How was that possible? It was seven in the morning when he finally fell into silence; how could he have been in this room so long? Time had evaporated. He was dry, talked out, lighthearted. He hadn't shared his life like this in years.

"I'm tired. Don't leave me until I fall asleep," she said.

"I won't."

She drew back the bedcovers and he lay alongside her, holding her hand in a possessive way. She closed her eyes. He watched her, wondered about her life — about which he knew so very little — listened to the rhythms of her breathing, and then moved very quietly when he was convinced she'd fallen asleep. He dressed, scribbled a note on hotel stationery: *I'll be in touch. Love, Frank.*

Then he slipped out of the room.

Outside it was cold and rain blew raggedly across Hyde Park. But he didn't notice the weather. He walked to his dented Camaro and drove in the direction of Soho and Golden Square. Back to reality, he thought. But reality, in inscrutable ways, had changed.

■

On Piccadilly he passed the tube station. It was still strung with scene-of-the-crime tape. A couple of uniformed cops stood idly in the entranceway. He turned the car into the back streets of Mayfair with the intention of avoiding any early morning traffic around Piccadilly Circus.

He felt energetic, wired. Brennan Carberry filled his thoughts and he had a fierce longing to turn his car around and go back to the Hilton, crawl into bed with her, live with her the rest of his days in mutual bliss. Here, George Nimmo, this is my resignation. Thank you and good night. But he knew he wouldn't do it, couldn't do it. He had never walked away from unfinished business; on the other hand, he'd never been this tempted before. Temptation at your age, Pagan, he thought. You ought to know better.

So why couldn't he just ascribe the incident with Brennan Carberry to the category of good sex and let it go at that? What was preventing him? You reach a point in your life when you're closer to the end than the beginning and you want something deeper — was that it? He tried to imagine a future that included Brennan Carberry, but he couldn't, and the failure troubled him.

He found himself in the vicinity of Grosvenor Square. He saw the US flag hanging limp from rain. The great eagle overlooking the embassy gleamed under streetlamps that were still burning even though dawn was in the sky. A few windows inside the embassy were lit.

He parked the car, got out, wandered toward the building. A man carrying a briefcase emerged from a car and went inside, passing the marine on security duty. Pagan strolled to the foot of the steps. The marine looked out at him from behind the glass doors. Pagan thought about Bryce Harcourt and Al Quarterman, visualizing them as they must have entered the building in the past. He gazed at the marine, whose expression was one of cheerless vigilance. Pagan walked to the corner, turned back the way he had come.

Why not, he thought. Why the hell not?

He went up the steps. The marine remained motionless. It was only when Pagan reached the glass door that the marine finally moved. His black face was impassive. Pagan pushed the door open and the marine said, "Is there something I can do for you." It wasn't a question.

Pagan took out his wallet. The marine studied the Special Branch ID, checking Pagan's face against the photograph. "I want to see the ambassador," Pagan said, a little surprised by his own nerve. But you needed gall at times. You needed brass.

"You have an appointment?" The marine handed back the wallet.

"No, I don't. But I think he'll see me."

"Yeah?"

Pagan looked beyond the marine. There was a photograph on the wall of the president. Various signs indicated the location of offices. VISA APPLICATIONS. PERMANENT RESIDENT APPLICATIONS. GENERAL IN-QUIRIES. US CITIZENS ADVISORY OFFICE. Somewhere a vacuum cleaner was running.

"You need an appointment to see the ambassador," the marine said.

"Do me a favor," Pagan said. "Just get a message to him that I'm here. Then we'll see what happens."

The marine looked reluctant but ushered Pagan to a chair and told him to wait. Pagan sat. The marine, walking crisply, vanished behind a door. While he was gone, Pagan leafed through some tourist brochures. Visit Florida. See the Everglades. Wonder at the Grand Canyon. The embassy was in the business of vigorously promoting tourism.

His thoughts ticked over into romantic fantasies in the course of which he and Brennan Carberry held hands in sight of Mount Rushmore or made love in a sailboat on some lonesome Minnesota lake as geese flew across the setting sun. While he leafed these glossy pages, various office workers entered the building, secretaries, receptionists, men in raincoats whose functions you couldn't guess. The place was coming to life.

"Mr. Pagan?"

He looked up. The man was young, bright-eyed, fresh-shaved, smelled of cologne. He wore a lapel badge that identified him as a vice-consul, *Butterworth, Peter.*

"May I see your ID, please?"

Pagan offered the young man his wallet. Butterworth looked at the photograph. "You understand the need for caution, Mr. Pagan. We get all kinds of strange people asking to see the ambassador."

"I'm sure you do," said Pagan, smiling in an understanding way.

Butterworth produced a lapel badge, which he clipped to Pagan's coat to identify him as an Authorized Visitor. "Follow me," he said.

Pagan rose, followed Butterworth along a corridor carpeted in dark blue; the walls were decorated with photographs of presidents past. Roosevelt, Truman, Eisenhower, Ford: these hung in neat alignment. This was unmistakably American territory. Pagan had the feeling he'd been whisked directly from London into the United States. He wondered what would happen if he suddenly took a wrong turning, slipped away from Butterworth, and roamed the hallways, opening closed doors, peering into rooms, looking for visible evidence of the Undertakers. Panic stations. Alarm bells. Armed marines.

Butterworth said, "This way," and escorted him inside an elevator. The American pushed a button. He said nothing as they traveled up; he looked once at Pagan and smiled in a kindly way. When they got out of the elevator, they walked another corridor, Butterworth opened a door, a middle-aged woman at a typewriter raised her face and regarded Pagan without any interest, and then, this time in a manner that was almost reverent, Butterworth opened another door.

Finally. The inner sanctum.

"Frank Pagan, Mr. Ambassador," Butterworth said, and withdrew.

William Caan got up from behind his large desk. He held out his hand for Pagan to shake; the grasp was solid and friendly, the contact prolonged.

"I've heard about you, of course," the ambassador said. He had the kind of accent Pagan associated with Harvard, flattened vowels, a certain crispness to the way he bit off words.

Pagan looked at Caan's impeccable hair, the unblemished skin. He was glossy. You had the feeling rainwater would simply slide off him. "I'm sorry I didn't make an appointment," Pagan said, and glanced around the office, which was decorated with framed photographs of more American landscapes. The Blue Ridge Mountains. The red rocks of northern Arizona.

"No problem." Caan went back to his chair. "Have a seat."

Pagan sat down facing the ambassador. "I wanted to say how sorry I was about Al Quarterman," he remarked. "It was the last thing I expected. I feel responsible." He was winging it, he knew, trying to exploit this encounter for anything it was worth.

"I hardly think you can blame yourself," Caan said. "You were doing your duty. Pursuing a line of inquiry."

"I thought Al might have some information." Pagan gave a little shrug. He needed an opening here, he needed to make a reference of some muted kind to the possibility of odd activities inside the embassy because what he wanted was to see Caan's reactions.

"I've already discussed this with your Home Secretary. And with your Mr. Nimmo. The meeting was cordial, Frank."

First name. Nice touch. Pagan looked into the ambassador's blue eyes. He had a sudden image of Bill Caan in shirtsleeves and Bermuda shorts, presiding over a barbecue, forking burgers and turning them, while happy families played softball on the lawn.

The ambassador reached for a paperweight on his desk, an onyx oval he stroked as if it were an oversized worry bead. "I understand the name of Carlotta has entered the frame."

Pagan nodded. Nimmo must have chatted freely with Caan. Sharing confidences. Caan was the kind of man with whom Nimmo would want to ingratiate himself. Yes, Mr. Ambassador. No, Mr. Ambassador.

Caan said, "I was surprised. I thought she'd gone to ground. Are you sure your information is valid?"

"I have good reason to believe it is."

"But you can't go into it."

"Not now."

"I understand," said Caan. He pulled his hand back from the paperweight. "If you locate Carlotta, there might be a tug of war. She's a fugitive, Frank. I'm sure our own authorities would like to put her back where she belongs."

"I'm sure," Pagan said. "It's a bridge we'll have to cross when we come to it." He changed the subject. He didn't want to be steered in the direction of Carlotta, although he was intrigued by the fact Caan had raised her name in the first place and was laying some kind of mild claim to the woman — if she were captured. Perhaps Caan was concerned that Carlotta might have too much to reveal. "What kind of work did Bryce Harcourt do here?"

"He was a researcher, but I'm sure you already know that," Caan said. "A good one too. I understand you had some cockamamie idea he was involved in other activities."

"It was a line of inquiry, nothing else," Pagan said.

"Lines of inquiry can go off at misleading tangents, Frank. They can lead to such things as doors being kicked down, for example," Caan said, and smiled. Christ, it was a great smile, Pagan thought. It was confident, open, charming. Caan could make a miser break free his lifetime hoard of coins from under the floorboards. Here, Mr. Caan, take it all. Give it to the poor.

"Frank, I run a complex organization here. There are a variety of departments. Immigration. Security. Commerce. I pride myself on knowing exactly what goes in every room of this building."

"I don't dispute it," Pagan said. "But you can see the complexity of my own problems, I'm sure. Somebody killed Quarterman, and I don't know why, I don't know who. People don't get assassinated for no reason, Mr. Ambassador."

"I can't help you with that one," Caan answered. "I'm no cop."

"My only intention was to ask Quarterman what he knew of Bryce Harcourt's life," Pagan said. "Is that reason enough for somebody to kill the man?"

The ambassador said, "We live in a complicated time, Frank. Something you know only too well yourself. We Americans are often blamed for events in which we were not involved. There are people in the world with grievances against us. There are grudges, and perhaps some of these are justified. I won't debate that matter here and now. But some people are resentful of us. Sometimes in foreign countries we're targets of animosity. Diplomats are kidnapped. Killed. I'm sure you know all this. Who can say what grudge somebody bore against Quarterman? He was an American. And in this world, Frank, that alone is often reason enough for murder."

"Maybe," Pagan said. "But it's the timing that bothers me. The fact he was shot in my company. The fact I had certain questions to ask. This worries me, Mr. Ambassador."

Caan surveyed his office, as if he suspected something were out of place, something moved by a cleaner. "I'm as perplexed as you are, Frank. Let me assure you — as I've already assured your Home Secretary — that I intend to make a thorough examination of Harcourt's background, and his relationship with Quarterman. And if I find anything that gives me pause for concern, you will be informed through channels."

Through channels, Pagan thought. That meant nothing. Channels were places where paperwork clogged like shit in narrow pipes. No. Channels weren't good enough. He studied the ambassador a second; the man was glib, you had to give him that. And he had the old pro's knack of making you feel you were the only important person in his world.

Pagan decided on a headlong approach, a lunge — what did he have to lose anyway? "I found a message on Harcourt's answering machine."

Caan smiled again. "This was after you'd kicked the door down, of course."

Pagan decided to let this one ride and go straight to the heart of the matter. "The message was a warning to Harcourt from a man called Streik."

The ambassador's expression didn't change. "What was the nature of the warning?"

Okay. Throw the ball up, see how Caan plays it. "Streik told Harcourt to get away from the Undertakers." There. Done. The ball hung in the air.

"The Undertakers?"

Pagan sat back in his chair and watched Caan, who stood up — perhaps a shade too briskly — and came around the front of his desk. He perched himself on the edge of the desk, swinging one leg back and forth. Pagan thought he detected a very slight alteration in Caan's expression, nothing he could quite describe; maybe he only imagined the change because he wanted to, but he had a sense he'd somehow touched a nerve. And then this small feeling of discovery passed because Caan was suddenly grinning.

"I think you've been kidded, Frank," he said.

"How?"

"The Undertakers," and Caan shook his head in exasperation. "Goddamn. I thought I'd scotched that nonsense a long time ago."

"Oh?" Pagan had the feeling that the situation was about to be turned around on him, that any tiny initiative he might have seized was going to be reversed.

Caan said, "I used to hear whispers *constantly* about some rogue outfit operating from this place. It was said they pulled some dirty stunts. They allegedly called themselves the Undertakers. When I first got here, I ran a fine-tooth comb through the embassy, Frank. Now, it's no great secret to say that some of the people here . . ." Caan leaned forward, drawing Pagan into his confidence. He reached out, touched Pagan's shoulder. "Well, let's just say their connection with diplomacy is minimal and leave it at that. But they're not breaking laws, Frank. They look after certain US interests that don't strictly fall into the category of diplomacy. But there sure as hell isn't any group in this building that goes by the name of the Undertakers, Frank. I can assure you of that."

He was good, Pagan thought. In one deft stroke, he'd admitted that a semi-clandestine element did indeed work in the embassy, *and* he'd eliminated the Undertakers, relegating them to the category of groundless rumor. Pagan felt as if he'd just witnessed a nifty piece of sleight of hand.

"So Streik's message to Harcourt was what — some kind of bad joke?"

"A bad joke. A bit of malice. The perpetuation of gossip. I don't know this Streik, so I couldn't possibly impute a motive to the man."

Pagan looked into the ambassador's face. Caan's legerdemain was impressive, but after every trick there was always a moment when you tried to figure out how it was done, a moment when the smoke cleared. And this trickery was too pat, too slick; it was a lacquered cabinet with false doors and concealed exits. Pagan longed to take an ax to it.

"I suppose I better scratch that lead," Pagan said. He got to his feet. "Well. Thanks for your time."

"The Undertakers," Caan said, and shook his head. "I can't believe that one's still doing the rounds."

He walked Pagan to the door, where he grasped his hand. "You need to ask me anything else, Frank, my door is always open to you."

"I appreciate that."

Butterworth appeared to escort Pagan out of the building. In Grosvenor Square, Pagan got inside his car and with one last glance at the embassy drove away. A pigeon flew into his windshield after he'd gone half a block, thumping the glass, sliding over the hood in a flurry of feathers. He wondered if this were an omen and, if so, of what kind.

■

It was ten A.M. when Foxworth met Alistair McLaren in a Victorian pub near Trafalgar Square. He'd waited for an hour the night before in a Soho pub, but McLaren, whose sense of time was as poor as his grip on reality, hadn't shown up, and now he was awfully apologetic about it, plunging into a rambling drunken story concerning a party in Greek Street that had led mysteriously to another party in Wimbledon, and you know, good lord, how these things can get out of hand . . . It was clear McLaren had been up all night drinking. He was a benign drunk with a gentle manner; he had a blood-red face and enormous uncontrollable eyebrows, a bear of a man. He clutched the brass rail that ran around the bar and often closed his eyes in mid-sentence as if seeking some tiny sober part of himself.

McLaren's drinking career had been a long one, involving hospitalizations, treatment centers, detox units, AA, the whole thing. The only reason he managed to cling to his job was because of his solid connections and the fact that people, for reasons of misplaced compassion, usually indulged him; he was just being himself, good old Alistair, basically a sound chap. He wasn't allowed to wander into any sensitive areas; his job description was strictly limited. He'd been demoted gradually over the years but was probably too addled to realize it. When you stripped him of any official titles he might have had, he was, Foxie thought, a filing clerk.

"So, Foxie, old devil, what have you been up to? Still slaving for Pagan, are we?"

"Still slaving." Foxworth ordered a brandy and a scotch for McLaren.

"Can't abide Pagan," McLaren said.

"He's not from your side of the tracks," Foxie said.

McLaren shook his large rugged head. "My dear fellow, class isn't involved in this. No, no, no, class is passé. Haven't you heard? All that bullshit has gone out the window." He made a gesture with his hand suggestive of a bird taking flight. "Pagan rubs me the wrong way. I like a man who knows how to enjoy himself. Have a bit of fun."

"I'm sure Pagan has his own definition of fun, Alistair."

McLaren slapped his glass down, picked up the new one. "I wouldn't want him as a drinking buddy, that's what I'm saying."

"I don't know. I've had a few good times with him."

"I can't quite imagine Pagan having a good time," McLaren said. "They say he's mad about vintage rock and roll. That tells you something right there. Stuck in the past. Glued to an old groove. Doesn't move with the times. Get with it." He clicked his fingers, as if to suggest he was with it himself; a man of the moment, the cutting edge.

Foxie, resisting the urge to defend Pagan because he wanted to be in and out of the pub quickly, said nothing. He tasted his brandy, then set his glass aside. McLaren was quiet for a while, searching the pockets of his old tweed suit for cigarettes. He found a broken one, lit it, couldn't get it going properly even though he puffed at it furiously.

"Cheers," he said, when he'd given up on the cigarette. "So you've come seeking favors."

"I need them," Foxie said.

"All this infighting's a bit of a cockup, don't you think? One department pitted against the other. You on one side, me on another, this branch of intelligence snubbing that branch, and on and on. If we had more cooperation, Robbie, we'd all be better off. What's wrong with a bit of bloody sharing anyway? We're on the same damn side, correct?"

"Correct."

"Under one flag, old son. It might be slightly tattered these days, but it's still one flag."

McLaren fished through his cavernous pockets, bringing forth all manner of items — streaks of cellophane, coins, matches, flakes of tobacco. "When you phoned, I went to the files. I think I found something for you. Took a bit of searching, all the same. You mind doing the honors while I rummage?" He nudged his empty glass toward Foxworth, who bought him a second shot, a double, even as he wondered about the shambles of McLaren's life.

"Thanks. Got it here somewhere for you." McLaren tasted his drink, then poked at the articles he'd stretched out on the counter. Foxie surveyed with some dismay the collection of garbage McLaren produced. Now McLaren was going through another pocket, fishing out more trash, more shreds and scraps and bits and pieces, a few creased baseball cards.

"What in God's name are you doing with baseball cards?" Foxie asked.

"Old hobby of mine. When the father shipped me off to Yale for a year after I flunked Cambridge, I fell under the spell of the summer game. Hot dogs and Coke and blue afternoons. Ah." McLaren smacked his lips. "Miss all that in a funny way. Miss the lazy humidity. America's a bit of a dream, really."

Now McLaren was going through the trouser pockets, the two front, the hip.

"Ah-hah. Got it." McLaren produced a crumpled sheet of paper and smiled triumphantly. "Here's what you're after." He pushed the sheet toward Foxie, who picked it up.

"This Streik," McLaren said. "Beats me why you're interested in him." He belched quietly, trying to suppress it at the last moment by tucking his chin into his neck. "Strictly small time. Delivered the occasional message for the CIA. Usually Prague, sometimes Warsaw. We used him once or twice on joint operations. Elusive bugger, though. No fixed abode. Last known address Manhattan."

Foxie looked at the paper, on which was scribbled an address on East Twenty-third Street. Useless, if Streik had vanished. Under the New York address was written a name he could barely read because McLaren's handwriting suggested the tremors of a hangover.

"What's this?" Foxie asked.

McLaren screwed up his eyes and looked at the paper. "Ah, yes. Audrey Roczak."

"Who?"

"Former small-time operative in Prague. Warsaw. Very long association with Jacob Streik. Best of pals. Maybe even more than that if you listen to gossip. If you're looking for Streik, you might try through her. Lives in Lyon."

"You don't have an address for her?"

"Sorry and all that. Just Lyon. Shouldn't be too hard, though."

Foxie nodded, moved away from the bar, most of his brandy untouched.

"I say, you're not leaving, are you?" McLaren seemed shattered at the prospect of drinking alone.

"Got to, Alistair."

"Is there no charity in that heart of yours?"

Foxie shrugged. He called to the bartender and set up another double scotch for McLaren and then he left the pub.

■

In his office, Pagan stood at the window and stared down at the square. Daylight, gray and scummy, caused the place to look neglected, like something imported from a dreary East European city. The only thing missing, he reflected, was a dismantled statue of Lenin. He was thinking of Caan, trying to suppress a small admiration for the way the ambassador had attempted to manipulate him. *Yes, we have some dubious characters in the embassy. No, there's no such thing as the Undertakers.* The first statement was a confidential admission designed to give the imprimatur of validity to the second.

A rhetorical trick, and Caan had worked it as well as it could be worked.

But Pagan wasn't buying. The strident, panicky tone in Streik's recorded voice impressed him more than Caan's silvery manner. Nor did Caan's weak explanations of Streik's message convince him.

He pressed his forehead against the glass; his thoughts drifted away from Caan, back to Brennan Carberry, back to the first meeting on the Embankment, the collision. She had caused more than a dent in his Camaro; she was doing a number on his emotions as well. She was fogging his brain, eroding his concentration, and he felt curiously destabilized. Somebody blows in out of nowhere and snags your heart and suddenly you're losing the thread of things and you don't really know why, you don't know your own mind, you don't know her, or whether in her scheme of things you're just some holiday recreation, the old shipboard romance that enhances a long cruise, a diversion . . .

He moved back from the window, ran a hand across his face, frowned, picked up the telephone, and even as he began to dial he experienced a feeling of resentment against himself, and a certain sadness, because he'd lost something essential from his life: he'd forgotten how to trust. He stopped dialing, put the phone back down. Don't do this, Frank, he thought. Leave it alone and see where it goes. But his hand strayed to the receiver again and he picked it up and this time dialed the number without stopping. It rang for a long time before it was answered. Pagan spoke his name.

He heard Artie Zuboric's voice, the bearlike growl of a man disturbed from sleep. "You any idea what time it is here, Pagan?"

"About five A.M.," Pagan said.

"Fuck's sake," Zuboric said. "I don't hear from you in what — five, six years, and you wake me in the middle of the goddamn night? This better be good, Pagan."

Pagan hesitated. You can still hang up, he thought. Apologize to Zuboric and put down the phone and forget you ever considered this.

Zuboric, who had no acquaintance with charm at the best of times, snarled. "I'm waiting, Pagan."

Pagan said, "I need a favor."

"Big or small?"

"Small," Pagan replied.

"Let's hear it."

Pagan made his request and Zuboric asked, "That's it?"

"That's it."

"Fuck you. You wake me for that? I'll get back to you." The line went dead abruptly and Pagan set the receiver down. Dogged by doubt, he wandered back to the window. Okay. It was done. Zuboric would get back to him. But he felt bad, sneaky, as if he'd done something underhand. He could call Zuboric again and tell him to forget it —

He looked down from the window.

A man in a dark green overcoat stood in the middle of the square, gazing up at the office. There was a moment of eye contact with Pagan and then the man drew from the folds of his overcoat a gun and raised it quickly, arm stretched, aiming at the window. Shocked, Pagan barely heard the two shots. Before he could react, he was aware of glass breaking all around him, chips of wood flying from the rotted old frame, fragments of plaster clouding the air about his skull — and then the man was rushing across the square in the direction of Lower James Street.

Pagan went to the drawer of his desk, took out his Bernardelli, and hurried from his office, striding quickly toward the stairs, rushing out into the street and heading in the same direction as the gunman, but there was no sight of him; already the figure in the green overcoat had vanished toward Piccadilly Circus.

Pagan kept moving anyway, looking this and that way through the crowds trudging up from the Circus, unaware of the startled expressions of those who saw him with the gun in his hand and shrank away, expecting the worst, a madman on the loose, a massacre in the making.

When he came to Piccadilly Circus, he gave up. Taxicabs, buses, cars, pedestrians, the place was choked. You could never find anyone here. He walked to the corner of Regent Street, where a vendor had on display an array of the morning's newspapers, one of which carried the lurid headline TERROR IN BERLIN, a proclamation that registered only slightly in Pagan's head because he was thinking of the man in the green coat, he was remembering the chase through the streets of Mayfair, the gunman who had shot Quarterman.

He gazed toward the statue of Eros, which seemed to fade into the threadbare morning light.

Are you sure it was the same man?" Foxworth asked.

"I didn't see him from the front when Quarterman was shot. So I can't be one hundred per cent. But I'm reasonably sure."

Pagan and Foxworth sat in a pub on Beak Street. It was jammed with midday trade. The air smelled of sausages, damp umbrellas, the stench of struck matches. The lunch had been Pagan's suggestion. He put down a half-eaten tuna salad sandwich. The acrid taste of gray fish and mayonnaise clung to his tongue like a fur.

"It's an interesting coincidence, don't you think?" Pagan asked. "An hour or so after I talk with William Caan, somebody takes a couple of potshots at me."

Foxie sipped his half pint of lager. "Caan doesn't like the direction of the investigation —"

"So he wants to . . . interrupt it," Pagan remarked. His voice was calm but the gunshots had shaken him. The marksman had come just a little too close.

"And you think he sent down an instruction."

"It's a reasonable assumption."

"To the Undertakers."

"Another reasonable assumption."

Foxie pondered this. On the circuitously careful walk to lunch, Pagan had brought him up to date on business, the talk with Burr, the interview with Caan, the putative existence of the Undertakers. Foxie had been overwhelmed by a sense of wheels spinning inside wheels, a carousal endlessly revolving.

Pagan was quiet for a time, listening to the roar of voices around him, the click of cutlery on plates, somebody telling a bawdy joke whose punchline hinged on some weak play on the word *beaver*. "It might be that the gunman's instruction was only to scare me. A warning to back off. Ease up a little. I don't know."

He picked up his scotch, tasted it, found it watery. He heard the shots again as you might hear faraway echoes. "I've been giving some thought to the idea that Caan might be a candidate for Carlotta's paymaster," he said.

"Except he'd be too cautious, too careful. Direct involvement would be out of the question for him, Frank."

"I'm not saying he'd *meet* Carlotta or pick up the phone and call her. He wouldn't go near her in a hundred years. He wouldn't make a silly move like that. I don't trust the guy, but I don't think for a moment he's the one *immediately* behind Carlotta. There's got to be somebody else. A go-between. Look. Imagine Caan wants to be rid of Harcourt. Maybe he doesn't want to involve the Undertakers in killing one of their own. Maybe he doesn't want it to be an in-house job. He prefers secrecy, a hired assassin, somebody *without* connections to the Undertakers. So he contacts a third party who brings in Carlotta . . . Possibly without Caan's knowledge or permission."

It was all very vague, Pagan knew. Straws, some short, some long, blew around in his head. "Even if it didn't happen like that, what it boils down to is the fact we have to keep as much information away from Caan as possible. If I feed everything to George, George sees it as his duty to spoon it out to Caan. And Caan, not content with the privilege of an inside track, wants to cover all his bases — which includes finishing me off along the way."

"If you're a target . . ." said Foxie, leaving his sentence unfinished.

"Then so are you."

"A shining thought," said Foxie.

"And I don't doubt for a moment they'll try again if we keep worrying them. You may be sure they're watching us."

Pagan shoved aside his sandwich and gazed around the crowded bar. You couldn't tell from superficial appearances if anyone in the pub was a potential killer. The plump man jammed in the corner balancing a pork pie, the long-haired kid in a leather jacket deftly rolling a cigarette, the laughing girl near the doorway. You just couldn't tell.

He took from his pocket the scrap of paper Foxie had delivered from the drunken McLaren and looked at it. "As to the business of Streik — this Audrey Roczak in Lyon. McLaren said she worked with Streik."

"He suggested they might have been closer than mere work-mates, actually. They ran errands in the Cold War days. They were postmen."

"At least Lyon narrows our inquiries down geographically."

"Except Audrey Roczak's not answering her phone," Foxie said. "I've been trying."

"You ever been in Lyon, Foxie?"

Foxie shook his head. "It's always had this weirdly inexplicable attraction for me, though."

"I hear it's a pleasant sort of town."

"I hear the same." Foxie watched a sly smile on Pagan's face.

"Billy Ewing can run the show from Golden Square in our absence," Pagan said.

"Nimmo wouldn't like that."

"I'm reaching the point where I don't give a shit what Nimmo likes." Pagan stood up, colliding with a pipe-smoking man in a wet tweed coat, who immediately said he was sorry in an exasperated manner. Pagan scanned the faces as he moved to the door. He thought a subdued air of desperation hung over everything; people had the expressions of mourners awaiting the entry of a corpse with whom they'd barely been acquainted.

He looked up at a small TV that played without volume above the bar. A plane wheeled along a tarmac, stopped, a door opened, a crowd of men in dark overcoats emerged, surveying the tarmac with the stiff stalk-necked movements of security guards the world over. And then Vladimir Gurenko appeared and began to descend, flanked by his protectors. He waved a hand, smiled for the camera, a breeze shuffled his already unruly hair. At the foot of the steps he was greeted by the prime minister, an overweight man whose customary expression was one of moral rectitude. He gave the impression of a mirthless life. Pagan, who had no great fondness for the PM — a party hack — felt a small admiration for the Russian. It was given grudgingly; Gurenko was a politician after all and, ipso facto, untrustworthy. But Pagan had always considered Gurenko something more than a product of the decrepit Russian system. He was a man of some courage and vision; he had stature — he had, Pagan thought, *soul* — in contrast to the pinheads running most of the governments of the world. Pagan remembered a famous photograph of Gurenko, taken in Red Square after a failed coup attempt by an assortment of superannuated generals and elephant-brained hardliners, depicting Gurenko with a bloodied bandage around his skull and a revolver in his hand and a wild look on his face. Pagan considered it unlikely that Gurenko had actually *used* the pistol in the course of events; but he'd enjoyed the symbolism of the Russian's stance. The photograph had come to represent Gurenko's determination for the future direction of his country. Pagan couldn't imagine, under any circumstances, the British PM with a pistol in his hand.

The man with the pipe stuck between his lips said to nobody in particular, "Once a Commie, always a Commie. Mark my words." He looked purposefully at Pagan, as if he longed for one of those interminable pub arguments that resolve nothing. "His people don't have enough food, they can't keep themselves warm in winter, and here he is traipsing round Europe like some bloody monarch. What's he playing at. Eh? Eh? Who does he think he is?"

Pagan wasn't about to be drawn into a dreary debate. He looked away from the TV, stepped out of the pub. He turned up the collar of his coat on the wet street. "Get us on the earliest flight, Foxie. I just need enough time to pack an overnight bag in case we have to stay in Lyon. Pick me up at my place when you're ready. And tell Billy Ewing he's minding the store."

"You're sure about this, Frank? It's a long shot."

"Without Jake Streik, what have we got?"

"A lot of nothing," said Foxworth.

"Precisely." He added, "And be careful."

"I always am." Briskly, Foxie moved off down Beak Street, while Pagan went to the car park where he'd left his Camaro earlier. He strolled around the car, got down on his knees and examined the underside, ran his fingers over the insides of the wheels. He neither felt nor saw any sign of interference, no hidden attachments, no devastating devices. He unlocked the door and, after a second of hesitation, turned the key in the ignition.

The car started at once.

■

He drove to Holland Park, went inside the house, headed down the corridor to the stairs. He passed the closed doors of Miss Gabler's apartment, hearing choral music issue from the old dear's antique record player. He took the stairs rapidly, climbing to the landing, where he let himself into his own flat and shut the door behind him.

He found a leather bag in his bedroom closet, tossed in two shirts, underwear, socks. From the bathroom he removed toothbrush, toothpaste, comb. Inside the living room he walked to the window, drew back the curtain, looked out in a guarded manner. Nobody moved in the colorless street. Nobody was obvious. Of course somebody could be sitting in one of the parked cars or watching from the small winter-dead park across the way. It was impossible to tell. He picked up the telephone, dialed the number of the Hilton, and was put through to Brennan's room. She picked up on the second ring, sounding breathless.

"I was running a bath," she said. "I knew you'd call. When can I see you?" The eagerness in her voice was touching.

He was quiet a second. He looked around the living room. He had a sense of something out of place, wasn't sure what. He surveyed the bookshelf — mainly paperbacks and the skinny volumes of poetry Roxanne had collected. These books always emitted a damp earthy scent whenever he opened one, which wasn't very often these days.

Carrying the phone, he walked to the kitchen door, nudged it open, glanced inside. The light above the sink was lit, throwing a yellow bloom into the room. He couldn't remember whether he'd left it on or not. He looked at the dishes arranged in the slats of the drying rack. For some reason their stillness, so utterly predictable, so ordinary, spooked him.

"Frank? Hello? You fall asleep?"

"Sorry sorry. I was thinking about something."

"You okay?"

"I'm fine." A lie. And it wasn't just because of the gunman he'd lied. He was thinking of the phone call to Artie Zuboric and chastising himself for his own dark doubts.

"So. When do we two meet again?"

"I'm going out of town for a day or two," he answered. "It isn't something I want to do."

"It's work. I understand."

"Do you know what I'd rather do? You want me to tell you?" He shut his eyes.

"Tell me."

"I want to come to your room. Lock the door. Take your clothes off. Slowly. Very very slowly. As slowly as possible. So softly you can hardly feel me doing it . . ."

"I'm approaching meltdown," she said.

"Then lay you down on the bed and fuck you until my heart gives out."

"The wires are burning, Frank."

"More than the wires." He had an erection. He supposed this was connected to the regression he was undergoing. The way he'd spoken to her, the words that had come tumbling out of him, the visual images that flowered in his head — this wasn't his regular kind of behavior, he didn't usually speak like some psycho phone freak in a vandalized callbox.

"I'm touching myself, Frank," she said.

He pictured her, perhaps naked, perhaps wrapped in a bathrobe, hair piled up and held carelessly in place with pins, a few blond strands hanging against her face.

"You have an amazing effect on me," she said.

"Hold the thought."

"I'm holding more than a thought, Frank. That's the problem."

He stared out into the street, looked at the tiny area of park, the empty flowerbeds awaiting spring, a couple of tired willows. Life should altogether be an easier proposition, he thought. The pieces should be made to fit. Doubts should be dispelled, shadows dispersed. But it didn't work that way.

"I'll be back from France in a day. Maybe two. As quick as I possibly can."

"France? I'm envious."

"Don't be. I promise I'll take you to Paris one day."

"And hold my hand on the boulevards," she said.

"The whole thing. I promise."

"Frank," she said, and was silent a second. "Tell me you're not playing games. Tell me this isn't some abrupt little affair."

"This isn't some abrupt little affair," he said. Call Zuboric back, he thought. Tell him to forget it. It isn't too late, is it?

She said, "I couldn't take disappointment. I don't handle it well. I'm not built for heartbreak."

"No disappointment. No heartbreak. I promise you."

When he'd put the receiver down, he was beset by the need to call her again at once and try to clarify his feelings — an elusive task — but instead he wandered the rooms of his flat, feeling a weird emptiness. He found himself in the kitchen, brooding beside the big humming refrigerator.

The kitchen is wrong, he thought. Something is altered here. He opened the drawers of the dresser, saw knives and forks where they were supposed to be, spoons in their allotted slots, everything the way he'd left it. And yet. He couldn't finger it. He couldn't place it. Maybe it was just the fact the light was burning over the sink; had he forgotten to switch it off when he'd hurried out the previous night? And now — was this just his imagination whispering that somebody had been here in his absence, somebody with an expert touch had turned the place over, looking for God knows what? He shivered. Had Bryce Harcourt felt like this when he'd told Victoria Canningsby he was being watched and followed — jumpy, hounded by seemingly irrational thoughts?

He reached back, touched his gun as if for reassurance, but the feel of the Bernardelli didn't assuage him. He picked up his leather bag, tossed in his passport, zipped the bag shut. And when he heard the sound of Foxworth banging the horn of his car in the street, he was happy to leave the apartment and lock the door behind him — even as he imagined strange characters emerging from closets and cupboards to continue their grim search of his possessions in his absence. Halfway down the stairs he heard his phone ringing, but he did not go back to answer it. Consequently he had no way of knowing that the caller was Artie Zuboric.

■

On the motorway to Heathrow, Pagan directed Foxie to an exit that led down some narrow suburban streets of terraced houses. "Park here," and he gestured to a space outside a corner grocery store whose steel-barred window was filled with assorted foods from England and the East, cornflakes and couscous, marmalade and jars of satay marinade, tins of custard powder and garam masala.

Foxie switched off the Rover's ignition. "Now what?" he asked.

"We'll sit a moment. See what happens."

Foxie looked at his watch. "Our check-in time is four-thirty."

"We'll make it." Pagan sat very still, looking now and then in the passenger-side mirror, seeing only gray houses. No traffic moved on the street for about five minutes, and then a delivery van unloaded some packages at the grocery store before pulling away again. After that, nothing save a few schoolkids screaming into view, swinging satchels around their heads as they passed the Rover. Foxie looked at his watch again.

"Satisfied?" he asked.

"I'm not sure." Pagan turned in his seat, stared the length of the street. It was all very ordinary. Streetlamps were coming on, burning against the fringes of a cold twilight. If anyone had been following them on the motorway, they hadn't come off at this particular exit. Pagan put his hands in his pockets. Another few minutes passed. Nothing, nothing at all. A light flickered on in the grocery window and created shadows from the steel bars. The small shop might have been built to withstand a siege.

"Okay," he said. "Let's move."

"Back to the motorway or what?"

"I don't think so, Foxie. Use the back roads."

"Time-consuming."

"We'll make the flight. Don't worry."

Foxie drove the Rover through more suburban streets, then skirted an industrial complex illuminated by ghastly orange lamps. Every now and then Pagan swung his head around to look behind. More suburban streets. TV lights fluttered behind windows. Then there were signs to Heathrow, and roundabouts clogged with traffic, and Pagan began to relax.

"I think we lost them," he said. "If there was anyone to lose . . ." It was odd how quickly you adapted your thinking to the possibilities of being followed. You developed a kind of force-field. You had your antennae in position to detect murderous interference.

They plunged into the tunnel to the airport, found a parking space, walked to Terminal 2. Inside the crowded building they checked in and passed through security, where Pagan was briefly detained by a bewhiskered official who examined his Special Branch identity card and his weapon. The man gave Pagan a knowing look, as if they were partners in a conspiracy.

In the departure lounge, Pagan ignored the NO SMOKING sign and lit a cigarette, which he puffed on reluctantly for a few seconds before stabbing it out. He stared at the departures screen, contemplating the vicissitudes of an investigation that had begun in an Underground tunnel and was now about to take him upward into the skies, from one extreme to another, as if the various bits of the puzzle had been scattered in a purgatorial place between heaven and earth.

VENICE

27

Messages came in by fax and modem, a flurry of them from different parts of the world. One originated in Berlin; Barron had already seen the TV pictures. A second relayed news from the Czech Republic. A bomb had exploded in Prague Castle, killing President Svobodin and four of his ministers. Barron had been in the castle in the days of the old regime, before Svobodin's reformers had come to power. He'd been given the whole tour, the picture gallery, the Church of Saint Vitus, the tomb of Wenceslas, the Bohemian crown jewels.

There were messages from Angola, from Somalia, one from Kuwait, where military representatives of the royal family, struggling with the unexpected depletion of currency reserves, were seeking to renegotiate terms. Another came from Mindanao: insurgents were busily accumulating arms in the interminable fight against the government in Manila.

The last message had been sent from Lyon. It simply said: *The Weed has been removed.* He was more relieved to read this than he might have expected. He'd known, of course, that Streik would be eliminated sooner or later, but something of the General's anxieties had clearly entered his system. He rose from his desk, studied the wall maps. The world, he thought, was burning like so much kindling.

He was about to leave the room when the telephone rang. This was his private line, a number known to only a very few. He picked up the receiver, spoke his name. The voice at the other end of the line echoed. Each word was repeated in a whispered way, creating a bizarre husky effect.

"I've heard something that disturbs me greatly, Tobias. Frank Pagan is looking for Carlotta. You didn't say a goddamn thing about Carlotta being involved. You didn't tell me how the whole business was going to be handled. I don't understand what's going on."

Barron didn't speak for a time. He had a jarring sensation in his head, as if a corkscrew had been twisted inside his skull. He curled the phone cord in his fingers. "How in God's name did Pagan get that information?" he asked.

"I have no idea."

"Can you find out?"

"I think I can cope with Pagan. But I'm not happy with the way this whole goddamn thing has been done. You never said anything about Carlotta —"

"Things happen." It was an inadequate response but the only one that came to mind. Barron put the receiver down. He left the room, locked the door, walked into the kitchen. Carlotta stood against the refrigerator, drinking a glass of the dark blood-orange juice she favored.

Barron looked at her. He had an uneasy sense of a fuse burning in his head, a spark attached to a cylinder of gelignite, a dangerous smoldering. He sat down at the long kitchen table. He clasped his hands in front of himself. He sought some inner calm, but it wouldn't come. He heard again the message on the phone, which seemed to repeat itself in his head in a sequence of troublesome little echoes.

Carlotta said, "Something bothering you, Barron?"

Barron stood up. How to approach this, how to raise the subject; he wasn't sure. He was walking on broken glass. It was best to come straight out with it, and if she flew into a defensive rage, he'd have to cope. He walked toward her. He placed his hands on either side of her face and looked into her eyes.

"Tell me, Carlotta. What did you do in London?"

"Is this weird question time or something? You know what I did. You sent me, after all. I did what you asked."

There was a thickness at the back of his throat. *"What did you do in London, Carlotta?"*

"You've got on your serious expression, Barron. The heavy one I don't like." She broke away from him, walked to the kitchen window, pulled the blind back. A gondolier with the small crabbed face of a gargoyle smoked a cigarette on the quay.

"I just had a phone call, Carlotta. From London."

"How nice," she said.

"No. It wasn't nice. Nice isn't even close. Will I tell you what I just heard? They have your name, Carlotta."

"Who has my name?"

"The cops. How did that happen? How do you suppose that happened?" He tracked her around the kitchen table.

"How would I know?" she asked.

"They're looking for you." He caught her wrists.

"Don't touch me, Barron."

"Somehow you've fucked up," he said, releasing her.

She looked challengingly at him. "Fucked up?"

"You must have been careless. You left something behind, didn't you? Something, some kind of clue, a hint, Christ knows what."

"Don't shout at me," and she covered her ears. "I didn't leave anything behind in London. I did the job. In and out. Nobody saw me. You know what this is? It's rumor, gossip, nothing."

"They just plucked your name from a hat? Is that what you're telling me?" He faced her, irritated with himself for losing control, but on a deeper level angry that he'd set her loose in London in the first place without knowing her plans. But she'd told him emphatically that if he wanted her to do the job, then he'd have to entrust it to her, the method, the details, everything — and he'd gone along with that, turning a blind eye as he usually did when it came to her.

"I don't know how you come by your information, Toby," she said. She edged toward him, dragging one foot behind her, play-acting. He knew this performance: this was the scolded child routine, the plunge into sulking, a funk she affected when things were getting away from her. "The source is impeccable," Barron said.

He watched her as she turned her feet inward, toes touching in a childlike way, hands clasped behind her back. Even the fact that she was wearing one of his white linen shirts, which was too long for her, contributed to an effect of smallness. But he wasn't buying into this performance. He said, "They're looking for you. Understand what I'm saying?"

"They're not going to find me, Toby. They don't know where I am." She was changing in front of his eyes. The chastised little girl had gone, replaced by someone cold and hard and contentious. She was defiant, shoving aside the world, forging her own reality.

"Your security must be screwed up," she said. "You can't blame me for your failings, Barron. Somewhere along the line you've got a leak."

"I don't think so."

"No? What makes you imagine your setup is perfect? Somebody spoke. Somebody said something in the wrong place. I won't be blamed for that."

Barron considered this. But it was impossible. Nobody had known of Carlotta's involvement. Not Kinsella, not Rhodes, not the General. And Willie Caan — Caan certainly hadn't been told in advance. Only Schialli had met the woman, but Schialli — even if he recognized her — would never have spoken. Nobody knew. Nobody had been told about Carlotta. You didn't just bandy about your association with somebody like her. You didn't want to hear the arguments against her — she was unstable, wayward, her mental state ballistic. You didn't want to listen to criticism of her.

"I don't think there's anything wrong with my security," he said quietly.

"God. You sound so fucking sure of yourself, Barron. You think you've got the perfect cover, don't you? You hide behind famous friends. You conceal yourself behind good deeds. You like to see your name in the gossip columns. But it doesn't work that way. Somewhere along the way your worlds overlap. And you're caught. You're exposed."

He was going to counter with something abrasive. He was about to say that she had no right to talk when it came to disguises and concealments and the alteration of identities — but he checked himself. He rarely won arguments with her in any event.

He went toward her, took her hands, held them against his chest. When he spoke he did so very quietly. "Carlotta. A lot of planning has gone into all this. All over Europe, in the United States, a great deal of money and time and thought has gone into this whole business. Understand me? Now the British police have your name."

She gazed at him wide-eyed. "I already told you. They don't know what I look like. They don't know I'm in Italy. I disappeared in France. I covered myself."

He shook his head. There was no way of getting his message across to her. There was no way of explaining the clockwork of a police inquiry, cogs turning, the availability of a large network of information. She just didn't want to listen. She was plugged into the moon.

"This cop Pagan," he said. "He has your name. That in itself doesn't worry me. It's all the rest of it that does. Sooner or later, probably sooner, wires will be buzzing across Europe, requests will go to Interpol, bulletins will be issued. It doesn't stop there, Carlotta. The FBI will be alerted, and God knows who else. Do you see?"

He gazed at her. It was futile to berate her. Instead, he had a sudden urge to protect her, as if she were some tiny vulnerable creature he'd found in a hedgerow. He wondered at the mysteries of the heart, the excesses, the surprises.

"Something must have gone wrong in London," he said very quietly. "Think. Try to think. Talk to me. Tell me how you did the job. Step by step."

She closed her eyes. She spoke in a strange monotone. "I watched Harcourt for a week in the beginning," she said. *Details*, she thought. *He wants details he isn't prepared to hear.* She wondered why she felt the need to spare him the truth.

"He didn't notice you?"

"Nobody notices me unless I want them to, Barron." She opened her eyes, looked at him without expression. "He had a habit of varying his routine. The variations were strictly limited. He wasn't the most imaginative human being I've ever had to deal with. He usually left the embassy between five and six o'clock. Sometimes he went home by tube. Sometimes he drove. Sometimes he caught a taxi. Once, he took a bus."

She paused. She sipped orange juice. Barron watched her face, the odd lack of expression.

"He spent his evenings in the company of women usually. Restaurants, nightclubs. One night he went to a house in St. John's Wood with a woman. I was parked outside, waiting. A man is sometimes vulnerable and not too attentive when he's just made love, Barron. His thoughts are elsewhere, he's just been laid and he's feeling exuberant, maybe he's even feeling omnipotent. When he left the house, he walked to his car. I watched him come out of the house. When he was about twenty feet from his car, I took my gun from the glove compartment and I approached him. At the last moment he turned his face, saw me coming under a streetlamp, he smiled at me — I was a mere woman, how could I possibly be a danger to him? I shot him twice in the heart. When he fell, I shot him a third time in the skull. I walked back to my car and drove away."

"And that was it?"

"The whole story, Barron."

"And nobody saw you."

"Give me some goddamn credit," she said.

"Are you absolutely sure Harcourt was dead?"

"For Christ's sake," she said.

Barron strolled the room, thinking that something in the woman's story didn't add up for him, an element was missing, out of place. He stopped moving, turned, faced her. It came to him suddenly: why hadn't he heard the news of Bryce Harcourt's murder from one or other sources of his information? Why hadn't there been a message, a report, even an item in a newspaper? Why hadn't Harcourt's name been mentioned in *anything* that came across the wires? It was a mystifying blank, which could only be explained if the woman's story were a lie — but why would she lie? What was she hiding?

Before he could say anything, he heard a sound from beyond the kitchen door. He raised a finger to his lips for silence, moved to the door, pulled it open.

The General stood there, dapper in his vicuña coat, his face red from the afternoon air.

"Your manservant let me in," he said quietly. "I'm sorry if I'm intruding." He looked at Carlotta and inclined his head very slightly in a gesture of greeting. But his expression was a cold one and the light in his eye hard as iron.

There was a moment of awkwardness, fragility. Barron didn't move; he smiled in a flustered way. He wondered how long the General had been on the other side of the door, how much he'd heard.

"Have I come at a bad time?" the General asked.

"Of course not, Erich." Barron stirred into action, stepped out of the kitchen, put a hand on the General's elbow and steered him across the sitting room. He hoped Carlotta would stay behind in the kitchen, but she had other ideas; in a contrary way she followed him, tracking him as he escorted the General to the sofa.

"No introductions, Tobias?" she asked.

"Introductions, of course, sure." Barron nodded at the old man. "Carla. This is General Schwarzenbach."

"Carla?" the General asked.

"Sometimes," Carlotta said.

The General looked puzzled. "Only sometimes?"

"What she means," Barron began to say.

"What I mean is that I change my name when it suits me," she said and sat alongside the General, touched the back of his hand flirtatiously. Barron was tense, coiled.

"A chameleon of sorts," the General said.

"You got it at the first try."

"How convenient to change one's name when one has the urge. But many people use different names for a variety of reasons, I'm sure. If they wish to disappear, if they have good reason to run from the law." The General looked at Barron. "Wouldn't you say so, Barron?"

Barron nodded. He needed to step in here, to stop the process of decay; he was convinced the old man had been lingering outside the door for many minutes. He must have heard it all, the argument, the mention of the London police, the talk about a leak in security. He wasn't a stupid man. If he'd been listening all along, he would have heard the name Carlotta. And, given the old man's attentiveness, he'd make assumptions, draw conclusions.

"A drink, General?" Barron asked.

"I think not."

"You don't imbibe?" Carlotta asked.

"I have my moments. This is not one of them." The General focused on her, narrowing his eyes. He smiled insincerely. "You know, you seem familiar to me. Have we perhaps met someplace before now?"

"Maybe. I meet a lot of people," Carlotta said. "But I'd remember you, General." She nudged the old man with her elbow. "If you're a general, where's your army?"

"Gone, alas."

"AWOL?"

"AWOL. I don't understand."

"Doesn't matter," she said.

"No. Tell me. I am anxious to improve my English."

Carlotta got up from the sofa, stared at Barron, then drifted to the window. "Absent without leave, General."

"Ah." The General appeared to absorb this term before he looked at Barron. "We must talk, Barron. We must talk privately."

Carlotta turned from the window. "Why? Tobias wouldn't send me out of the room. Would you, Tobias? You wouldn't eject your poor little Carla, would you?"

She was playing a game, enjoying herself. She came close to Barron, placed a hand on his thigh. "Don't send me away," she said. "You aren't some kind of male chauvinist beast, are you, Tobias? You don't subscribe to the notion that the place of women is in the kitchen, do you?" She kissed his cheek with an exaggerated smacking sound.

Barron said nothing. He heard an alarm in his head. What had caused some vague sense of familiarity in the General? Was it possible that somewhere in the past Carlotta's path had crossed his?

The General was rising from the sofa. "Is there a place we can talk alone?" he asked.

"Of course."

Carlotta stepped in front of the General. She seemed flushed, excited. Barron knew this mood of animated mischief; it was a kind of high for her. When she was determined to provoke reactions, when she was flying willfully into a scenario of her own design, he had no way of dealing with her. The General appeared bewildered and irritated.

"Boys will be boys," Carlotta said. "I'll make myself scarce. What do you want me to do, Tobias? Rustle up some chicken soup? Make tea? Do tell."

"Carla," he said.

"I do a wonderful gâteau, General. You should taste it. Want me to whip one up, Tobias?"

"Carla, please." She was heading toward the outrageous and he wasn't sure how to stop her.

"Please? I take it that's an acceptance? Let me go find my apron. I can't bake a cake dressed in one of your good shirts, Tobias. Can I? Not one of your best linen numbers. I'm so messy in the kitchen, General." Her voice was high, her sentences quick.

Barron looked at the General, who was shaking his head. "This is not a good time for us, Barron."

"Whaddya mean, General? It's a great time." Carlotta danced in front of him, poked him in the chest. "You were listening at the door, weren't you? You naughty old General. Tsk-tsk. Bad boy."

"I'm sure the General is too good-mannered to listen in on other people's conversations, Carla." Why didn't she leave? Why did she continue to play-act?

"Yeah? You too good-mannered, General? He doesn't look it to me, Tobias. I think he's an old rascal." She prodded him again, laughed in a theatrical way. The General was very still, glaring at Barron, holding him responsible for this woman's unacceptable behavior. But there was more in the General's expression, a certain guarded slyness Barron didn't like.

"I'll make coffee," Carlotta said. "Don't you run away, General, you hear?" She was drawling her words in a Southern fashion now. She walked into the kitchen, closing the door behind her.

Barron stood against the spinet. "She's an old friend," he said, thinking up lame excuses. "She's been through some bad times recently. Divorce, you understand. She's visiting me from America, a short vacation, a couple of days. I apologize for her behavior." He wanted to steer the subject away from Carlotta. "I have news of Streik."

The General said, "Streik. Yes. It was Streik I came to ask about —"

"We found him. It's taken care of. You have nothing to worry about now."

"Nothing to worry about," the General remarked.

"Streik's out of the way. He's gone. He needn't concern us."

The General made a gesture of finality, as if Streik were consigned to history, an unimportant matter. "The world is too small these days. People come and go. They meet, they part, they live their separate lives."

Barron wondered what the old boy was talking about.

"And sometimes we forget the people we've met. The places we've seen. I had a position of great authority at one time in life —"

"I know, I know —"

"Let me finish. My work involved a great number of acquaintances, assistants, associates, informers. Their names were kept on record, their photographs filed. I sat on top of a vast mountain of information. Another man might have found it too much to digest. But I was blessed, you see, with an astonishing memory. And it served me well. It served me very well." The General nodded in the direction of the kitchen. "Your strange friend, Barron. Divorced, you say. Just arrived from America to forget her marital distress, is that it?"

"Yes."

The General smiled and tapped the side of his skull in a knowing way. "I think not."

"I don't follow you, General."

"Barron, Barron. Do you take me for a fool?"

"Never," said Barron.

The General took a step toward Barron. He was still tapping his head. "In here, Barron. All locked away in here. All very easy to open, if you have a key."

The kitchen door opened. Carlotta came out carrying a tray. Barron sensed immediately a change in her mood, a lowering of the temperature in the room.

"Instant coffee," she said. "I couldn't find the tea."

She laid the tray on a coffee table, smiled at the General. This is wrong, Barron thought. On two small counts. Two small domestic counts.

There is no instant coffee in the kitchen. And she knows where the tea is kept.

She knows this place, this apartment.

It is going wrong.

"I brought biscuits. You like biscuits, General?" she asked. "Chocolate chip cookies. Tobias has a weakness for them, don't you, Tobias?"

The General stared at the tray. Carlotta moved quietly behind him. Barron's point of view was obscured by the old man's bulk for a moment. He didn't see Carlotta move, he was conscious only of the way the General gasped suddenly for breath, how his expression changed from one of keen attention to pained astonishment, how he swung around, turning toward Carlotta, a hand raised in the air, the gesture of a man clutching for support where no support is to be found.

"Dear God," the General said. "Dear God."

He went down on his knees, gripped the edge of the coffee table, toppled the tray, cookies fell around him, little brown discs in disarray. He tilted his head toward Barron, his eyes large with horrified surprise. Barron watched the knife go in a second time, then a third, heard flesh tear, saw the General slump to his hands and knees and try to crawl out of Carlotta's range, saw blood spurt and drip across the carpet.

The General slithered toward him as Carlotta struck again and again. Blood covered the General's face, ran over his scarf, spilled from the side of his face. He crawled as far as the place where Barron stood and he clutched the cuffs of Barron's trousers, smearing them. Carlotta brought the knife down directly into the back of the General's neck and the old man moaned, dropped his hands from Barron, turned over on his side, said something inaudible in German, and then lay still. But he was breathing, if you could call it that, his chest heaving, mouth open, throat rattling thickly. Carlotta shoved the knife between the old man's ribs and drew it downward in a ragged line, an autopsy performed by a psychotic.

She stood over the body. Her white shirt was streaked with the General's blood; her legs were daubed with red. It was in her hair, her face, as if she'd been targeted by spray paint. Immobilized, Barron watched her go down on her knees alongside the General.

"I met him once," she said. She might have been speaking to herself. "The only time I was ever in Berlin. He had a job he wanted me to do. It didn't work out. It didn't suit me. And I didn't like those STASI types. I could never have worked with them. He knew me as soon as he saw me, Barron. What else could I do?"

Barron stepped back, appalled, stricken by a sense of having stepped inside a viciously bad dream. None of this was real, none of this had happened. He couldn't take his eyes away from the lurid sight of the dead man, the red-stained carpet, the blemishes in the General's clothing. He was transfixed, paralyzed, trapped in a vision of red, red everywhere. The whole room might have been leaking blood. It was changed in his perception now, altered by murder, the echo of violence.

"Forgive me. I forgot," she said. "You have no taste for this kind of thing."

He couldn't speak. He closed his eyes. He had an after-image of blood. He saw it all over again, the General crawling across the carpet, Carlotta following him, the knife rising and falling, the cutting sound of steel on flesh, the ripping of cloth. He couldn't breathe. He had a barbed feeling around his heart. The air in the room seemed to reek of the stench of an abattoir, the stuff of death.

Carlotta stood up. She let the knife fall from her fingers. It dropped against the side of the General's face, where it reflected red light drably. Barron opened his eyes, turned his face away.

"Well?" she asked. "What was I supposed to do? Let him walk? He couldn't be trusted, Barron. Maybe he wouldn't blow the whistle immediately. Maybe he'd wait for the right moment. But one day he'd talk, he'd say I was associated with you, he'd know about my role in this. Don't you see? He would have had a lock on us for as long as he lived. I did this for you as much as for me."

Was she trying to say that this act of murder was a means of protecting *him?* He couldn't accept this. With trembling fingers he poured himself a large shot of cognac, which he tossed back rapidly; the fierce heat of the brandy made him feel sick and unsteady. His arms and legs tingled. He set his empty glass down, ran his hands across his face.

"Queasy?" she asked. "Are we upset, Tobias?"

He glanced at the knife that lay propped against the General's cheek. Then he looked at Carlotta, whose face was expressionless. She came across the floor and pressed her bloodstained body against him, her arms circling him, her damp red hands touching his skin.

"Now you know," she said. "You know it's no goddamn abstraction, Barron. It isn't fax messages and phone calls from distant places. It isn't men droning around a table and weapons being fired in faraway countries. It's here and now. It's reality. And you don't like it, do you? Just what the hell did you think, Barron? Did you just imagine you were immune, you had some kind of protection, you could pass on instructions and sleep easy and make believe you didn't have any direct responsibility? Sweet Christ."

I did this for you as much as for me.

"Look at him, Barron. Look at him." Her tone was strident.

Barron had a bizarre feeling of dislocation, as if his skull were not attached to his body, as if his body were elsewhere. She pressed her hands on either side of his face and turned his head so that he couldn't avoid looking at the body of the General who, in death, appeared to have deflated.

"I think you're ready now to hear the real truth about the death of Bryce Harcourt," she said.

LYON

28

It was nine o'clock and raining when Pagan and Foxworth took a cab from Lyon Airport. Foxworth gave the cabdriver Audrey Roczak's address on Rue de Marseille, which lay on the east bank of the Rhône, close to the university. They crossed the river by the Pont Galleni. Where the Rue de Marseille intersected the Rue Salomon, the driver stopped the cab. Foxie stepped out first and erected his umbrella and held it over Pagan's head, but umbrellas were useless in this kind of downpour. Foxie paid, and the taxi pulled away.

"Bleak," Foxie said.

"If you're a tourist," Pagan remarked. "What number are we looking for?"

Foxworth had it memorized. They walked a few yards, passing the darkened windowfronts of various stores, a plumbing-supply shop, a glasscutter's, a small shuttered bistro in which chairs were inverted on tables and a man pushed a broom back and forth.

Audrey Roczak's apartment was situated over the bistro. Tiny nameplates were stuck on a door. Pagan flicked his cigarette lighter and held it against the names and when he found ROCZAK, he pressed the bell, holding his finger upon it for a good thirty seconds. There was no response, nothing from beyond the door.

"Now what," said Foxie, shivering under the umbrella.

Pagan looked the length of the dismal street. Rain ran down the side of his face, pounded his overnight bag. "Either we find a warm place to sit or we ring every bloody bell on this door until somebody answers." The street didn't look too promising. There were no welcoming café lights nearby, no pension, no signs of life save for passing traffic. He turned his attention back to the buzzers, of which there were six, and he rang each in turn.

The door was eventually opened by a small woman dressed in what seemed to be a garland of ostrich and peacock feathers. The face that peered from the center of this flamboyant arrangement was small and nut brown, shriveled. The reek of camphor overwhelmed Pagan.

Foxie said, "*Bon soir. Nous cherchons Audrey Roczak.*"

"What a *deplorable* accent you have," said the small woman in English. "You're English. Home Counties, I'd say."

"Well, yes," said Foxie. "Surrey."

"I can always tell, *always*. I'm from Kent. But that was long ago." The woman shuffled her feathery attachments and looked at Frank Pagan. He was reminded of a decayed bird, something stuffed and stuck in the window of a taxidermist long gone out of business. The little blue eyes were alert, though, and probing. "And who are you?"

"Police," Pagan said. He showed his identity card.

"London police? Oh, I say. London policemen looking for Auders. Well well. Whatever has she *done?*" The little woman held the door wide, allowing Pagan and Foxworth to step inside the hallway out of the weather.

"The standard phrase is that she might be helpful in our inquiries," Pagan said.

"Oh, I *do* like that. You sound like a man in a detective story. Have you read Dorothy L. Sayers?"

Pagan admitted he hadn't.

"I daresay she's gone out of fashion rather. The old body-in-the-library stuff does seem *rather* tame when you've got fellows dashing around with tommy guns or whatever they're called. Why don't you both come this way and we'll dry you out a little?"

Tommy guns, Pagan thought, and glanced at Foxie, raised his eyebrows, then followed the feathery woman along the hallway to a large room where a hundred or so framed and signed photographs of old film and theater celebrities hung on the walls. In one corner sat a black-lacquered grand piano, drowned by arrangements of plants and even more photographs. Chinese paper lanterns, screens adorned with dragons, a collection of filigreed seashells — the impression was of eccentric clutter and nostalgia.

"My name's Deirdre Chapman," the little woman said. "Of course, you wouldn't have heard of me. Why should you? You're both too young." She gestured at the pictures on the walls. Pagan recognized Maurice Chevalier, Edith Piaf, Jean Gabin, and some defunct crooners, like Frankie Laine and Rosemary Clooney; all the pictures were signed to Deirdre with one or another form of affection. "I had my heyday in the music halls. I was *quite* the chanteuse in my time. Why don't you put your bags down and come closer to the fire and tell me all about Auders?"

Deirdre Chapman poured three glasses of sherry from a decanter and placed them on a wickerwork tray. "Help yourself. I don't want to hear any of that can't-drink-on-duty business."

Both men took the sherry. "Cheers," Pagan said, and glanced at Foxworth, who was looking bemused.

"Married a Frenchman, in case you're wondering why I'm in *this* particular town," the woman said. She fluttered in a way suggestive of a coquette with marvelous memories. *I wasn't always old, boys.* "I sang in Paris toward the end of my career. We retired down here. Henri died three years ago. I *do* so miss the old blighter, bless his heart."

Deirdre Chapman sat in a lime green wicker chair close to the fire. "Now. What *has* Auders gotten herself involved in?"

Pagan tasted his sherry, which was rich and warming. "As I said, we don't think she's done anything. We're hoping she might answer a few questions, that's all. But she doesn't seem to be at home."

"Oh, I'd be *ever* so disappointed if you'd come all the way to Lyon just to ask a few *questions*. I was sort of hoping for a grand scandal." Deirdre Chapman gazed at Pagan. "If you were to ask me about Auders, I'd say she's a woman with a past."

"How do you mean?"

"An aura of, well, mystery surrounds her. She's definitely *not* what she appears to be. The cats and the oil paintings do not fool me.

One look at her and you can just *feel* she knows all *kinds* of secrets."

Pagan wondered if it was worth the time pursuing Deirdre Chapman's talk of auras and feelings, or if it would merely prove to be an unenlightening ramble down the byways of her imagination. She lived alone, she missed her dead husband, she read detective fiction; the ingredients were all there for a ragout of speculation. "Has Audrey ever done or said anything . . . out of the ordinary?"

"You're not *following* me, are you? I'm talking about instincts and insights. I'm talking about intuition. She doesn't *have* to do anything out of the ordinary to be an object of mystification, does she? No no. It's in her manner, do you see? It's in her eyes."

"What's in her eyes?" Pagan asked wearily.

"The weight of grave secrets. If you saw her, you'd understand what I'm *trying* to *tell* you." Deirdre Chapman brandished her glass of sherry as if Pagan's obtuseness exasperated her. The nut-brown little face seemed to develop a snout as she tilted her head upward to survey him.

Pagan slumped into silence. He'd let Foxworth pick up the slack. Foxie had more patience with dotty people anyway. He had better manners in general.

"When did you last see her, Mrs. Chapman?" Foxie asked.

"It's Madame Delacroix, actually. But you wouldn't be expected to know that. How could you?"

Foxie smiled gently. You could see Foxworth guiding tour parties of aged persons around ancient monuments, answering questions in a measured manner.

"Well. I saw Auders only yesterday. It must have been late afternoon. Let's say it was five o'clock. Yes. She was coming down the stairs in a *great* rush. Which was rather unusual, I must say, because she's normally an *unhurried* sort of person. I asked her where she was going in such an *ungodly* hurry and . . . *This* is very uncharacteristic of her. She was actually quite *brusque* with me. Normally we'd have a little chat, nothing of great *import*, don't you know? But yesterday . . ."

"So she said nothing?" Foxie asked.

"Well she muttered *something* about having to buy oils before the art shop closed and then she was gone! Just like that!" Deirdre

Chapman clearly found the recollection unsettling, a major disturbance in a life that was otherwise routine.

"Oils," said Foxie.

"Oils. She dabbles in painting. Oh, lord, great *dreary* things, all blacks and browns. I don't believe she's picked up a brush in months. Showed some of her work to a dealer and he *wasn't* encouraging. Big blow to her ego. American, you see. They always seem to have ego problems, don't you think?"

"So you haven't seen or heard from her since she left," Foxie said.

"No, I haven't."

Deirdre Chapman poured herself another glass of sherry, a tiny amount. She offered the bottle. Both Pagan and Foxworth declined.

"Was she carrying any luggage?" Pagan asked.

"A purse, I do believe. That's all. The cats worry me rather. She has about six or seven of them upstairs. And if she *didn't* come back last night, how are the animals to be *fed?* It simply isn't like her to *leave* the cats alone."

Pagan set down his empty glass on the table. Fatigue gnawed on him. When had he last slept? "Has anyone been asking for her?"

"Apart from yourselves, no."

"Are you sure you have no idea where she might have gone?"

"Well. She does have a little studio not so very far away. She might have gone there."

"Do you have the address?" Pagan asked.

"I can tell you where it is, but I don't have the *actual* address."

"We'd be obliged," Pagan said, and took out his notebook, anxious to be gone from this room, which was having a deleterious effect on his senses — the stench of mothballs, stale feathers, furniture wax, the ghostly photographs of long-dead smiles. The crypts of other people's keepsakes made him uncomfortable.

"Fire away," he said, pencil poised over open notebook.

Deirdre Chapman stood up. Her feathers appeared to wilt, as if the imminent departure of her unexpected visitors made her unhappy.

"Now then. Let me see. Do you know this city?" she asked.

Pagan shook his head.

"Do you have a car?"

"No."

"Then you'll need a taxi. Ask the driver for Vieux Lyon. Get him to drop you off at the Place Saint-Jean. Are you getting this down?"

Pagan said he was. Deirdre Chapman went on, "There's a narrow street just *beyond* the Place. Now I can't *quite* remember its name, but on the corner of the street is a café called Bip. Write that down. Pass the café, keep going, oh, perhaps twenty meters or so, and you'll come to a small shop that sells puppets."

"Puppets," Pagan echoed in a dutiful way.

"The window's filled with all *kinds* of dolls and puppets. Guignol and the like. Above the shop is Auder's studio."

Pagan shut his notebook. Foxworth, sensing Frank's growing impatience, seeing his look of quiet weariness, thanked the woman. Reluctantly, she escorted them along the hall to the front door. Rain still pounded the street demonically.

"This has been *fun*," Deirdre Chapman said. "I do so hope you find what you're looking for."

"So do I," Pagan said.

"And I do hope Auders isn't in any deep bother." Deirdre Chapman raised her face, cheek turned toward Pagan, for a farewell kiss. Thinking the matter more than a little theatrical, Pagan bussed her quickly, and Foxie did the same, and then the door was closed and Deirdre could be heard singing "My Funny Valentine" as she went drifting back to her room of memories.

Foxie opened his wet umbrella and held it aloft.

"I think we should find a bloody taxi before we drown," Pagan said.

"Strange old thing, Deirdre," Foxie said.

"Strange is right. I kept resisting the urge to feed her bread-crumbs."

■

They were obliged to walk several blocks before a taxi appeared to take them to the Place Saint-Jean, where they looked for the Café Bip. Pagan tried to imagine himself into another season, Lyon in high summer, the sidewalk tables crowded by tourists, parasols, carafes of wine being lazily drunk in the sunlight. It was difficult; you couldn't foresee this rain — so merciless, so severe — ever stopping. The city had an abandoned feel to it despite the lights in restaurant windows and the people who hurried into doorways for shelter and the occasional gust of music that blew out into the night.

They walked past the Café Bip into a narrow street, hardly more than a passageway, where they found the shop Deirdre Chapman had described. In its palely lit window a variety of wooden puppets gazed out with a certain malign indifference. They had a disquieting effect, as if they were simply awaiting an infusion of some dreadful life; a windowful of small zombies. Pagan surveyed them a moment, then followed Foxie, who had paused outside a door adjoining the shop.

"This would appear to be the place," Foxie said, and he looked up, seeing a lit window across which a thin curtain was drawn. He examined the door, couldn't find a bell, only a large iron knocker in the form of an animal's paw. He banged it a few times against the wood, waited. Nothing happened. Pagan, who stood beneath the umbrella, stared in a morose way at the sturdy door.

"I don't think it's the kind we can just kick in, Foxie."

"I'd say not."

"Keep hammering."

Foxie repeated the act of raising and dropping the iron upon the wood. Pagan moved to the edge of the sidewalk and stared up at the curtained window. Nothing was visible, no shadow moved.

"What now?" Foxie asked.

Slicks of rain slid from a spoke of the umbrella and slid around Pagan's nostrils. "Let's wander around behind the building," he suggested. "There might be some rear access."

They walked to the end of the street, turned into another passageway, fumbled down a darkened lane which appeared to be the back of the building in which Audrey Roczak had her studio.

"This would be it, I think," Foxie said. He indicated a short flight of ancient stone steps that rose to a door. Pagan considered the aesthetics of rear entrances, how unlike their front counterparts they usually were, poor relations, places where garbage was stacked and concealed. You could have roses and ivy and bloody Doric columns at the front and all manner of rusty detritus at the back.

They climbed the crumbling steps to the door. Above the door was a darkened skylight. Foxie tried the handle. Locked. "We could use a flashlight right now," he muttered. "This might be the wrong place. What would happen if we battered the door down only to discover a harmless bourgeois family dining away quite merrily on potatoes lyonnaise?"

Pagan gave the handle a twist. There was a certain amount of play in the lock, a space between jamb and catch. If he had a strong object he could insert into the tiny space . . . He was considering this when abruptly a light came on and the door flew open and a stout red-haired woman in a long skirt stood there with a gun in her hand.

"Fuckers," she said. She leveled the pistol directly at Pagan, who, assaulted by the glare of electric light, flinched and stepped back. Looking directly into a gun was like gazing into an infinity of darkness. Your own.

"Miserable fuckers," the woman said. She held the gun in such a way it was obvious she knew how to use it, and even more apparent that she wouldn't think twice about pulling the trigger. Pagan looked more closely at her now, conscious of large earrings, a wide lipsticked mouth hardened in anger.

"Miss Roczak," he said.

She raised the gun very slightly, directing it toward Pagan's head. He looked at her: Audrey Roczak, one-time minor operative in the grim cities of Eastern Europe, a carrier of messages, letters left in drops, passwords and codes and safe houses, an imagination fevered by the temperature of the times.

"Miss Roczak," he said again. The gun could go off. Quite easily. "We're looking for a man called Jake Streik."

"Never heard of him," she said.

Pagan sighed. "Try a little harder," he suggested.

"You're not listening to me, fella."

"On the contrary. I'm listening hard. But I'm not believing."

"You don't quite get it, do you? I never heard of Jake Streik. Never. You've got thirty seconds to back off before I employ this," and she waved the pistol at Pagan, then at Foxie.

"You and Streik," Pagan said. "Old comrades in arms. Prague, was it? Warsaw? Come on, Audrey. You're not going to fire that gun. You know it. We know it. All we want is some information about your old pal Jake. We believe he's in trouble —"

"Yeah, right, and you want to help Streik, whoever he is."

"If we can," Pagan said.

"Twenty seconds," she said.

Pagan raised his hand. "I'll show you some identification."

"All the ID in the world wouldn't make a damn bit of difference to me. Keep your hand away from your pocket. Don't take chances, I'm not in the mood."

Pagan said, "We've come from London. From Scotland Yard —"

"And I'm Anastasia."

"Audrey," Pagan said. "*You* know Jake's in trouble. *We* know he's in trouble. The Undertakers want him, don't they?"

Audrey Roczak was quiet a moment. She kept the gun level, but the expression in her eyes altered just a little. The mention of the Undertakers appeared to have softened her somewhat, caused her a small flash of doubt.

"Okay. Let's see your plastic," she said. "Do it slowly."

Pagan took out his wallet, handed it to the woman, watched her flip it open and glance at it in the light.

"Frank Pagan," she said. "Good old Special Branch." She looked at Foxworth. "Who are you?"

Foxie produced his own ID, passing it to Audrey Roczak, who scrutinized it carefully, as if all forms of laminated identity cards were suspect. Pagan wondered how many times in her own history she'd used false documents. She clutched both cards and looked from Pagan to Foxworth, then back again. You could see uncertainty working through her, little fissures opening.

"You're not from the Undertakers," she said.

Pagan shook his head. "All we want is to talk to Jake Streik."

She was silent for a long time. With her face tilted to one side, she appeared to be listening to the rattle of rain falling on plastic trash sacks. "You say you want to help him."

Pagan nodded.

Audrey Roczak, with a slight gesture of the gun, indicated that they should step inside. She kicked the door shut quickly, then walked to the foot of a staircase, where she paused.

"You're probably too late," she said in a dry manner.

■

Knock knock knock. Streik thinks the sound is coming from the unspeakable pain in his chest but then in a moment of clarity understands it issues from the external world, whatever that is nowadays. Edges are fudged, things come and go, there are tidal movements in his head. Pain has this diabolical way of diminishing your humanity, you dwindle until you're nothing more than the goddamn embodiment of your hurt, you're a tiny figure spied through a keyhole of agony. *Knock knock knock.* The sound changes along the way to *Rap rap rap*, thunderous, echoing, urgent, and although he is possessed by the desire to get up and do something about it — what? he doesn't know — he finds he's crippled, incapable of moving, his mouth and throat dry, limbs wasted, and even his heartbeat, to which he tries to listen, is as faint as the footfall of a mouse. I am dying, he supposes. The thought, initially so gratifying, turns around, and then he panics, opens his eyes, looks around a room he's never seen before, unlit candles stuck in dusty wine bottles, stalactites of wax, easels, jars of paint brushes, old crushed paint-streaked newspapers on the floor.

Dying. Well. It isn't so good. You couldn't say a lot in its favor. You wouldn't want to write home about it. Hello, folks, wish you were here. His head slumps back against what is presumably a pillow, then he calls out hoarsely for Audrey — *he remembers Audrey now* — but there isn't an answer. He gazes feebly into light from a ratty fringed lamp shade hanging low from the flaky ceiling. He's never, *never* in his entire life, felt so utterly alone.

But here she is. Here's Audrey now. She comes to the sofa where he lies and stoops over him, fusses with the sheet that covers his body, a red sheet in fact, and her earrings dangle forward from her face and create glassy flickers of light.

"Jake," she says, and she's a long way off, oh babe. "Jake. Can you hear me?"

He nods his head, but what an effort.

"Jake, listen. This man is from Scotland Yard. Special Branch. He wants to talk to you."

Streik raises a hand, but it falls back. The trap of gravity. Scotland Yard, he thinks. His head is filled with confused images of lonesome mountains and bagpipes and whisky, then he makes the true connection. The guy who looks down at him is okay, concerned gray eyes, firm mouth, but Streik sees his own death in the man's look of pity.

"Aud," Streik says. "Something. For the pain."

Audrey looks helpless, goes away, comes back with tablets which she places on his tongue. A bolt of pain — you couldn't call it pain, it's gone way beyond that now — crucifies him to the sofa.

"Frank Pagan," the guy says.

The name's remotely familiar to Streik. But then again, any name might be *remotely* familiar when you're dying, when your memory's shot. How can you say for sure you've ever heard the name before?

"Can you hear me, Jake?" Pagan asks.

Streik moves his head, blinks, licks his lips. He sees Audrey in the background somewhere, her big reliable body shimmering under the light.

"You and Bryce Harcourt," says this Pagan.

"Bryce," Streik mumbles.

"I need to know what you were involved in. Can you tell me that, Jake?"

Audrey says something in a tone of voice that is one of vague complaint. Streik can't catch the words. Anyway, he's thinking about Bryce, about London.

"Bryce," he says. "He okay?"

"Bryce is dead," says Pagan.

Dead? Streik wonders. Somehow he isn't as surprised as he wants to be. He feels only a slight regret. When you're dying, maybe you want everybody else to join you. Come, share the amusement of it all, participate in the big black party, this way to the horrors.

Pagan leans closer. "Can you talk to me, Jake?"

"Yeah." Streik's voice is a croak.

"What did you and Bryce do together, Jake?" Pagan's breath has a faintly sweet smell, a light boozy aroma.

"Money," Streik says.

"Money?" Pagan seems to be bringing his face closer all the time to Streik.

"Millions."

"You took it to Bryce, is that it? You took it to the Undertakers."

Streik tries to nod, thinking how complicated this dying is, it isn't the simple business everybody tells you it is, but under that there's the deeper complexity of communicating to Pagan the intricacies of arrangements between himself and Bryce, the trips from America to London, the diplomatic bag routine, they were sacks not bags, sacks and sacks, all tagged, all secure, beyond the penetration of customs agents. PROPERTY OF THE UNITED STATES OF AMERICA. He panics again, and says, "Aud, help me, Aud, I'm fucking dying, I'm dying."

She is holding his hand. He thinks of priests and sickbeds and last rites and the smell of death and suddenly he wants absolution for the German hitchhiker, but priests are like cops, you can't find one when you need one.

"You'll pull through," she tells him.

The lie is enormous in her eyes.

"Yeah yeah," Streik says. The second *yeah* — that's a wasted word, a ruined breath.

"Who gave you the money in the first place, Jake?" Pagan asks.

Streik thinks Bryce is suddenly in the room, he sees Bryce's face float above him, a pale looming balloon. "Bryce," he says. "What's it like, old buddy? What's it like?"

Pagan says, "Try and concentrate, Jake. You were saying where the money came from. Remember?"

"Money?" Back to earth, bump, no Bryce, no cheery word, hallucination.

"Where did you get it? Who gave it to you?"

"Yeah, well," Streik says. Lips cracked. Tongue swollen. "Different . . . guys."

"You know any names?"

"Guy called Monty Rhodes . . ."

"Rhodes? Is he connected to the Undertakers?"

Streik groans. "He runs the US end."

"Anyone else? Any other names?"

"No names. Faces." Streik has a flutter in his chest. He imagines small sharp teeth gnawing on the bloody tissue of his heart, claws hooked into his liver. He's out on a tide now, floating to a dead estuary. He thinks he sees Montgomery Rhodes in his black shades waving to him from the shore.

"What was the money for, Jake?"

Streik remembers but before he can say anything, the sheet lightning of pain convulses him, and he moans, clutches his chest, tries to be sick, his mouth filling with sticky strands of saliva. Now Audrey is holding a wet rag to his forehead and the pain ebbs for a time and Pagan's face, which had gone out of focus, comes swimming in again, and Streik has a wondrous moment of clarity in which everything seems suddenly very very simple.

"Bryce and me," he says. "We knew."

"Tell me, Jake," says Pagan. "Tell me what you knew."

Streik looks at Audrey, and she nods, it's okay, you can talk to this man. There's some real odd weather in Streik's head, first a blizzard, then dippy rainbows. He looks into Pagan's gray eyes. He hears Audrey say something to Pagan about quitting with all the questions, can't you feel the guy's pain for Chrissakes, but Pagan isn't about to stop, you can see it in his face, he wants the rest of Streik's deathbed narrative.

"Money all over the place," Streik says. "Spread like fucking manure."

"What was the money for?"

Memory seeps like sewage through a leaching field. Memory dies with the body. Streik thinks of all the blackness awaiting him. A nostate. A nothing. He looks into Pagan's face.

"Oh, man," says Streik. Why isn't this Pagan grasping the fucking point? Does he think there's all the time in the world? "Chaos . . . weapons . . . you name it . . ." Streik feels a deepening lethargy, which has to be death, has to be, no two ways about it, and he's panicked again, doesn't want to go, isn't ready, hasn't prepared himself for a confrontation with the Maker, but maybe there isn't a Maker, and if there isn't, he doesn't have to carry the guilt about the German into eternity with him, does he . . .

Streik has the need to touch something, to anchor himself, so grips the sleeve of Pagan's wet overcoat. "The way these guys think. Peace is bad for business. You don't do business when you got stability . . ."

Hold the coat, Jake. Keep holding. Don't let go.

Pagan asks, "Where does Carlotta come in, Jake?"

Streik opens his mouth. Carlotta, he thinks. Carlotta rhymes with oughta. Carlotta oughta mean something, but it doesn't. Petrified by darkness, he stares into Pagan's face, shakes his head, he's slipping, he's going, his candle is being snuffed out, oh God don't let it be like this, I don't want to go, please please don't take me, let me dally and linger and I promise to be gooooood from now on . . .

But his hand slips from Pagan's sleeve, falls to his side, his head rolls on the pillow, he gasps, shudders, feels the quietly insistent pressure of oblivion.

"I didn't mean to shoot the kid," he says inaudibly, and closes his eyes. His thick lips part with a soft fleshy sound.

■

Audrey Roczak, her eyes red-rimmed, drew the sheet across Streik's face. Pagan stepped back from the dead man, listened to rain on the window. He was conscious of Foxie at his side. Nobody spoke for a time. Then Audrey Roczak, lighting a Gitane, said, "I knew he wasn't going to make it. At least I thought he could die here, where nobody could find him. I guess the old busybody *la chanteuse* told you I might have come here. Old fraud. All those photographs. She signed them herself. She never knew any of those people. Even her dead husband's a fiction. She's a spinster from way back." Audrey Roczak looked more sad than angry. "Jake had papers stuffed in the trunk of his car. You're welcome to them. He sure as hell doesn't need them." She picked up a purse from behind an easel and, reaching inside, pulled out a wad of sheets, which she handed to Pagan as if they were distasteful to touch. It was a bulky collection.

"Maybe they'll be some help to you. I don't know."

Pagan folded the papers, tucked them carefully in the inner pocket of his coat. He'd look at them later, when he was out of the dead man's presence.

"Poor bastard," she said. "All he ever really wanted was to belong to something. And half-assed espionage was the only club that would have him. Terrific, huh?"

Pagan gazed away from the body of the fat man. Death had compressed the room. He stared at the canvases stacked against one wall. They were as somber as Deirdre Chapman had said, infinitely depressing in a way that had nothing to do with their artless quality.

Audrey Roczak sucked on her cigarette. "One thing's damn sure. You work for the Undertakers, you can't count on a fucking pension at the end of the day."

Pagan could still feel the pressure of the dead man's fingers on his sleeve. He wanted to get out of this wretched room, out into the rainy air.

"Well, Frank Pagan," the woman said. "Have you learned anything? Or do you have questions for me?"

It happened before Pagan had time to answer, the shattering of glass, the frame of the window buckling, the curtain blowing back — it happened quickly, frighteningly, an outburst of red-purple flame, a cracking sound followed by dense smoke that sucked everything out of the world.

VENICE

29

In choppy darkened waters beyond the island of Murano, the engine of the launch was silenced. Schialli stepped down to the stern, balancing himself delicately against the robust sway of the vessel. Barron watched him reach down to grab the General under the shoulders. He grunted with the weight of the dead man. Carlotta, in a long black waterproof coat, took hold of the General's ankles.

Barron tried to think of the General as something that had never been human, but pictures kept flickering through his mind, staccato images, the knife going into the General's back, the dying man's hands on the cuffs of his trousers, the way Carlotta had looked at him and said, *It's reality. It's no abstraction.* Reality now was the sight of Carlotta and Schialli raising the corpse of the General and lowering it over the stern and letting it slide into deep water, where it drifted away on unpredictable currents like a great dead fish.

Schialli clambered back to the wheel, started the motor, turned the launch around in the direction of Venice. Carlotta shook her hair free and leaned her body against Barron. By the pale stern light she looked vibrant; the whip of rain had colored her cheeks. Her eyes were bright.

"You see, Toby. Easy. Simple."

"Yes," Barron said.

"When he washes up on some beach, nobody will be able to identify him. No papers. Nothing. An accident. A suicide. A pauper's
grave. The matter is ended. The menace is over."

Yes, yes. Barron gazed toward the lights of Venice. He imagined
the General's body twisting and turning on the tides, sucked under
by whirlpools, snapped at by predatory sea creatures. He heard water splash against the hull of the launch and for a moment imagined
the General rising from the dead, fingers on the handrail, white face
emerging. He had a sense of things getting away from him. He felt
the slick material of Carlotta's wet coat against his flesh as she raised
a hand to the side of his face in a gesture of intimacy. He didn't
move. Did she think this murder enhanced their relationship? that
he was somehow closer now to her own dark world? that the death
of the General was a bridge between them? Come inside *my* world,
Tobias. Be my partner in the unhallowed places *I* haunt. Hold hands
with me at the gravesides of all the dead.

He thought about the death of Bryce Harcourt, and he remembered Carlotta's voice. *You want me to get rid of a guy and you don't
want it to be obvious, right? So how do you achieve that? Most people would
go with the idea of an anonymous gunman, say, a guy that comes and goes
in the dark. Boom and over with. But that's banal, Barron. That lacks
imagination. Besides, it draws highly focused attention. You get cops crawling all over the place because you've given them one corpse, and one corpse
is manageable, they can cope with that, they can investigate that. So, you
create a situation that isn't manageable, you give them an investigation
that has them stretched to their fucking limits, that's how you do it. You
confound them, Barron. You give them a goddamn catastrophe. You make
it so they can't see the woods for the trees.*

A catastrophe. The woods for the trees. You confound them. He
tried to see this reasoning from her point of view, but it was like
looking into a distorted mirror. Her logic was beyond him; and because he couldn't comprehend it, it was unassailable. For a second
he had a flash, a glimmer into her reasoning, but then it became
eclipsed. All he could think of was the train exploding, all he could
think of was pain and death.

*It was brilliant. Everybody thinks the Irish or some other terrorist outfit
did it. Everybody leaps to that conclusion. So they're off and running in all*

the wrong directions. He'd seen in her eye a light of demonic intensity such as you might associate with people who have undergone a holy experience. Her fervor was religious, her focus so narrow it suggested a laser incinerating everything before it.

To kill Bryce Harcourt she'd killed more than a hundred people.

He tried to get his mind around that fact but all he could hear was Carlotta's voice ringing in his ears. *If you don't want to get your hands dirty, don't play in the mud, baby. Stick to what you do best. Lock yourself in your little room and read your faxes and make your phone calls and hold your clandestine meetings and keep track of your messengers and go out and do those good deeds you seem to believe in — but when it comes to death, Barron, leave it. Leave it to other people, leave it to the experts.*

Leave death to other people, he thought. The experts. Like herself. She was correct, of course. She was perfectly right. He was an organizer, not a killer. He was an orchestrator, not an assassin. People died; that was not his responsibility. It was an abstraction, a matter of numbers. People died in all kinds of ways, in earthquakes and accidents, by bomb and gunfire. The world went on. That's what it came down to in the end.

But —

He stared at the lights of the city, and he shivered. Venice seemed distant, a trick of light, a mirage of sorts. He thought: You made all the connections yourself. You established the networks. You introduced the Undertakers to Kinsella and his associates, those bland-faced captains of the munitions industries, those contractors and subcontractors of death, men whose fortunes came from making the machinery of war, from armaments and computer systems designed to guide missiles. You brought the General and his European friends into the alliance because there were mutual interests, great profits to be made. You passed on instructions and commands, joined the wires together. You. Only you. You wanted the power that comes from being at the center of things. You enjoyed all the toy soldiers at your disposal. You moved in elevated circles, magic restaurants and exclusive clubs where restaurateurs shook your hand and club owners ushered you to your own table, you walked in the hushed hallways of power, and the boy who'd begun life dumped on the doorstep of a convent in goddamn Poughkeepsie to be raised by nuns was dead and buried, he'd ceased to exist, he'd risen like a rocket without leaving traces of his origins. *Yes, yes.*

But in the beginning it had all been so simple, paper transactions, discreet meetings with men like the General and Kinsella and Caan, disembodied voices on phone lines. It had involved incidents in distant cities, events you might have watched, in a detached fashion, on a newsreel in a darkened cinema. He remembered once seeing a scratchy old film of British soldiers, faces masked against the stench of decay, bulldozing the victims of Belsen into pits, and he'd felt at the time he was watching something staged, an affair with only a tangential connection to the real world. He'd never been truly connected to anything, he thought, not to history, not to himself, not to the women who'd paid for his services.

"Forget it, Barron. It's over. It's done. It's luggage, Barron. Let it go."

Yes, he'd let it go, he'd have to, what choice did he have? He looked into Carlotta's face, stunned by her expression of innocence. This was nothing to her, a boat ride through darkness to a fabled city, a quick pleasure cruise. Already the General had been consigned to memory.

The woman touched the back of his gloved hand. "Poor Tobias. You never once saw the true picture. Now you smell the blood, babe. And you can't stand it, can you? You just can't stand the stench."

A night bird flew above the launch, circled hungrily, then was gone. Barron looked at the lights of Harry's Bar and of the Bauer Gruenwald Hotel and thought of Kinsella and Rhodes in their suites. He thought of them waiting for Helix to happen, Rhodes sipping cognac, Kinsella tossing down whisky sours as he walked up and down his big comfortable sitting room, perhaps fielding phone calls from his associates, his colleagues who waited anxiously for news in Bermuda or Coral Gables or Washington or wherever men of inconceivable wealth and devious political ambitions gathered. Men who wanted the profits to be harvested from turmoil.

Men like himself.

Carlotta turned her face toward him, kissed him passionately. The kiss disturbed him, and not just because the night air had chilled her lips. He was drawn down into her mouth, he felt the restless flick of her tongue against his gums, heard her excited breathing; he had a sense of being embraced in the depths of a sepulchre. Her hands moved inside his overcoat, fumbled with his belt, searched for him, found nothing. The kiss seemed to set a seal on his corruption.

"Something wrong, Tobe? Equipment failure?" She drew away from him, laughing quietly. "Can't quite cut it, huh? Not in the mood? Too much on your mind?"

He said nothing. He looked back the way the launch had traveled and he was thinking again of the General rising and sinking in waters the color of a black moonless night.

Carlotta slung an arm around his waist. "Never mind. It's only a small failure. You'll get over it. Everything passes, Barron. Everything decays. Remember that." She stepped away from him, leaning against the rail, studying the water. Everything decays. She was so very composed, so certain of herself. She was flushed with confidence. He felt lost and dizzy.

Schialli turned off the Grand Canal, docked the launch, tied it. He assisted Carlotta to disembark. Barron followed. They went to the apartment, where Schialli unlocked the door. Inside the elevator the silence was interrupted only by the creak of pulleys as the cage rose in the shaft. The apartment was cold. The room in which the General had been stabbed smelled of the cleaning fluid Schialli had used to remove bloodstains from the carpet.

Schialli disappeared in his solemnly quiet manner, leaving Barron alone with Carlotta. "You see," she said, gesturing around the room. "Life goes on. Nothing's changed."

Barron poured himself a shot of bourbon and walked to the fireplace, where with one swift motion of his hand he swept aside all the photographs from the mantelpiece, causing them to fly through the air and settle here and there in mounds of broken glass. Marcos, Arafat, Caan, Bush, the others — they lay in a shattered heap.

"Breaking free, are we?" she asked. "Destroying the past? Or just yourself?"

Barron looked across the room at her. The chemical smell assaulted him. He wanted to say something, but no words came. He

sat in an armchair and tossed back the drink and surveyed the
wreckage on the floor. She dropped her coat, came toward him,
lowered herself on the arm of his chair and ran fingers through his
hair. He pulled his face away from her.

"The arrows of conscience, Tobias? Oh, God. To think I had you
down in my book as the kind of guy nothing ever touched. Mister
Cool in the transcendental white suit. You sailed along, you could
walk on water, you could even fly. Now something's singed your
poor old wings. Now you can't get off the ground. Sad, sad Tobias.
You don't see the world the way it is. It's violent. Violence comes
more naturally to the beast than charity, or spontaneous acts of
kindness, or love. Violence is what we all do best, whether we like
the fact or not."

He looked past her, seeing the place where the General had finally come to rest. Where Schialli had doused and scrubbed, the
rug was discolored, pinkish. She moved her body, spread her legs,
sat on his lap with her skirt drawn up to her thighs. He felt the
warmth of her against his knees.

"Come on, Tobe. Come on. Touch me. Feel me." She took his
reluctant hand and slid it under the skirt and drew it up the soft
texture of her inner thigh. She directed his fingers and thrust them
inside her and tossed back her head. "Come on, what are you waiting for, you want to fuck me, don't you? You want to fuck it all out
of your system, don't you? Come on, Tobe. Screw me. Screw me."
She pushed aside his coat and unzipped him. He remembered the
knife going in and out, the ripping of flesh, the old man crawling
across the carpet. He thought of an Underground carriage blasted
into nothing.

She tugged at him, pulling him to the floor. He allowed himself
to be drawn on top of her, felt his fingers push her skirt up beyond
the waist, and then — possessed by a dreadful need — he tore her
underwear aside, entered her, rolled over and over with her as he
fucked her with brute determination, without tenderness, seeking
an unattainable release from the violence he'd seen in this room.
They twisted, turned, rolled. He stared into her eyes, she looked
back without flinching, as if she were saying, *Go on, fuck me, hurt me
if you think you can.* And he wanted to, he wanted her to feel pain.

He forced himself deep into her and she kept saying, *Harder harder harder*, as if nothing could satisfy her.

He shuddered inside her and then lay silent and still. He listened to his heartbeat and the way his blood drummed. Depleted, he saw that he lay in the precise place where the General had died. He saw the discolored patch of carpet under him. He didn't move. He lowered his face into her neck. He felt imprisoned by the woman's presence.

After a time she slid out from under him, stood up, straightened her skirt, then knelt alongside him. She touched the back of his neck. "There, there. You feel better now. Don't you? You feel so much better." She stroked his cheek. Her tone of voice was condescendingly proprietorial.

He raised himself wearily on an elbow.

His thoughts were suddenly filled with the rush-hour crowd in the London Underground, with death in Berlin, the explosion in Prague. His head was crammed with images of planes and ships ferrying guns into Cuba, Ireland, Somalia, South Africa, the Philippines, the theaters in which he operated, all the projects he'd so nicely code-named as if the reality behind the sweet-sounding names could be masked by words. He had a feeling of being underwater, his oxygen running low.

Carlotta took his hands between her own. "You have to move on. You can't dwell on what's past. You listening to me? Lesson number one. You don't come back from the dead."

He turned over on his back, looked up at the chandelier, an intricate maze of mauve Venetian glass.

"Lesson number two. When you've buried the dead, you go on living." She took from the pocket of her blouse the Russian identity card he'd given her, and she tossed it on the rug. "Now. Suppose we discuss this. Suppose we talk about this Alyssia Baranova and what the future holds in store for her."

He picked the card up, felt the smooth laminated surface. Carlotta observed him, saw the way his fingers shook. She had a sense of having triumphed over him, dynamited the struts of his self-confidence. He was riddled now with the woodworm of uncertainty, his self-assurance had been eroded, his complicity was complete. All the airtight compartments of the man had been punctured.

And now, now she had control. And control was freedom. She'd liberated herself from him by bringing him down into her own world. Suddenly she was thinking of London, the Underground tunnel, then the blood-rich room, the scissors. She thought: I killed to free myself. To liberate myself from Barron. I left my own mark. And it had nothing to do with Barron. The scissors in her fist, the fist in the air, the dull mirror effect of old silver. And then she had a flash of Frank Pagan, the keen young officer who hadn't been able to take his eyes away from her legs inside the interrogation room, who'd escorted her to a hotel room, she remembered the smell on him, the musk men emitted when they wanted to fuck her, the vibrations they sent out like signals. He wouldn't be so young anymore, and maybe the edge of his eagerness had gone, he might have become jaded, the gloss of youthful ambition buffed down, cracked. She thought of the writing on the lamp shade; she wondered what effect it had had on him. He'd remember her, of course, and maybe he'd remember the sharpness of his desire, the way she'd played with him. The way she was still playing with him.

She tapped the ID card. "Suppose, Tobias, we talk about Helix."

■

Later, he locked himself inside his office and sat staring idly at the most recent influx of messages. He had a sense of the world buzzing out of control all around him, a big wayward puzzling place. He sifted the faxes with less than his usual enthusiasm, looked at the electronic wall maps as if he no longer understood their meaning. It was as if he'd created a mosaic years ago and now he'd forgotten the reason for its design. He felt, in a fashion that depressed him, possessed by death. *Lesson number two. When you've buried the dead, you go on living.* His private telephone rang. He picked it up slowly. He recognized the voice immediately.

"I have some new information concerning our friend Pagan."

Barron didn't speak.

"Unfortunately, our best efforts didn't work. The man seems to have been born under a lucky star."

Barron leaned back in his chair. The wall maps blinked in a way suggestive of distant stars beginning to go out.

"I had to pull my people out. I don't like them being overexposed, if you know what I mean. So the ball's in your court, Tobias."

Barron was still silent. He listened to the rest of the caller's story.

"You still there?" the man asked.

Barron said that he was.

"It's up to you now, Tobias. You understand me?"

"Yes," Barron said.

"Can you do it?"

"Of course."

"No fuckups."

"No fuckups."

"And no more theatrics."

"No theatrics, William."

The line was severed. Barron put the receiver back in place, but only for a moment.

LYON

30

Pagan disliked hospitals, the smell, the hush of wards, the fuss of nurses. The French doctor who examined his neck was a scrawny fastidious man with a conscientiously attentive manner. He spoke in perfect English, which somehow made Pagan all the more irritable.

"A lucky man, Mr. Pagan. A very lucky man."

Pagan agreed. "Sure, I'm lucky as hell, but I want to know about my associate, I'm not interested in some superficial burn on my neck, for God's sake." He tried to get up from the bed on which he lay, but he'd been given some kind of painkiller that made him weak and groggy, and they'd taken away his clothes, dressing him in one of those ridiculous hospital gowns whose only purpose appears to be that of humiliation. He looked around the room, a narrow pale green coffin. His clothing hung on wall hooks.

"It's not what I would call superficial," the doctor said, peering at Pagan over his half-moon eyeglasses.

A nun appeared in the doorway; her crucifix glinted in the light of the lamp on the physician's desk. She frowned at Pagan, who said, "Will somebody tell me about Foxworth?"

"Ah," said the nun, an attractive young Vietnamese woman. She wagged a finger at Pagan. "You are the stubborn one." She glided inside the room. She appeared to consider herself more of an authority than the doctor on the subject of Pagan's neck. She examined the gauze dressing that had been applied just below Pagan's jawline. She had a gentle touch. Pagan could barely feel her fingertips. He knew that if he were to turn his head too sharply, or incline it at a certain angle, there would be painful friction. So: he'd walk around stiff-necked for a while, what the hell, he wasn't going to lie in this goddamn hospital.

"There is the matter of shock," said the nun. "You must take things easy. Maybe tomorrow you can go."

"I want to see Foxworth," he said.

The physician shrugged. "Your friend was less fortunate, Mr. Pagan."

"What does that mean?" For a moment Pagan was beset by the numbing possibility that Foxie had been killed in the fire-blast, but he refused to entertain the prospect. He remembered the ambulance, Foxie slipping into unconsciousness, the attendants who applied an oxygen mask to his mouth. He remembered a wild ride through the streets of Lyon, the wail of a siren, the way Foxie had been rushed off on a gurney whose out-of-whack wheels rattled with the clank of iron on iron. These recollections were misty, distorted. The painkiller was doing a number on his thought processes.

"He was a little closer to the flames than yourself," the nun said. By lamplight, her olive skin appeared darker than it was. She had high cheekbones and long eyelashes; Pagan wondered what had driven her into the embrace of Christ.

"I want to see him," Pagan said.

"You can't get out of bed," the doctor remarked.

The nun was a little more lenient. "If you get up very very carefully, I will take you to your friend. Here," and she held out her hand to clasp Pagan's, assisting him from the bed. The doctor complained in French, but the nun paid him no attention.

"Lean against me if you need to," she said.

He propped himself against the nun, who put an arm around his waist for support. Together, they moved slowly along a green-walled corridor bedecked with crosses and religious medallions. Inside a glass case stood an elaborate plaster Mary, her arms held out, palms turned upward. Imitation flowers sprouted all around her; at her feet was a cracked plaster lamb in need of paint.

The nun opened a door. In a darkened room Foxie lay surrounded by pillows. His arm, hanging over the bedsheets, had been wrapped with plastic that contained cubes of ice, some of them melting already. He turned his face when Pagan approached the bed; he had the zoned look of a man on heavy-duty medication. His lips were cracked and dry, his pupils dilated. At the corners of his mouth were small white flecks of saliva. The unscalded arm was attached to an IV drip.

"What happened, Frank?" he asked. "All I remember is some bloody explosion."

Pagan sat on the edge of the bed. The nun hovered discreetly nearby. "He needs rest, Mr. Pagan. Peace and rest. He has severe burns."

Pagan stared into Foxie's face. On his forehead were fierce red scorch marks where fire had licked the skin. But Foxie too had been fortunate. An inch or so lower and the flames would have blinded him.

"You're not looking your best, old friend."

"I'm not feeling my best. I drift in and out of things. We *are* in France, right?"

"We're in France." Pagan said. He tried to concentrate, clear his head, but whatever they'd injected into him had been strong.

Foxie grimaced. "Jesus, I'm sleepy."

"Drugs," said Pagan.

"I'm not complaining. All things considered, I don't feel *too* bad . . . Actually, I could get quite used to this."

Pagan gazed for a time at the ice packed against Foxie's arm. Foxworth closed his eyes and for a few seconds seemed to float off into drugged sleep, but the eyes fluttered open. "Audrey Roczak," he said. "What about her?"

Pagan shook his head. "I'm told she took the full blast."

"Poor thing." Foxie craned his neck and glanced down at his burned arm with an expression of distaste. "What are we to make of Streik, Frank? What was he telling us?"

The nun touched Pagan's shoulder. "Now I must insist," she said. "Your friend needs sleep. We must leave him in peace."

"Am I to be stuck here, Frank?"

"It looks that way. I'll talk to you later."

"They followed us, didn't they?" Foxie asked. "Bloody Undertakers had our number all along."

"It would seem so, Foxie."

"Please," the nun said.

Pagan stood up shakily, followed the nun out of the room and back into the corridor. "How long will you keep him?" he asked.

"Hard to say. A week perhaps. It depends on the doctor's opinion."

A week, Pagan thought. Shuffling along the corridor in frail hospital slippers, he stared into the meek face of Mary, whose features were rendered slightly obscure by the way light refracted on the glass oblong in which she stood. He had never been a religious man, nor was he miraculously about to be converted in a French hospital where nuns went silently back and forth in earnest pursuit of Christian service, but if he'd been a believer he might have offered a word of gratitude to the madonna that he'd survived, with so little injury, the incendiary device that had been tossed through the window of Audrey Roczak's studio. But he had no hallelujahs, no hosannas in his heart.

"Come," the nun said. "Back to bed."

He followed her obediently inside his narrow sick-green room. He lay down. The nun watched him.

"Promise me," she said. "You will not make any effort to leave until tomorrow."

"I promise," he said.

The nun smiled, went out of the room. He looked up at the ceiling. *What are we to make of Streik?* Foxie had asked. *What was he telling us?* Pagan, his body trembling as if only now he was experiencing the blast, the outrage, the leap of flame, the sight of Audrey Roczak's dress on fire, closed his eyes. What indeed was he telling us? Money came to Streik, from Streik it went to Harcourt, and from Harcourt to . . . Pagan replayed the conversation in his mind, or what he remembered of it, but his synapses were acting like tiny acrobats who kept falling arse-backward. Money, he thought. Millions of dollars, according to Streik.

He swung his legs over the edge of the bed. The pain in his neck throbbed. He felt strangely delicate, his relationship with the world fragile. He moved to where his clothes were hanging. His holstered gun was suspended underneath his shirt. He put his hand into the inner pocket of his overcoat and took out the folded papers Audrey Roczak had given him. He carried them back to bed, lay down, looked at them. His eyes ached.

The writing was very neat, each letter carefully inscribed; Streik had obviously been concerned with keeping a detailed account because he'd guessed that one day a reckoning would come. There were dates, names, places.

Washington, July 6, 1993, three bags picked up from Montgomery Rhodes, amount $2.5m.

New York City, two bags received from unknown man September 5, 1993, amount $2m black Buick Vermont plates # 865 AX7.

Norfolk, Virginia, four sacks amount $4m received from unknown woman September 20, 1993, red Chevy West Virginia plates # 12RP925.

Pagan sifted the papers; there were about twenty sheets in all, and the man called Rhodes figured in three of them. Streik had been aware of the amount involved in each transaction; obviously he would have been accountable if any had gone missing en route. Jake Streik must have seen this record as a way of covering his ass in the event of some misfortune — but in the end these papers had been of no help to him.

Pagan worked at focusing his thoughts. The question is, he wondered, what am I going to do with this information? The license plates would probably be dead ends; rented cars most likely, hired by men carrying fake licenses. And even if the cars hadn't been rented and were lawfully owned, what benefit was that to him? The men who'd delivered the cash to Streik would claim they'd never heard of the guy, that the whole thing was a fiction made up by a dreamer. Streik, like the Undertakers, was deniable.

And where was all this alleged cash anyway? It might as well be orbiting a distant sun; without evidence, you had nothing. Even if he could somehow prove that Streik had ferried money to the Undertakers, and thus into the US embassy, he ran again into that other insuperable obstacle: diplomatic privilege. Money, guns, drugs — diplomatic bags could contain anything. And if by some miracle he could demonstrate that the money had found its way into the embassy and was then 'spread like fucking manure,' as Streik had claimed — spread where? he wondered — he had nothing in the way of substantiation. He was empty-handed. Flat, busted. If he spoke to Nimmo about all this, he could predict the man's reactions, he could hear the outrage of Willie Caan at such dangerous allegations, he could hear teacups breaking inside the hushed rooms of the Foreign Office. He'd be put away, banished, ridiculed. Permanent quarantine. *The Undertakers? My dear fellow, I think you're missing a rung on the old ladder. I believe you're a sandwich short of a picnic.*

The burn on the side of his neck buzzed angrily. He folded Streik's papers, felt sleepy, fought against the sensation. Streik's diction, his ellipses in speech. *Peace is bad for business.* Whose business? Pagan wished he could focus harder.

The Vietnamese nun came back inside the room looking agitated. "Mr. Pagan, there are policemen who want to see you. I have tried to tell them you're in no condition for visitors, but they are very persistent."

The gendarmes, he thought. Of course there would have to be cops. An explosion in the middle of Lyon was the kind of thing that would quicken their interest. He stuffed Streik's papers under his bedsheets.

"I can't keep them away from you," the nun said.

Pagan shrugged. He was floating again. "Send them in," he said. Chewing on her lower lip, her expression one of charitable concern — an angel of mercy, he thought — she opened the door. At once the room was filled with stern men, some of them in uniform.

And in the center, *yo*, stood George Nimmo.

■

Pagan had a moment of light-headedness, one of those jarring displacements of self caused by the combination of drugs and the appearance of George Nimmo. He looked at the crucifix on the wall, which he found too finely detailed, as if it had been cloned from a cell of Christ and not carved from simple wood.

"Pagan," Nimmo said.

Pagan involuntarily touched the dressing on his neck and winced. "George. Good to see you."

"What the hell are you doing here? What in God's name have you been up to?" Nimmo's face was red. He was closer to apoplexy than sanity.

"It appears I got too near to a fire," Pagan remarked.

"And now you're well and truly burned," said Nimmo, his hands clenched in anger. "Well and truly."

Pagan thought: you had to give George some credit for maintaining control of his voice, even if his body revealed his true mood. Nimmo stepped forward and for a moment Pagan had the absurd thought George was about to raise a fist and strike him, but that wasn't Nimmo's way; he wasn't a man of action, he preferred to work with papers and memos and have quiet words in the right ears. His ax was a bureaucratic one.

"Why are you in France? Why wasn't I informed? Why did I have to hear of your reckless misadventures courtesy of the Lyon police department?"

Pagan said nothing. Drugs distanced him from Nimmo's wrath. He was more interested in Streik's dying words than in George Nimmo's full-blown rage. Even as Nimmo went on snapping and fuming, Pagan was still hearing echoes of Jake Streik.

"These gentlemen," and here Nimmo gestured to the congregation of law-enforcement officers, "are demanding to know your business in their jurisdiction. And rightly so. You don't come blundering into somebody else's backyard and bring down all kinds of destruction. You don't carry on like that, Pagan. There's protocol involved. You didn't inform me. You didn't inform these good men. No, you went in feet-first as usual, you went your own damn way without regard. You're a walking disaster, Pagan. A disgrace. And I'm taking you back."

"Back where?"

"Where do you think?" Nimmo stepped very close now. The hands were still fisted, the knuckles drained of blood.

"Is this your way of saying I'm off the investigation?" Pagan asked. He raised eyebrows in a form of mock innocence.

"Don't play silly buggers with me," Nimmo said. "You know damn well what I mean. I wouldn't let you direct traffic in Kensington High Street, never mind the investigation of a bomb attack."

"I'm getting the picture," Pagan said. It was strange how he managed to draw strength from Nimmo's words; the more Nimmo railed at him, the better he felt, the harder his resolve became. "Too bad," he added. "Just as I was making headway."

"Headway. Is that what you call this?" Nimmo made a snorting scornful sound and gestured around the room. "For the benefit of our French friends here, what exactly are you doing in Lyon?"

"Following a lead."

"And? And? I'm listening."

"Obviously somebody didn't like what I was doing, George." For a second he had the mischievous urge to toss out the name of Caan, to throw the ambassador onto the bonfire of Nimmo's anger, but he resisted.

"This so-called lead — I daresay it had something to do with your raging paranoia about our American friends?"

"Hardly raging, George. Let's just say there's a connection between the death of Bryce Harcourt and my business in Lyon."

Nimmo unclenched his hands finally and turned to look at the assembly of French cops. He was putting on quite a little show for them, berating Pagan before their very eyes, dismissing him. Nimmo knew how to play to the gallery.

"And this mysterious connection will lead us to Carlotta, will it?"

"Perhaps."

Nimmo paced around in circles, hands clenched behind his back. "At considerable expense to Special Branch — to say nothing of serious injury to your colleague — you pursue some nebulous lead which, in the final analysis, may or may not have something to do with Carlotta. Pardon me if I don't see the logic."

Nimmo was quiet for a moment, apparently gathering his strength for a renewed assault. But instead he appeared to lose his momentum and stepped back among the clutch of French cops, where he held a hushed conversation with a man in a long heavy overcoat, who was seemingly his opposite number in Lyon. Pagan experienced weakness again. What happened now? Did he go back to

London handcuffed to George Nimmo? Would he be escorted to the airport, there to await the next flight home? Pensioned off, banished to his flat in Holland Park. The bright side of that fate was the fact he'd have all the time in the world for Brennan Carberry, whose face drifted tantalizingly through his head. Enticing as this was, he thought: no way. Nimmo wasn't going to cast him aside. He wasn't about to quit now. *Rock and roll, Frank. Keep on trucking.*

Nimmo took a couple of steps toward the bed. "Right. We're agreed."

"Who's agreed what, George?"

"You spend the night in the hospital. First thing in the morning, we catch the early flight to London." He came even closer to the bed, "Think yourself lucky you're not being locked up, Pagan."

"I bless my good fortune," Pagan said.

Nimmo shook his head. "You won't be blessing anything when we get back home."

"What do you intend, George? Public disgrace? Pagan in the pillory? Behavior of Rogue Cop Humiliates Commissioner? I can see the tabloids."

Nimmo ignored this. He went out of the room, followed by the contingent of French police. Alone, Pagan lay motionless. He reached under the sheets, grabbed Streik's papers, spread them across the bed. Talk to me, Jake, he thought. Tell me more. Take me to a place beyond these scraps of detail. Show me the whole thing. Come back from the grave and *speak* to me. He looked at the papers in the attitude of a man awaiting news trumpeted from a disembodied voice at a seance.

Bryce Harcourt and Jake Streik. Carlotta and her Underground bomb. The transfers of vast sums of money. The Undertakers. Caan's complicity. He had more slippery hoops in the air than he could handle. His brain wasn't up to it. Whatever drug they'd pumped into him had a tidal way of coming and going. Moments of clarity and focus were eclipsed by lassitude and confusion.

He stared at Streik's handwriting. His head was clapped-out again; sleep murmured in his ears.

Chaos, he thought. If peace was bad for business, then chaos was good — if you were in the kind of business where profits were to be made from anarchy. He found himself thinking of William Caan, whose fortune, according to Martin Burr, had come from computerized weapons systems. What was it Burr had said so long ago? Scrap a new missile and a whole industry suffers? And all the subindustries, all the research and development boys start to hurt as well. Factories close, weeds grow through concrete, FOR SALE signs mushroom, former highly paid executives sign on for welfare, ruin all the way down the line.

Because peace is bad for business.

This trail of thought faded out on him. Caan eluded him, drifting away like a wisp of woodsmoke on a dull afternoon. His insight came to an end in a thicket of half-formed notions and tangled deductions. I'll come back to it, he thought. I'll rest, then I'll come back to it.

He shut his eyes, saw a fierce afterimage of Nimmo's flaccid features, opened his eyes again at once. He didn't want Nimmo occupying his head. No. He decided that what he really wanted, what he *needed*, was to speak to Brennan, this was the druggy urge that fluttered through him now. He longed to hear her voice, make a soothing connection with her, envisage her lying across her bed in the room at the Hilton with the telephone pressed to her lips. *I don't want you to worry,* he'd say. *There's been a small accident.* Maybe he wouldn't mention it at all. Maybe he'd say what he'd considered saying before, that he loved her — an ambitious statement, one of consequence and commitment, a declaration and a risk.

He raised his face. There was a telephone on the bedside table. He doubted if it was connected to anywhere beyond the hospital switchboard, but he'd try it anyhow. He fumbled for the receiver and, to his surprise, heard a dial tone. He called the operator, had himself transferred to international inquiries, and was presently patched through to the Hilton in London, where a receptionist answered. Pagan asked for Brennan's room number. Dismayed, he heard her line ring unanswered, on and on. He replaced the receiver, dropped his head back against the pillows and wondered where was she at this time of night. The explanation's simple, he thought. She'd gone to a theater because that's what Americans in London did. And now she was sitting in the hotel bar nursing a nightcap and thinking thoughts of him. There: perfectly acceptable. So why didn't it silence his concern?

He felt drowsy again, but the drift toward sleep was disturbed by recurring images of Brennan and her empty room. With the lover's unbounded optimism, he dialed the Hilton again. There was still no answer from her room. He left a message with the operator, settled back, shut his eyes. She wouldn't go away. She was there. She was in front of him constantly. He tried to remember if he'd obsessed over Roxanne, but that whole history was strangely lost to him. He floated into shallow sleep, fought against it, forced himself awake. He needed to think. He needed to be alert. Rhodes, he thought. Who the hell was this Rhodes character who figured in Streik's deathbed thoughts? It seemed to him a matter of the utmost urgency to find out; Rhodes suddenly dominated his sluggish brain.

He reached for the telephone and dialed Billy Ewing's line at Golden Square. The Scotsman was in a spluttering mode. "Frank? Where the hell are you? It's like some bloody palace coup is going on here, for God's sake. Gladstone and Wright are installed in your office, going through your notes, rummaging through everything they can lay their hands on . . . They even had me in there for questioning. They're like the bloody Gestapo. What did Pagan tell you? What secrets are you keeping from us? And now we've got some tight-arsed bastards from Nimmo's special staff going through the whole place. Jesus."

"Call it the end of a very short era, Billy," Pagan said. "I've got a small job for you."

"Frank, I was to let them know the minute you made contact —"

"You wouldn't do that, would you, Billy?"

"What do you think I am?"

"Run a name for me. Rhodes. Montgomery Rhodes. An American. See if we've got anything on him. And then call me back as quick as you can at this number . . ." Pagan looked at the phone, read the digits to Ewing. "I don't know the area code for Lyon. Look it up."

"Listen, Frank, I'll do what I can, but I'm not sure they'll even let me within a hundred yards of a computer the way things are.

They've taken over. Everything. It's like the invasion of the body snatchers."

"Stay calm. Do what you can, Billy."

"Don't hang up, Frank. There was a message for you. I took it myself. Guy called Zuboric from New York. Grumpy character."

Zuboric. Pagan had almost forgotten. He shut his eyes. "And?"

"I'll read it for you word for word."

Ewing read in an intoning, ministerial way. No, Pagan thought. Zuboric's got it wrong. It doesn't make sense. A confusion of names, a blip in the system, a hiccup. No. No. He asked Ewing to repeat it, but before Billy could respond, the line — whether severed by the hospital, or more likely by an eavesdropper in Golden Square — had gone dead. Pagan slumped back against the pillow. He shut his eyes again. Sometimes computers went mad, gremlins made mischief of the system, viruses played havoc with the links — and what came out was skewed, false. Sometimes data was inaccurately stored by the operator, a keyboard struck wrongly, a letter out of place. You heard such things all the time. You heard of mistakes, bank statements sent to the wrong person, electricity bills that amounted to impossible sums of money, you heard all kinds of computer horror stories —

And Zuboric's message —

Zuboric's message had to be one of them. Misinformation. Yes. That was the word.

But somehow he knew otherwise. And somehow he'd known all along. He kept his eyes shut. He didn't want to open them. Didn't want to think.

"Frank . . ."

He shifted his head, licked his dry lips. He had one of those moments when the border crossing from reality to fiction shifts, when you find you have a visa valid for neither the dream world nor the waking one. But the touch of her fingers on the back of his hand was real enough, and so was the sound of her whispered voice, and the way lamplight created flares and shadows in her hair, which she'd rearranged, pulled from her face so that no careless strands fell upon her brow. She was sitting on the edge of his bed. She wore a black leather jacket, black T-shirt, faded blue jeans. She looked, he thought, both beautiful and austere, and despite the devastating message he'd received from Artie Zuboric, he was filled with a yearning to touch her.

"Frank . . ."

He was about to speak her name but then he realized that his world had changed in a matter of seconds, that he didn't know her name. "You were killed in a skiing accident in Vermont in 1988. Your neck was broken when they carried you off the slopes. DOA. Brennan Carberry doesn't exist."

VENICE

31

The plane from London landed at Marco Polo Airport at eight minutes before three A.M. Swarmed by security personnel, Gurenko disembarked and was escorted down the gangway to a car that carried him a couple of hundred yards to the dock. Everything was done with all the frenzied haste of a polka. He was hustled, Budenny at his elbow, pressured along by a variety of underlings, their ears plugged to listening devices, their lapels wired. They created a large human pool around him. The photographers and journalists awaiting his arrival had no opportunity to get near him. He was swept onto the launch, which was encompassed by a dozen craft, each manned by a contingent of guards, some Russian, others Italian.

When he was seated in the lounge of the launch, he lit a cigarette and attempted to move the curtain from the window in preparation for his first sight of Venice — but Budenny, forever paranoid, forever alert, advised him against it on the grounds that such an act might expose him.

"Expose me to what?" Gurenko asked.

"You never know," Budenny said.

Gurenko puffed away at his cigarette with a show of resentment. All his life he'd wanted to see the lights of the city along the Grand Canal, and now he was to be denied the pleasure. The Palazzo Loredan, the Farsetti, the Grassi, the Ca' Foscari — and he wasn't allowed to draw back the curtain and look. He was a lover denied the sight of his mistress's face.

He walked up and down the narrow curtained lounge. He had the sensation of traveling inside a sealed box. All this security was overkill. He crushed out his cigarette. "I feel caged," he said. "And very very frustrated."

Budenny smiled. "It's exactly how you're supposed to feel."

"I've dreamed of this city for years, Budenny. When I was a student, Venice was where I wanted to be. Not London, not Paris, always Venice . . . During all the years when foreign travel was difficult for us, I would read histories of the place, look at photographs, study books of paintings. Magnetism, Budenny. And now you won't let me look out the damned window."

Budenny said, "I have responsibilities. Besides, you'll get the chance to see what you want to see. Sit down. Be patient." Budenny opened a folder, studied a typed schedule. "Luncheon with the Italian prime minister and his cabinet members. A private meeting with the prime minister after luncheon — who, incidentally, would have preferred to meet you in Rome, but he seems, good fellow that he is, to understand your artistic interests. After the meeting, a quick tour of Venice before you head for Berlin in the evening."

Quick, Gurenko thought. Like a tourist. He wanted the impossible, probably: the time in which to embrace the whole place. Even in London, when he'd spent five hours with the dour British prime minister, and then two hours with Caan, the US ambassador — a glossy character altogether, a smooth New World product who reassured him that democratic reform in Russia had priority on the US agenda of foreign affairs — he'd been thinking of Venice. Then in Paris, where he'd eaten a late dinner with the president and talked of Russia's future with a confidence he wasn't sure he felt, he'd caught himself drifting. When the Frenchman was interrogating him on the subject of popular support for the new Russian constitution, his mind had now and then wandered.

He regarded Budenny a second. In his well-tailored gray suit, white shirt, and bright flowery tie — a blinding length of silk — he was so different from the old Vassily that if you looked at a photograph of Budenny taken ten years ago, you'd be staring at a quite different man, a colorless Party functionary dressed in the kind of shapeless baggy clothes that resembled rejects from a zoot-suit factory. Now he subscribed to fashion magazines published in London and New York; he made shopping trips to foreign cities — Amsterdam, Milan, Paris — and always returned with boxes of shirts and suits and shoes. In recent years, Gurenko thought, he'd become something of a dandy. He'd also acquired implanted teeth to go with the clothes and the blow-dried hair. Budenny could *never* understand the attraction of Venice. You could explain until there was a heatwave in Siberia, and he'd still never grasp it. His life was all schedules and anxiety. He lived like a man whose eyes are forever looking sideways.

The launch was slowing now. The motor of the craft was silenced; the hull knocked against a quay. Gurenko, again surrounded, squashed by his human shields, was assisted out of the launch to the jetty, then escorted under a barrage of umbrellas to the lobby of the hotel. He had an impression of marble, chandeliers, a thick red carpet underfoot. Otherwise, his view was strictly limited. He suddenly thought of a phrase from a poem he'd read at university, something from Max Eastman, written in the 1920s. *Fear is the only danger.* Old Max, a bolshevik New Yorker who'd written in Russian as well as English, was correct. Budenny and his security buffoons should have read that poem.

And now he was jammed inside an elevator, rising to the upper floor of the hotel, where every room and suite had been reserved for the Russian party. There he'd be trapped until it was time to be ushered back into the world.

Inside the elevator, squeezed between Budenny and his guards, he had a moment of stifling dizziness. The elevator doors slid open, the hotel manager stood in the hallway, obsequiously stooped, a fake smile of welcome on his face. *We're so proud to have you stay with us,* et cetera, et cetera, and Gurenko nodded, returned the smile after a fashion, and then was whisked down the corridor to his own suite of rooms: two bedrooms, two bathrooms, a sitting room filled with flowers and baskets of fruit and wine chilling in a silver container.

Under Budenny's scrutiny, the security guards checked the rooms, as they'd done so many times before Gurenko's arrival. They swept the place with electronic devices, examined the telephones, sampled the fruits, sipped the wines, explored the bunches of flowers — what did they expect to find? transmitters concealed in petals? tiny explosives stuffed in stems? — then departed, seemingly satisfied, or as close to satisfaction as they were likely to get. Gurenko, overwhelmed by their zeal, their mute dedication, was left with Budenny. Exhausted, he slumped on the sofa and put his legs up.

He remembered another phrase from Eastman's poem. *But they are feeble and their watch is brief.* He was about to quote it for Budenny's sake — but poetry was pointless in Budenny's world, a luxury for the very few, an artsy-fartsy pastime for those of a sensitive nature.

Budenny pressed the remote control for the TV. There was a dazzling chorus of dancers, bright-faced young men in bullfighting suits and leggy girls in abbreviated skirts — a garish spectacle, just the kind of thing Budenny would enjoy. Gurenko felt the frustration rise in him again. Stuck here in front of a stupid TV — when all around him in the city lay great works of art, creations of genius. Lost opportunities: what a life.

"Nice, very nice," said Budenny, eyeing the dancing girls.

Gurenko picked up the remote control and pressed the off button. "But not to my liking," he said.

Budenny laughed. "Pretty girls. One should always appreciate them. To my mind, *they're* the real works of art. Not stuffy old canvases hanging on a moldy wall."

Gurenko looked at the dead screen. He concluded that Budenny's soul was a lost cause. "Tomorrow's schedule," he said. "I'm looking forward to the Scuola di San Rocco."

"Of course you are."

"A lifetime ambition, Budenny. A lifelong yearning. You wouldn't understand that."

"I have other kinds of longings," said Budenny.

Gurenko rubbed his hands together briskly and smiled. The Tintorettos would be all around him in their luminous glory. *The*

Adoration of the Magi. The Flight into Egypt. The Slaughter of the Inno-cents.

Budenny yawned, covered his mouth with his hand. "I'll leave you. Let you get some sleep. If you need me, my room is next door."

Gurenko said good night, watching Budenny go. Alone, he undressed, opened his suitcase, took out a brown bathrobe. Then he lay down on the bed. He picked up a small guidebook to Venice, flicked the pages until he came to the Scuola. *The Crucifixion,* in his own modest view the painter's best work. *The Miracle of the Manna, The Punishments of the Serpents.* He knew he'd experience the kind of awe that always overcame him in the presence of genius, that reverential hush of his heart, the dumbstruck silences of his mind. Great art had a way of putting things in perspective for him; it reminded him of his own mortality.

He closed the book, opened a small plastic bottle, and dutifully swallowed two multivitamin capsules as Svetlana had instructed him.

■

Vassily Budenny locked the door of his suite. He rubbed his hands together briskly. His blood pressure was high, his pulses too fast, his heart quick. Earlier, on the flight from Paris, he'd gone inside the toilet and taken a mild tranquilizer. He'd studied his face in the mirror for such a long time he'd experienced a sense of unfamiliarity in the reflection; he might have been looking at a stranger. What will history have to say about Vassily Budenny? Would it vilify him? Applaud him? Or would there only be silence? Perhaps his role would never be known, perhaps a century might pass before his significance was discovered. What did it matter?

Historical judgments lay in the hands of people as yet unborn. It was an odd consideration. Even as he'd gazed at himself in the mirror, he'd imagined a coupling on some double bed in a strange city, two people copulating in Minsk, say, the passage of sperm from man to woman, the fertilization of the egg, an embryo that would become a historian of the future, an eager young man or woman whose eventual academic labors would be a doctoral thesis on the life and times of Vassily Budenny. Heroism or denunciation — it made no difference. His patriotic duty was clear.

He lay down on the sofa, kicked off his shoes, turned on the TV, enjoyed the dancing girls. Pert little asses. Poor Gurenko, he thought. The man would have been happier as the administrator of an obscure province, scribbling poetry in the evenings, contemplating the mystery of moths that, attracted to light, fluttered under his desk lamp.

LYON

32

Just who the fuck are you?" Pagan asked. He looked into the girl's face and thought: Some things you couldn't absorb at once. You needed time and distance. You had to be far away from the epicenter of the blast before you grasped the extent of the damage. She was gazing at him with a serious expression.

"You didn't trust me," she said. "You had to do some checking, didn't you? You couldn't stop yourself."

"Old habits."

"Bad ones," she said quietly.

A smell haunted him, fiery turpentine, canvases devoured by flame. His unruly thoughts stampeded. He was unable to harness them. He thought: Fool. Middle-aged and pathetic. A lonely man too careless with the remains of his heart. He remembered how they'd made love, that passion.

"Who are you?" he asked again.

She was quiet. She appeared to be gathering herself for an explanation of some sort, and although she seemed calm, Pagan had the feeling it was a superficial thing that required enormous effort. He was sensitive to other people's anxieties, but not, seemingly, to his own. He'd staggered blindly into an affair with this girl, he'd plunged without pause, and when he'd taken a step back to survey his situation, it was too late. Questions crowded him. *Her identity.*

The fact she knew where to find him in Lyon. Her motive for lying. For the facade, all the sweet words.

"Brennan Carberry was convenient," she said. "She served her purpose."

"You got a copy of a dead girl's birth certificate, then applied for a passport in her name." Pagan heard himself speak in a flat fashion, one that belied his bewildered anguish.

"The paper game," she said. "You know how easy it is to play. One phone call gets you a copy of a birth certificate. The rest is plain old sailing."

Plain old sailing, he thought. He had a flash of her body in the hotel bedroom. The image was curiously inverted in his head, and strange, as if he were looking at the behavior of another person altogether, another Frank Pagan. He felt drained, all energy depleted. Systems down, wires disconnected.

She moved as if to lay her fingers across his wrist. He pulled his hand away quickly. He said, "*I couldn't take disappointment. I don't handle it well. I'm not built for heartbreak.*"

"You have a good memory, Frank," she said.

"Some things just stick," he remarked. "Especially bullshit." He had a surge of raw bitterness, a sharp awareness of loss.

"You think that's all it was?"

"It was a bad script," he said. "Who wrote your lines for you? Or did you manage to make them up on the spur of the fucking moment all by your little self?" He reproached himself for the crude anger in his voice, but what was he supposed to do? Stay detached? He didn't have the capacity for icy disinterest. She'd lied to him, and the lies ran deeper than the matter of assuming the identity of a dead woman: How had she known where to find him? What exactly was being played out here in a hospital room in a rainy French city?

She stared into his eyes. He detected in her look a quality of melancholy he wanted to believe was genuine — but he set the notion aside. She's fake. An actress. Everything about her is false. Nothing else is worth remembering.

"It was planned," he said. "Planned from the start. Right?"

"You're quick."

"The way you ran into my car. The way you infiltrated my life. The way you were supposed to make me . . . feel. All that was deliberate. More extracts from the same bloody shabby script. Did you rehearse it beforehand? Did you run through your lines with your script director or whoever the hell it was? Frank Pagan, pushover, been on his own too long, shouldn't be too hard to crack open his shell, bring a little light into his dreary life. Oh, sure, just get him into bed and screw him until he sees rainbows and starts hallucinating about the possibilities of love." He caved into the anger completely now. He recognized it was not one emotion pure and simple, but several tributaries of feeling — pain, sadness, humiliation.

"It started like that." She smiled at him rather gently. "But I was beginning to like you. I was beginning to have feelings. Dangerous things."

Feelings, he thought. Even now he had the urge to reach for her, the longing to hear her say, *Hey, I'm joking* — a cruel one, but a joke just the same. Hah hah, let's get on with our lives, Frank. But he knew it wasn't going to be like that.

"Who instructed you?" he asked. "Who pressed your button and set you in motion? Who told you to play this role? What's the point behind it?"

She didn't answer the questions. Instead she said, "I want you to understand, Frank." She reached for a large leather purse. She set it in her lap, opened the clasp, put her hand inside. She removed a document from her purse, which she placed before him, but he didn't want to touch it, whatever it was.

"Look at it," she said.

He didn't move. In small back rooms of his head he heard the angry slamming of doors, keys turning in heavy locks. Rooms he'd never visit again.

"Look at it . . ."

Slowly, his hand unsteady, he reached for the document. It was an American passport. "So what," he said.

"Look inside."

He flipped the passport open. He stared at the page where her photograph was located. She looked innocent and vibrant with youth and she was gazing into the camera in a straightforward manner. There was no guile about this face. You would put your faith in those features. *And I did*, he thought. *I truly did.*

He raised his eyes, stared at her, said nothing.

"Look at it closer," she said.

What was he supposed to see? He wasn't sure. He gazed at the picture again, and then his eyes strayed to the passport owner's name. But he'd reached a place where names had no validity, they shifted, you couldn't expect stability.

He said the name aloud and it didn't sound right. She stared at him, waiting. He spoke the name again.

Katherine Cairney. But when you said anything long enough or looked at the particles of a word hard enough, they gave up any references to the real world. *Katherine Cairney*. It might have been an anagram whose solution was too dreadful to discover.

"You killed my brother, Frank."

Brother . . . This statement baffled him. Language was tunneled by flaws.

"Patrick Cairney was my brother," she said. "And you killed him. You killed him, Frank."

Patrick Cairney. *Jig*. Pagan sagged back against the pillows, letting the passport slither from his hands. He wished the medication would kick in again and free him from the straitjacket of this bad dream.

"I was only supposed to watch you, Frank. That was my brief. Keep an eye on him. Report anything he does, anything he tells you. Get inside his head. Get information. The rest . . . the rest came kind of naturally because I was drawn to you."

Drawn to me, he thought. Like a crow to carrion. Blood on a wet road and the fevered beat of wings and claws in his dead flesh. "Your brief," he said.

"Yes," she said.

"Who the hell briefed you?"

"It doesn't matter."

"It matters to me."

She shook her head. "It's not important now. The situation's changed." She put her hand back inside the purse and brought out a small gun attached to which was a silencer. Pagan stared at the weapon, which seemed toylike, plastic, and his mind went scurrying into dead-end passageways. She pointed the gun at him and he turned his face to the side a moment.

"I'm to be killed," he said. "And you're the designated hitter."

She tightened her hand on the gun. He strained forward a little. "I don't give a shit what anybody told you, I didn't shoot your brother."

"Sure, Frank," she said. "You tracked him, you hunted him down. You pulled the trigger. You did that, Frank."

Pagan looked at the girl's face, this stranger's face, this Katherine Cairney. "Listen. And listen well. I went after Patrick. My job was to bring him in. That was the extent of it. I didn't want him dead. That was the last damn thing I wanted. He was a key IRA player. But I didn't pull the trigger. He was shot by his own stepmother, for Christ's sake. I didn't do it. That bitch Celestine killed him." He thought: *I already told you that in another lifetime.*

"Jesus Christ. You're still clinging to that crap. That was the official line, Frank. That was pablum dispensed to satisfy the public and let the police and the Feds walk away without blood on their hands. Pure fabrication. And you're still sticking to it —"

"Who told you I killed him? Who are you working for anyway?" he asked. "What are they paying you?"

"There's no pay —"

"You work for nothing, is that it?"

"I work for the Cause."

"Ah, of course, the Cause, forgive me for letting it slip my mind. The precious Cause, capital C. Patrick Cairney's Cause." His voice was hard with forced sarcasm. He closed his eyes a moment; connections were rippling outwards from some central point, only he couldn't quite detect the core, the place where the surface of water broke and where disturbances were created. Rings were interlocked with other rings, and they kept shimmering. If she was working for what she called the Cause, where did the Undertakers figure in this? Who had sent her here to Lyon? Ambassador Caan? Nimmo could have updated Caan on the situation and Sweet William might have turned the heat up on the girl. Pagan's gone too far, Caan might have said. It was possible . . . The world seemed to him a great sphere of derangements in which he was doomed to search for loose connections that, in the end, would always elude him.

She pushed the gun toward him, a strange little motion of the hand, as if some force had compelled her from behind. Pagan looked directly into her eyes. "Are you capable of killing?"

"Perfectly capable."

"You've done it before."

"Yes."

He found the cold certitude in her voice shocking. "In what circumstances?"

"Does it really matter?"

He glanced at the wall, the place where his raincoat hung; he thought of the holstered pistol dangling under the coat, but he'd never be able to reach it before she pulled the trigger. What he needed was space, room in which he might maneuver. He said, "I'm curious, that's all. I just want to be sure you know what you're doing. I don't want you to botch it. The last thing I need is some amateur shooting me in the wrong bloody place. I have this quite understandable aversion to lingering pain caused by a misdirected bullet."

She was quiet a moment. "You don't need to worry about that, Pagan."

"Your last victim died swiftly, is that what you're telling me?"

"Yes."

"And what had this unfortunate done?"

"His name isn't important, Pagan. He was just somebody in the States who had betrayed the Cause, that was all. The job was entrusted to me, and I did it."

"And you shot him how — from close range, the way you mean to shoot me? Or did you use a rifle?"

"A revolver. From a range of ten feet."

Pagan sighed. "Brennan, Katherine, whoever you are, what the hell do you think you're involved in here? The Cause, for Christ's sake. The good old murderous Cause. Let me see if I can guess. You made regular contributions to NORAID or some fund-raising group that specializes in tugging soft Irish hearts in exile, and somewhere along the way they pressed you into active service, and when they were sure of your loyalties, they put you through some basic training and gave you a target to hit, and now you're about to kill again — based on the absurd lie that I shot your brother. Well, I'm sorry about Patrick, but I didn't kill him." Pagan paused, but knew he had to keep talking, because the longer she listened the longer he survived. That simple.

She said, "You're so full of shit. You haven't got a clue, Pagan."

"No? Let me keep guessing. Stop me when I get it wrong. Shoot me when I step out of line. Here's what I see. A young girl who's brought up by a father who happens to be the principal American fund-raiser for the IRA. He talks of old glories, the bold fight for freedom, he throws in the Easter Rising because that's always good for a quickening of the heartbeat. God, it's wondrous stuff. Comrades in arms. Fighters. Hard men of courage. He force-feeds you martyrs, great old tales of heroes shot down in cold blood by the Brits. Maybe you even learn a few rebel songs on Daddy's lap, and it's cute, you're like some little Shirley Temple mouthing songs she doesn't even understand —"

"You're wrong, you're way off —"

"But the old songs have nothing to do with reality, they don't have a bloody thing to do with the way people have been dying in Ireland or England, do they? Anyway, you're nicely indoctrinated at an early age — exactly the way your brother must have been — and you grow up believing in all the garbage you've been fed. And now somebody's playing you like a bloody instrument. Somebody's spooning out lies, stirring the truth around, manipulating you into acts of murder —"

"You have no idea, Pagan. You think you know so much." She pressed the gun into his chest and he tilted his head back, squinting down at the silencer and wondering if he'd gone too far, goaded her more than was good for him. There was a delicate balance here and he didn't know which way it was going to shift and his heart was a jackhammer.

"I'm not blaming you," he said. "You can't help yourself. You've been brainwashed and your brain's been hung out to dry —"

"Shut up —"

"And you don't know how to distance yourself from Daddy's old stories, do you? You're a prisoner of a history that was never as romantic as your father led you to believe. It was sordid and squalid and too many people have died for nothing. And here's a small irony, love, if you're in the mood for it. You're not even *Irish*. You're an *American*, you don't know Ireland, you might think you do, but you only see it from a distance and your view is so limited it's laughable —"

"I suppose *your* view is the only acceptable one," she said. "Why don't you just shut the fuck up?"

"Why? Am I bothering you?"

"I don't need to listen to you moralize. It's trite, Pagan. It's trite and it's tired."

"You don't *want* to hear anything that undermines your creed, because it's inviolate, it's beyond criticism. Would you like me to describe what my wife looked like after she'd been blown up by one of your bombs? You want details of that? You want to hear what was left of her? You want me to tell you what it felt like going down to the morgue and identifying the remains of Roxanne? Merry Christmas, Frank. Here's a little present from the IRA. Enjoy."

"It's war, and there are always casualties, because that's the way it is —"

"Casualties of war? A woman standing at a bus stop on Christmas Eve? Right. She's an enemy. She's most definitely an enemy. Let's blow her and a few other Christmas shoppers to pieces. You never know. Instead of gift-wrapped boxes in their bags, they might be carrying guns for the Loyalists." He was weary suddenly, talked out, depressed by memory. He looked into the girl's face. Her expression was one of annoyance and determination; her loveliness was altered, as if it had been an illusion from the start. He remembered how, when he'd first met her, she'd been upset by the story of Roxanne's death. Another piece of playacting, that's all. I'm sentimental, Frank. I weep at movies. I'm a little softhearted. More lies. Lies all the way along the line. And you, Pagan, you paid the price of admission, you willingly picked up your ticket and entered the hall of mirrors.

"I'm genuinely sorry about your wife," she said.

"Excuse me if I doubt the sincerity of that." He could still smell the morgue if he tried hard enough, a medicinal aroma suggestive of bleach. He could still see the white tiles, the steel drawers where they stored the dead.

"Think what you like, Pagan. It doesn't matter to me. Nothing you say changes what I have to do."

"I didn't imagine it would. Not for a moment. You have your orders, don't you? And you have to carry them out like the good little foot soldier you think you're supposed to be." He looked into the girl's face, glanced down at the gun she held against his ribs. He thought: It would take a sudden movement, it would have to be swift, a blurred motion of his hand. But it was chancy, the turn of a card, she only had to squeeze off one shot and that would be the end of it. A sense of timing was the thing — and lately he'd lost his. He was tense, wondering if he could pull it off, wondering if he had time and space, wondering about the contest between his reactions and hers.

"You know, I feel sorry for you," he remarked.

"Spare me your pity. I don't need it."

"I also feel regret. I thought we had something real between us. For a while, you uplifted me."

"We had a nice moment, that was all. It's over."

"It was more than a nice moment for me. I was starting to feel some sense of . . . call it life, if you like. Funny, don't you think? I'm talking about life. And you're about to end it."

"Yes. I'm about to end it," she said — and he thought he heard a tiny note of regret in her voice. Or maybe that was just what he wanted to hear. Something undeniably human.

"Then why don't you just pull the goddamn trigger?" He stared into the eye of the gun, half-expecting the blast. *This is the last sound you'll ever hear, Frank.* He raised a hand, indicated the center of his chest. "Here. What they call," and he paused, weighing the next word, "the heart. You know where the heart's located, don't you?"

She drew the gun back from his ribs a matter of a few inches.

"Good thinking," he remarked. "Otherwise you'd get my blood all over yourself. And we don't want that, do we? Executioners don't stain themselves with their victim's blood."

She looked into his eyes. "You're through talking."

He gazed at the gun; time was seeping away. He imagined he heard shutters being slammed across windows. Total darkness. Move, he thought. Move yourself. She was still pulling back from him, but the gun never wavered, she held it steady, directed toward his chest. She was two feet away at best. Force yourself to move, Pagan, or this is the place where the train finally stops. This is the terminus, the last station. The gun stayed firm in her hand. In her mind, he thought, I am already dead, this murderous little bitch is already walking the corridors to the exit, gun securely tucked inside purse . . .

"Mr. Pagan?"

He hadn't heard the door open.

The Vietnamese nun stepped quietly inside the room. She held a tray with a glass of water. "Time for your medication," she said, then noticed the girl, the gun, and she was suddenly very still.

The girl turned her face to the intruder and Pagan, in a flurry of bedsheets, forced himself up, lunged forward, seized her hand and twisted the gun to one side and a silenced shot went off with the sound of air rushing from a puncture. The shot struck the nun in the forehead. The tray clattered, the water glass broke, the small woman — Pagan's angel of mercy — dropped to the floor, surrounded by the collapsed folds of the white habit she wore. Enraged, Pagan forced the girl's hand down, twisted it, making the gun slip from her fingers. She fought back with fierce determination, clawing at his face and neck. She tried to bring a knee up into his groin but he sidestepped her, slapped her across the lips, knocked her down on the bed, slapped her again. She rose quickly, rushed him, punching wildly, blows he parried for the most part against his arms. He backswiped her and she dropped on the bed and he picked up the fallen gun. He walked to where the nun lay. He looked at her wide eyes, the pleasant mouth slightly parted; blood ran over her forehead and along her eyebrows.

"Another casualty for your side," he said. "Another accident — isn't that what you'd call it?"

"I didn't make it happen." Breathless, she was sitting on the edge of the bed. "You forced the shot."

He walked back to the bed and shoved the gun directly under the girl's chin. He resisted the deranged impulse to shoot her where she sat. But that was what he wanted to do — eliminate her, snuff her out, just blow her away. He thought how frail she looked all at once, her features collapsed in dejection and uncertainty. Another man might possibly have found in himself reservoirs of forgiveness, might have made allowances for her background, her indoctrination, the way she'd been misled and manipulated, might have taken into account the way she'd lived under the mythic shadow of her famous brother: another man might. A saint maybe. But Pagan didn't have that expansive generosity of spirit when it came to Katherine Cairney; it had been killed inside him. It had been injured years ago in a foul-smelling morgue; and in the last twenty minutes it had been fatally wounded. His anger was like a vast field with no horizon. He pushed the gun into her soft flesh until her neck was distended. "Talk to me," he said, and his voice was tight.

She closed her eyes. She said nothing.

"*Talk*."

"I don't have anything to say."

He forced her down on the bed, his knees pressed into her body, the full weight of him upon her, and he thrust the gun deeper into her skin. And he remembered the last time they'd been in a bed together and he thought how his tenderness and affection had been corrupted. Was that what angered him more than anything else? The dead woman on the floor, who'd walked into all this innocently, seemed like a tragic coda to his emotions.

"Who briefed you? Who gave you your instructions?"

"Why the hell should I tell you?"

There was, Pagan thought, a limit to all things. And he'd reached his. He was prepared for the descent into brutality. He was ready to do real violence. It was strange how the heart could turn like this. It was weird and disturbing, the dark reactions you found in yourself. He raised the gun and held it in the air the way you might hold a knife before you plunged it downward. He thought of the butt smacking against bone, hard metal slicing open this lovely deceitful face. He knew what he must look like through her eyes — demented, beyond the reaches of reason, infinitely dangerous. And he knew she'd never encountered anyone in his condition before.

She stared up into the gun, as if she were already seeing its descent and feeling it come down on her face with shattering impact. She was afraid — he could see it in her eyes, smell it on her; all the bravado was falling away. On one level she seemed to understand that he wasn't going to kill her just yet. But she also understood there was going to be pain instead, and pain wasn't what she wanted to encounter.

"Answer me," he said. He moved his arm higher, more threateningly. He was outside of himself, a spectator, fascinated by what he saw and at the same time repelled by his own behavior. The beast set free, the cage broken. Pagan unhinged.

"The name wouldn't mean anything to you."

"Try me."

"Goddamn you, let me up, I can't breathe."

"Too bad."

Blood was rushing to her face. She was struggling. She spoke in a gasp. "Tobias Barron."

"Barron," he said.

The name was one he'd seen in gossip columns, columns he never read because they were no more than fluff, idiocy, documenting the comings and goings of that class of people for some reason deemed celebrities. But somehow these columns infiltrated your head even if you never actually read them; pictures came at you as you skipped newspaper and magazine pages, and the brain, that insomniac limpet in the skull, stored all manner of needless trivia, including the names of flimsy celebrities.

"The well-known philanthropist. The walking charity. Mister Goodheart. Friend to the famous. And he gave you your instructions. He told you what to do."

She tried to push him away, then gave up. He enjoyed listening to her fight for air even if he didn't like himself for it.

"What did he tell you exactly?"

"You were an enemy of the Cause . . . you needed to be kept under surveillance . . . . Please. Let me get up."

But he wasn't ready yet to release her, he wanted her under him, to keep up the pain of pressure.

"I can't . . . breathe," she said.

"You already told me that."

He looked down into her eyes, remembering something else about Barron now, something that floated up to him from a submerged place in the mind, the photograph taken of Carlotta in Rio, the teasingly familiar face of the man walking alongside her.

Barron.

Barron and Carlotta . . .

. . . his mind was back into the tunnel, he saw the wreckage, the body bags aligned on the platform, he imagined Carlotta threading her way slyly through rush-hour crowds on her murderous mission. That was no IRA brutality, no sectarian savagery carried out in the name of the struggle against English occupation; the Cause wouldn't have employed Carlotta if they'd wanted to blow up a train, they'd have used their own killers, people close to the heart of command, because strangers couldn't enter the inner sanctum. Carlotta's instructions hadn't come out of Dublin or Belfast. They'd been issued elsewhere.

"You've never heard of Bryce Harcourt or Jake Streik, have you? You've never heard of an outfit called the Undertakers."

"I don't know what you're talking about . . ."

He released the pressure on her. He stepped back from the bed, reached quickly for his clothes. She watched him with a look of frightened uncertainty. She'd seen something savage in him and she had no way of knowing if the animal had been incarcerated or if it was still loose. He tossed aside the hospital gown, pulled on his shirt, strapped his holster in place and put the girl's weapon in the pocket of his coat, everything done quickly.

"You've been used, love," he said. "Used and abused. Welcome to the club."

She was coughing into her hand, a series of quick spasms. When she stopped, she raised her sleeve to her lips. "I'm not following you —"

"Used, abused, and sold down the river," he said. "Here's the way it is. Barron sends you out on what he *says* is IRA business because he knows you'll go along with it. He plays on your sympathies for all they're worth. Maybe he's associated in some way with your so-called Cause. Fine. But it's more than that. It goes way beyond the IRA. It goes into areas you couldn't even start to guess. You've been taken. Swindled. Call it what you like. What it comes down to is this: you're a stupid little girl who's way out of her depth."

She coughed again and shook her head rapidly. "You don't know anything —"

"This is what I know. Listen and digest. The Undertakers work secretively out of the US embassy. They handle vast amounts of money, apparently with the knowledge of the ambassador. Where this cash comes from, I don't know yet. And I don't know where it goes. Maybe a fraction finds its way into the treasury of the IRA, I'm not sure. But the rest . . ." He shrugged. "The money was handled mainly by two men. One called Streik, the other Harcourt. Streik's dead. Harcourt was killed in the Underground bombing, courtesy of a certain Carlotta. Presumably you've heard of her."

"I know her reputation, sure. What the hell are you getting at?"

"I don't suppose Barron ever informed you of a plan to kill a hundred people on a subway carriage, did he?"

"We had nothing to do with that," she said. "You can't possibly believe that."

We, he thought. *We.* She belonged. She was up to her neck. Only she didn't know the true nature of what she belonged to.

"Carlotta planted that bomb. And right now I'm starting to think she was working under instructions from your master — Tobias Barron."

She shook her head. "No way. Absolutely no goddamn way. You're really going downhill fast, Pagan."

"Why? If he's capable of giving you the order to kill me, why wouldn't he be just as capable of giving Carlotta a mandate to blow up an Underground carriage? You think he'd be deterred by the numbers of casualties involved? Is that what you think? One or two murders are acceptable. A hundred — unthinkable. Oh dear, such delicate sensibilities. Christ's sake. Open your eyes."

"You don't know Barron. He wouldn't sanction death on that scale. You're out of your mind."

"Maybe. Maybe I'm mad as a fucking hatter," Pagan said. "I must say I find your belief in him touching. In the circumstances, I'm naturally a little more sceptical." He paused, assessing the look on her face, the same fretful apprehension. "Did he ever tell you why the simple order to keep me under surveillance was upgraded to an execution command?"

"He said you knew too much."

"Too much about what?"

"I didn't ask. I assumed he had good reasons."

"I'll tell you what his good reasons are. I'm getting too close to him, I'm beginning to trespass in forbidden areas. I'm gatecrashing his private party, and he's uncomfortable. I know about Carlotta, for one thing. Which isn't conducive to his peace of mind — or he wouldn't have sent you here. He knew the *first* attempt to kill me in Lyon had been botched. So he sends you out in the hope you have what it takes to finish the job."

Pagan stared at her. The desire to hurt her had gone out of him; the outburst of rage was diminishing. Anger of such intensity was hard to sustain. It damaged your system, devoured all your energies. He was calmer now, but troubled by the uncharacteristic way he'd yielded to the notion of brutality, the way he'd snapped.

"Do you know where Barron is?" he asked, and his voice was quiet, but it took an effort.

She shook her head.

"I'm expected to believe that?" he asked.

"Believe what you like," she answered.

He moved toward her, looked down at her. "I don't want to hurt you," he said. "But I will. You know I will."

She said nothing. He wondered if he could find the energy to strike her again and what it would cost him. He decided to try another tactic. "You think I'm lying about Barron. Maybe I am. But you're not sure. You don't know. You think I'm wrong when I tell you how he manipulated you. Maybe so. But if I were you, I'd want to find out. I'd want to know if I'd been manipulated. I'd want the truth. Of course, you wouldn't be interested in the truth, would you? It wouldn't fit into your scheme of things. It might interfere with your nice little black-and-white picture of the world."

"Of course I'm interested in the truth —"

"Well then?"

"Is this the civilized approach, Pagan?"

"Would you prefer the other way?" he asked. "I'm capable of it. You know that."

She raised her face. "I know that now," she said.

He finished dressing. He picked up Streik's papers, which had fallen from bed to floor, and carefully placed them in the pocket of his coat. "What's it going to be?"

She didn't speak. She looked at him with what he took to be the contempt of somebody grudgingly defeated. "I have a telephone number, that's all."

"Call him. Tell him you killed me."

"And then what?"

"Tell him you want to see him."

"If he doesn't agree?"

"Tell him it's important. Impress that on him. Convince him. Act it out. You're talented in that direction."

She ignored the barb. She placed her hands on either side of her face. Her hair had become unpinned and was falling across her shoulders and she resembled nothing more than a vulnerable child who had strayed by circumstance into a place where she was lost. But he wasn't going to be drawn into that picture frame; he wasn't going to be touched by an outbreak of sympathy.

"There's the phone," he said, and gestured toward the bedside table. "Call him now."

She picked up the receiver, started to dial, then set it down again. "I can't," she said.

"You don't want to take the chance I might be right," Pagan said. "Good old Barron. Can't do any wrong, can he?"

"Fuck you."

"You already did," he remarked.

She picked up the phone again, dialed, tapped her fingers on the bedside table as she waited for an answer. Then he heard her say that Pagan was dead. She was convincing enough; her voice had a quiet shocked quality. He heard her ask for a meeting. She listened in silence for a while, then she hung up. She scribbled something on a notepad.

"It's arranged," she said.

"Where?"

"Venice."

He walked toward the door, looked down at the dead woman, felt the weight of a terrible regret. But this wasn't the time to linger and be trapped by feelings.

The corridor was empty. Dim lights lit the way to the exit. He gripped the girl by the elbow.

"Now what?" she asked.

"We visit Barron."

They started off down the corridor, walked past the reception desk, which was unoccupied, then stepped out into the street.

John Downey emerged from the shadows. "Fancied some night air, did we? A little stroll in the dark? See the sights?"

Shit. "It crossed my mind, John."

"Afraid not." Downey, who wore a cavernous raincoat, had his hands in his pockets. Pagan didn't doubt he had a gun stashed away. "Strict instructions from Mr. Nimmo. You stay where you are. Been a little wayward, haven't we, Pagan? Been a little stupid."

"Depends what you call stupid, John," Pagan said. He didn't have the heart to confront John Downey. He doubted if he had the strength.

Downey shifted his weight, glanced at the girl dismissively. He was a solid man; the sunken cheeks and the vanity of the waxed mustache might have misled you into thinking he was a pushover, past his best. But Downey could play rough when he had to; his penchant for adding a sharp physical dimension to interrogations was well known. He stared hard at Pagan; you could see in the look the malignant gleam of old resentments. He would have liked nothing better than to shoot Pagan.

"One wrong move, Pagan. That's all I'm waiting for."

Pagan raised his hands in a gesture of appeasement and acquiescence, knowing that if he was going to get past Downey he was going to have to be quick, because if he missed he wasn't going to get a second chance. He half-turned away, his arms still raised slightly in front of his body. Now, he thought. It has to be now. He moved the left arm with all the strength he could gather and chopped John Downey in the larynx. It wasn't brilliant, but it was forceful enough to knock Downey back against the wall. Pagan struck a second time, slamming a fist into the side of Downey's jaw, hearing a cartilaginous creak as Downey's head swung back and struck the wall. Pagan kicked him in the stomach and Downey slumped to the ground at an unusual angle, as if the joints that held his skeleton together had been severed. Even then he tried to get up, driven by brute stubbornness, by his hatred of Pagan. Pagan lashed out with the foot again, aiming it directly into the side of Downey's head, and Downey fell backward.

Pagan stepped over him, moved away, breathing hard. There was fire under the dressing on his neck, a pulse of flame. He reached for the girl, who had watched the brief flurry of action in a wide-eyed way, and grabbed her arm.

"Do you have a car?" he asked.

"I rented one."

"Then let's get the hell out of here. Fast."

VENICE

33

The morning weather in Venice was unexpectedly sunny, almost springlike, if you chose to ignore the fact that the temperature was only four degrees above zero. The rain had gone, the sky was clear. The pastel shades of the city had been refreshed overnight. Shadows formed in the squares. At least for the moment the dead city of winter had passed; hardy tourists hired gondolas, crowds strolled on the Rialto or gathered in the Piazza San Marco, where they stood around in awe, and when awe subsided they fed the pigeons with breadcrumbs purchased at extortionate prices from vendors.

Barron stepped out onto the balcony of his apartment. Leaning against the handrail, he looked down into the canal below. He wondered where the currents had taken the General's body. Out to sea, Carlotta had said. Out to sea and long gone. But Barron was beset by the strange notion that the corpse would eventually somehow drift just under his window, that he'd look down and see the General's sea-bleached face staring up at him. All night long he'd imagined the body rolling with the tides, water billowing in the General's clothing.

He went back indoors. Carlotta was coming down the staircase from the bedroom. She wore a navy blue business suit, the skirt knee length, dark shoes brightly polished. She had very little makeup on her face. She'd tinted her hair and now it was black and severely parted.

"How do I look?" she asked.

"Businesslike," Barron answered.

She came to the bottom of the staircase. "You had a restless night. You didn't sleep well."

"I drifted in and out."

"Nervous?"

Nervous didn't quite describe it, Barron thought. He watched Carlotta cross the floor toward him. It was strange how she adapted the movements of her body to the kinds of clothing she wore. In loose-fitting garments she seemed angelically at ease, flowing. In tight skirts she walked provocatively, her hips thrust at an aggressive angle. In her present attire she appeared to have developed a rapid walk with shorter steps than usual; you almost expected her to advise you on investment matters. Angel, slut, businesswoman, mass murderer; there were no limits to Carlotta, and because there were no limits, there was no core, nothing you could ever pin down and say: *Here, this is the real Carlotta. This is who she really is.*

"Well, Barron," she said. She tapped a cigarette on the surface of a silver cigarette case. "This is the day. And the sun is shining. How appropriate." She looked from the window, lit her cigarette. She stuck the case back inside the small purse she carried, which matched her suit. She turned, faced him, smiled. There wasn't a trace of uneasiness about her. She was calm, deliberate. This is Carlotta in her element, he thought. This is how she comes to life — by being somebody else, in this case a Russian security operative named Alyssia Baranova.

She stepped toward him, blew smoke directly past his face. Every gesture, every move — total confidence.

"Well? Nothing to say?" she asked.

"You know what you have to do," he answered. "There's nothing you've forgotten?"

"We've gone over everything." She laid the palm of a hand tenderly against the side of his face. "It's going to be very simple, Barron. There's nothing in the world to worry about. Anyhow, frowning ages you. And you don't want to look your age, do you?"

He smelled scent on her fingertips.

"Think of it as just another day," she said. She pinched his cheek lightly between thumb and forefinger. The gesture, seemingly so innocuous, made him feel like a patronized child. His relationship with this woman had more complex passageways than an anthill. You went one way, found yourself in a chamber you'd never seen before. You went another, came to a dead end, backtracked, passed through rooms only vaguely familiar to you, and yet all the while you could detect the spoor of the woman, the scent that compelled you to keep searching for her. But you never found her because she wasn't there.

"Just another day," he said.

"Exactly." She moved away from him. Looked at her watch. Took from her purse a compact, flipped it open, regarded her face a moment in the mirror. Suddenly stern, eyebrows drawn together, she surveyed Barron over the rim of the mirror. "Alyssia Baranova. I was probably raised in Smolensk. My father was, let's say, an engineer. My mother taught in a nursery school. She was more liberal than my father. When I was ten, she sent me to ballet classes, but I didn't have the talent for that. What then? Well, I went to university, studied languages, became fluent in French and German. And then I was recruited by intelligence. The bare bones of a life."

She smiled, seemingly pleased with her invented history. She might never have been Carlotta. She put the compact back inside the purse.

"And when I'm no longer Alyssia Baranova? What happens next?"

"We go away on an extended vacation. Tonight."

"And then? Do we live happy ever after, Barron?"

"We try."

Barron watched her go toward the door. He had an urge to detain her, to keep her from going out of the apartment, as if some part of him, a relic of conscience, wanted to bring everything to a dead stop. But he didn't speak. It was too late to change anything now. He'd played his part. He had nothing more to do with events.

"Later," she said. And she went out, leaving her casual word of departure hanging in the air. Later. He walked up and down the room, stopped at the mantelpiece, remembered all the photographs he'd broken. Earlier, he'd watched Schialli silently sweep away shattered glass, and he'd felt nothing, no regret, no touch of sadness. He had a sense of having outlived the usefulness of his souvenirs.

He went back on the balcony, back out into the sun, whose cold harshness burned upon the deteriorating buildings of the city. He felt a peculiar menace in the brightness.

He looked at his watch. He thought of the girl calling from Lyon to say that the business with Pagan was finished with, and he wondered why she wanted to see him. She was always a delight, of course, she always had been — and he permitted himself a moment of nostalgia, remembering her father, Harry Cairney, the business he and the old man had done together, Harry raising money for his beloved Ireland, Barron supplying weapons. Life had seemed altogether simpler in those days. And then he thought of the son, Patrick, but that memory was thin, a handsome face, dark determined features, nothing more.

He looked down into the waters of the canal and pondered Rhodes and Kinsella in their hotel suites, anxiously awaiting news of Helix. And then he turned and, shivering, went back indoors. He looked toward the fireplace, his attention drawn by scraps of colorful paper that had been discarded in the grate. Gift-wrapping paper that depicted clowns and elephants and seals, the paper the General had given him. The pictures seemed forlorn to him, and joyless, as if the object that had once been wrapped inside the paper had bleached all the childish merriment from the illustrations.

He struck a match and applied the flame to the paper and watched the characters darken and curl and turn finally to black ash.

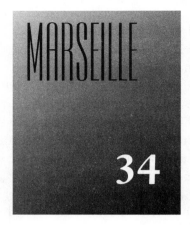

MARSEILLE

34

Pagan saw no future in going to Lyon Airport — which was the first place he'd be apprehended as soon as the dead woman was discovered or Downey had recovered awareness. For much the same reason he decided against the Geneva airport as a destination; it was close enough to be placed quickly under surveillance. So he told the girl to drive to Marseille, two hundred and fifty kilometers away.

To forestall the possibility of conversation that would have been either stilted or recriminatory, he turned on the radio and for a few minutes there was jazz, before the station drifted and an Italian baritone voice fused uncomfortably with Dizzy Gillespie. Now and then he looked out the window, fighting sleep; he avoided the girl's face. The tension inside the vehicle was like a third passenger, somebody having a quiet nervous breakdown in the backseat.

The girl turned off the radio. Pagan had the feeling she was about to speak, and wished she wouldn't. He didn't want to hear what she had to say; it had gone beyond that. Silences were preferable. He looked at the reddish glow of the dials, then peered at the highway, here and there seeing farmhouses, the outlines of barren trees, small cafés. A chill dawn sun hung in the sky.

He found himself wondering about the girl's reports to Barron, the phone calls. How much had she revealed anyhow? How had she phrased her reports? *I've got him exactly where I want him, Tobias. I really think he's falling in love with me. He tells me practically everything about his work.* These were depressing considerations. He couldn't dwell on betrayal; it was like sucking on an orange spiked with arsenic.

Barron, he thought. And his anger rose up again, sickening him. Barron, do-gooder, benefactor of the meek, the underprivileged, the starving. And what else besides? Connected to Carlotta, and presumably to the bomb, and so to the Undertakers; hence to William J. Caan. The sharp cogs, the teeth of a very complicated machine. And all the while Barron sprayed garlands of goodwill around the wretched planet, he opened clinics, schools, bestowed his blessings on the needy. It was terrific cover.

The girl glanced at him. "I want you to know how I got involved with Barron."

Pagan said nothing. He made an indifferent gesture with his hands. He didn't care.

She didn't speak again for a few miles and then it was as if she were addressing herself. "It seems sometimes that I've known him forever. He used to come regularly to our house in upstate New York. He'd lock himself away with my father for hours. I was just a kid, what did I know? Two grownups discussing business, that's all. When business was over he was . . . playful, I guess is the word. He liked games. Croquet. Checkers. He taught me chess moves. Whenever he came to visit, he brought presents."

"Good old Uncle Tobias," said Pagan wearily.

Undeterred by his tone, the girl continued. "I went away to boarding school for a while. During summer vacations, I'd go visit him in Coral Gables. He always had time for me. He'd drive me around in this big convertible he had. Take me to restaurants. I was maybe thirteen, fourteen, and he treated me like an adult. He was never anything but kind to me . . ."

Pagan didn't want to hear any more recollections of Uncle Tobias. "Very nice," he said. "I'm happy for you. I'm delighted you've got all these lovely memories to sift. Long sunshine days in Florida. Teaching you chess. Open-air restaurants. Very nice."

She glanced at him and he looked away. He said, "And the sweet little girl grows up to be a killer. Uncle Tobias was a terrific influence. A real role model."

"I made my own decisions, Pagan. He didn't force me into anything."

"He approached you with a proposition. Get me the dirt on Pagan and don't worry if you have to sleep with him to do so — it's all part of the ongoing struggle for justice. He pimped for you and you cruised along with it. Then there's another proposition. *Katherine, my dear, I'm afraid you're going to have to kill Pagan. You don't mind, do you, Katherine?* Or did he call you Kate?"

"I'm trying to explain," she said.

"And I'm wondering why you feel this burning need. I don't give a shit —"

"I don't believe what you said about Barron, Pagan. That's why. What you tell me doesn't square with what I know about him."

"You're trying to defend a man who orders you to shoot me? You're trying to tell me he's basically good, is that it? I'm not buying, love."

There was anger in the girl's voice. "Look. He was kind to me, goddammit. After my father died . . . shit, I couldn't begin to tell you. You wouldn't listen anyway."

"You've got that right," he said.

She tightened her hands on the wheel, gassed the car, overtook a convoy of cumbersome trucks in a reckless way. Then she braked slightly as if her anger had dissipated. "Your perspective is just so goddamn narrow, Pagan. You've been chasing terrorists for so long it's warped your judgment. You see things that aren't there. You impute motives to people who don't deserve to be maligned. This Carlotta, this bomb on the Underground, you've got that all wrong when you blame Barron. Okay, he wanted *you* out of the way, but he'd have a sound reason, because he wouldn't order death unless it was necessary, and even then he'd be unhappy about it —"

"Mister Conscience," Pagan remarked. "Even as he tells you to off me, he's wringing his hands and blowing his nose into a hankie and his eyes are watering."

"You're a shit," she said.

"When it comes to people like you and Barron, I'm more than a shit. I'm a monster."

"You could never understand the part he played in my life." The girl stared at him a second before returning her eyes to the road. "I was fifteen when I understood that Barron was helping the Cause. I knew about my father's involvement before that — how could I not have known? It was all around me. When my father died, I went to live in Barron's house in Florida for a time. When I was seventeen, and pretty damn bitter about the way both my father and brother had been killed, Barron asked me to run an errand for him. A simple thing, really. I was to deliver an envelope from Belfast to New York. I jumped at the chance. I didn't know what it contained, I didn't care. I assumed it was money, a check maybe, I don't know. All I knew was I was making a contribution . . . And it excited me, Pagan. I was doing something *real*."

Pagan said, "And one simple errand leads to another. Then another. And then to murder. By which time you're ready for your next assignment — namely, Frank Pagan."

She nodded her head. "I was happy to be asked. Do you understand that? I knew your name, of course. I knew about you and Patrick. I wanted the job, Pagan. And when it came down to killing you, I wanted that as well."

Pagan stretched his legs, felt his neck throb, tried to adjust his position in such a way that the friction of collar against burn would be alleviated. He stared from the window, seeing apartment buildings and an industrial development. Somewhere a factory stack was burning and ragged red cinders rose into the sky. Beyond, over the Golfe du Lion, the sun was cloudy, a forlorn old biddy of the sky.

"Now you're trying to convince me Barron's a liar," she said. "And I'm not ready to accept that. Not on your word alone, Pagan. No way. What are you running on anyway except some wild stories, some flight of goddamn fancy?"

Pagan glanced at her profile and felt a slight sadness. She was lost to him. But it was unproductive to think about that; that road led nowhere. She came into your life, she went out of it again, and amen. Sadness was irrelevant. He had to put himself in a place beyond feeling. Cold storage.

At Marseille Airport, she parked the car. Pagan stuck her gun with the silencer in the glove compartment. They went inside the terminal building, walked to the Air France desk. When he stated his destination, the putty-faced woman behind the console looked at him in a surprised way. "I'm afraid there's no direct connection, sir," she said. "You need to go through Rome."

"What about another airline then? What about Alitalia?" he asked.

The woman patiently punched her keyboard. "Alitalia has no direct flight either. You would have to fly through Milan on that airline. Sorry."

Sorry. Pagan realized he'd fallen into a trap of assumptions. He'd come to Marseille because it was the closest major city to Lyon, and he'd assumed, wrongly, that a direct flight to Venice would be instantly available, he'd buy a ticket, flash a passport — presto, a window seat, coffee, a quick flight.

"What's the earliest connection we could make?" he asked.

"For Rome, nine twenty-five. You'd arrive there at ten forty-five. That would get you to Venice at fourteen twenty-five." The woman tugged at her eyelashes, one of which came off on the tip of her finger like the leg of a spider.

"Okay," Pagan said. "We'll go through Rome."

He watched as she tapped her keyboard. The printer, whirring into life, issued two tickets. He paid cash, stuck the tickets in his pocket, then, followed by the girl, wandered around the terminal. It was eight-thirty according to the departure screens. A brief time to kill. He got some coffee from a machine, thought about smoking, changed his mind.

He looked in the window of a shop selling souvenirs of France, jars of Dijon mustard, baguettes, wines. He perceived his own reflection in glass. Pallid, worn down. In the same window the girl seemed like a ghostly shadow standing beside him. It was, he thought, an appropriate little cameo — a faded snapshot, a creased item you carried in the back of your wallet.

He sat down, finished his coffee. The girl sat alongside him. Pagan crushed his cardboard cup, dropped it in a wastebasket. He gazed at the information screens, pondered faraway destinations.

"When we get to Venice, what then?" she asked.

"We go to Barron's."

"Together?"

"You step inside — I'll be right behind you, armed and ready. He's expecting you. I'll be the surprise."

"Just like that?"

"Yes."

"I don't like it."

"Why? Do you feel you're betraying Barron? Is that what you feel?"

"Maybe."

"My heart aches," he said.

She pressed her hands between her knees and looked at the floor and was silent a long time. When she spoke her voice was quiet. "In a strange kind of way I'm sorry we —"

"I don't want to hear it," Pagan said. "You have any regrets, keep them to yourself. Spare me."

She raised her face, looked into his eyes. She said nothing. His attention drifted to the doorway of a newsstand, where there was a rack of the morning's papers. The headlines concerned the devastation that had taken place in Prague, the assassination of Svobodin and several of his ministers inside the Castle. A picture showed smoke rising from the building.

Pagan, tired of bombs and destruction, weary of hatreds, allowed his eye to wander across the front pages of various newspapers — Italian, French, English. There were photographs of Vladimir Gurenko, looking small and startled, perhaps even vaguely deranged, by the flashbulbs of cameras. Three separate photographs — Gurenko shaking hands with the British prime minister, Gurenko in the presence of the French president.

And the third — Gurenko being greeted by Ambassador William Caan on the steps of the US embassy in London. Caan looked positively beatific, glowing in the Russian's presence. Gurenko wore a stressed-out labored smile, that of a man obliged to carry on his back the burden of a nation splintered by factions.

Pagan rose, stared at the ambassador's handsome face, then lowered his eyes and glanced at the text accompanying the pictures. The words he read caused a darkness to stir at the back of his brain.

He'd been too preoccupied with the tunnel, and with Brennan Carberry, and Streik, and Carlotta, to pay anything but the most superficial attention to what was going on in the wider world. He'd been drawn so far down into his own depths that the movement of politicians was remote from him, like an ancient clock he heard from time to time ticking asthmatically in a distant room.

Caan greets Gurenko.

Gurenko, according to the text, was on his way to meet the Italian prime minister in Venice. *A lover of art, the President will visit the Scuola di San Rocco . . .*

Venice. Wintry Venice.

Where Tobias Barron resides . . .

Where Carlotta may be . . .

He seized a newspaper from the rack and gazed at the photographs and he had the curious sense he was in some way seeing *beyond* them, he was looking into another dimension, as if what he held in his hand was not a record of the recent past but an insight — slim and tenuous — into the future.

The girl stood behind him, looking over his shoulder. "What's wrong?" she asked.

He wondered what his expression revealed. He stuffed the newspaper back in the rack. "I hope it's me," he replied.

VENICE

35

She walked quickly through the narrow streets. Here and there flags fluttered. Festive Venice: the city was welcoming the president of Russia. The wind in the shiny plastic bunting made whiplike sounds, as if the air were filled with birds of prey. Sunlight in the *campos*, fat women strutting in fur coats, kids running back and forth. Happy ever after was what Barron had said. What did he see in the future for them? Some Caribbean island where they'd grow ancient together? Walks along glistening beaches? Meals eaten on stuccoed terraces?

That wasn't happiness, not for her. That was boredom. Barron's little world. And she didn't want to belong to it anymore. She'd outgrown him, she'd unshackled herself from him. He was weak, and she wasn't. She'd seen the weakness in him when the General had been killed. She'd seen fear and horror in him when she'd told the truth about the death of Bryce Harcourt. And why had she protected him from that truth in the first place? *Because he couldn't face it. Because he didn't have the detachment of true ruthlessness.* She'd outstripped him; that was what had happened. Life with him would be burdensome now. Relationships were fragile things, and this one had broken. It was that simple. Barron was no longer significant in her eyes. She felt nothing in this recognition, no sadness, no sense of an ending, no emotional rupture; if she experienced anything, it was a faint sense of disappointment in him for his lack of strength. He didn't like the taste of death in his mouth.

She was happy right now, happy *doing what she was doing*, she was vibrant with the idea of death. Her blood rushed. She was electric, on fire, it seemed to her that anyone looking at her would see around her an aura of flame, a burning in the depths of her eyes. Barron could never begin to understand her. Barron, despite his ostentatious trappings of power, his machinery and his networks and his money, had no courage when you got right down to the place where he lived. What could he offer her in the future? No, she needed more than anything Barron could give her.

She crossed a small bridge, heard the click of her own urgent footsteps. When she reached the Rialto, she barely noticed the shoppers perusing the silk scarves and T-shirts and costume jewelry on display. These things belonged in another world, one that didn't have anything to do with Alyssia Baranova from Smolensk. She was a tourist in this place, a stranger, she was merely passing through. She turned her face up, looked at the sun, blinked.

On the other bank of the Grand Canal she found herself moving in the shade of an alley, passing cafés, conscious of voices raised in small talk. Alyssia Baranova wouldn't understand Italian. She wouldn't know how to go inside a café and order a drink except by pointing to a menu and nodding her head in the silly apologetic way tourists had. She might be thinking of her father, the engineer, and wondering how he was surviving the ravages of winter in Russia. Or her mother, her careworn mother with the grooved forehead and the intricate network of wrinkles around her lips and the hands that were chapped and cracked by the cruelty of the season. Alyssia Baranova might stop and pick out a picture postcard and pay for it in the clumsy manner of foreigners who don't understand currency. Yes, these were the things Alyssia would do.

She emerged from the alley into the direct white flash of sunlight falling on a small square. The Scuola wasn't far away. She looked up, saw banners being shifted by the wind. She was aware of policemen now, scores of them, and soldiers standing idly around in groups with their automatic rifles held lazily against their bodies. Certain alleyways had been cordoned off. Venice, vigilant host, protector of the man called Gurenko. She smelled all around the inherent decay of the city, the odor of canals, the creeping damp of old stone lapped for centuries by water.

She walked to the Campo San Rocco, where already journalists and cameramen were gathering. Armed soldiers thronged the square. The reporters, the TV analysts, the commentators, the cameramen — they strained to get closer to the Scuola. Here and there angry words were traded; a soldier seized the camera of a particularly persistent photographer and threw it on the ground, where it shattered.

Alyssia Baranova had to show her identity card to an armed guard before she was allowed access to the doorway of the building, a somber place corroded by fog and damp in winter and heat in summer.

It was exactly two o'clock.

The interior of the building, the gloomy main hall, was chilly, despite the body heat generated by the milling security personnel. She understood that the preservation of the Tintorettos depended on the temperature. Too much heat might crack or damage them. She passed through a metal detector, had her ID card scrutinized by a silver-haired Russian security agent in an Italian double-breasted suit, who smiled at her. She understood: this was the one. This was the one who had cleared the way for her. There were going to be no obstructions, the machine had been lubricated.

She entered the hall. A long table had been placed in the center, ten chairs on either side. All around her Russian security people, thirty men and women, scanned the walls with electronic sweeping devices. They were thorough: walls, the floor, the chairs, the table, everything. Perched on long aluminium stepladders, agents examined the ceiling. There were lengths of thick black electric cable across the floor. Portable consoles, attached to the electronic devices, depicted graphs, like those machines you saw measuring heartbeats in hospitals.

She raised her face, looked up at the paintings, which meant nothing to her; there was no artistic appreciation in Alyssia Baranova's character. *The Adoration of the Magi. The Circumcision.* The mystic nature of the works was lost to her. Their dark colors, enlivened here and there by flecks of red and gold, didn't touch her.

Somebody approached her, fussing, worried, mumbling, a small man with rimless glasses, seemingly the curator. "I do not approve, I do not approve," he was saying as he rushed back and forth, making sure that nobody actually laid a hand on any of the art. "Clumsy people, such clumsy people, what do they care that this is all so *priceless?* Why did they choose *this* place when they could have chosen so many others? Politicians. Pah. Pah. They think the world revolves around them."

Alyssia Baranova, pretending not to understand, moved away from him. She attached herself to the security personnel, buried herself amongst them, pretending to be officious, looking this way and that with an expression of grave concern. She melted into the crowd; perfect camouflage. She had the ability to appear busy, to look fussed, under pressure.

"Are you new?"

Alyssia Baranova turned. The woman who'd asked the question was in her middle thirties, prettified by too much lipstick and rouge. She had a rather stern expression.

"I haven't seen you before," the woman remarked.

Alyssia smiled in a quiet way. "I was brought in at the last moment," she said.

"That accent," the woman said. "Are you from Leningrad?"

"I lived there for a time. But my parents moved around." Alyssia shrugged. She hadn't expected conversation. Her Russian, which she hadn't used in a long time, was still fluent.

The woman glanced at the silver-haired man in the doorway, then turned her face back to Alyssia, and her expression was one of knowing slyness. "I think I see."

"See what?" Alyssia felt a very slight alteration of her heartbeat. "What do you see?"

"You're one of his latest," the woman said.

Alyssia shook her head. "Whose latest?"

"My dear. He picks us up and drops us when he feels like it. It's nothing to be ashamed about. You're Budenny's new playmate."

Why deny it? Just go along with it all. "I didn't think anyone knew," she said coyly.

The woman laid a hand on Alyssia's arm. "His appetites are enormous. Everybody knows that," and she laughed, although the sound was dry and brittle and perhaps even a little envious. "Good luck. You'll need it. And stamina. You'll need that also."

Alyssia moved away, walking to the rear of the gray-stoned hall. There she turned and looked in the direction of the man called Budenny, who was gazing back at her across the big room. Was that a wink, that flutter of eyelid? Budenny had turned his face away from her now. She felt like an excited participant in a clandestine love affair. Should she blush?

She made herself busy, going down on her knees, examining woodwork with her fingertips, scrutinizing it with a professional air, checking for anything the electronic sweepers might have missed — although, of course, they would have missed nothing. *You can't miss it. You go there after the electronic boys have worked the area.*

She coughed, took a handkerchief from her pocket, raised it to her lips, then she stood upright and made her way across the hall. She passed close to *The Assumption of the Virgin* and walked toward the doorway. Budenny looked at her — but it was difficult to read his expression. One eyebrow raised, he inclined his head toward her.

"You're the one with the head cold," he said.

"Yes," she answered.

"It's the season. Go back to your hotel. Take it easy."

"I will. Thank you."

He dismissed her with a languid gesture of a hand. She walked out of the Scuola. She crossed the Campo San Rocco, pushing past soldiers and journalists. When she was free of the area, she looked at her watch. Two-thirty. Her work was done. She went over the Rialto and decided to stroll across the Piazza San Marco. Perhaps she'd even stop for coffee at the Florian in the archways. Then she'd go back to Barron's apartment on Calle dei Avocati, and the fiction that was Alyssia Baranova would cease to exist because she'd fulfilled her function: she'd started the clock called Helix ticking.

VENICE

36

Frank Pagan and Katherine Cairney arrived at Marco Polo Airport at four o'clock and walked through the terminal, where a large contingent of local police wandered vigilantly around. They were looking, Pagan knew, for the kinds of weirdos, fruitcakes, ax-grinders, fringe radicals, and conspiracy theorists who tended to congregate where prominent politicians appeared — the kind of people cops tended to lock up for the night just as a precautionary measure.

At the dock they boarded a launch headed for the city. In Rome, where they'd been obliged to spend time in the terminal waiting for the connecting flight, the sky had been gloomily overcast; here, in Venice, the sunlight was unexpected, almost caustic. Pagan observed the other passengers aboard the launch — a pair of ruddy backpacking Finns who looked impossibly healthy; a loud Englishman, armed with high-powered binoculars, who spoke at his timorous wife as if language were more a barrage of missiles than a means of communication. *By God, I remember coming here with Bob Duffy, what a time we had of it in those days, got to know Venice like the back of my bloody hand*, the Englishman was saying.

Pagan stepped onto the deck. The girl came after him. Despite sun, there was no trace of warmth. He shivered, stuffed his hands in his pockets, and thought that this might have been romantic in other circumstances — the glories of Venice, an attractive girl at your side. But not now.

As the launch approached the Grand Canal, where sunlight picked at the threadbare fabric of the waterside palaces, he thought of Barron, tried to *imagine* his way inside a man about whom he knew practically nothing. He turned to look at the girl, who had found in her purse a pair of amber-tinted glasses that made her appear remote and sullen.

"Is Barron likely to have protection?" he asked without looking at her. "Guns. Bodyguards."

She shrugged. "I guess that's something you'll have to find out for yourself, Pagan."

He gripped her arm. "Try again."

She smiled coldly at him, shaking her arm free. "I only ever visited him in Florida. I didn't notice any gunmen hanging around. He had a cook and a maid. I don't remember anything else. Maybe he's got a whole goddamn arsenal in Venice. How would I know?"

He gazed along the banks of the Grand Canal, seeing wind-tossed banners here and there. His Italian was almost nonexistent, but he understood the sense of the proclamations. Gurenko was being officially welcomed to the city. More, he'd been given the freedom of Venice, whatever that honor meant. VENICE GREETS GURENKO.

Pagan's uneasiness, which had dogged him on the flight from Marseille to Rome and hounded him on the leg to Venice, persisted as he stared at the flapping banners under which pedestrians strolled innocently in sunlight. It was almost as if he could smell in the air the gathering scent of disaster the way you might sense thunder in the distance before you heard it. He pushed the sensation into the back of his mind, a useful cellar where bottled notions sometimes fermented over time. But now they kept bubbling instantly back at him: Gurenko, the photographs in the newspaper at the Marseille airport. If Carlotta was here, if she could blow up a London Underground train, what did another body matter?

If she was here . . .

They disembarked some yards from the Rialto, wandered along the bank. He had picked up a tourist map at the airport and was trying to study it, shielding it with his body from the wind. What he saw was a twisted network of streets and waterways. Unknown cities always dislocated him, even when they were laid out in a comprehensible way — but he couldn't figure out the logic of Venice. He glanced down at the surface of the canal, where barges loaded with fruits and vegetables skimmed past, the mosquito-like buzz of *vaporetti*, the labored motions of *sandoli*. Then he concentrated again on the map, running a fingertip over it.

"I've found the street," he said finally. "We have to cross the Rialto and head for the Piazza San Marco." The wind flapped at the map, blowing it awkwardly back against his face.

"You're in charge, Pagan. Lead the way."

They walked a few yards, reached the Campo de la Pescaria, where the street ran with the blood and slime of gutted fish from the seafood market. The entrails of squid, squashed prawns, mullet bones, scraps of eel, discarded eyes — these were cast aside and pilfered by cats. He and the girl moved cautiously past unidentifiable pink organs, mounds of wrinkled fish skins, scales. Somebody was hosing these relics aside and the air was filled with the ancient scent of a long-dead ocean.

They crossed the Rialto and entered a maze of streets and alleys, some of which opened quite unexpectedly into startling squares. Pagan had a sense of wandering through cramped tunnels that led to boxes. It was, he supposed, apt — this awareness of a maze, of going blindly, of not knowing if the direction he was following would turn out to be correct. He could be perfectly wrong; the picture taken of Carlotta and Barron was years old, after all. There might no longer be any relationship between the pair — but why then had Barron sent down the execution order? The murder of Pagan made no sense unless it was examined in the context of his being a menace, a threat to whatever Barron was involved in . . .

They came to the Piazza, where nuns led a procession of schoolkids across the square and tourists snapped photographs of the basilica and the Campanile. In the failing coppery light the Piazza had an ephemeral quality. Pigeons floated and fluttered, people strolled under the darkening archways, artists sold their insipid watercolors.

In the center of the vast square he paused, glanced at the girl, saw dying sunlight strike the lenses of her glasses. A curious breathlessness affected him, as if everything conspired in this place to induce a contrary sense of peacefulness. He imagined drawing the girl toward him and kissing her on the forehead and plunging into the warm welcome of amnesia. How convenient it would be, he thought, to forget the reason he'd come to this city, to set aside the girl's treachery and take her to a little pension with a high cracked ceiling and peeling cornices and a big brass bed that creaked to the act of love.

A wind came up, sloughing across the square, blowing papers and breadcrumbs and discarded tourist leaflets — and the banality of these objects snapped him out of his reverie. He listened to the flap of flags and the crackle of bunting and his frame of mind was replaced by an unfocused sense of urgency.

He thought of Gurenko again. If he were assassinated — what would the consequences be? For starters, chaos. *Chaos.* The fragile Russia whose factions Gurenko barely managed to hold together would come instantly unglued, and voracious vultures would bicker over the corpse, hardliners as well as reformers, the old strife between change and familiar sterile stability — even civil war.

Pagan, sensing the origins of a headache, a throbbing pain behind his eyes, zigzagging lines coursing across his perceptions, heard Streik's voice again. *Peace is bad for business.* Bad for business — if your business happened to be weapons of death.

And that was William J. Caan's line of work. It was, according to old Martin, the basis of his fortune.

He thought he had it just then, the fine connections, the loose pieces that formed the picture. You created a line that led from Caan and the Undertakers to Carlotta, and in the center of that line you placed the middleman, Tobias Barron, who had commissioned Carlotta to kill Bryce Harcourt, who perhaps didn't like what he was involved in, who was scared like Streik and maybe ready to blow the whistle . . . He thought he had it, but it was elusive even yet, because if there was no association between Carlotta and Barron, there was nothing.

He walked under the archway, kept moving, the girl at his side. He consulted the map. "We turn left here," he said, and they entered a street of pizzerias, trattorias, grocery shops in whose windows hung hams and sausages; Pagan had a stab of hunger. He couldn't recall when he'd last eaten. The sun was beginning to abdicate the sky and the city was fringed by growing darkness.

"We need to find the Calle della Manola," he said. The wind seized his coat and he shivered as he entered a square, a mysterious space, shadows lingering around its perimeter, where plaster flaked from terra-cotta walls.

They crossed a short bridge and then came to another square, the Campo San Angelo, where a drunk singing to himself lurched out of nowhere into Pagan's path. Pagan, his nerves strident, reached back for his gun, but the drunk swayed away from him, and staggered into an alley.

"We're almost there," he said. He stopped, examined the map to be certain, then headed across the square toward a somber narrow passageway which the sun didn't penetrate.

"This is it. The Calle dei Avocati," he said. And paused, because suddenly whatever small assurance he'd had seemed momentarily to desert him. It was as if he were caught up in one of those weird dreams in which you were completely alone in a place of strangely angled buildings, where streets were crooked and led nowhere, and misshapen faces gazed at you from dim windows, and you experienced the kind of choking panic that forced you awake.

They entered the passageway.

Lamps had come on suddenly. Their light accentuated the delicacy of the girl's features. She was hesitant now and he wondered how he'd react if she stubbornly refused to do what he'd asked of her when she reached the threshold of Barron's house — but he didn't want to consider that possibility. Huddled against the renewed force of wind, they searched for the number, which turned out to be a dark four-storied building adjoining structures of a similar kind. The door was of solid blackened wood; the upper panel had been carved in the form of two ferocious lion heads so realistic they looked as if they were in a feeding frenzy. He thought of Audrey Roczak's studio in Lyon — his life seemed to have become a sequence of implacable doors, rooms from which he was excluded, secret places.

"Ring the bell. I'll be right behind you. Don't try to warn him in any way. Don't even think about it." He took his gun from the holster and held it, half hidden, in the folds of his coat.

The girl looked at him, didn't move.

"Ring the bell," he said again.

She stared at the ground, shifted her feet.

"For Christ's sake," he said, impatient. He reached past her, stuck his thumb on the doorbell, heard it ring deep inside the house. Then he stepped a couple of feet away.

The man who opened the door was not Tobias Barron. He was pallid, slightly stooped, dressed in a black suit. He didn't see Pagan at once, only the girl.

"Signorina Cairney?" he asked.

The girl nodded. There was no enthusiasm in the gesture. Tense, Pagan anticipated an erratic act on her part, a warning shout, perhaps a surreptitious sign of caution. But she simply stepped into the doorway.

"Come, you are expected," and the man opened the door a little wider —

Which was the moment Pagan chose to make his appearance, moving forward swiftly, gun out, barrel held directly to the side of the man's head.

"Back up," Pagan said. "Back up, keep your hands at your sides. You understand me?"

The man looked at the girl uncomprehendingly. "Who is this?"

Pagan stepped inside, kicked the door shut. He was aware of a large flagstoned vestibule where a chandelier of mauve Venetian glass threw a glittering confection of lights.

"Who is this?" the man asked again.

The girl said nothing. Her expression was despondent.

"Where's Barron?" Pagan asked. He stared into the sallow features of the man, the dark-brown eyes that registered confusion and alarm.

The man stepped away, disconcerted. Pagan was conscious of a stone staircase beyond the reaches of the light from the chandelier.

"I asked you a question," Pagan said, and reached out, prodding the barrel of his gun into the man's forehead. Pagan's imagination sprinted — perhaps an alarm system was set into the flagstones and needed only the pressure of a foot to activate it, perhaps there was a form of hidden signal which, once given, would bring down all kinds of grief in the shape of armed men swarming from the upper floors.

"Don't make me ask again," Pagan said, and pressured the man's brow with the gun. The girl, hands in the pockets of her leather jacket, was gazing toward the stone staircase, her attention drawn there by a movement in the upper shadows.

A figure appeared in the gloaming. The man in the dark suit turned his face toward the stairs and flicked both hands in a gesture of uncertainty. The figure on the staircase moved, stepped down into the reaches of the light from the chandelier. He continued to descend and halfway down paused, one hand on the banister rail, the other tucked in a pocket of his jacket.

Pagan regarded the tanned features, the expression of calm, puzzled by the way celebrity seemed to create a nimbus around those who had achieved it. It had something to do with the surprise of recognition, the photograph becoming flesh, substance behind image.

"Katherine," he said. "And Frank Pagan. Surprise surprise." He looked at the girl, frowned, inclined his head a little. The voice was deep, a salesman's voice in a way, the kind that might persuade you into signing elaborate life-insurance policies you didn't need. If he was surprised by the appearance of Pagan, he managed to conceal it. He said, "You disappoint me, dear girl."

Katherine Cairney said nothing. Barron seemed disinclined to descend further, enjoying his lofty viewpoint.

"I'm glad we can dispense with introductions," Pagan said.

Barron smiled. He had, Pagan noticed, a certain easy smooth charm. "I've been following your recent career with interest, Pagan. But you know that by this time," and he nodded toward Katherine Cairney, to whom he addressed his next remark. "I think I asked too much of you, didn't I? You weren't quite ready, I'm afraid. Your brother's blood doesn't seem to flow in your veins, Katherine."

At the mention of her brother, the girl stepped toward the foot of the stairs and looked up. "You told me Pagan shot Patrick. Which Pagan denies."

"Of course he *denies* it. What do you expect him to do? Confess?" Barron asked. He took one step down, smiling at the girl. "You don't believe him, surely."

"I don't know what the hell to believe."

"You pain me," said Barron.

The girl said, "If you've lied to me, Tobias . . ." She didn't finish her sentence. There was an odd tone in her voice, in part hope, in part the dread of disappointment.

"Let me point out that you're the one that has lied to me," he said. "You claimed Pagan was dead. And here he is in the flesh. Right before my eyes. Let's not argue about lies, Katherine."

"Tell her, Barron," Pagan said. "Tell her the truth. Explain how you used her for your own purposes. And when you've done that, tell her about the bomb in the train, tell her about Carlotta."

Barron looked at Pagan. Then, as if Pagan had never spoken, he said, "Katie, Kate, when I told you Pagan killed your brother, I wasn't lying. Why would I lie to you anyway? We go back a long way together. We're practically family."

Family, Pagan thought. He studied Barron's expression and saw there a look of bruised dignity, a man offended. Barron was good, you had to give him that. He was an operator. Manipulation came easily to him.

Pagan persisted. "Tell her about Celestine. Tell her the way it really was, Barron. Explain to her that Celestine, the lovely Celestine, shot her own stepson."

Barron smiled at Pagan, then turned his face to Katherine. "Why have you even *listened* to this man, Kate? Why have you manufactured this pointless meeting? Patrick's dead. And Pagan killed him. Not Celestine. *Pagan.* That's the way it happened. I don't feel any need to argue the matter further. And I don't feel the slightest obligation to defend myself against these stupid accusations."

Katherine placed a foot on the first step, as if it were her intention to climb and confront Barron, and Pagan was agreeably surprised by her determination. She wasn't going to be pushed aside easily.

"It's not just Patrick," she said. "What about these other things? What about Carlotta? What about the Underground bombing?"

"Pagan's in the business of accusations, my dear. That's what he does for a living."

"You're not answering me, Tobias."

Barron smiled. Perfect white teeth. "How long have you known me, Katherine? Years? And how long have you known Pagan? A few days?"

Persuasive, Pagan thought. Voice confident, manner comforting. Yes, you could trust Tobias Barron. It would be the easiest thing in the world for an impressionable young girl.

"Your late father was one of my dearest friends, Katherine. On more than one occasion he asked me to keep an eye on you if anything should ever happen to him. And I did. I looked after you. I cared for you. Do you deny that?"

She shook her head. "I don't deny it."

"But you still have doubts."

"Yes, I have doubts because you're still not *answering* me, Tobias. You're evading my questions."

Barron descended another step, stopped. He raised a hand, palm outward. He looked weary for a moment, and sighed, and his shoulders slumped a little. "This kind of conversation is tedious to me," he said.

"She simply wants some straight answers," Pagan said. "That shouldn't be too difficult for you, should it?"

The girl's hands were clenched tightly at her sides. "This stuff about Carlotta — do you deny that? Do you deny you know her? Tell me, for Christ's sake. Do that much, at least."

Barron was silent. He looked down at her as if he wanted to confide in her some irrefutable truth, some ponderous bit of advice. He said, "I meet all kinds of people, Katherine. I travel the world, I shake hands, I give little speeches. All kinds of people drift past me."

"What the hell is that supposed to mean? Is that a yes?"

Barron shook his head. "All I'm saying is this: If I ever met the woman in question, I don't remember it. Isn't that enough for you?"

"No, it's not enough. You're playing goddamn games with me, Tobias."

"I don't play games," he said.

"Then give me a straight answer! Do you know this Carlotta? Did you have something to do with the bombing of the Underground? Did you? Answer me."

Barron appeared to consider these questions. "You sound just like your friend Pagan, dear. He must have rubbed off on you. Pity."

"Just give me some fucking answers." The girl's expression was stressed, her voice gritty in a way Pagan had never heard before.

Barron came down another step, glanced at Pagan. "Do you need to point your gun like that? I don't keep weapons in this house, so your gun is a little superfluous."

"I think I'll hold on to it anyway." Pagan studied Barron a moment. The man's features, when you saw them in the light emitted by the chandelier, seemed to sag a little. The impression of youthfulness was fractured. He might have been a small-time actor awaiting the ministrations of a makeup artist. Handsome, certainly, but tired, worn down, in need of a brush stroke, a touch of paint.

Pagan asked, "Where is she?"

"Christ, you don't give up, do you, Pagan?"

"I just want to know where she is," Pagan said. He looked at Katherine Cairney. She appeared confused, somebody presented with a message written in impenetrable code. Sweet Uncle Tobias; was she wondering if he had feet of clay? if the distant noises she heard inside her head were the clatter of idols falling? He felt sorry for her — but the feeling was remote, at one remove from himself.

"I'm sorry, Pagan. I haven't a clue what you're talking about. I can't help you."

"I think you can," Pagan said. "You're the one calling the shots, aren't you? You finance her. You meet her bills."

"Really, this kind of wild conjecture is tiresome," Barron said.

Pagan moved to the foot of the stairs. "I don't think it's wild, Barron. On the contrary, I think it's so near the mark it's unhinging you. Let's pluck a name out of the air and see what you make of it, right?"

Barron drew a hand across his forehead in the manner of a man suffering a mild headache. "I don't have time for this, Pagan."

Pagan said, "Start with Bryce Harcourt. You and your friends — and I'm assuming William Caan belongs in that category — want him out of the way because he's getting pretty damn strung out about all this cash going around, he's no longer predictable, so you commission Carlotta. Get rid of Harcourt for me. And she goes about it with a vengeance, which is the biggest understatement of my life. Afterward, because she hasn't *quite* had her quota of kicks, because a hundred people on a train isn't *quite* enough to satisfy her rapacious appetite for destruction, she slices up some poor hooker —"

"Hooker?" Barron asked. "I don't understand what you're saying."

"You didn't know about that? You weren't informed? Your sources of information must be slipping, Barron. Let me edify you. Carlotta killed a prostitute in Mayfair and left a personal calling card behind addressed to me. You must know enough about her to realize she thinks it's fun to slice somebody up with a pair of scissors. It's a lark. It's a day at the beach for her. Even then, she wants some extra spice, so why not leave a message written in blood behind — it makes the joke funnier still."

Barron was silent for a time. You couldn't read anything in his expression. He was skilled at camouflage. Even the vague weariness that created an aura around him might have been designed for effect.

Pagan said, "Where is she?"

Barron moved down a couple of steps.

"She's here in Venice with you. She's here with you because this is where the action is. Right?"

Barron looked at his wristwatch. "Action, Pagan?"

"Gurenko. An assassination. Stop me if I err," he said. Finally giving voice to this notion imbued it with a sharp credibility for him. Gurenko. Marked for death. *Peace is bad for business.* There was an equation somewhere. There was a design even if its strands were still twisted.

Barron looked distant, as if he were elsewhere, thinking thoughts that had nothing to do with whatever Pagan said. Then his mood appeared to alter, his face shadowed over, and Pagan had the notion that somehow the news about the vicious death of the hooker had touched him. But he rejected this idea. If Barron had commissioned Carlotta to destroy the Underground train, what was the blood of one young girl in Mayfair to him? Maybe Barron was one of those people who had a way of separating atrocities, placing them in different boxes, some labeled Necessary, others stored under the rubric Needless. Or maybe he was immune to death, as coldhearted as Carlotta herself.

Barron had arrived at the bottom step, then moved across the flagstones, pausing some feet from Pagan. "Assassination. Another wild surmise, Pagan. Not what you'd expect from a trained cop. Or are you a hunch-player? Is that what you are?"

"Sometimes."

"Hunches," Barron said with a trace of scorn. "You need something more solid than that. But you don't have anything, do you, Pagan? You don't have evidence. You have absolutely nothing to connect me with Carlotta. You have nothing to substantiate this ludicrous notion about an assassination. You say this Carlotta, with whom I'm allegedly associated, killed some whore in London. But you don't have Carlotta, Pagan, do you? You don't have Carlotta to verify any of this. Let me tell you what you are, Pagan. You're a lunger. Life's one headlong rush for you, isn't it? You jump into deep waters and you don't know the first thing about the currents. You don't even know how to swim. You're drowning. Look how easily you drowned in our pretty little friend here . . ." He swept a hand toward the girl. "If you honestly believe in this bug-eyed assassination theory of yours, why don't you pop down to the local cops and speak your mind? Tell them what you suspect. Let them have a look at this patchwork quilt of your suspicion. You'll find them at Parrochia di San Zaccaria, if that's any help to you. I'm sure they'll listen. Better still, find Gurenko and have a quiet word with him, if you can get within an inch of the man. And even if you do, you better have a damn good story before you open your mouth." Barron looked at his watch again. "I understand that he's scheduled to look at some paintings shortly."

Pagan realized he was being goaded, pushed. He tried to dredge up something he might throw back in Barron's face, a piece of solid evidence, anything to defuse the man. But he had nothing to use, nothing convincing, certainly nothing that would alarm Barron. He could toss all kinds of darts — the names of Streik, Caan, the Undertakers — but none had force enough to pierce Barron. Even his earlier mention of Caan had brought no noticeable reaction from Barron.

Barron drew the cuff of his sleeve over his watch. "Now, if you don't mind, I have a few things to attend to," and he moved toward the girl. He raised his hand, stroked the side of her face.

"You make me sad, Katherine," he said. "You'd rather believe what this policeman tells you than anything I have to say. Pity."

"You told me Pagan was a danger to the Cause, he had to be killed —"

"And you doubted me —"

She closed her eyes a moment. "I don't know what I believe any more. You. Pagan. And now this talk of an assassination —"

"That's a figment of Pagan's brain. A cop's delusion." Barron sighed, and let his hand fall from her face. "Katherine. Katherine. My precious little Katie." His voice was almost a whisper. Pagan had a flash of the girl as a child strolling across a sunlit croquet lawn with Uncle Tobias. Hand in hand, moving under a willow tree, the pungent drift of barbecue smoke; halcyon times. Dross now, and gray skies.

Pagan leveled the gun at Barron; overhead, the chandelier appeared inordinately bright, a shower of gold coins. "You still haven't told me where to find her," he said.

"This conversation is over," Barron said. Ignoring the weapon, he moved toward the staircase. He climbed a few steps. Pagan, who felt the situation sliding away from him, raised the gun, fired it upward. The bullet crackled in the bulbs of the chandelier and glittering fragments of glass showered the air. A cloud of plaster floated down amidst the shards.

"That was an old piece," Barron said without any obvious feeling. "I'm sorry you did that."

Pagan was assaulted by the need to fire the gun again and again into anything — the antique chairs, the remains of the chandelier that swung wildly above him, the paintings on the walls.

"Eighteenth century," Barron remarked. "Very difficult to replace." He shook his head, turned, and continued to climb.

And then, out of nowhere, she materialized above Barron, her arms folded across her breasts. She was hardly visible in the poor light. Barron became aware of her and stopped halfway up the stairs. *"I asked you to stay out of sight,"* he said.

She moved a few steps toward him. Her manner was one of aggression, confrontation. Her voice was quiet, but Pagan, even from his distance, could hear a tremor of rage behind her words. "You're letting him walk? You're letting him stroll *out* of here? And that girl? You're letting them leave?"

Barron answered her in a subdued way. "What can he do? What can he possibly do? Nobody is ever going to listen to him. He doesn't worry me."

Her face, which Pagan realized time had barely touched, turned toward the few remaining bulbs of the chandelier. She looked directly down at Pagan, and he was reminded of the interrogation room, the hotel, the easy way she'd stirred him. He stood very still. Her surprising appearance had frozen him. She might have taken substance out of the shadows, a good conjuring trick, an illusion that for a moment left you incredulous.

"He doesn't worry you," she said to Barron, mocking him. She was still staring down at Pagan, who imagined her inside the Underground station, placing the explosive on the tube, vanishing in the rush-hour crowds, doing her scissors number on the sad girl in Mayfair. She was all illusion. She was created by mirrors and vanished in drifts of colored smoke.

"He doesn't worry you," she said again to Barron, her voice rising a tone. "You're above all that. Is that it? You're still untouchable. You still don't see jeopardy. You're out of tune, Barron. Pagan and this girl, this bimbo, walk out of here — and then what? He just forgets his whole conversation with you? You think he's going to stop at

this point? Investigation over. Dead ends. He strolls away empty-handed. Is that what you think?"

Barron shrugged her words aside. "He's got nothing. He can *prove* nothing. He can *do* nothing." He held one arm up, showing her his watch. "Tick tick tick. Listen."

"Barron, Barron," she said, and her voice now was softer and her tone just a little sad. "You still live in that dreamworld of yours, don't you? After everything that's happened, you're still locked inside your own little tower where you think nobody can touch you. You fool. You poor sad fool. You haven't learned a goddamn thing."

Barron turned his face in Pagan's direction and Pagan had a sense of wills locked in conflict, Barron's pitted against Carlotta's, and he understood there could only be one winner. All at once a new dimension opened up for Pagan: the concept of a close relationship between Barron and Carlotta. He couldn't imagine it somehow. He reached for it but couldn't grasp it. He remembered her face and manner, the bewitching way she cast spells without effort, her forceful sexuality, and he wondered if Barron had been enchanted the way he himself had been years ago. He wondered about the complexity of their world, how hard they might have warred. If there was affection between them, if there was love, it was of a kind he couldn't begin to understand: the raw meat of emotions tossed into an arena where Carlotta and Barron fought over the scraps and entrails like animals.

He put his foot on the first step, the gun pointed upward. He was aware of Katherine Cairney standing nearby. He was conscious of her anger, her pale face. He went up another step.

"Carlotta," he said, and he jerked the gun.

Carlotta stared at him a moment. She looked hard, determined. She had the kind of eyes you couldn't stare into for long because they were unflinching. And then she changed again, smiling at him, the features suddenly soft. But he knew her deceptive abilities, the way her surfaces mutated.

"Is this the bit where you arrest me, Pagan?"

"Something like that."

"Do you have time for these legal niceties?" she asked. "Do you have time?"

He looked up into her smile. She moved so quickly, so unexpectedly, his eye couldn't follow her. He heard her say *Catch me, Pagan,* and then she laughed, a curious clipped sound, and shoved Barron in the center of his chest and — surprised, mouth open — he lost his balance, tumbling backward and rolling over and over, arms upraised, skull striking stone. He collided briefly with Pagan as he fell. Pagan stepped aside and Barron, calling out Carlotta's name, continued to tumble until he came to a stop at the foot of the staircase.

Carlotta had already disappeared. He could hear her footsteps on another flight of stairs and the sound of her voice coming through the darkness at him. *Catch me, Pagan. Catch me.* A message in blood on a lamp shade, a voice rolling through a big house. He scrambled upward, hearing her just ahead of him on a third flight of stairs. He needed light, he was running blind, his only sense of direction the sound of the woman racing upward. A dull bloom fell from streetlamps through windows here and there, but it was too thin to be useful. He kept going, climbing, hearing the sound of doors slamming shut, one after another, as if she were trying to confuse him into thinking she'd vanished inside one of the many rooms of the house. He was beyond thought, out of reason's range, he was motion, nothing more, he was trapped inside Carlotta's game of hide-and-seek and had no way of knowing quite what the rules were, whether she was intentionally leading him to some place where she'd corner him — or if she were simply using up his time. Breathing hard, he kept going, kept chasing, he had no choice other than to find her because that was what everything came down to in the end, the capture of Carlotta. He approached yet another set of stairs. This had to be the uppermost floor of the building, there were surely no more stairs after this unless you believed the structure had infinite levels, a trick place designed to cheat the senses. Another door slammed above him, then another, then another.

Carlotta was here and everywhere, and her voice floated around him as he reached the place where, finally, the stairs ended.

She stood in silhouette in the open doorway of a lit room. She was very still. He couldn't see if she was armed, and had the thought that maybe on her ascent through the house she'd picked up a gun from somewhere: he didn't trust Barron's statement that there were no arms in the place. He stepped toward her. He spoke her name in a hoarse, tired whisper.

"This is what I call a merry dance," she said.

"It's over," Pagan said.

She shook her head. "It's not over, Pagan," and she stepped back inside the room, kicking the door shut even as he lunged forward at it. He charged into the room beyond, seeing her rush toward glass doors. Suddenly she stopped and turned toward him.

Her arms hung at her sides in an aspect of surrender, a gesture that made him instantly wary. It was damned hard to connect the appearance of this woman with her murderous history, that was the trouble Pagan had had years ago, and the trouble he was having now. She looked at him with an expression of such translucent innocence he was forced to remind himself of what she'd done.

"Come quietly," he said. He was back inside the interrogation room, he was watching her slender legs, hypnotized by her eyes, drawn down into the sight of her graceful fingers, remembering how she'd behaved in the hotel room ten years ago, the way his blood had rushed, the thoughts of betrayal he'd entertained.

"And if I don't? Do you shoot me?"

Pagan didn't reply.

She said, "I don't think so. Most people are weak, Pagan. Like Barron. Like yourself. You have fronts you assume. Barron likes power because he finds it an elevating drug. Plug him into the power source and he feels strong, complete. That's his front. You like law and order, because you can't cope with chaos. That's your front. I knew that about you years ago, and you haven't changed. But I surprised you back then, didn't I, Pagan? I gave you something to ponder. I showed you a dark side of yourself and you didn't like what you saw."

"You're right. I didn't like it," he said.

"But it's part of you, Pagan. It's a part you choose to ignore because that way you're not inconvenienced by unwanted urges. You can sail along undaunted by your own demons. You just deny their existence. Dead simple. Frank Pagan, cop, upholder of the law, good citizen, boy scout. But there's something else murmuring in a corner of Pagan's heart. Something he doesn't want to face. Relax,

Frank. We all have our little monsters. The trick is to recognize them. When you've done that, living with them is easy. Every now and then you just turn them loose and let them do what they have to."

"You turned them loose in London all right," he said.

"I gave them a field day, Pagan. I gave them what they wanted — their freedom. You should try it sometime." She moved nearer to him and he was conscious of her scent, the way her silk dress clung to her body, the boldness in her eyes. "You've never forgotten our meeting, have you? It's stuck with you. And every so often it surfaces and you wonder what's inside you, if you're capable of betrayals and lies and infidelities, and your whole little world tilts just slightly. You wanted to fuck me that day."

"Yes . . ." Funny: the admission didn't embarrass him.

"You wanted it so goddamn bad I could smell it on you."

"It was long ago —"

"But not so very far away, Pagan." She stared at the gun. "I left the message in London as a reminder. I wanted you to remember that I'd done a number on you ten years ago, and that I could still do it. I had you climbing a very uncomfortable tree back then. And I have you climbing one now."

"I don't think so," he said. "Things change."

"Not the underlying things, Pagan. They don't change. There's still the same dark corner in you. You keep it hidden. But it's there. And I've got news for you: it's never going to go away."

The same dark corner, he thought. He wondered if she was right. She came closer still to him. She reached out, caught his lapel, rubbed the material between thumb and forefinger. She looked at the gun and said, "You'd rather fuck me than shoot me, Pagan."

"I don't think so," Pagan said.

She smiled and it was dazzling. "I know you, Pagan. You don't like to admit that, but I know you. And the reason I know you is because we're opposites. You think of rules, I don't. You worry about things making sense. I don't. What you see as endings are only beginnings. It's all a matter of perspective. Yours is very different from mine." She stepped back from him, raised one hand, studied her fingernails, which were glossy and pink. "The very things you'd find precious, I see as worthless. Love is a joke. Kindness is *always* self-serving. Human life has all the value of a counterfeit coin. You see a train packed with people. I see only one face. You see an eminent politician, and I see a man who means nothing in the general course of things."

An eminent politician. "It's going to be like the Underground again, isn't it? The same thing's going to happen."

"You're the detective. You figure it out."

"When is it due to go off?" he asked.

"When is what due?"

"Don't screw with me, Carlotta. *When is it due to go off?*" he asked again.

She moved back from the table and turned toward the glass door. He couldn't see her face now. He had the feeling she was about to do something, produce a weapon from somewhere and wheel around with it in her hand, more sorcery. But all she did was to point across the room to a door and say, "Unlock that and guess what you'll find. The soul of Tobias Barron."

Pagan gazed in the direction she'd indicated and in that second when his attention was diverted, she struck the glass doors with her body, burst her way through them with a force he couldn't have imagined, and he went after her even as glass sprinkled the air around his face, he pursued her out to a small balcony and saw her leap the handrail and jump into the darkness of the canal below, avoiding his outstretched arms. He heard the splash as she struck water. He went to the rail and looked down, but the canal was black and although a few foaming circles of white water broke the surface, he could see no sign of the woman. He called out her name a couple of times, imagined he heard an incomprehensible response from a place beneath him, thought he saw a movement along the narrow ledge that bordered the canal — a cat, that was all, a white cat slinking through the night for prey.

He turned back into the room. Katherine Cairney was standing in the doorway, watching him. He was beset by the urge to move quickly.

"I have to go —" And he rushed past her without touching her, hurrying down the stairs, down and down, back to where Barron lay on the flagstones at the bottom. His cheekbone had splintered flesh. His lips had been cut by his teeth, which were no longer perfect. Across his forehead were a series of blue-red indentations where his skull had struck the cutting edge of stone. Pagan stooped over the man.

"How long have I got?" Pagan asked.

Barron coughed blood. His expression was distant. When he spoke, his broken voice came from a faraway place. "Strange. I was asking that very question of myself . . ." He groaned, raised a hand feebly in the air. A look of pain contorted his face. He was dying, and he knew it; Pagan felt nothing, no compassion, no sense of pity.

"How long have I got, Barron?"

Barron managed a tiny counterfeit smile which contained an element of malice; on the threshold of dying, he was still trying to maintain some small hold on control even if it were slipping quickly away. "The clock ticks, Pagan. Tick tock. Ticktocktick. Too fast. Far too fast for all of us."

"How fucking long is it going to tick?"

Barron shut his eyes and for a moment Pagan thought he'd lapsed into the finality of unconsciousness, but then he coughed again — a harsh deep hawking sound — and he whispered hoarsely, "A little more than twenty minutes . . . a little less than thirty."

Barron's deathbed statement: inexact, enigmatic, barely audible. Barron turned his face to the side, his eyes open now, and unseeing. In death he seemed shrunken, dissipated. Pagan stepped away and hurried across the flagstones and out into the night.

VENICE

37

Gurenko was cold. In the underheated main hall of the Scuola he sat at the center of the long table, facing the Italian prime minister, a small bald man delighted that his country was playing host to the Russian president, and that Venice in particular had been selected as a meeting place. Hadn't it once been a crossroads of Europe, a forum for men of vision? He rambled on about democratic ideals, then segued into the subject of great art. It was, Gurenko thought, an altogether boring speech, most of which he managed to tune out.

Every now and then he would gaze away from the Italian, his eye drawn — where else — to the paintings on the walls. They excited and startled him. Even though he thought he'd known them intimately, his experience had come secondhand, from photographic plates in art books, which did no justice to the originals. He could *hear* the paintings; they spoke to him in subtle whispers.

As soon as the prime minister finished his speech, it was planned that Gurenko would stroll from one picture to the next, studying each in the company of an expert — an ax-faced man with a handlebar mustache — whose task was to point out the salient features of the works. Gurenko would ignore the expert. He didn't need a lesson in art history. No, he'd enter each painting as he came to it, he'd move into the dimension between the frames, he'd lose himself in the profoundly delicate combinations of shadow and color.

A dozen security people stood along the wall, watching. They were happy with Venice as a venue. It was an island, easily protected. A couple of official photographers held their cameras in a reverential way.

Gurenko, his bones beginning to lock, rearranged his position. The cold was feathered by damp and the air had a suggestion of mildew. It was this dampness and chill that Budenny had used as an excuse for his absence. Claiming a headache and the onset of a cold, he'd remained in the hotel. Fictions, Gurenko thought. He was probably watching TV, feet up, vodka in hand. Maybe he'd found himself a girl for amusement.

The Italian prime minister had apparently finished his speech. His aides and associates and the prominent dignitaries who'd gathered in Gurenko's honor applauded. Gurenko clapped his hands too, more from relief than appreciation. He got to his feet and was at once surrounded by people — the prime minister, his deputy, the mayor of Venice, the art expert, a number of hangers-on. Why couldn't he be left alone to wander the Scuola? Why did they press in on him with such eagerness to please?

"This way, Mr. President," said the art expert, and took Gurenko gently by the elbow, leading him toward the paintings.

Gurenko smiled. He'd suffer this fellow, but he wouldn't listen to him. Great art was something you explored alone. It was a private experience, a communication between yourself and a painter long dead. There was, he thought, an element of a séance about the business, a spiritual affair.

■

Time was a series of small collapses. Time was disintegrating, like paper eaten by acid. Pagan rushed across the dark of the Campo San Angelo and hurried along the Calle della Mandola, where he came to a bridge leading to the Campo Manin. He had no idea where the Scuola di San Rocco was located or if Gurenko was even going to be there. The newspaper he'd seen in Marseille Airport had mentioned the place, and Barron had casually remarked that the Russian was scheduled to view some paintings; it was a matter now of luck and timing — but how to proceed?

This side of the Grand Canal, the other — Venice lay around him in the manner of a formless labyrinth, a place beyond the skills of any cartographer, blind alleys, side streets, bridges, a cold intricate perplexing city. He was panicked by his lack of geography. He reached the Campo Manin, thinking, *the Scuola, how the hell do I find the damn place.* He kept hearing Barron say, *Tick tock . . . More than twenty minutes, less than thirty . . .*

Okay, you just go up to somebody and ask and hope whoever it is speaks reasonable English. Among the pedestrians he stopped in the Campo Manin he was luckless three times, somehow managing to choose winter tourists, a Turk, a middle-aged American couple trawling the historic places of Europe, a slender long-haired girl in a metal-studded leather jacket who spoke only Italian, *Non capisco, non capisco.*

When he encountered an elderly man carrying a rolled umbrella, his luck changed. The man was a retired professor of literature, who walked with less speed than Pagan would have liked, but who was prepared to show him the way to the San Angelo *vaporetto* station, where he would be ferried across the Canal to San Toma, and from there it was a short walk to the Scuola. There would be signs. The alternative, on foot, would mean crossing the Rialto and going by way of Campo San Polo, a long way around through a *parrochie*, a neighborhood, in which it was easy to get lost.

They left the Manin, loosely followed the course of the Rio di Luca for a short distance, reached the Grand Canal, where the retired professor indicated the *vaporetto* station. There was no sign of activity. "Here you must wait," he said.

"I can't wait," Pagan replied. He looked across to the opposite bank. What was the distance? Fifty yards, a hundred? It was frustratingly short.

The elderly man smiled as if impatience were a character defect he'd managed to eliminate from his own life. "The signor could always swim."

"It crossed my mind," Pagan said. He imagined going into the water, ploughing desperately to the other side.

"Of course, there is always the expensive water taxi," said the professor. He nodded his head toward a small launch docked some yards away.

Pagan moved toward the launch, looked down into the cabin, where a white-haired man in a heavy sweater and muddy boots was chewing on a *tramezzi*. The professor, eager to help the anxious Englishman, followed. He spoke to the taxi driver in Italian; there was haggling, which increased Pagan's impatience. How long did he have? How much time had evaporated since he'd left Barron's apartment? Eight minutes? Nine? His mental clock was awry.

The professor said, "For twenty thousand lire, he'll take you across. It's exorbitant. We must haggle more."

Exorbitant or not, Pagan agreed to the price, stepped down inside the launch, thanked the man. The driver started the motor, the craft throbbed violently. Pagan turned, facing the other bank, beating the palm of his hand on the brass rail. This rushing, this motion — he stared at the lights on the other side as the water taxi vibrated so vigorously it shook his bones.

"San Toma," the driver said.

The crossing had taken about a minute, certainly no more. Pagan crammed some money into the driver's hand.

"Sterling, sorry," Pagan said, and he skipped up onto the bank, grasping a wooden rail for support. He'd given the driver everything he had, about seventy pounds, not bad for a minute's work. He hurried away from the taxi, looking for the signs the professor had mentioned, couldn't find them in the thin scattered lamplight. He walked quickly, sometimes breaking into a sprint. Finally he came to a small blue plaque with arrows, one of which pointed to San Polo, the other to San Rocco. How far? he wondered. The city seemed to gather itself around him, the hunched buildings, the narrow lanes, a corral in which he'd become enclosed.

He knew he'd reached San Rocco when he saw the congregation of police and security personnel and the harsh arc lights rigged up by TV reporters, people milling restlessly in the street, vendors selling coffee and tea and sandwiches, the whole circus of security and publicity and sustenance that follows the president of an important nation. The Scuola itself was lit by a series of electric beacons, which played crisscross upon the surface of the building and created the impression that the structure was floating a few feet off the ground.

Pagan saw at once that it was going to be difficult to get close to the building because armed guards behind a yellow tape blocked the way, but he had little choice except to try. He shoved forward, pressing past photographers and media hawks and members of the footloose clan that call themselves stringers. He heard complaints on either side as he pushed his way forcefully through — *Rude bastard, where do you think you're going, Hey buddy, watchit.* He elbowed people aside, causing hot coffee to spill down the front of somebody's coat. He reached a point where he could go no farther because he'd come face to face with an Italian soldier who immediately stuck an automatic rifle in Pagan's chest.

Pagan raised his hands to show they were empty, then, miming caution, reached inside his coat for his identification — at which point the soldier undid the safety catch on his rifle and prodded Pagan hard. The soldier, you could see, had quickly reached his limits. He was under orders to take no prisoners. His imagination had been fired by his superior officer, who had given long lectures on certain radical elements in Italian society — extreme rightists, remnants of the Red Brigade, hard-line Communists who felt Gurenko was betraying the muddy ideals of Stalin. Pagan could belong to any such murderous outfit.

"Look," Pagan said, flashing his ID, which might have been a library card for all the soldier knew.

"Look," Pagan said again. "For God's sake."

The soldier seemed alarmed when a couple of nearby journalists, having witnessed this exchange, crowded around, firing all kinds of questions, trying to get a look at Pagan's identification, sniffing as they always did at the periphery of any story that might alleviate their tedium. They'd followed Gurenko from London to Paris and now to Venice, and they were due to track him to Bonn next, and Brussels after that, and so far the statements that had emerged from his meetings with heads of state invariably amounted to the usual platitudes. Here, for their diversion, was a little human drama, and it galvanized them.

They wanted to know what Pagan was trying to do here, did he have sinister intent, was he merely demonstrating against Gurenko, was he a radical or what, what was the goddamn scoop? The soldier popped Pagan again with the rifle, forcing him back. One of the journalists, a wild-haired Irishman from Radio Telefis Eirrean with booze on his breath, muttered something about the inherent brutality of the military mind. It was, Pagan thought, getting out of hand, the whole situation drifting away from him, the scribblers clustered at his side, the guard in front of him. It had begun to assume a raggedness he hadn't expected. And the shadow of time passing clouded his brain. How many minutes were left to him? He could make no headway with the soldier, and the journalists were clamoring abrasively for information. The soldier stuck his gun into Pagan's flesh again, this time with a look that meant he intended to use the damn thing, he had a heavy responsibility. Nobody was allowed under the tape unless they'd been authorized.

A man in a navy blue coat appeared just behind the guard. Tall, bespectacled, with an air of control about him, he was the kind who took charge of matters in a quiet, unflustered way. He seized the identification card and studied it and then said, "You are a long way from home, Mr. Pagan."

He raised the yellow tape and allowed Pagan to pass under it. Pagan's admission to a forbidden area agitated the hacks, who pleaded for information, firing questions, bitching, whining, wondering just what the hell was going on and what was so special about this guy who'd been allowed under the tape and into the sacrosanct space beyond.

Pagan was led to the side of the Scuola, where a swarm of Italian security agents immediately surrounded him and began frisking. His holstered gun was discovered and confiscated. The bespectacled agent still had Pagan's ID in his hand.

"My name is Androtti," he said. "I am in charge of security here. Your name is well known to me, of course, Pagan. Your long pursuit of Jig most memorably comes to mind . . . Your career has been an interesting one. Not altogether exemplary in terms of discipline,

perhaps . . ." He shrugged indulgently, as if he shared Pagan's distaste for the strictures of operating against terrorism by the book.
"We do what we can in a hard world, do we not?"

A hard world, Pagan thought. About to get even harder. "We can
discuss these things some other time, Androtti. Not now." He heard
a hoarse strident tone in his voice. He wondered briefly how he
looked to the Italian; a madman, a demented creature blown in out
of the darkness. "I've got to get inside the building."

Androtti took off his glasses, rubbed the lenses in the folds of his
scarf. Slowly, fastidiously, irritatingly. Androtti wasn't listening to
clocks. He had no way of hearing the tiny cogs that marked the
motion of seconds. "Inside the building?"

Pagan said, "Now." He stepped past the Italian and began to
move toward the entrance to the Scuola. Androtti caught him by
the arm and held him.

"Why?"

"If I don't get inside, Androtti, let me tell you very quickly what's
going to happen: Gurenko and everybody else around him goes up
in one amazing blast of fire. It's as simple as that."

Androtti brought his face very close to Pagan. "Are you trying to
say that the building is not secure?"

"In a word," Pagan said.

"No, this I find very difficult to believe. The Russians have declared
it safe. My own people have also verified this. And now you appear
from nowhere to tell me that we might have overlooked something?"

"That's exactly what I'm telling you."

"How? How is it unsafe? An explosive device?"

Pagan, assailed by the potential sense of a sudden eruption, an
image of the dark sky over Venice lit by a great sunburst of destruction, moved toward the doorway. Minutes, he thought. He imagined a bell in a steeple, the whirring of machinery, the clang of an
iron clapper about to strike. Time had become a series of rigid images that made grinding sounds inside his head suggestive of a welding tool slicing through metal. *More than twenty minutes, less than
thirty.* Barron could have been lying, a dying prevarication. But you
had no choice except to work on the assumption he'd been telling
the truth. Tick tock.

He stepped quickly toward the entrance, which was protected by soldiers. The night was loaded, the darkness charged. It was one of those situations that demanded a headlong plunge into action. What had Barron called him? *A lunger.* Okay, fine, he was a lunger, but sometimes that was what you needed to be; time-consuming explanations gained you nothing. He kept moving toward the lit doorway of the Scuola. The Italian hurried after him. Pagan was conscious of the phalanx of security personnel that gathered around him.

"Pagan," Androtti said. "How certain are you?"

Pagan had reached the entrance. The soldiers stared at him. Their faces, illuminated by electric light, were red from the raw night air. "I'll put it to you like this, Androtti. I'm not here for the benefit of my fucking health."

Androtti stared into Pagan's face as if he were searching for a visible sign of dementia. He said, "Very well," although there was a tiny element in his voice of doubt. But Pagan was known, Pagan had a reputation, admittedly one riddled with a certain recklessness, and if he was convinced that the Scuola was unsafe, then Androtti had no intention of standing in his way. He began to issue instructions in rapid Italian, his tone suddenly urgent.

The soldiers stepped aside and Pagan, followed by Androtti and his brigade, entered the Scuola. *Inside,* Pagan thought. *This is only the first step. What next? What now?* He stared across the large cold hall. Clusters of men surrounded one of the paintings. Somewhere in the midst of this throng was Gurenko. Pagan glimpsed him a moment — smaller in life than in his photographs — and wondered if there was time for people to be evacuated from the Scuola. He had a sense of being suspended in a place where time was an arbitrary measurement controlled only by Carlotta's chronometer, which ticked in an arrhythmic way, now fast, now slow, sometimes not at all.

Androtti was at his side. "Show me, Pagan. Show me what it is that panics you."

Show me. Pagan was struck by a paralysis of indecision. There were too many options. Too many places to look. Behind paintings, under chairs, beneath the table in the center of the room, on some high stone ledge, perhaps even in the upper room of the building. *Where did you put it, Carlotta? Where the hell did you put it?*

The crowd of about twenty or so milling around the painting on the far side of the hall seemed unaware of the entry of Androtti and his agents because they were too engrossed in the Tintoretto. They created a knot of concentration and gushing admiration. Somebody could be heard saying . . . *The magnificence of shadow, do you see* . . . The magnificence of shadow, Pagan thought. What I want is light, bright light, X-ray light. Shadow is the last thing I need.

"Well, Pagan? Where is this danger?" Androtti asked.

Pagan scanned the room. Clocks. Thin sands falling through an hourglass. Tides rushing over pebblestones. He realized he was sweating even though the air in the room was chill. He worked inside Carlotta's head, tried to see the room through her eyes, tried to imagine a place she'd think safe. A purse, a briefcase on an Underground train at rush hour. But the Scuola wasn't a carriage. He didn't know where to look, where to begin.

"Tell your men to start searching, Androtti. It doesn't matter where. Dark corners. The upholstery of the chairs. Behind paintings. I can't do this on my own. I need your help. You might also give priority to a complete evacuation of this place."

Androtti appeared to ponder this suggestion. He'd yielded some of his territory to the Englishman by allowing him inside the Scuola, but he wasn't going to surrender any more than he deemed necessary. To permit Pagan inside the building on the basis of the man's reputation as a counterterrorist agent was one thing; to ask Gurenko and the other dignitaries to leave was another. The prospect of rushing someone so important as Gurenko out of the Scuola in an unseemly manner didn't appeal to him. If Pagan was wrong about all this, if he'd made a mistake or was acting on unreliable information, Androtti was the one who'd be blamed for causing needless panic. On the other hand . . . Androtti had the expression of a man with his head caught in a vise.

"Do it," Pagan said. "Do it, for Christ's sake. Don't waste time. Get them out of here."

"You're not running things here, Pagan. Let me remind you of that. Now. Can you at least describe the alleged object we're looking for?"

Pagan shook his head. He didn't know. Explosive devices came in all shapes. "It's bound to be small and well hidden. That's all I can tell you."

Androtti spoke quietly to his men, who began to move around the Scuola discreetly, as if the object of their search were a lost tie pin, a wedding ring, something innocuous. The magnificence of shadow, Pagan thought. Something in the phrase suggested the inside of Carlotta's head, a place of elaborate shaded edifices, of cryptic bowers. He walked past the table, dragging the tips of his fingers under the surface, feeling only hard wood, a fragment of which splintered and pierced his skin.

Notice the extraordinary use of red in this instance . . .

Red, Pagan thought. He looked at his fingertip, saw a spot of blood. It was nothing compared to the blood that would be shed if he didn't find what he was looking for. He was conscious of Androtti and his men surreptitiously exploring the place and he wondered how long it would be before their search was noticed by Gurenko's group, and curiosity was aroused, and then panic, people scurrying toward the exit and out into the night. He sucked the tip of his finger, tasted his blood. His head was filled all at once with a sea of blood, as if the explosion had already taken place, and there was flame, charred flesh, screaming, and the Scuola had become a furnace similar to one inside the Underground carriage —

Keep looking, keep looking, he told himself. Androtti, always an inch or so behind Pagan's shoulder, had a vulturous presence, a predator's restrained urgency. "Who is supposed to have placed this explosive, Pagan?" he asked.

Pagan didn't answer, didn't hear, he was still trying to imagine Carlotta coming inside this big stone-cold hall, trying to see her move toward a hiding place. How had she made it past security to begin with? False papers? Inside assistance? Some combination of the two? It didn't matter. *She steps inside the Scuola, she strolls across the stone floor, maybe she stops and checks out a couple of paintings, maybe not, maybe she's too focused for that kind of indulgence, she's thinking of one thing only, she's thinking of the secret place where she can plant the device. Okay, maybe she doesn't have much time, she has to do the job under the eyes of the security people, so she needs someplace within easy access and yet a place that isn't immediately obvious to the casual eye . . .*

Ticktockticktock.

He heard somebody say, *Observe the gold in this detail, you can almost feel the surface of the precious metal, how wonderful it is . . .*

Pagan thought: *She steps inside the Scuola, she has no time for all this artistic detail, no time to enjoy the colors of Tintoretto, she knows precisely where she's going as soon as she enters the place because it isn't the kind of thing she'd leave for the last minute. Planned, exact. Nothing left to chance. Within easy reach and yet not obvious.* His mind blurred, he was consumed again by the sound of clocks; even the harsh noise of somebody coughing on the other side of the hall suggested to him the discordant echo made by a skewed pendulum. *How much time did he have?* He glanced at the group around the painting, seeing Gurenko again, the rapt expression on the man's face.

He looked at Androtti and whispered, "I'll say it again, Androtti. Evacuate the place. Get everyone out of here. Immediately. Look, even if I'm wrong, even if I'm barking mad, it's a precaution you have to take. If this building blows . . ." Pagan didn't finish his sentence.

The Italian looked across the hall at the crowd clustered around a painting. He beat a hand against his thigh in a gesture of indecision: better to be safe but . . . The problem was the orchestration of evacuation, how it could be achieved in an orderly fashion. Pagan, who didn't wait for the Italian's response, *couldn't* wait, continued to move. He found himself going in the direction of the altar. *She comes this way,* he thought. *She passes the great Corinthian columns of the hall and she moves toward the altar because here there are more shadows.* He didn't turn when he heard the sound of Androtti's voice.

"*I must have your attention, please,*" Androtti was saying to the group. "*One moment. Please. One moment.*"

The cluster of people around the painting turned slowly.

"Due to unforeseen circumstances, we have to leave the building for a time. This is a precautionary matter, nothing to cause alarm."

Somebody asked, "What circumstances?"

"Please," Androtti said. "We will escort you outside for a short time, and then you may return."

The group, with Gurenko in the center, didn't move at once. In the manner of most human gatherings, it had developed an indecisive collective will. Gurenko had a look on his face of displeasure, like that of a man interrupted in the middle of a very good dream.

"If you will follow me," Androtti was saying.

A few people took tentative steps toward Androtti, others shuffled their feet, others still remained immobile. Gurenko was particularly reluctant. Androtti clapped his hands to instill a sense of urgency and order. If Pagan was aware of any of this, it was something he registered on the edge of his consciousness. He was moving in shadows. Candles flickered around the altar, shuddering darts of light whose power barely illuminated a gold cross just ahead of him. Divine intervention, Pagan thought. I need a little of that now.

His skin was damp, his nerves stressed, his mouth a dry hollow. He felt small and utterly insignificant and vulnerable under the great ceiling. *If it goes up now.* He thought of the impact, the blast, the flame, columns toppling, paintings seared from the walls. Keep going. Keep looking. Don't stop. Don't think. Keep searching. He moved toward the cross, clambering over a collection of wooden pews. *She goes for the bold strokes,* he thought. *She goes for the grand gestures, the theatrical. Remember that.* He was drawn forward, sucked toward the candle flames; light was dispersed all around him in a sequence of fragmented reflections like images seen in the broken shards of a mirror. It could be anywhere, he thought. *Anywhere.* He fumbled hastily along the pews, feeling the undersides, groping, wondering again about time, thinking how time had broken down into quantities too small for him to understand, microseconds, nanoseconds, fractions whose measurements required a machine more sophisticated than a simple human brain. Time had become a viscous substance, quicksand into which he was sinking. More than twenty, less than thirty. He must have used up ten or fifteen minutes getting here from Barron's house, perhaps another five actually gaining entrance to the Scuola: what did that amount to? His mind was numb. He'd lost his hold on the relationship of numbers to one another. Addition and subtraction were suddenly beyond him. Ten minutes from Barron's place to here, ten, twelve, fifteen, he wasn't sure, the numbers kept breaking down inside his head and all he could hear was Barron's voice — *The clock ticks, Pagan. Far too fast for all of us.* Okay. Concentrate. Calculate. At most, he must have used twenty minutes. Maybe twenty-one. Twenty-two. And counting.

On his knees, he searched between the pews, possessed by the feeling that each time he plunged his hand into shadow he was reaching for something that existed beyond the limits of the material world. A mythical object. A thing in another dimension. His damp hands were covered with fine dust. He crawled along the floor. *The grand gesture*, he thought. *The theatrical.* Something extravagant.

He got to his feet and looked back across the hall where Androtti was still trying to organize his group of evacuees. There was resistance going on. Androtti was making imploring gestures, Gurenko was stubbornly pointing at the painting just behind him; a conflict of interests and desires. People arguing with one another in different languages. Misunderstandings. Just get them the hell out, Pagan thought. At gunpoint if you have to. *Just get them out of this place.* He wiped sweat from his eyes and went to the altar and looked at the cross.

Something was wrong with it. He wasn't sure what. Not immediately. He reached out to touch it and then realized it was marginally off-center, as if it had been moved recently and replaced a fraction of an inch out of its original position. At the base of the cross could be seen a spidery line of polished wood, brighter than the slightly dusty surface on which the artifact stood. He touched the thing, ran his fingers down its facade, then reached behind it and felt —

A hard cylindrical object. His fingertips encountered a strip of tape that held the thing in place against the cross. He stepped behind the cross, saw dark duct tape pressed against gold, and under the tape a cylinder of black plastic four inches long. Sweat ran into his eyes; a curious fog rolled through his head. He needed expert help. He needed somebody like Dick McCluskey to be here, somebody who understood these things, who knew how to render them useless, he needed somebody who understood primers and acid and retaining devices and plungers and sparks and plastique, but he didn't have anyone; you're on your own, Pagan. Solo. *This is up to you now. And maybe you have only a minute, two minutes, three. Beyond that: zero.*

"What are you doing?"

The man who had asked the question wore rimless glasses; his florid face was flustered. He emerged from shadow and reached out and gripped Pagan's arm.

"Are you trying to steal this priceless artifact?" the man asked.

Pagan shrugged himself free. He didn't have time for human impediments. He didn't have time for obstructions. He didn't have time for anything.

"You think you can come in here and steal this cross when nobody is looking, yes? I am curator here. You have no permission to touch anything. You are breaking the law."

Pagan placed one hand in the dead center of the man's chest and pushed him away. The man's glasses slipped down his nose.

"Get out of my fucking way," Pagan said.

The curator grabbed Pagan a second time. Pagan shoved him back and the man lost his balance, going down on one knee, breathing hard, his red face darkening. Then, tiresomely resilient, he got to his feet. He lowered his head and, bull-like, made a quick little lunge at Pagan, who side-stepped him nimbly and brought the flat of his hand down against the back of the man's neck. The curator sprawled on the floor and immediately got to his feet again. Dear God, Pagan thought. He couldn't afford this kind of conflict.

The curator, who had lost his glasses, came back at Pagan. "Thief," he said, blinking furiously. "Thief."

"Stay away from me," Pagan said.

"This place is my responsibility, everything here is my responsibility," and the man bunched his hand into a fist and swung it at Pagan's head. The attempted blow was easily parried. Pagan brought up his knee sharply and felt the bone sink into the softness of the man's scrotum. The curator groaned and slid down between the pews and lay with eyes watering and hands covering his groin. It was apparent he wasn't about to rise again immediately, but he'd cost Pagan time — at least another minute, perhaps more — and the contretemps had drawn the attention of Gurenko's security personnel, who were beginning to move inquisitively in Pagan's direction. There would be a question and answer session at the very least; a prolonged interrogation at worst. I need that, he thought. *I have all the time in the bloody world for a nice little sitdown and chat.*

Aware of two raincoated figures moving toward him, he began to work quickly. Trying to still his hands, he picked at the edge of the tape, freed the object from the cross, and the cylinder — with tape attached — slipped into his hand. He felt that he was holding his own death in his palm. How did you dismantle these things without blowing yourself up? How did you deactivate them? A small puzzling cylinder of destruction, so harmless in appearance, so utterly mystifying; finally so terrifying.

The two men stood about three or four yards from him now. One of them asked a question in Russian, which meant nothing to Pagan, who looked in Androtti's direction for assistance. Androtti was otherwise engaged. He had a hand on Gurenko's sleeve and was trying to draw the man in the direction of the doorway, and Gurenko, like a stubborn child unwilling to be dragged from his favorite toy, was pulling in the opposite direction. Exasperated voices were raised, explanations were being demanded, protocol had been seriously violated: there was outrage in the atmosphere.

Pagan looked at the security men, one of whom asked another question even as he produced an automatic weapon from a shoulder holster and pointed it directly at Pagan. It's slipping away, Pagan thought. Everything. Time dies. The Scuola itself seemed like some huge stone clock that ticked all around him, reverberated inside him. He had minutes at most. Two, three, one. Perhaps only seconds. He was acutely conscious of the device in his hand, which he held as if it were precious glass because he had no way of knowing if it would explode were he to drop it, or if it slipped from his unsteady hand and struck the floor; he imagined acid eating through wire even as he gripped the thing, he thought of a spark igniting the plastique, the physics of terrorism; why hadn't he taken the time in his life to understand the science of destruction? Too busy chasing the people who made these things to understand precisely *how* they were made. Too preoccupied with the consequences of terrorism rather than the instruments of terror themselves.

He gazed at the Russian with the gun. He raised the hand that held the device. Duct tape adhered to his fingers. He was tethered to destruction. He moved away from the cross and, walking past the pews, reached the man with the gun. The Russian was staring at the device. He stepped back from Pagan and lowered his weapon an inch or so, frowning at the object Pagan held, seemingly aware of its function, as if he'd encountered something similar in the past. Perhaps in a security training manual, perhaps in the field, it didn't matter; he recognized its capabilities.

"This is about to go off," Pagan said. "Do you understand me?"

The Russian glanced at his associate, a tall muscular man who made the gesture of a throat being slit with the tip of his finger.

"Do you understand me?" It seemed to Pagan that he was speaking very slowly, as if in a dream of alienation where nobody understands what it is that you are trying to tell them and no matter how damned hard you try you can't convey meaning. He pantomimed a watch, tapping the back of his wrist with an urgency that wasn't exaggerated. Perhaps the Russians had some rudimentary knowledge of English, perhaps the device simply scared them; they stepped aside and Pagan moved past them in the direction of Androtti, who by this time had released Gurenko and was talking rapidly in Italian to another dignitary. Pagan glanced at the Russian president. A moment of brief eye contact: Pagan saw a certain flinty determination in Gurenko's face, a hardness of purpose. If he'd been informed that the Scuola was a dangerous place to be, he was the kind of man

who'd want proof before he responded. He lived with danger all the time; perhaps he'd become immune to menace.

"Androtti," Pagan said.

The Italian turned, moved toward Pagan. "They are unwilling to leave, I can't seem to get it into Gurenko's head that —" Androtti saw the device just then in Pagan's hand and he was suddenly pale: a man in a nightmare.

"I don't suppose you happen to have an explosives expert at hand?" Pagan asked.

"It will take twenty minutes to get one here."

"If we're lucky, we have twenty seconds." Pagan continued to walk, hurrying past Gurenko and his group, heading for the doorway. Androtti followed.

Pagan wondered if the device would be affected by the warmth of his skin, if the heat of his flesh would hasten the process that was going on inside the cylinder. Maybe. He didn't know. He felt a heightened terror. He was a walking bomb. The object in his hand seemed to emit a radiance of its own, and he considered the idea of taking a chance and stripping the thing down and trying to dismantle it; he'd be going into it blind, but blind people built clocks and tuned pianos, didn't they? Blind people had all kinds of instincts. He imagined pulling the duct tape away, gently breaking open the plastic case, and then what? What puzzles would he see in the intestines of the thing? What conundrum of wires and springs? And how in God's name would he deal with them? The device seemed to be emitting more heat with each moment he held it. He had the illusion that what lay in his hand was a burning coal, a red-hot cinder. Too hot to hold. Sooner or later he'd have to let it go.

Both men were outside now. Reporters thronged around and the cold night air smelled of onions and garlic and ground coffee. Androtti tugged on Pagan's sleeve and asked, "What do we do with it?"

"There's only one thing I can think of," Pagan replied, and he began to trot briskly, Androtti still following him, glasses clouded with condensation, coat flapping at his calves.

"You're going to dump it," Androtti said.

Pagan said nothing. Clear of the Scuola now, away from the observations of newshounds, he broke into a run. Androtti kept up with him, his breath hanging in chill little clouds. They entered a quiet street which led to a small bridge over the Rio della Frescada. Ungathered laundry, stiffened by the night air, hung across the canal. Inverted shirts, palely lit from windows, were ghostly presences. Pagan leaned from the bridge and tossed the device from his hand and heard it strike the black water, and then he retreated quickly, moving away from the bridge with Androtti rushing at his back.

They returned to the side street, where Androtti asked, "Will it go off underwater?"

Before Pagan could hazard a guess, he heard the sound of water erupting in a great frothing surge suggestive of lava bursting in the sky. The side street was lit briefly by a column of bright flame that rose up from the canal for twenty feet before it flickered and died like a huge firework in the shadows of the bridge. Laundry was whipped back and forth, ropes shuddered, there was the sound of windows breaking and anchored boats battering against stone and tiles being ripped from rooftops, and then the noises faded and the night was momentarily becalmed — before the street was filled with anxious people driven outdoors by the blast.

"Thank God," Androtti said, and slumped against a wall in the manner of a man overcome by exhaustion.

Pagan could hear echoes of the explosion. The burn at the side of his neck had begun to throb. But he felt it only distantly.

"You know what this makes you?" Androtti asked.

Pagan shook his head.

"A hero."

A hero, Pagan thought. He felt no elation, no relief, no sense of achievement. Instead, he was haunted by emptiness and exhaustion. He'd reached the limits of himself, and he was drained, more than drained. Androtti took Pagan's gun and ID card from his pocket and handed them back to him. "Your property," he said, and was quiet for a moment. "We need to sit down together, Pagan. I need to hear the whole story. How you got on to this business. How it started. Who is responsible. A great many people will have questions for you, Pagan. And a great many people will have gratitude to express."

Pagan said, "It may take some time."

"I have time," said Androtti.

"Tomorrow," Pagan said.

"Why not tonight?"

"I'm tired, Androtti. Dog-tired."

"Telephone me at nine in the morning. Here." He produced his card and Pagan took it.

"Nine sharp," Pagan said.

"Don't forget."

■

Pagan walked back to Barron's house on the Calle dei Avocati. The night was a black wind-blown void. He traveled backstreets, passageways, crossed the Rialto, then the dark square of San Marco. He had the sense he was being followed, observed, that Carlotta dogged him, although whenever he turned to look he saw nobody. Imagination, he thought. He was going to carry her presence around inside him for a long time. He would half-expect to see her whenever he turned a corner or sat in his car at a traffic light, or he'd notice her waiting under the trees of the grim little square across the street from his apartment. A kind of haunting manufactured from the notion that she was at liberty in the world. She was free.

When he reached the Calle dei Avocati, he saw that the door of Barron's house was open. He stepped inside. Somebody had tossed a sheet over Barron's body. There was no sign of the servant, no sign of Katherine Cairney. Broken glass crunched under his feet as he walked toward the stairs. He paused to look down at the sheet; a makeshift shroud.

He passed on, climbed the stairs until he came to the room from whose balcony Carlotta had jumped. Night had entered the space, carrying the smell of an ancient mildewed basement. He wondered about Katherine. Where was she? Had she seen and heard enough and then walked away from here?

He looked at the door which led, according to Carlotta, to the soul of Tobias Barron. It was shut, probably locked. He moved toward it, tried the handle; it yielded. Katherine Cairney sat on a swivel chair and turned her face when Pagan stepped inside. Drawers had been opened in filing cabinets, folders removed, papers spread across the desk. An ungainly length of fax paper hung from her hand.

"What happened?" she asked.

"Everything's fine," Pagan answered, wondering if he had the inclination to expand on this, but then his attention was drawn away from the girl to the room. On electronic wall maps colored cursors moved, blinking like tiny tics of anxiety. Computer screens were lit, displaying a series of menus, curiously named — floral, herbal, delicate names.

"I found the key to this room on Barron," she said. "I'm glad I did." She handed Pagan the roll of fax paper, which he took and studied slowly. He read and reread. Where did everything begin and end? It went beyond this room, beyond Tobias Barron, it spread in threads so intricate it might take years to unweave the magnitude of Barron's work.

"I've been trying to imagine him sitting here," she said in a quiet voice, "the whole world spread out in front of him." Her voice was expressionless. She might have been reciting from memory some meaningless doggerel. "I've been trying to feel what he must have felt with all this at his fingertips."

She gestured toward the folders, then at the roll of paper dangling in Pagan's hand. "It makes interesting reading." She looked small, depressed. "Wherever there was chaos, that was where you'd find Barron doing business. Requests for arms from Somalia. Angola. Cuba. Bosnia . . . You name it, Barron was involved in it somehow. And when there wasn't sufficient chaos to suit him, it seems he was very busy igniting it, funneling dollars from sympathetic contributors into all the fragile places he could find. Berlin. Prague. Moscow. The idea apparently was to destabilize weak regimes, provoke bloodshed, stoke the fires of anarchy and disorder. A sound investment. You throw in a few million dollars here and there to create conditions that suit your purpose and you reap dazzling benefits in the sales of arms. You can read it for yourself. It's all there. And God only knows what's in the computers . . ."

Pagan tilted back his head and looked up into the strip of fluorescent lighting, his attention drawn there by a vague noise. A dying moth, born too soon in the cold year, adhered to the glowing tube. Its wings thrummed.

"Requests for money and matériel from Germany. Georgia. Poland. Afghanistan. Acknowledgments of cargoes dispatched to South Africa, Guatemala, Panama . . . and Ireland. Dear old Ireland." She paused, smiled in a sad way. "He supplied any cause that could come up with the cash. At least you can always say that much about Barron. He didn't take sides. IRA. Loyalists. It didn't matter to him. He catered to them both."

She indicated the desk, the open drawers, the folders. "And then there's all the other stuff, requests for endowments, charity donations, good causes everywhere — Calcutta, Mozambique, Peru, they come from all over the world." She drew a hand over her face, a tired gesture, containing an element of disappointment and puzzlement.

"I thought I knew him," she said, and she shook her head.

Pagan looked at the screens. Experts would come here and break into the system, gathering all the secrets of Barron's harvest, examining every stalk, tracing the roots of whatever Barron had planted. *Peace is bad for business*, he thought. Yes. In all human history, there had never been profit in peace. It was a profoundly depressing consideration.

"I can't imagine it ever being completely unraveled," she said. "I can't imagine the people with whom Barron did business are simply going to wither away. Whatever he was involved in . . ."

"It's not going to be stopped overnight," Pagan said.

"No, it's not."

On the desk beside one of the computers was a framed photograph of Carlotta, a studio shot, posed. Her hands were carefully positioned, fingertips touching just under her lips. Scrawled across the photograph were the words *For Barron, Love Carlotta*. Pagan picked up the picture. Love, Carlotta, he thought. He set it back down. He felt chilled. He imagined her somewhere in the city, cold and wet, walking the darkened bank of a canal, seeking a place where she might hide for a time and then, when she was ready, resurface. In what form, though? he wondered. And where?

The girl rose from her seat. Pagan stared at her. She came very close to him, reached out, laid her fingers on his arm. Then she dropped her hand to her side and shrugged. She stepped past him, moved to the door, hesitated there.

"What do we say to each other now?" she asked.

Pagan wasn't at all sure. He wasn't sure if there was anything left to say.

"You were right about Barron. I was wrong," she said.

"That doesn't make me feel good," he replied. The urge was there; through all the layers of his fatigue, through all the reasonable objections he could think of, the urge to touch her was still there.

"Who knows?" she said. "Maybe we'll run into one another somewhere along the line. Maybe we'll have a reunion and a glass of wine and look back at this with some kind of detachment. Or bewilderment. Whatever."

"Maybe."

He turned away, gazed in the direction of the balcony. He wanted to look around, but he didn't — not when he heard her move, not when he heard her footsteps on the stone staircase, not even when the sound of the big front door slamming shut reached him. He gazed down into the motionless canal and wondered about loss and renewal. The house held and trapped the echo of Katherine Cairney's departure and there was a sad quality in the way it finally faded.

Epilogue

■ It rained for days, an endless drumming that made drainpipes roar and gutters flood. Even so, Pagan sensed it was the last outrage of winter, a dying squall; in the air was a hint of spring, a freshness on the night wind. After his meeting with Androtti, the details of which aroused the interest of the Central Intelligence Agency, MI6, Special Branch, and investigators representing the security interests of various foreign governments, he'd left Venice and skipped from place to place, from city to city, staying one step ahead of those who chased him with questions.

Pagan took the view that anything they wanted could be found inside Barron's computer system, or in Streik's papers, which he'd left with Androtti, and that he was entitled to his privacy; besides, he had no great fondness for seeing his name in print, nor did he enjoy the prospect of interrogations, the wholesale intrusion and ransacking of his life — which had suddenly become public property. Gurenko wanted to see him. The Italian government had undying gratitude to express because he'd saved priceless works of art in the Scuola, to say nothing of the reputation of the country's security forces. He was in the papers constantly, and longed for anonymity.

He followed the news, the unfolding story of Barron's life and times, the scary designs of the man, the pyramid of terror he'd created. The press, indulging its propensity to pop psychology, spoke of a man who represented the black-and-white aspects of the human soul — the former epitomized by the chaos he'd created and the weaponry he'd sold, the latter by his valuable acts of charity. *Did he not represent the dichotomy in every man's heart?* one hack asked rather grandly.

Bullshit, Pagan thought. Barron hadn't done any good deeds except in places where he could also do bad ones. The perfect balance. He knew the economics of what he was doing. He sold to anyone wanting to buy. Where business was poor, he had his friends pump in money to make sure it picked up again. It was deadly simple. It was predatory, and cunning.

From one rainy city to the next, slogging journeys by train, by bus, Pagan traveled in an aimless manner into obscure corners of Europe, where he'd install himself in small hotels under assumed names, pretending he spoke no English. He was just a stranger who came and went. He stopped shaving. Some days he lay in bed and listened to the rain, and when it was time to move on he sneaked off under cover of darkness, even though he knew his anonymity was not everlasting. Sooner or later he'd have to surface. But only when he was ready.

In Saint-Etienne he read that William J. Caan had been taken into custody, although no reason was given. In Clermont-Ferrand he read that a number of agents of the US Defense Intelligence Agency had been suspended from duty, a small item on an inside page. By the time he reached Limoges, scandals were dominating the headlines of the world press — prominent businessmen arrested in America and the UK, law-enforcement officers jailed in Germany, politicians under house arrest in Russia; Fidel Castro had denounced the ease with which American weapons found their way into the hands of Cuban guerrillas, a member of the Kuwait royal family had committed suicide — the old poisoned-chalice routine, Pagan noticed. A couple of four-star generals had taken early retirement from the Pentagon — for "budgetary reasons" it was reported. And in London a man called Montgomery Rhodes, described as "an American security expert," had been found in a sleazy bed-and-breakfast joint near Euston, wrists slashed, an incomprehensible suicide note discreetly placed under an HP sauce bottle.

It was never made plain that these events were linked to Tobias Barron directly, but his name occurred in several of the reports, usually in a vague aside or the kind of innuendo that fooled nobody. Sometimes Carlotta's name appeared; she'd been seen in Mexico City, Los Angeles, New Orleans, and once by a mushroom-eating commune leader in Montana. A wisp, an enigma, her profiles in the press were invariably melodramatic; she was linked with satanic cults, volatile charismatic movements, and every conspiracy going. Old lovers emerged from the dry rot of her past to sell revelatory first-person accounts of their sexual experiences with her. One was an impecunious marquis, another a fashion designer, another a former runway model from Pakistan. By general consent, Carlotta was reported to have been more than a little fond of sexual accoutrements and experimentation, which involved cross-dressing, disguises, assignations in curious places — graveyards, churches, and in one alleged instance an empty coffin in a funeral parlor. These accounts, though published under different names, all seemed to have been penned by the same hack scribbler and were charged with tabloid clichés.

Pagan, who didn't care if the lurid histories were true or false, kept moving. He had come to favor the bus as the best means, because the trips took longer. You could draw a rug over your lap and ride through hours of lonely darkness surrounded by sleeping passengers.

From Rouen, Pagan placed a phone call to Foxworth at his home number in London.

"Where the devil are you, Frank?" Foxie asked.

"Somewhere in France."

"And that's all you're saying?"

"That's all."

"Everybody and his uncle is looking for you."

"Let them look. Are you recovered?"

"Sick leave. I'm reading Anselm. Then it's on to Thomas Merton. I'm considering a career in mysticism. Are you coming back to London?"

"Soon," Pagan answered.

"Nimmo's going around like he's about to get a bloody knighthood or something, Frank. His halo is *gleaming*. It dazzles all who come in sight of it. He's the man whose stroke of genius brought Frank Pagan back into the fold, after all. And just look how well it turned out. He was on the telly the other day saying more or less that he knew your present whereabouts but he understood your need for privacy."

"Good luck to him," Pagan said. Nimmo: the name was a small dull echo in his head.

"I've had reporters phoning me to ask about you, Frank. What was he like to work with? What kind of man is he? What can you tell us? Any little thing of human interest. You're *famous*."

"Fame lasts about ten minutes," Pagan remarked.

"Of course, I tell them rotten things, your dictatorial attitude, your despotic ways, your notorious rudeness." Foxie laughed quietly. "You're missing some of the fun, though. The CIA has practically *seized* the US embassy, causing all manner of uproar. Nobody can get near the place. Apparently they've uncovered documentation that is utterly damning to Caan. The House of Representatives is conducting an extensive inquiry, the Home Secretary has lodged a complaint about abuse of diplomatic privilege and the way Caan used the embassy as his personal conduit for cash, and the whole thing's a bloody circus. I lie awake at night and I can hear the whisper of the ax, I swear it."

Pagan moved on again. Sometimes, in a remote way, he contemplated the future, but that was an unreadable map. When he reached Paris he booked into a hotel on the Rue Mazarine; from his window he could see the corner of the Boulevard Saint-Germain. He thought about Katherine Cairney. He'd promised her Paris; a lifetime ago. Now and then she entered his thoughts, and sometimes he found himself brooding over her, wondering where she might be and if she was thinking about him in much the same way — but he disliked the romantic impulse behind these indulgences. She was gone. History. A memory. Nothing could come of all that now.

Even so, when he left his hotel on the Rue Mazarine and strolled along Saint-Germain to Saint-Michel, he could feel a shadow of her.

He wandered down in the direction of the Seine, crossed over into the narrow streets of the Ile de la Cité, and there he was particularly struck by her absence.

He went inside a small café and drank coffee and thought it ironic, if you were in the mood for such interpretations, that he was back where he'd been before she entered his life: on his own. Whether it was Paris in the rain, a street in Dublin, or watching a full moon rise over Alba — he was alone, and loneliness was an abscess.

He wondered if this was his destiny, to go through life unattached. He finished his coffee and set the cup down and stared through the rainy window at the street. He found himself entertaining the idea that the girl, like a heroine in a romance, would materialize in the rain and come running over glistening cobbles in his direction, losing a shoe and laughing about it and not giving a damn —

Nothing in life happened that way.

He played with the edge of his cup, opened a pack of cigarettes, tore off the cellophane. He struck a match, watched it go out, dropped it in the ashtray. Absorbed in his thoughts, he didn't notice the woman passing outside, a slender figure dressed in a man's black pin-stripe suit, hat drawn down over her forehead. She took her hands from the pockets of her pants. They were gloved in black silk.

The woman glanced at him through the window and then moved on through the rain. By the time Pagan left the café, the street was empty.